Aldeburgh Studies i
General Editor: Paul

Volume 3

On Mahler and Britten

Donald Mitchell, London, 1994

On Mahler and Britten

ESSAYS IN HONOUR OF
DONALD MITCHELL
ON HIS SEVENTIETH BIRTHDAY

EDITED BY

Philip Reed

THE BOYDELL PRESS
THE BRITTEN–PEARS LIBRARY

First published 1995 by The Boydell Press, Woodbridge
in conjunction with
The Britten–Pears Library, Aldeburgh

ISBN 0 85115 382 8

Aldeburgh Studies in Music
ISSN 0969–3548

The Boydell Press in an imprint of Boydell & Brewer Ltd
PO Box 9, Woodbridge, Suffolk IP12 3DF, UK
and of Boydell & Brewer Inc.
PO Box 41026, Rochester, NY 14604–4126, USA

A catalogue record for this book is available from the British Library

Library of Congress Cataloging-in-Publication Data applied for

This publication is printed on acid-free paper

Printed in Great Britain by
St Edmundsbury Press Ltd, Bury St Edmunds, Suffolk

Contents

CONTENTS

CONTENTS

List of Illustrations

List of Abbreviations

ABL   Alma Mahler-Werfel, *And the Bridge is Love* (London: Hutchinson, 1959)

AMEB   Alma Mahler, *Gustav Mahler: Erinnerungen und Briefe* (Amsterdam: Allert de Lange, 1940)

AMML²   Alma Mahler, *Gustav Mahler: Memories and Letters*, tr. Basil Creighton, ed. Donald Mitchell, 2nd edn (London: John Murray, 1968)

AMML³   Alma Mahler, *Gustav Mahler: Memories and Letters*, tr. Basil Creighton, ed. Donald Mitchell, 3rd edn (London: John Murray, 1973)

AMML⁴   Alma Mahler, *Gustav Mahler: Memories and Letters*, tr. Basil Creighton, ed. Donald Mitchell and Knud Martner, 4th edn (London: Cardinal, 1990)

AMWB   Alma Mahler-Werfel (ed.), *Gustav Mahler Briefe, 1879–1911* (Vienna: Zsolnay, 1924)

ASL   *Arnold Schoenberg: Letters*, tr. Eithne Wilkins and Ernst Kaiser, ed. Erwin Stein (London: Faber and Faber, 1964)

ASSI   Arnold Schoenberg, *Style and Idea*, ed. Leonard Stein (London: Faber and Faber, 1975)

BC   Christopher Palmer (ed.), *The Britten Companion* (London: Faber and Faber, 1984)

DMBA   Donald Mitchell, *Britten and Auden in the Thirties: The Year 1936* (London: Faber and Faber, 1981)

DMCN   Donald Mitchell, *Cradles of the New: Writings on Music 1951–1991*, selected by Christopher Palmer, ed. Mervyn Cooke (London: Faber and Faber, 1995)

DMPB   Donald Mitchell, 'The Origins Evolution and Metamorphoses of *Paul Bunyan*, Auden's and Britten's "American Opera"', in W. H. Auden, *Paul Bunyan: The Libretto of the Operetta by Benjamin Britten* (London: Faber and Faber, 1988): 83–148

DMPR   Donald Mitchell and Philip Reed (eds), *Letters from a Life: The Selected Letters and Diaries of Benjamin Britten 1913–1976*, Vols 1 and 2 (London: Faber and Faber, 1991)

GM¹   Henry-Louis de La Grange, *Gustav Mahler: Chronique d'une vie*, Vol. 1 'Les Chemins de la Gloire (1860–1900)' (Paris: Fayard, 1979)

GM²	Henry-Louis de La Grange, *Gustav Mahler: Chronique d'une vie*, Vol. 2 'L'Age d'Or de Vienne (1900–1907)' (Paris: Fayard, 1983)
GM³	Henry-Louis de La Grange, *Gustav Mahler: Chronique d'une vie*, Vol. 3 'Le Génie foudroyé (1907–1911)' (Paris: Fayard, 1984)
GMB	*Gustav Mahler Briefe*, ed. Herta Blaukopf (Vienna: Zsolnay, 1982)
GMB¹	*Selected Letters of Gustav Mahler*, tr. Eithne Wilkins, Ernst Kaiser and Bill Hopkins, ed. Knud Martner (London: Faber and Faber, 1979)
GM(E)	Henry-Louis de La Grange, *Mahler*, Vol. 1 (London: Gollancz, 1974)
GMUB	Gustav Mahler, *Unbekannte Briefe*, ed. Herta Blaukopf (Vienna: Zsolnay, 1983)
GMZZ²	Kurt Blaukopf, *Gustav Mahler,* tr. Inge Goodwin (London: Allen Lane, 1973)
HK	Herbert Killian (ed.), *Gustav Mahler in die Erinnerungen von Natalie Bauer-Lechner* (Hamburg: Karl Dieter Wagner, 1984)
HOBB	David Herbert (ed.), *The Operas of Benjamin Britten* (London: Hamish Hamilton, 1979)
MCPR	Mervyn Cooke and Philip Reed, *Benjamin Britten: Billy Budd* (Cambridge: Cambridge University Press, 1993)
MDS	Kurt Blaukopf, *Mahler: A Documentary Study* (London: Thames and Hudson, 1976)
NB-L	Natalie Bauer-Lechner, *Recollections of Gustav Mahler,* tr. Dika Newlin, ed. Peter Franklin (London: Faber Music, 1980)
NL	Norman Lebrecht, *Mahler Remembered* (London: Faber and Faber, 1987)
PFL	Donald Mitchell and John Evans, *Pictures from a Life: Benjamin Britten 1913–1976* (London: Faber and Faber, 1978)
SSLD	Donald Mitchell, *Gustav Mahler: Songs and Symphonies of Life and Death: Interpretations and Annotations* (London: Faber and Faber, 1985)
WY	Donald Mitchell, *Gustav Mahler: The Wunderhorn Years: Chronicles and Commentaries* (London: Faber and Faber, 1975)

Library siglia

A–Wn	Austrian National Library, Music Collection, Vienna
GB–ALb	The Britten–Pears Library, Aldeburgh
GB–Lbl	The British Library, London

Acknowledgements

First and foremost I must warmly thank all the contributors to this volume. They have given freely of their services and lavished much care and time on their articles. Without such willing co-operation, the book would have remained an idea only. That the *Festschrift* takes such handsome form is due to the generosity of the Trustees of the Britten–Pears Foundation, whose support of the project has been unswerving from the outset. At the book's planning stage I was much assisted by Paul Banks (General Editor of the Aldeburgh Studies in Music series), and subsequently by Marion Thorpe and Kathleen Mitchell. I am further indebted to Prof. Banks and Hugh Cobbe (Chairman of the Britten–Pears Library Committee), for their support in allowing me what amounted to 'sabbatical' time from my other Library duties in order to see the volume through the press. Thanks must also be made to Chris Banks (Curator of Music Manuscripts, British Library); the staff of the Britten–Pears Library, Aldeburgh; Sir Rupert Hart-Davis; Belinda Matthews and Lucy Vickery (Faber and Faber Ltd); and Nick Winter (St Petersburg).

I am deeply indebted to Jill Burrows not only for her excellent typography and the provision of a superb index – a service she has rendered DM many times over the years – but also for acting as a constant source of sound advice on a wide variety of matters related to the volume's production. I have, I'm sure, tested the bounds of our friendship on many occasions while working on the *Festschrift*. Acknowledgement should also be made to Michael Durnin, who set the music examples, and to Richard Barber and his staff at Boydell & Brewer.

I must extend warm thanks to Lady Nolan and the Trustees of the Britten–Pears Foundation for permission to reproduce Sir Sidney Nolan's *Abraham and Isaac* (1967) as the jacket illustration.

Grateful acknowledgement is made to Britten's principal publishers, Boosey & Hawkes (Music Publishers) Ltd and Faber Music Ltd, for permission to reproduce excerpts from works of which they are the copyright holders. Extracts from *Billy Budd* are Copyright 1951 and 1952 by Hawkes & Son (London) Ltd, Revised version © 1961 by Hawkes & Son (London) Ltd; extracts from *Canticle II* are Copyright 1953 by Boosey & Co. Ltd; extracts from *Peter Grimes* are Copyright 1945 by Boosey & Hawkes Ltd; extracts from *War Requiem* are © 1962 by Boosey & Hawkes Music Publishers Ltd. All are reproduced by kind permission of Boosey & Hawkes Music Publishers Ltd. Extracts from Shostakovich's *Lady Macbeth* are © 1935 by Boosey & Hawkes Music Publishers Ltd for UK, British

xi

Commonwealth (excluding Canada) and Eire, and are reprinted by kind permission. Extracts from Shostakovich's Fourteenth Symphony are © 1970 by Boosey & Hawkes Music Publishers Ltd for UK, British Commonwealth (excluding Canada) and Eire, and are reprinted by kind permission. I am indebted to Faber and Faber Ltd for permission to reprint Christopher Palmer's contribution (Chapter 21), originally published by them in *The Britten Companion* (1984); to Boosey & Hawkes (Music Publishers) Ltd, the Trustees of the Britten–Pears Foundation and the Austrian National Library for permission to reproduce the pages from Britten's composition draft of Britten's *Billy Budd*; and to the British Library for permission to reproduce the leaf from Mahler's Ninth Symphony. The draft of Auden's *Ode for St Cecilia's Day* (Chapter 19) is © 1995 by the Estate of W. H. Auden. All quotations from Britten's and Pears's letters and diaries are © 1995 the Trustees of the Britten–Pears Foundation and should not be reproduced further without prior written permission.

Finally, I and my fellow contributors join together in offering Donald our warmest congratulations, love and good wishes as he enters his eighth decade. We hope very much that *On Mahler and Britten* will bring him much pleasure.

Philip Reed
Suffolk, March 1995

Donald Mitchell: A Chronology

1925   *6 February* Born in London.

1930–42   Educated at Brightlands Prep. School and Dulwich College, London.

1942–3   While awaiting National Service, works at the Lime Grove Studios of Gainsborough Pictures (1928) Ltd, as advisory reader of new fiction and novice writer of screen treatments in the office of Harry Ostrer.

1943–5   Registers as Conscientious Objector. War-time service in Non-Combatant Corps.

1946   Teaches at Oakfield School, London, publishes first articles, and gives first broadcasts for BBC.

1947   Founds *Music Survey* and edits it (from 1949 with Hans Keller) until it ceases publication in 1952.

1949–50   At Durham University with Arthur Hutchings and A. E. F. Dickinson. Among his fellow students are Peter Evans and Eric Roseberry.

1952   Publication of *Benjamin Britten: A Commentary on His Works from a Group of Specialists*, edited by DM and Hans Keller.

1953–7   Contributes to the musical press and monthly to the *Musical Times* and *Musical Opinion*.

1956   *January* Marries Kathleen Livingston. Publication of *The Mozart Companion*, edited by DM and H. C. Robbins Landon.

1958   Publication of DM's first volume of Mahler studies, *Gustav Mahler: The Early Years*. Becomes music books editor at Faber and Faber; DM builds up a prestigious list.

1958–62   Editor of *Tempo*, the Boosey & Hawkes house-magazine.

1959–64   Member of the music staff of the *Daily Telegraph*.

1961   The Bruckner Society of America presents DM with its Gustav Mahler Medal of Honour.

1963   Publication of DM's *The Language of Modern Music*.

1963–4   Music adviser at Boosey & Hawkes with particular responsibilities for contemporary music and the acquisition of contemporary composers. Peter Maxwell Davies and Nicholas Maw join the Boosey & Hawkes list.

1964   Music critic for *The Listener*.

1965   Founding managing director of the newly created publishing house of Faber Music Ltd (vice-chairman, 1976; chairman, 1977; president, 1988–95). Apart from publishing new works by Britten, DM builds up a remarkable list of contemporary composers.

1968   Publication of DM's edition of Alma Mahler's *Gustav Mahler: Memories and Letters*.

1971–6   After a year as a visiting fellow, DM becomes first professor of music at the University of Sussex.

1971   DM is elected a publisher Director of the Performing Right Society.

1973   Honorary MA at University of Sussex. Becomes a director of Faber and Faber (Holdings) Ltd.

1975   Publication of DM's second volume of Mahler studies, *Gustav Mahler: The Wunderhorn Years: Chronicles and Commentaries*. The volume is dedicated to Britten. Becomes a director of the English Music Theatre Company, the successor to the English Opera group.

1976   *December* Benjamin Britten dies. As one of his four executors (the others were Peter Pears, Isador Caplan and Leslie Periton), and later as a senior trustee of the Britten–Pears Foundation, DM plays an increasingly significant role in promoting Britten's music through performances, recordings, lectures and publications.

1977   Doctorate at Southampton University with a dissertation on Mahler. Appointed Director of Academic Studies at the Britten–Pears School for Advanced Musical Studies, Snape (retiring in 1990) and council member of the Aldeburgh Foundation (retiring in 1994).

1978   Publication of DM's pictorial biography of Britten, *Pictures from a Life* (with John Evans).

1979   Delivers the T. S. Eliot Memorial Lectures, *Britten and Auden in the Thirties*, at the University of Kent, Canterbury; subsequently published in 1981.

1983   DM and his wife, Kathleen, visit China on an inter-governmental exchange. DM gives a series of pioneering lectures on Britten at the Conservatoires in Beijing and Shanghai.

1985   Publication of DM's third volume of Mahler studies, *Gustav Mahler: Songs and Symphonies of Life and Death: Interpretations and Annotations*. Becomes a governor of the National Youth Orchestra (until 1990).

1986   Appointed chairman of the Britten Estate Ltd and a director of the Britten–Pears Foundation.

1987   The International Gustav Mahler Society in Vienna awards DM its prestigious Mahler-Medaille. Retires from full-time activities at Faber Music. Publication of DM's handbook on Britten's *Death in Venice*. Elected joint deputy chairman of the Performing Right Society.

1988   Becomes a governor of the Royal Academy of Music.

1989–92   Chairman of the Performing Right Society.

1990   The University of York, where DM is a visiting professor, confers the honorary degree of Doctor of the University on DM.

1991   Guest Artistic Director of the Aldeburgh Festival which features music and drama from Japan and Thailand, reflecting DM's long-standing study of and interest in non-Western music, of Thailand in particular. Publication of the first two volumes of *Letters from a Life: The Selected Letters and Diaries of Benjamin Britten*, edited by DM and Philip Reed, for which the editors receive a Royal Philharmonic Society Award in May 1992.

1992   Honorary Member of the Royal Academy of Music.

1992–4   Vice-President of the International Confederation of Societies and Authors and Composers (CISAC).

1995   *6 February* Publication of *Cradles of the New*, a major selection by Christopher Palmer and Mervyn Cooke of DM's writings on music spanning more than forty years. Appointed a visiting professor in the department of music of King's College, University of London.

           May Mahler-Feest, at the Concertgebouw, Amsterdam, marking the 75th anniversary of Mengelberg's 1920 Festival. DM is executive chairman (with Henry-Louis de La Grange and Eduard Reeser as fellow chairman) of the symposium *Gustav Mahler: the World Listens*. Editor-in-chief of the Festival Programme Book and co-author with Edward Reilly of the texts accompanying the published facsimile of Mahler's Seventh Symphony.

Foreword

MARION THORPE

Dear Donald,

Mahler and Britten – two composers specially close to your heart, to whom you have devoted unbounded enthusiasm, profound insight and original thought. May the contents of this book, written by your friends and colleagues from many lands, give you pleasure and perhaps some amusement. It is a tribute to you on your seventieth birthday, in recognition of your many achievements; it is also an indirect appreciation from the composers themselves, without whom these articles would not have been written!

Britten was a devotee of Mahler's music – and dare I say that had Mahler been able to hear the works of the later composer, he would not have disapproved! Your friend and my father, Erwin Stein, was a champion of both composers and formed a remarkable link between them over a span of years. From a young age, at the beginning of the century, Erwin followed every new work that Mahler wrote and attended all his performances at the Vienna Opera. Some thirty years later he, with you and a handful of others, recognized Britten's genius. Neither composer had an easy ride with the critics of their time, who found fault in ways now quite incomprehensible to us. Ben used to say: 'I know the weak spots in my music, but no critic has yet pointed to the right place.'

In this country, Mahler's works were sadly neglected, and came to full recognition only after the Second World War. In the early 1940s both Britten and Stein made reductions for smaller orchestras of movements from Mahler's symphonies in order to give easier access to the vast scores and facilitate performances. Britten arranged the second movement of the Third Symphony ('What the wild flowers tell me') and Stein the *Andante moderato* from the Second Symphony. This pioneering exercise may well have contributed towards bringing Mahler's music to the notice of the British public. Your scholarly studies of Mahler's compositions have helped towards a deeper understanding of his works and now of course his music is widely performed to appreciative and enthusiastic audiences all over Britain.

Ben and my father discussed Mahler's music in detail and would frequently play through the symphonies – *vierhändig*. My father's recollection of Mahler's tempi, phrasing and shaping were crystal clear, and coincided closely with Ben's conception of the music. Listening to them together, the combination of my father's authoritative rendering and Ben's expert piano-playing brought these symphonies to life – much more so than some of the performances one hears today!

Both composers were of course also performers of music other than their own, and their rare creative insight made their performances unique. My father often spoke of Mahler's interpretations of Mozart – particularly of the production of *Le nozze di Figaro* at the Vienna Opera. We remember some unforgettable Mozart events at the Aldeburgh Festival – especially Britten's conducting of *Idomeneo* and the Requiem.

We have also heard Britten conducting Mahler – what would one give to hear Mahler perform *Death in Venice* or the *War Requiem*?

Dear Donald, your fellow Trustees present this book to you, with every good wish for the years to come.

I

On Mahler

1

Mahler and Viennese Modernism

PAUL BANKS

In his autobiography Stefan Zweig wrote of his youth in Vienna during the last years of the nineteenth century that

> Anything that was not yet generally recognized, or was so lofty as to be obtainable only with difficulty, the new and radical times, provoked our particular love . . . To have seen Gustav Mahler on the street was an event that we proudly reported to our comrades the next morning as a personal triumph.[1]

By the end of his ten-year tenure at the Vienna Hofoper (1897–1907) Mahler had evoked admiration from many forward-looking critics and musicians, but an examination of the history and foundations of such responses to Mahler's work in the opera house and as a composer reveal some interesting limitations and paradoxes.

For Mahler to have been appointed Director of the Hofoper in Vienna at the age of thirty-seven was a remarkable achievement:

> A man of thirty was . . . regarded as an unfledged person, and even one of forty was barely considered ripe for a position of responsibility. Once, when an exception occurred and Gustav Mahler was appointed Director of the Imperial Opera at thirty-eight [sic], the frightened whisper and astonished murmur went through Vienna that the first artistic institution of the city had been entrusted to 'so young a man'.[2]

This appointment thrust Mahler into prominence in one of the most culturally aware capitals in Europe, yet when he arrived there in 1897 he had no connections with the intellectual and artistic élite of the city, he disliked meeting people for the first time,[3] his lower-middle-class, provincial origins

---

1 Stefan Zweig, *The World of Yesterday* (London: Cassel, 1943): 42.
2 Ibid.: 37.
3 See AMML⁴: 293. When invited to dinner by Bertha Zuckerkandl (see below) he accepted with the proviso, 'Keine Gesellschaft, sonst laufe ich davon.' Bertha Zuckerkandl, *Oesterreich intim. Erinnerungen 1892–1942*, ed. Reinhard Federmann (Berlin: Propyläen, 1970): 41.

were only thinly disguised[4] and his circle of friends consisted chiefly of relatively unknown musicians and academics he met during his student years in Vienna (1875–83).

This comparative isolation might have continued but in the summer of 1900, during a visit to Paris with the Vienna Philharmonic, he met the wife of Paul Clemenceau at the Austrian Embassy.[5] Sophie Clemenceau (née Szeps) was Viennese, and her sister, Bertha Zuckerkandl, supported the Secession and later the Wiener Werkstätte both as an art critic and as a hostess; when Sophie visited Vienna in the autumn of 1901 Mahler was invited to dinner at the Zuckerkandls', and that evening met Gustav Klimt and Max Burkhardt for the first time, and was introduced to Alma Schindler, who in March 1902 became his wife. Alma had been bred into the very social stratum that bred and nurtured much of the most stimulating creative work produced in Vienna during the *fin-de-siècle*. She was the daughter of a painter, the admired landscape artist Emil Jakob Schindler (1842–1892), her step-father, Carl Moll, was a member of the Secession who introduced Mahler to many of its members, such as Koloman Moser and Alfred Roller, and her composition teacher was Alexander von Zemlinsky, through whom Mahler eventually got to know Schoenberg, Berg and Webern.

The first five years of Mahler's activity at the Hofoper seem to have attracted little attention from the artists and critics of the Secession, but as a producer Mahler was primarily concerned with controlling the music and movement on stage, rather than stage setting. The same had been true of his directorship at Budapest (1889–91), and at Hamburg (1891–7) Mahler had no control over design, which was entirely in the hands of the impresario, Bernhard Pollini. Although Mahler inherited Wagner's ideal of artistically integrated productions of opera, he may have been hampered by a lack of interest in visual arts:

> Mahler had no native feeling for painting; his mind was too much under the domination of literature. Yet by degrees, through much looking and an exorbitant desire to know all that there was to be known, he began to derive pleasure from pure painting and the ability to judge it. Moll, Klimt, Roller and Kolo Moser disputed the right to be his teacher.[6]

Nevertheless Mahler was already voicing his exasperation with various design aspects of productions as early as January 1898,[7] and on 1 August 1900, before his fateful meeting with Alma, he appointed Heinrich Lefler (1863–1919) 'head of set design, artistic adviser and costume

4   GM²: 158.
5   This account is based on AMML⁴: 3–5, and GM²: 156–8. See also GM(E): 664–6; Bertha Zuckerkandl, op. cit.: 41–3, and Bertha Szeps [=Zuckerkandl], *My Life and History*, tr. J. Summerfield (London: Cassell, 1938): 151.
6   AMML⁴: 160.
7   NB-L: 110–11.

designer'.[8] How the two men met remains shrouded in mystery,[9] but Lefler was an artist of considerable ability, and possessed a forward-looking (though hardly radical) outlook. Trained in Vienna and Munich, he was a founder, with Josef Urban and other colleagues, of the *Hagenbund*, a group of artists which declared its independence from the Künstlerhaus in November 1900; adopting a creative stance which might be crudely located as somewhere between traditional academicism and the Secession, the group continued until 1939.[10] Lefler's appointment at the Hofoper united diverse design functions in the hands of one artist – where previously they had been handled by separate craftsmen such as Antonio Brioschi (chief scene painter, 1885–1920) and Franz Gaul, who as head of the technical department specialized in costume design until his departure in 1900 – and was thus a step towards the achievement of artistically integrated productions.

Although it is possible that the significance of Lefler's appointment has been underestimated (indeed it is worth recalling that their collaboration resumed when Mahler conducted *Die verkaufte Braut* at the Metropolitan Opera in 1909)[11] it is undeniable that the high point of Mahler's work as a director of opera, and his creative contact with modernism in the visual arts, was in his collaboration with Alfred Roller (1864–1935). Known initially as a draughts-man, Roller was appointed a Professor at the Kunstbewerbeschule in 1899, and was already a leading figure in the Secession, a frequent contributor to its journal, *Ver Sacrum*, and a designer of posters for its exhibitions. One of the most striking was that for the Fourteenth Exhibition (15 April – 27 June 1902), a celebration of Max Klinger's *Beethoven*, with decorations by Roller and Klimt, and music for the opening organized by Mahler. It was almost certainly Carl Moll, the composer's new father-in-law, who drew him into the event and introduced him to Roller. By May they were discussing a new production of *Tristan und Isolde*, which was given its première on 21 February 1903, and even before this fruit of the collaboration was seen, costume designs by Roller were used for a new production of Weber's *Euryanthe* first performed on 19 January 1903. Roller left the Kunst-bewerbeschule, and was placed in charge of the Vorstand des Aus-stattungswesens on 1 June 1903. His relatively brief collaboration with Mahler resulted in a series of epoch-making productions:

8   Wolfgang Geisenegger, 'Set design and costumes', in Andrea Seebohm (ed.), *The Vienna Opera* (New York: Rizzoli, 1987): 191.
9   There is a possibility that the appointment was initiated by the Emperor. See Randolf Carter and Robert Reed Cole, *Josef Urban: Architecture, Theatre, Opera, Film* (New York: Abbeville Press, 1992): 17.
10 For accounts of the early history of the *Bund*, see ibid.: 31–4, and Hans Bisanz, 'The Visual Arts in Vienna from 1890 to 1920' in Robert Waissenberger (ed.), *Vienna 1890–1920* (Secaucus: Wellfleet Press, n.d.): 109–70.
11 See Zoltan Roman, *Gustav Mahler's American Years 1907–1911: A Documentary History* (Stuyvesant: Pendragon Press, 1989): 145–50 and 223, and *Annals of the Metropolitan Opera: Complete Chronicle of performances and Artists* (Basingstoke: Macmillan Press, 1990): 174.

Table I

Wagner	*Tristan und Isolde*	1903
Verdi	*Falstaff*	1904
Beethoven	*Fidelio*	1904
Wagner	*Das Rheingold*	1905
Pfitzner	*Die Rose vom Liebesgarten*	1905
Wolf-Ferrari	*Die neugierigen Frauen*	1905
Mozart	*Così fan tutte*	1905
Mozart	*Don Giovanni*	1905
Mozart	*Die Entführung aus dem Serail*	1906
Mozart	*Die Hochzeit des Figaro*	1906
Mozart	*Die Zauberflöte*	1906
Goetz	*Der widerspenstigen Zähmung*	1906
Wagner	*Die Walküre*	1907
Gluck	*Iphigenie in Aulis*	1907

In these stagings Mahler was able to accomplish at the Hofoper a synthesis, prefigured in Wagner's writings, but achieved visually in twentieth-century terms: 'The whole of modern art has to serve the stage. Modern art, I don't mean just the *Sezession*. It's a question of all the arts working together. Traditional methods are simply worn out; modern art must embrace costume, accessories, the whole revitalization of the work.'[12]

I shall argue later, this statement is more ambiguous than it may at first seem, but, nevertheless, it is not surprising that critics sympathetic to modernist trends began to show an interest in the work of the Hofoper. By the autumn of 1904 Hermann Bahr – 'the spokesman, the organizer, the catalyst, and the major critical theorist of the young artists in Austria'[13] – was asserting that in the Mahler–Roller productions a new scenic ideal, striven for by Wagner, Appia, Fortuny, Olbrich and Moser, was attained for the first time, and was using these productions as a critical yardstick.[14] Later the art critic Ludwig Hevesi also turned his attention to some of Roller's designs for the Hofoper,[15] and Peter Altenberg wrote short pieces on the productions of *Das Rheingold* and *Die Walküre*.[16]

What is noticeable is that it was an interest in the visual rather than any musical components of the Mahler–Roller productions which initiated

12 Part of an interview given by Mahler to the *Illustriertes Extrablatt* in September 1903; see Peter Vergo, *Art in Vienna 1898–1918* (London: Phaidon, 1975): 158.
13 Donald G. Davidau, 'Hermann Bahr, The Catalyst of Modernity in the Arts in Austria during the fin de Siècle', in Petrus W. Tax and Richard H. Lawson (eds.), *Arthur Schnitzler and His Age* (Bonn: Bouvier, 1984): 30.
14 See Hermann Bahr, *Glossen zum Wiener Theater (1903–1906)* (Berlin: G. Fischer Verlag, 1907): 48–9.
15 GM[1]: 544, 757, 759, 770, 1036, 1038 and 1041.
16 Reprinted in Werner J. Schweiger (ed.), *Das große Peter Altenberg Buch* (Vienna: Zsolnay, 1977): 310–12, 308–10. 'Unser Opernhaus' (ibid.: 305f.) contains an appreciation of Roller's *Tristan*.

modernist awareness of Mahler, and subsequent assessments of Mahler's place within modernist cultural developments in pre-war Vienna have tended to accept the unambiguous, but slightly imbalanced image of Mahler's contribution as Director of the Hofoper that resulted. His achievement as an innovator (or at least an instigator of innovations) in staging could be easily placed within a modernist account of the history of theatre and the visual arts, but sympathetic music critics saw the importance of his operatic career less in terms of an historical context and innovation, but rather as a striving for, and frequent attainment of the highest artistic standards.[17] Such a perception was certainly grounded in Mahler's avowed intentions, but also had the advantage of avoiding problems of interpretation stemming from, on the one hand, the lack of any appropriate historiographical model for developments in the musical aspects of operatic performance during the period from 1890 to 1907, and on the other from underlying ambiguities in Mahler's position.

The *Illustriertes Extrablatt* interview suggests that the motivating force behind Mahler's operatic activity was not primarily a commitment to modernism and the new, but an allegiance to the Wagnerian concept of the *Gesamtkunstwerk*. The first part of this interpretation is borne out by an examination of the repertoire of the Hofoper between 1897 and 1907 which offers convincing evidence that Mahler was not greatly concerned with the promotion of new works.

Table II[18]

Year	New Productions	New Stagings	Vienna Premières	World Premières
1897–8	6	1	4	0
1898–9	6	0	4	1
1899–1900	7	0	3	1
1900–1901	3	3	2	0
1901–2	2	1	2	1
1902–3	1	3	2	1
1903–4	4	1	3	0
1904–5	2	2	4	0
1905–6	2	6	1	0
1906–7	4	3	3	0
Total	37	20	28	4

17 E.g. Richard Specht, *Das Wiener Operntheater von Dingelstedt bis Schalk und Strauss: Erinnerung aus 50 Jahren* (Vienna: Paul Knepler, 1919), and Erwin Stein, 'Mahler and the Vienna Opera', in Harold Rosenthal (ed.), *The Opera Bedside Book* (London: Gollancz, 1965): 296–317. Specht (1870–1932) was a literary and music critic sympathetic to Arthur Schnitzler, Mahler and Richard Strauss; Erwin Stein (1885–1958) was a pupil of Arnold Schoenberg (see also pp. viii–ix above, and chapter 12 below).

18 Derived from Franz Willnauer, *Gustav Mahler und die Wiener Oper* (Vienna: Jugend

Table III

Year	Vienna Premières	World Premières
1897–8	Smetana: *Dalibor*	
	Tchaikovsky: *Eugen Onegin*	
	Bizet: *Djamileh*	
	Leoncavallo: *Die Bohème*	
1898–9	Rezniček: *Donna Diana*	Goldmark:
		Die Kriegsgefangene
	Haydn: *Der Apotheker*	
	Lortzing: *Die Opernprobe*	
	S. Wagner: *Der Bärenhäuter*	
1899–1900	Rubinstein: *Der Dämon*	Zemlinsky: *Es war einmal*
	Tchaikovsky: *Jolanthe*	
	Giordano: *Fedora*	
1900–1901	Reiter: *Der Bundschuh*	
	Thuille: *Lobetanz*	
1901–2	Offenbach:	Förster: *Der dot mon*
	Hoffmanns Erzählungen	
	Strauss: *Feuersnot*	
1902–3	Tchaikovsky: *Pique Dame*	Mozart: *Zaide*
	Charpentier: *Louise*	
1903–4	Puccini: *La Bohème*	
	Wolf: *Der Corregidor*	
	Verdi: *Falstaff*	
1904–5	Delibes: *Lakmé*	
	Blech: *Das war ich*	
	d'Albert: *Die Abreise*	
	Pfitzner: *Die Rose vom Liebesgarten*	
1905–6	Wolf-Ferrari: *Die neugierigen Frauen*	
1906–7	Erlanger: *Der polnische Jude*	
	d'Albert: *Flauto solo*	
	Saint-Saëns: *Samson und Dalila*	

Any interpretation must be cautious, but the record of world premières is unimpressive: during ten years only one full-length opera by a contemporary composer (*Es war einmal*), two one-act operas and an unfinished opera by Mozart. Richard Specht was defensive about this aspect of Mahler's reign in Vienna[19] and it contrasts with the innovative repertoire of Mahler's concerts in America in 1909–11, which reflect a wide-ranging interest in new

und Volk, 1979): 255–72. This table excludes ballet (a genre that interested Mahler very little) and repertoire operas. The headings are attempts at English equivalents for Willnauer's classifications *Neueinstudierung*, *Neuinszenierung*, *Erstaufführung* and *Uraufführung*. Here and elsewhere in the essay the titles of works are given in the form under which Mahler performed them.

19 Op. cit.: 47f.

orchestral music.[20] But mitigating factors need to be taken into account. Of the twenty-eight works new to Vienna, eighteen had been composed within ten years of their first performance there and were thus in every sense contemporary. Furthermore Mahler certainly contemplated the production of a number of other new operas, e.g. Dvořák's *Rusalka*,[21] Max von Schillings *Moloch*,[22] Strauss's *Salome* and Zemlinsky's *Der Traumgörge*.[23]

If Mahler was relatively unsuccessful in promoting new operas, it is also notable that one of his main efforts (again not wholly successful) was to increase the number of operas in the repertoire by Mozart, thus anticipating the future by looking backwards. The modernist critic might have commented (and it would be interesting to explore the reasons why they did not) that most of Roller's innovative designs for Mahler's production were (to make the point as provocatively as possible) used as display cases for exhibits in a museum. Mahler himself offers an answer in his interview when he talks about the need to replace traditional methods in order to revitalize the work. Such words are indicative of a serious artist faced with the fact that opera repertoire was increasingly dominated not by 'new' works, but by a relatively stable and limited number of standard works which modernist productions could help to keep fresh.[24] The extent to which Mahler acquiesced in the stabilization of repertoire or struggled against it only to be defeated by external cultural pressures is an issue which awaits additional evidence for its illumination.

Further ambiguities emerge from an examination of Mahler's handling of the music itself. He was one of the first conductors to reinstate the harpsichord to accompany recitatives in Mozart, as in the 1901 *Così fan tutte* and the 1906 *Hochzeit des Figaro*:[25] in German-language opera houses the practice of replacing *secco* recitative with spoken dialogue in Mozart had become almost universal during the nineteenth century and as late as 1915 Otto Klemperer was criticized for restoring recitatives in a production of *Figaro* in Strasburg.[26] Yet this 'innovation' (which, again, looks backwards),

20 See Roman, op. cit., *passim*, and Knud Martner, *Gustav Mahler im Konzertsaal* (Copenhagen: privately printed, 1985).
21 GM²: 293.
22 Ibid.: 514–15.
23 GM³: 94.
24 The decline in the number of works in the repertoire was noted disapprovingly by Karl Kraus (*Die Fackel* 83 (October 1901): 22–4). It must be admitted that the interpretation of Mahler's repertoire offered here is not supported by Franz Willnauer who, in his paper 'Mahler und das Opernschaffen seiner Zeit', in Carmen Ottnet (ed.), *Oper in Wien 1900–1925* (Vienna: Doblinger, 1991): 85–100, argues that Mahler's whole activity at the Hofoper shows a consistent involvement with contemporary opera. One source of the divergence of views may stem from the fact that I do not consider Wagner, though still immensely influential, to have been a standard bearer of modernism in 1897, but rather one of the foundations of the repertoire. Indeed in some circles he was already considered *passé* – see AMML⁴: 79.
25 GM²: 10 and 791.
26 Peter Heyworth, *Otto Klemperer, His Life and Times*, Vol. 1 (Cambridge: Cambridge University Press, 1983): 97.

with its apparent concern for the authority of the text, and the performance conventions of Mozart's day, has to be set alongside the addition of a new scene in *Die Hochzeit des Figaro*,[27] and new interludes to cover scene changes in *Così*,[28] and Mahler's general practice of removing most ornaments, including the appoggiaturas, from the vocal parts.[29] The concern for the textual integrity of Wagner's stage-works which led to the restoration of passages normally cut in Vienna has to be set alongside the recomposition of the end of Smetana's *Dalibor*. Such provocative changes may be understood most positively as attempts by Mahler to achieve a viable music drama, drawing on a complex network of underlying assumptions in which nineteenth-century notions about the status of the text, and the performers' relationship to it co-existed with some prefiguration of ideas which became influential in the twentieth. In fact Mahler anticipates the two major strands in late twentieth-century responses to the stabilization of repertoire: on the one hand offering new ways of hearing familiar works through stylistic innovation grounded in a genuine interest in performance practice of the past ('authenticity') and on the other new ways of seeing such works through an anachronistic willingness to restage and even recompose existing works in contemporary terms.

Whatever the discrepancies we may now discern between the motivating forces behind Mahler's re-creative work and modernist interpretation of it, for the artistic avant-garde in Vienna the significance of his directorship at the Hofoper was profound. Mahler was important to modernist artistic circles in Vienna, not just because he promoted scenic innovations, but because he was seen as a leading figure sympathetic to their cause within the Monarchy's cultural establishment. Thus his resignation from the Hofoper in 1907 was a severe blow to forward-looking artists, and inspired an address, presented to Mahler by some committee members of the *Vereinigung schaffender Tonkünstler in Wien*;[30] the list of sixty-nine signatories – which included Peter Altenberg, Hermann Bahr, Max Burkhardt, Hugo von Hofmannsthal, Felix Salten, Arthur Schnitzler, Stefan Zweig, Josef Hofmann, Gustav Klimt, Max Kurzweil, Kolo Moser, Ludwig Bösendorfer, Julius Epstein, Julius Labor, Lilli Lehmann, Oskar Nedbal, Heinrich Schenker, Arnold Schoenberg, Sigmund Freud, and Ernst Mach – makes it clear that the importance of the event was apparent far beyond theatrical or musical circles.[31] When Mahler left Vienna for America on 9 December 1907 a specially invited group of writers, musicians and artists assembled at the station to bid him farewell. As the train departed it was Klimt who summed things up: 'Vorbei!'.[32]

---

27 WY: 419–22.
28 GM²: 11.
29 Stein, op. cit.: 305, and GMZZ²: 173. Blaukopf compares Mahler's action with Adolf Loos's statement in 1908 that 'Lack of ornament is a sign of spiritual strength'.
30 The text appears in French translation in GM³: 37–8.
31 See ibid., and MDS: 248.
32 See Paul Stefan, *Das Grab in Wien* (Berlin: Reiss, 1913): 92, and GM³: 175. The farewell was organized by Anton Webern, Paul Stefan, Karl Horwitz and Heinrich Jalowetz.

Fig. 1

INHALT

Contents pages from *Gustav Mahler: Ein Bild seiner Persönlichkeit in Widmungen*

What was over, having united those present, was Mahler's contribution to Viennese culture as a re-creative artist. His creative life was by no means finished, but as a composer he had always been controversial, and on the whole had attracted less support from the avant-garde. In 1910 Mahler was

Fig. 1 (cont.)

fifty years old and Paul Stefan, a music critic sympathetic to modernism, edited a small *Festschrift* for the composer – *Gustav Mahler: Ein Bild seiner Persönlichkeit in Widmungen*[33] – which in its structure (though not so consistently in its content) reflects the Viennese modernist perception of Mahler: two-thirds of the volume are given over to contributions relating to his activity as a conductor of opera. (See Fig. 1. The choice and placing of the Klimt reproduction perhaps has a significance beyond the expediency of book design. It has often been assumed that the figure of the knight in Klimt's great Beethoven frieze was modelled on Mahler, and the placing of this precise image at the end of a book which begins with a photograph of Rodin's bust of the composer does nothing to discourage such assumptions. Mahler first met Klimt early in November 1901; the frieze was created for the Fourteenth Secession Exhibition which opened on 15 April the following year.)

It is not Bahr's contribution, but the detailed account by Oskar Bie that articulates the modernist view of Mahler's opera productions, and this is counterpointed by Hagemann's article which identifies the Wagnerian influence on Mahler's ideals. Hauptmann's brief text is unusual in asserting a link between Mahler's creative and re-creative work. The section entitled

33 Munich: R. Piper, 1910.

Der Komponist contains only two notable items: a warm and generous tribute from Alfredo Casella, and the only contribution to discuss the music, by Bruno Walter. Considering his aversion for most twentieth-century music it is interesting to find Walter stressing the 'new' as well as the traditional in Mahler's music. Some of the pieces by fellow composers are perfunctory in the extreme (one, Paul Dukas, admitted that he knew only a single composition by Mahler) and the Viennese composer who might have made a significant contribution – Schoenberg – was apparently not approached. It is symptomatic of Mahler's status as a composer that, as was pointed out by the Viennese music and theatre periodical *Der Merker*, not one of Mahler's major works was performed in the Austrian capital in 1910.[34]

Mahler's music was not, however, without its admirers, particularly among young musicians and music-lovers,[35] including many of the members of the group centred around Arnold Schoenberg. Berg and Webern, his most able pupils, got to know Mahler's music by playing piano transcriptions *circa* 1902,[36] and they soon became convinced of its aesthetic value. All three subsequently manifested their responses to Mahler's *oeuvre* in different ways: Berg chiefly in his own music,[37] Webern principally as a great conductor of Mahler,[38] and Schoenberg in his writings.[39] Because of the importance of Schoenberg's theoretical works, and the frequent references to Mahler within them, they have played a crucial role in moulding subsequent

---

34 *Der Merker* 2/14 (April 1911): 616. Later in 1911 Schnitzler declined to contribute to a Mahler issue of the journal (one of whose editors was Richard Specht), but suggested that a Mahler cycle played by the Vienna Philharmonic would be an appropriate *Lebensfeier* (as opposed to a *Totenfeier*) – see Schnitzler, *Briefe 1875–1912*, ed. Therese Nickl and Heinrich Schnitzler (Frankfurt a. M.: Fischer, 1981): 664.

35 See, for example, Maria Komorn, 'Mahler und die Jugend', *Neues Wiener Journal* (31 August 1930), quoted in MDS: 225.

36 See Hans Moldenhauer, *Anton Webern: A Chronicle of his Life and Work* (London: Gollancz, 1978): 39, and the 'Verzeichnis der von Berg studierten "Orchester- und Kammermusikwerke auf Klavier zu 4 und 2 Händen" aus den Jahren vor 1904', in Rosemary Hilmar, *Alban Berg, Leben und Wirken in Wien bis zu seinem ersten Erfolgen als Komponist* (Vienna: Böhlaus Nachf., 1978): 173–82. Berg's marginalia in this list indicates that he heard one of the first two performances of *Das klagende Lied*, which were given on 17 February 1901 and 20 January 1902.

37 See N. Chadwick, 'Berg's unpublished songs in the Österreichische Nationalbibliothek', *Music and Letters* 52/2 (April 1971): 123–40, H. F. Redlich, *Alban Berg, Versuch einer Würdigung* (Vienna: Universal, 1957), particularly pp. 93–101, and Douglas Jarman, *The Music of Alban Berg* (London: Faber and Faber, 1979).

38 See Moldenhauer, op. cit. Mahler exerted some influence on Webern's creative work (see Elar Budde, 'Bemerkungen zum Verhältnis Mahler–Webern', *Archiv für Musikwissenschaft* 33/3 (1976): 159–73) and Webern mentioned Mahler in a series of lectures on the development of modern music (published as *Der Weg zur neuen Musik*, ed. Willi Reich (Vienna: Universal Edition, 1960)), but perhaps only as a result of Schoenberg's advice (see Schoenberg's letter to Webern dated 22 January 1931 in ASL: 146–7).

39 Principally the *Harmonielehre*, and in essays contained in *Style and Idea*; there are no significant differences of emphasis or content in the other important works such as *Structural Functions of Harmony* or *Fundamentals of Musical Composition*.

perceptions of how the members of the Second Viennese School understood Mahler's music, and saw their relationship to it.

Schoenberg's activity as a teacher and theorist may be typical of his generation of *fin-de-siècle* artists[40] but he contrasts strongly with Mahler, who never theorized publicly, and was less than enthusiastic about those who analysed his music.[41] In assessing Schoenberg's writings about Mahler it has to be remembered that his relationship to the older composer was more complex and more ambiguous than that of Berg and Webern. When asked by Alma Schindler, probably late in 1901, if he were going to attend a performance of the Fourth Symphony, he retorted, 'How can Mahler do anything with the Fourth when he has already failed to do anything with the First?'[42] Schoenberg was introduced to Mahler by Zemlinsky soon after Mahler's marriage and in December 1904 heard and was impressed by Mahler's Third Symphony, which was being rehearsed for its first performance in Vienna.[43] Nevertheless this experience seems not to have completely convinced Schoenberg of Mahler's creative stature, for on 29 December 1909 he wrote (after hearing the Vienna première of the Seventh Symphony): 'I am now really and entirely yours',[44] and in a letter to Olin Downes dated 21 December 1948 admitted that between 1898 and 1908 he had failed to appreciate Mahler's music.[45] In the same letter Schoenberg wrote: 'Between 1925 and 1935 I did not dare to read or listen to Mahler's music. I was afraid my aversion to it in a preceding period might return'; and in an essay entitled *My Evolution* written in 1949 he pointed out that he came to understand Mahler's music at a time when it could no longer influence his development.[46] This complex history together with Schoenberg's own reference to himself as Saul (ASSI: 455), and extraordinary hyperbole in his address

---

40 See *Arthur Schnitzler and his age*: ix.

41 Mahler may have relaxed his attitude over the years. The Berlin journal *Die Musik* published notes about new works to be performed at festivals organized annually by the Allgemeine Deutsche Musikverein. In 1902 Bruno Walter's note on the Third Symphony, given its first complete performance at that year's event, was withheld at Mahler's request (see *Die Musik* 1/17 (June 1902): 1563), but the journal did contain an extended description by Ernst Otto Nodnagel of the Sixth Symphony, given its first performance at the 1906 Festival (*Die Musik* 5/16 (May 1906): 233–46).

42 AMML⁴: 78. In his note to this passage Knud Martner argues persuasively that in fact Schoenberg indicated a lack of interest in the First because the Second had failed to achieve much, but in any case Alma makes it clear that when he *did* eventually hear it Schoenberg didn't like the First either.

43 See his letter to Mahler dated 12 December 1904 (AMML⁴: 256); Mahler replied the following day (GMUB: 182). Schoenberg must have attended rehearsals because the performances took place on 14 and 22 December.

44 AMML⁴: 325.

45 ASL: 264.

46 In ASSI: 79–92. This statement contradicts (and no doubt corrects) the impression given in Schoenberg's 'Notes on the Four String Quartets' [1936] (reprinted in *Schoenberg, Berg, Webern, The String Quartets: A Documentary Study*, ed. Ursula von Rauchhaupt (Hamburg: Deutsche Grammophon Gesellschaft, 1971): 35–63) that Schoenberg was influenced by Mahler as early as 1897.

Gustav Mahler given at Prague, Munich and Vienna in 1912 and (even more extreme) 'Gustav Mahler: in Memoriam'[47] suggests that profound ambivalence continued to cloud his relationship to Mahler's music. Peter Franklin, in a stimulating discussion of the 1912 address, has gone so far as to question whether Schoenberg ever cared a great deal for Mahler's works.[48]

Schoenberg refers to Mahler throughout his theoretical output, but the majority of the specific, technical references are concerned with only two aspects of Mahler's music: his use of irregular phrasing in the structuring of his themes, and, more frequently, Mahler's use of dissonant harmony. That these two should be concentrated on is not surprising, as they are aspects of his own music that Schoenberg discusses at length, and, as he admits, 'In every case where human understanding tries to abstract from divine works the laws according to which they are constructed, it turns out that we find only laws which characterize our cognition through thinking and our power of imagination.'[49] Moreover, in his use of irregular phrasing and dissonant harmony Mahler is placed between, on the one hand, Brahms and Wagner, and on the other, Schoenberg, in a rigidly evolutionist view of music history: 'Nothing is definite in culture; everything is only preparation for a higher stage of development.'[50] The close of the extended essay on Mahler includes the assertion that 'this is the essence of genius – that it is the future ... Mahler was allowed to reveal just so much of the future'.[51] Such a conceptual framework was doubly satisfying from Schoenberg's point of view: he was able to trace his links in the Austro-German tradition via, among others, Mahler; and his own music, in so far as it represented the future towards which Mahler was striving, validated his predecessor's achievement.

In his 'search for ancestors'[52] Schoenberg imposed on Mahler a teleological view of his *oeuvre* which is not entirely convincing or particularly revealing. After all Schoenberg admitted that he was not interested in Mahler's music until 1908: until then it was not part of his musical past. Moreover, viewed in a strictly evolutionary way, Mahler's music, like any other, loses much of its individuality; there is a danger that it will be reduced to the status of a transition – as is the case in Allan Janik and Stephen Toulin's influential *Wittgenstein's Vienna*.[53] Its relation to its past, often complex and highly

47 'Gustav Mahler', in ASSI. In a letter to Carl Moll (16 November 1912) Schoenberg rejected the idea of publishing the essay, saying that despite revisions he was not satisfied – see Ernst Hilmar (ed.), *Arnold Schoenberg Gedenkausstellung 1974* (Vienna: Universal Edition, 1974): 248) and ibid.: 447–8 (originally published in *Der Merker*).
48 *The Idea of Modern Music: Schoenberg and others* (Basingstoke: Macmillan Press, 1985): 82.
49 'Gustav Mahler', in ASSI: 452.
50 Arnold Schoenberg, *The Theory of Harmony*, tr. Roy E. Carter (London: Faber and Faber/Faber Music, 1978): 97. Mahler's concept of music history was broadly similar (see his letter to Gisella Tolney-Witt, 7 February 1893, in GMB1: 147–9).
51 ASSI: 471.
52 James L. Rolleston, 'The Discourse of Abstraction: Thinking about Art, 1904–1914' in *Arthur Schnitzler and his age*: 123.
53 New York: Simon and Schuster, 1973: 108–9.

original, is ignored, as are those innovations which have no future.

The opening of Mahler's First Symphony (a work that, as indicated earlier, Schoenberg decisively rejected), composed between 1884 and 1888 (revised 1893-6 and in 1906), illustrates some relevant features. Even in its 1893 version (which differs significantly in orchestration)[54] it was strikingly original despite and even because of the unmistakable reference to the opening of Beethoven's Fourth Symphony. At this time the use of earlier works as models which were elaborated and transformed was by no means uncommon,[55] but in Mahler's music the model is often not obliterated; past and present audibly co-exist. This was a provocative procedure in an age when artistic value was closely associated with originality, and such techniques, together with Mahler's use of quotation (as in the third movement of the First Symphony with its explicit reference to the Bruder Martin/Frère Jacques canon) and musical clichés borrowed from popular genres such as the march, waltz and ländler, evoked repeated critical denunciations for lack of originality, banality and triviality.[56]

Schoenberg was well aware of such criticism, and defended Mahler against some of these reproaches. He argues that

> Art does not depend on the single component part alone; therefore music does not depend upon the theme . . . The inspiration is not the theme, but the whole work.[57]

The defence against the charge of banality seeks to dismiss the whole issue; Mahler's 'themes are actually not banal'.[58] Schoenberg admits that once he too found these themes banal, but on closer examination now finds them full of subtleties and beauties. Such a defence, while doing justice to the processes in Mahler's music, doesn't address the surface references to commonplace musical idioms and thus overlooks one of the most subversive aspects of Mahler's art as a symphonist: his radical expansion of the range of musical styles to be incorporated in the genre. In the early works in particular, popular and folk musics appear in a relatively unbowdlerized form, so that they create an usually strong confrontation with more overtly sophisticated symphonic material.

The four fanfares near the beginning of the First Symphony provide a relatively obvious example of unsophisticated music, and also illustrate some other characteristic features. Fanfares are one of a group of musical patterns Mahler derived from military music, and, like the trumpet flourish in Act II of Beethoven's *Fidelio*, usually announce an imminent arrival. In musical

54 See WY: 215-17.
55 Charles Rosen, 'Influence: Plagiarism and Inspiration', in Kingsley Price (ed.), *On Criticizing Music* (Baltimore, The John Hopkins University Press, 1981): 16-37.
56 See the reviews of the première of the First Symphony quoted in GM(E): 204-7, and Hanns Gutmann, 'Der banale Mahler', *Anbruch*, 12/3 (March 1930): 102-5.
57 ASSI: 458.
58 Ibid.: 455.

content, the fanfares at the opening of the First Symphony, like most, are musically simple – arpeggios around a simple chord – but their functional significance is more complex. The first set is deprived of its associated instrumental colour and is played not by trumpets (or possibly horns) but by two clarinets and bass clarinet.[59] The result is bucolic rather than military. All four sets are dissociated from the rest of the texture, the first, harmonically (a B♭ arpeggio over a dominant pedal in D minor), the rest, spatially, with the three trumpets placed in the very far distance.[60] Spatial separation of sound groups is a common feature in opera, but its employment in a symphony (even after Berlioz's *Symphonie fantastique*) was an unusual event. In the First Symphony it is used briefly and in a relatively unsophisticated way. There is some evidence that Mahler intended the third and fourth fanfares to be played nearer the orchestra (his instructions are not entirely clear, and such an intention is rarely fulfilled in performance), but the Second Symphony takes the technique further, employing brass instruments at different (and changing) distances on either side of the orchestra in a complex sound-world: another extension of means.

So the fanfares in the First Symphony are presented at first as sound events isolated from the rest of the musical texture, as evocative but apparently decorative features which fail to announce any musical appearance; it is only later that they reappear in more conventional guise. Although they are absent when the slow introduction returns (bars 113f.) they play a crucial role at the climax of the movement (bar 358). Not only does their reappearance (played by trumpets on-stage for the first time) give the dominant preparation recapitulatory weight, but for the first time they do indeed herald an arrival: that of the tonic key with its new thematic articulation first adumbrated, *ppp*, at the centre of the movement. On this level the process of transforming the fanfares' function from a decorative to a structural role is typical of this movement, but the fanfares also have another, deeper structural significance for the movement. The main tempo of the opening of the Symphony is *Langsam*, but this contrasts with the faster tempo of the fanfares and the cuckoo calls and at two points the two tempi overlap (bars 32, 47) – an extraordinary effect which appears far more prominently at a crucial formal juncture of the opening movement of the Third Symphony (bars 633f.: unfortunately most performances manage to emasculate the passage). Moreover the first three sets of fanfares have *accelerandi* marked. An examination of the tempo and dynamic structure of the movement as a whole (see Table IV) reveals what is obvious to the innocent ear: that the underlying (or is it overlaying) process of the movement is a simultaneous *accelerando* and *crescendo* which is heard twice, from bars 1 to 151 and from

59 In the 1893 version this dissociation was not present: the fanfares were played by four horns. See WY: 216.
60 This latter dissociation was, again, not present in the 1893 version, and was not added until the first edition of 1899. The third trumpet should almost certainly be placed nearer the orchestra than trumpets 1 and 2.

Table IV

Bar	1	53	59	63	110	135	151	159	163	180	189	207
Tempo	Langsam. Schleppend	Allmählich und unmerklich in das Hauptzeitmass übergehen	Im Anfang sehr gemächlich (♩=wie zum Schluss die ♩)	Immer sehr gemächlich	Von hier an in sehr allmählicher aber stetiger Tempo-Steigerung bis zum Zeichen*	*Hier ist nach allmählicher Steigerung ein frisches, belebtes Zeitmass eingetreten	Noch ein wenig beschleunigen	Etwas zurückhalten	(♩=wie früher die ♩)	Etwas zurückhaltend	Immer noch zurückhaltend	Sehr gemächlich
Time Sig.	4/4		2/2		2/2				4/4			2/2
Dynamics	ppp	pp/p	pp	pp	pp/p < ff	$fffff$ > pp			ppp/pp		pp	ppp/ppp
Key	i^v		i^v	I	V [V^v]	V			I^v	♭III		I

ACCELERANDO

RITENUTO

Bar	220	232	257	275	279	331	337	352	358	364	378	416	437	443
Tempo	Etwas bewegter, aber immer noch sehr ruhig	Von hier an wird das Tempo bis zum Zeichen *in sehr allmählicher unmerklicher Steigerung belebt	*Hier ist wieder das Zeitmass 'Gemächlich' eingetreten	Ganz unmerklich etwas zurückhalten	Etwas gemächlicher als zuvor	Von hier ab bis zum Zeichen* unmerklich aber stetig breiter werden		*Vorwärts drängend	a Tempo (Haupt-	Etwas bewegter zeitmass)	Von hier ab wird das Tempo bis zum Zeichenø in unmerklicher, aber stetiger Steigerung immer Lebhafter	øHier ist bereits ein ziemlich frisches Zeitmass eingetreten, welches jedoch noch immer etwas zu steigern ist	accelerando	Schnell (bis zum Schluss)
Dynamics	pp	pp/p	p/pp	p	pp	p/fp	langsames crescendo	ff	ff	f	p/mf cresc.	ff	fff	ff
Key	I → V	V	♭V [=♯III] ♭III					I^v	I					

ACCELERANDO — RIT.

RITENUTO — ACCELERANDO

ACCELERANDO

ACCELERANDO

bar 220 to the end (despite the *ritenuto* in bars 331–51, which serves to add weight to the preparation for the return of the tonic, the sense of a pre-dominant *accelerando* is not compromised), and that this is at least as important as tonal and thematic processes in the formal articulation of the movement. Thus even at the opening of the Symphony the fanfares are not merely non-functional gestures, but anticipations of later events and crucial form-defining processes. Interestingly, the first published score of the work incorporates similar processes in the second movement. Here the first appearance of the Scherzo material is also organized as a double *accelerando* (bars 1–108[?], 118–69), of which only a single statement reappears after the trio.

The structural use of tempo and tempo changes, the use of acoustic space and the incorporation and transformation of popular music in a genre of high art were not aspects of music which much interested Schoenberg as a creator;[61] like most composers in the Austro-German tradition, his main technical concern was with pitch – harmonic and melodic organization. In Mahler's first three symphonies a flamboyant and radical expansion of the means available went hand in hand with a more-or-less traditional concern for economy and coherence in the handling of thematic material and harmony. In the later works he shows increasing interest in and mastery of pitch relationships and it is in that area that his most far-reaching explorations were carried out – his growing interest in Bach from *circa* 1900 onwards is a related phenomenon. Thus as Mahler matured he became more like Schoenberg's image of him, as is rather aptly revealed by his 1906 revision of the first movement of the First Symphony, in which he inserted the sub-stantial repeat shown in Table IV: this compromises the elegant simplicity of the original conception (defined to a considerable extent by non-pitch elements) and brings to the fore references to conventional form-building processes dependent on pitch, and particularly tonal functions. At the same time Mahler removed the structural first *accelerando* from the second move-ment of the Symphony, thus also severing a non-pitch connection between it and the first movement. None the less Mahler never quite fitted Schoenberg's model: the form-defining role of tempo modification was not entirely abandoned, as the Eighth Symphony (Part II) and Ninth Symphony (first movement) make clear. If Mahler were allowed to reveal just so much of the future, Schoenberg was interested in exploring just so much of the territory opened up by his predecessor. As a good Darwinian, Schoenberg might have expected some developments to remain unexploited: innovations without a future, but innovations none the less.

If there is a tendency for modernist criticisms of Mahler's operatic career in Vienna to underestimate the conservative, stabilizing aspects of his tenure,

---

61 There is one famous exception – the incorporation of *O du lieber Augustin* into the second movement of Schoenberg's Second String Quartet, composed in 1907–8, before the composer's rapprochement with Mahler's music.

then conversely Schoenberg's account of his creative work, while seeking to emphasize the forward-looking elements in Mahler's music, overlooks much of his early radicalism, some of which stems from his novel approach to his musical pasts, some from his exploration of techniques which remained unexploited by his immediate successors. James L. Rolleston has argued that before talking about the art of the *fin-de-siècle* we should examine closely the way we think about history, not least because 'when it comes to thinking about our own century, it seems that the search for ancestors takes priority over the need to discriminate'.[62] In trying to achieve an understanding of Mahler's contribution to, and place in, Viennese culture it may indeed be necessary to dispense with inappropriate historiographical models and break down some conceptual categories: the composer who exploited acoustic space in his own music was the conductor who added off-stage instruments to Beethoven's Ninth Symphony,[63] the composer who used *accelerandi* as a form-articulating device in his First Symphony, was the conductor who applied the same device to Beethoven's *Leonore* Overture No. 3.[64] As Schoenberg wrote: 'The productive man conceives within himself a complete image of what he wishes to reproduce; the performance, like everything else he brings forth, must not be less perfect than the image. Such re-creation is only slightly different from creation.'[65] Perhaps a post-modern age offers a particularly sympathetic environment in which to attempt yet again to understand the full range of Mahler's achievement.

62 Op. cit.: 123.
63 J. B. Foerster, *Der Pilger: Erinnerungen eines Musikers,* tr. Pavel Eisner (Prague: Artia, 1955): 385.
64 GM(E): 257.
65 ASSI: 465.

2

Gustav Mahlers Sprache

HERTA BLAUKOPF

Abstract

While Mahler's music has been thoroughly analysed, his relation to language has found next to no attention. Examples pointing to Mahler's specific use of language are presented in the hope that this may trigger further in-depth research. Mahler was born in Bohemia and brought up in Moravia where both Czech and German were spoken. Extant documents prove that German (his mother tongue) was the only language in which he was able to express himself adequately – when we exclude the language of music. He used the Austrian idiom, but not the Viennese dialect of the lower classes as has been suggested by a non-Viennese contemporary.

Mahler's early poetry, e.g. *Das klagende Lied*, reflects the Romantic fashion then prevailing among young people in Vienna. The *Lieder eines fahrenden Gesellen* show that about six years later he had overcome such imitative eclecticism. A surprising feature, especially in the second of these songs, is the frequent use of interjections. There is evidence that Mahler favoured such 'non-verbal' communication also in private conversation.

The rhythm and the intonation of a few letters written by Mahler in 1879 show that they contain many musical elements. In a letter written immediately after the completion of his Fourth Symphony (1900) the rhythm of characteristic melodic figures of the first movement of this symphony can be traced.

A further feature of Mahler's language is his gift for jokes and puns which, in his lifetime, became even more popular than his music.

* * *

Mit Mahlers Musik hat sich die Wissenschaft in vielen Jahrzehnten analytisch auseinandergesetzt; Mahlers Sprache, auch für ihn das primäre Kommunikationsmittel, blieb so gut wie unbeachtet, sieht man von Untersuchungen der von ihm vertonten Texte ab. Angesichts der Breite und Vielschichtigkeit des Themas vermag diese Studie nicht viel mehr, als einige Richtungen künftiger Forschung zu zeigen und vielleicht auch Anregungen zu geben.

In dem kleinen böhmischen Dorf Kalište, dessen Bewohner tschechisch sprachen, wurde Gustav Mahler geboren; in der mährischen Stadt Iglau, einer deutschen Sprachinsel in slawischem Umland, wuchs er auf. Seine Muttersprache, wörtlich genommen, war deutsch, wie in den jüdischen Familien Böhmens und Mährens in der Regel deutsch gesprochen wurde, und Mahlers Mutter, von der wir einige Brieftexte kennen, verstand es, sich flüssig, anschaulich und recht korrekt mitzuteilen. An den Iglauer Schulen, die Mahler besuchte, wurde ausschließlich in deutscher Sprache unterrichtet.

Mahlers Cousin Gustav Frank hingegen gab 'böhmisch' als Muttersprache an,[1] als er in Wien die Akademie der bildenden Künste bezog. Das hatte seinen Grund: in Vlašim, wo Frank aufgewachsen war, gab es keine deutschen Schulen. Der Erstunterricht (sechs Jahre) in tschechischer Sprache[2] mag ihn bewogen haben, diese als Muttersprache zu bezeichnen, obwohl in seiner Familie deutsch gesprochen wurde. Es gibt hingegen keinen Bericht und kein Dokument, aus denen hervorginge, daß Mahler Tschechisch sprach oder verstand, nicht einmal in jener rudimentären Form des 'Kuchlbemisch' (Küchenböhmisch), die im alten Österreich, besonders in Wien, vielen zu Gebote stand und häufig scherzhaft gebraucht wurde.

In der deutschen Sprachinsel Iglau (tschechisch: Jihlava) verständigte man sich in bairisch-österreichischer Mundart, wobei sich im Laufe der Jahrhunderte einige Besonderheiten herausgebildet hatten. So etwa lautete der schriftdeutsche Kuckuck dort 'Gugug' und das Verbum klagen wie 'glagn', um nur zwei für Mahler nicht unwichtige Lexeme anzuführen.[3] Da war es zur Wiener Mundart nicht weit. Wenn Mahler in späteren Jahren seiner Frau gegenüber den Ausspruch tat: 'Ich bin dreifach heimatlos: als Böhme unter den Österreichern . . .'[4] usw. usf., so konnte sich dies kaum auf seine Sprachwurzeln beziehen. Man sprach in Wien nicht viel anders als in Iglau.

Der Musikkritiker Ferdinand Pfohl, der sich mit Mahler in dessen Hamburger Zeit anfreundete, seiner aber nicht eben freundlich gedachte, berichtete in späteren Jahren: 'Er hielt immer an der österreichischen Mundart fest, wälzte sich in der breiten Trivialität des Wiener Vorstadtdialektes.'[5] Der erste Teil dieser Erinnerung wirkt durchaus glaubhaft. Mahler drückte sich in österreichischer Umgangssprache aus, die unter den Gebildeten der Städte gesprochen wurde und durch Autoren wie Arthur Schnitzler, Joseph Roth und manche andere in die Literatur einging. Norddeutschen mochte sie mundartlicher klingen, als sie war. Daß Mahler sich aber eines breiten Wiener Vorstadtdialektes bedient hätte, ist völlig

1 Archiv der Akademie der bildenden Künste, Wien, Aufnahms-Listen 1877–1878, Bd. 100.
2 Briefliche Mitteilung (9.7.1994) von Prof. Jiři Rychetsky (Humpolec), dem ich hiemit herzlich danke.
3 Vgl. *Die österreichisch-ungarische Monarchie in Wort und Bild, Mähren und Schlesien* (Wien: Hof- und Staatsdruckerei, 1897): 174.
4 AMEB: 135.
5 Ferdinand Pfohl, *Gustav Mahler: Eindrücke und Erinnerungen aus den Hamburger Jahren*, hg. von Knud Martner (Hamburg: Karl Dieter Wagner, 1973): 17.

unglaubhaft, denn dieser war unter der jüdischen Bevölkerung Wiens verpönt, und Mahler hatte während seiner Wiener Jahre 1875 bis 1883 gewiß keinen Umgang mit Menschen der unteren Schichten, die solchen Dialekt sprachen. Anzumerken ist, daß Ferdinand Pfohl, obwohl in Hamburg tätig, kein Norddeutscher war, sondern Deutschböhme, allerdings aus dem Egerland, wo man anders sprach als im südlichen Iglau.[6] Diese historisch gewachsenen Nachbarschaften unterschiedlicher sprachlicher Kulturen, ihr Reichtum an Idiomen und Dialekten, an Vokabular und Metaphorik wurde erst durch die Nationalismen in unserem Jahrhundert vernichtet.

In der 1. Klasse des Gymnasiums, in das Mahler im Alter von neun Jahren eintrat, stand bereits Latein auf dem Lehrplan, ab der 3. Klasse auch Altgriechisch.[7] Im Zeugnis der 4. Klasse findet sich als einzige lebende Fremdsprache die französische mit der Benotung 'Vorzüglich', eine Rarität in den durchwegs schlechten Schulergebnissen des Gymnasiasten Mahler. Seine Leistungen im Französischen hielten sich allerdings nicht auf diesem Niveau. In den Zeugnissen der 7. und 8. Klasse, die er, bereits in Wien am Konservatorium, als 'Privatist' absolvierte, taucht diese Sprache, im Gegensatz zu Latein und Griechisch, nicht mehr auf. Immerhin scheint er imstande gewesen zu sein, sich französisch verständlich zu machen, wenngleich unbeholfen und fehlerhaft: 'Mon Français est une chose singulière . . .'[8]

Ein wenig Englisch eignete er sich erst als Zweiunddreißigjähriger anläßlich eines Gastspiels in London an.[9] Ob er in der Lage war, fünfzehn Jahre danach, als er nach New York reiste, an diese Elementarkenntnisse anzuknüpfen, wissen wir nicht. Vermutlich hat er in Amerika, wo immer es anging, Deutsch gesprochen. Da in den amerikanischen Orchestern dieser Zeit viele Deutsche saßen, war die Verständigung kein Problem. Die Wiedergabe eines Interviews, das Mahler der Zeitschrift *The Etude*, Philadelphia, gab, vermerkt ausdrücklich: 'Mr. Mahler gave his opinions to our interviewer partly in German and partly in English. Consequently it has been impossible to employ his exact phraseology.'[10] Die New Yorker Tageszeitungen, die Mahler interviewten, teilten nicht mit, welcher Sprache man sich bedient hatte.

Als Mahler im Jahre 1888 Operndirektor in Budapest wurde, verpflichtete er sich nicht nur, die königlich ungarische Oper als nationales Kunstinstitut zu führen, sondern auch selbst Ungarisch zu lernen. Es

6 Vgl. *Die österreichisch-ungarische Monarchie in Wort und Bild, Böhmen* (1. Abt.) (Wien: Hof- und Staatsdruckerei, 1894): 605f.

7 Diese Angaben und die folgenden entstammen den Katalogen des k.k. Staats-Obergymnasiums zu Iglau, Bezirksarchiv Jihlava.

8 Brief an Alfred Bruneau, ohne Datum, zitiert nach: Henry-Louis de La Grange (Hg.), *Mahler et la France* (Paris: Musical Revue du Châtelet, 1989): 47.

9 Vgl. Brief v. 9. Juni 1892 an Arnold Berliner sowie dessen Anmerkung, zitiert nach GMB: 99.

10 *The Etude*, Philadelphia, Mai 1911, 301, zitiert nach Zoltan Roman, *Gustav Mahler's American Years 1907–1911* (Stuyvesant NY: Pendragon, 1989): 442.

gelang ihm nicht, falls er es überhaupt ernstlich versuchte. Bei feierlichen Anlässen sagte er einige knappe Sätze in ungarischer Sprache auf, die er auswendig gelernt hatte.[11] Als ihn der Komponist Wilhelm Kienzl in Budapest aufsuchte, gestand Mahler, wie groß seine 'Sehnsucht nach deutschem Gesange' sei.[12] Der Sprachphilosoph Fritz Mauthner, ein Altersgenosse Mahlers und Deutschböhme und Jude wie er, hat die These aufgestellt, daß Gefühle wie Heimatliebe oder Patriotismus letztlich die Liebe zur Muttersprache seien.[13] Mahlers Sehnsucht nach deutschem Gesang wäre demnach seine Form des Heimwehs gewesen. Die Sprache, in der Gustav Mahler beheimatet war, ist uns in Form von Versen überliefert, die er zur Vertonung bestimmte, in Zeugnissen von Zeitgenossen und in tausenden Briefen.

Eigene Dichtung vertont

In Mahlers Wiener Studienzeit gab es einige Jahre, in denen er laut Aussage einer von ihm approbierten kleinen Biographie, den Gedanken an musikalisches Schaffen aufgegeben hatte und Dichter werden wollte.[14] Diese Krise muß in die Zeit von 1877 bis 1879 gefallen sein, als er die *Ballade vom blonden und vom braunen Reitersmann* schrieb, die später zum *Waldmärchen* wurde, und die anderen Teile des *Klagenden Liedes*. Es gibt keinen Hinweis, daß das Poem von Anfang an zur Vertonung bestimmt war.

Wir befinden uns in der Ära des Historismus; Hans Makart malte seine immensen Historienbilder; in Wien wurden ein Parlamentsgebäude im griechisch-antiken Tempelstil errichtet, ein gotisches Rathaus und eine Renaissance-Universität. Kein Zufall, daß sich auch die jungen Poeten des Landes, und fast jeder Jüngling fühlte sich als Dichter, an der Vergangenheit orientierten, und dies umso mehr, als die deutsche Romantik in Österreich erst mit einer Verspätung von Jahrzehnten rezipiert wurde.[15] Märchen und Sagen lieferten nun die Stoffe; Volkslieder, alte Moritaten und die Kunstpoesie der Romantischen Schule die Form. Auch Mahlers Texte zum *Klagenden Lied* sind archaisierend in Fabel und Sprache, mit einem obsoleten Vokabular, das Richard Wagner so eindrucksvoll aktualisiert hatte. So werden wir im *Waldmärchen*, während in Mähren und rund um Wien die österreichische Schwerindustrie entstand, mit holprigen Versen in eine mittelalterliche Märchenwelt entführt. Keine Wendung und keine Vokabel erinnern an die Umgangssprache ihres Autors oder gar an den von

11 Zoltan Roman, *Gustav Mahler and Hungary* (Budapest: Akadémiai Kiadó 1991): 68.
12 Wilhelm Kienzl, *Meine Lebenswanderung* (Stuttgart: Engelhorn, 1926): 135.
13 Fritz Mauthner, *Die Sprache* (Frankfurt: Rütten und Loening, 1906): 37.
14 Vgl. Richard Specht, *Gustav Mahler* (Berlin: Gose & Tetzlaff, 1905): 17.
15 Vgl. Herta Blaukopf, 'Die deutsche Romantik und Mahler', in *The Seventh Symphony of Gustav Mahler: A Symposium* (Cincinnati: The University, College-Conservatory of Music, 1990): 6ff.

Pfohl vernommenen Wiener Vorstadtdialekt. Wir finden dagegen das an Wagner gemahnende 'wonnigliche Weib', überdies auch eine 'wonnigliche Nachtigall', die gängige Inversion 'O Ritter mein' (anstelle von 'mein Ritter') und das ebenfalls wagnerische 'Wähnen'.[16]

Die Musik freilich, die Mahler im Jahre 1880 dazu ersann, war trotz der Jugend und Unerfahrenheit des Komponisten in keiner Weise irgendeinem historischen Stil oder Richard Wagner abgelauscht, sondern preschte vor in die Zukunft, und das bereits durchaus Mahlerisch.[17] Wenn Mahler anläßlich der Revision seines Jugendwerks zu entdecken glaubte, daß der Tonfall des Textes dem *Wunderhorn* verwandt war, das er damals noch gar nicht gekannt hatte,[18] so zeigt dies, wie sehr die Wiener Luft der 1870er Jahre von deutscher Romantik vernebelt war. Das gilt in besonderem Maß für die Atmosphäre an der Wiener Universität, unter deren Studenten nach der Gründung eines deutschen Kaiserreiches die alte deutsche Sagenwelt und eine deutschnationale Gesinnung in Mode kamen.

Sprachlich weitaus origineller, reifer und persönlicher erscheinen uns die Verse der *Lieder eines fahrenden Gesellen*, die freilich sechs Jahre später entstanden sind. Obwohl Mahler alle Texte als eigene reklamierte, ist heute bekannt, daß das erste Lied zum überwiegenden Teil aus dem 'Wunderhorn' stammt. Die Änderungen und Erweiterungen, die er hier erstmals an einem der von Clemens Brentano und Achim von Arnim gesammelten und bearbeiteten alten Lieder vorgenommen hat, zeugen von Phantasie und Stilgefühl. Das gleiche gilt für die drei original Mahlerischen Texte. Der Dichter-Komponist war aus dem mittelalterlichen Märchen, das im *Klagenden Lied* und auch in dem nicht vertonten Textbuch zur Oper *Rübezahl* beschworen wird, ins neunzehnte Jahrhundert gesprungen. Denn der fahrende Gesell ist er selber, der vierundzwanzigjährige Musikdirektor Gustav Mahler, mit dem glühenden Messer des Liebesschmerzes in der Brust. Er bedient sich freilich einer literarischen Sprache, die sich das *Wunderhorn*, die Märchen der Brüder Grimm und auch die romantische Lyrik eines Wilhelm Müller, der durch Schuberts Vertonungen Unsterblichkeit errang, angeeignet hat. Das Vokabular ist der gehobenen österreichischen Umgangssprache keineswegs fremd, wenn man von dem um des Reimes willen gewählten norddeutschen Schellen (statt Läuten) absieht.

Dieser Wortschatz genügte ihm aber nicht, denn er schaltete, besonders im zweiten Lied, Naturlaute und Ausrufe ein, die unmittelbare Gefühls- und Lebensäußerungen darstellen, jedoch nicht Sprachzeichen im engeren Sinn sind. 'Ziküth! Ziküth!' singt das Vöglein im ersten Lied, 'Zink! Zink!' und 'Ei du! gelt?' ruft der Fink im zweiten, und der fahrende Gesell selber

16 Eine Analyse des Textes und seiner Quellen findet sich bei Susanne Vill, *Vermittlungsformen verbalisierter und musikalischer Inhalte in der Musik Gustav Mahlers*, Frankfurter Beiträge zur Musikwissenschaft, Bd. 6 (Tutzing: Schneider, 1979): 18ff.
17 Vgl. Brief Mahlers an Max Marschalk, 4.12.1896, in GMB: 183.
18 Brief Mahlers an Natalie Bauer-Lechner, Autograph in der Hebräischen Universität, Jerusalem.

übernimmt die Musik der Vögel und das Läuten der Glockenblumen und bricht vor Lebenslust in das eine None umspannende 'Heiah!' aus. Der Schmerz des dritten Liedes tut sich immer wieder im Halbtonschritt eines 'O weh!' kund, das nicht Wort sein will, sondern Seufzen, Ächzen und Stöhnen.[19]

Diese Überfülle an Interjektionen korrespondiert mit dokumentarischen Hinweisen auf Mahlers Alltagsdiktion. Pfohl erinnerte sich, daß Mahler häufig solche nonverbalen Interjektionen gebrauchte. Wenn ihn etwas überraschte, besonders interessierte oder wunderte, stieß er einen 'vogelhaft quakenden Laut: ah-ah-ah!' aus, 'dessen regelmäßige dreimalige Folge er mit beschleunigtem Tempo und steigender Tonlinie fast zur Klangwirkung des "Hurra!" erhob . . .'[20] Dieser Pfohlschen Beschreibung kann man vermutlich trauen, denn eine vokalisch und rhythmisch variierte Interjektion dieser Art finden wir in einem Brief, den Mahler im Jahr 1900 aus Paris nach Wien richtete. Ein verärgerter Mahler, der sich über den Trubel der Weltausstellung mokierte und ihr gesellschaftliches Zeremoniell, in dem Musik 'unerhört deplaciert' wirkte: 'Es ist mir geradezu komisch, wenn ich den Taktstock ergreifen soll.' Und darauf folgt, in einer Zeile für sich stehend, ein 'O! O! O! O!'[21]

Mahler hat insgesamt vierundzwanzig Kompositionen geschaffen, die auf Texten aus *Des Knaben Wunderhorn* beruhen. Durch Collagen, selbst erdachte Verszeilen, Austausch einzelner Wörter, Umstellungen, sprachliche Modernisierungen etc. schuf er aus dem vorliegenden Rohmaterial die zur Vertonung geeigneten Texte. Seine Quellen und seine Vorgangsweise sind ausführlich dokumentiert worden.[22] Deshalb muß hier ein einziges Beispiel genügen, bei dem es sich überdies um ein einziges Wort handelt. Im *Wunderhorn* findet sich ein Lied mit dem Titel *Wer hat dies Liedlein erdacht?* 'Liedlein' ist ein Diminutiv von Lied. Obwohl es sich bei der Silbe -lein um eine alte Verkleinerungsform handelt, wirkte sie schon zu Mahlers Zeit unnatürlich und geziert, weil in Österreich und in Bayern seit langem oder immer 'Liedel' im Gebrauch stand, eine Form, die in diesem 'Wunderhorn'-Text, neben 'Liedlein' sogar vorkommt. Als am 6. Februar 1892 die Klavierfassung entstand, überschrieb Mahler sie, seiner Vorlage folgend: 'Wer hat dies Liedlein erdacht?'[23] Wenig später aber, als er das erdachte Liedlein für Orchester setzte, gab er ihm den heimatlich lautenden

19 Kritische Gesamtausgabe der Werke Gustav Mahlers, Bde. 13 und 14, Teilband 1, *Lieder eines fahrenden Gesellen*, hg. von Zoltan Roman (Wien: Weinberger, o.J. 1982).
20 Pfohl, a.a.O.: 16.
21 GMB: 246f.
22 s. Renate Hilmar-Voit, *Im Wunderhorn-Ton, Gustav Mahlers sprachliches Kompositionsmaterial bis 1900* (Tutzing: Schneider, 1989), sowie Kritische Gesamtausgabe der Werke Gustav Mahlers, Bd. 13, Teilband 2b, hg. von Renate Hilmar-Voit (Wien: Universal Edition, 1993).
23 Autographkopie in der Internationalen Gustav Mahler-Gesellschaft.

Titel 'Wer hat dies Liedel erdacht?'[24] Er empfand mit gutem Recht, daß das 'Liedel' besser zu dem 'Mädel' passe, das aus dem Haus herausschaute. Lange vor der Drucklegung, im Oktober 1893, wurde dieses Lied in einem Orchesterkonzert uraufgeführt. In Hamburg, wo man weder Liedeln noch Liedlein singt. Und so besann sich Mahler auf den norddeutschen Diminutiv -chen und ließ in das Konzertprogramm drucken: 'Wer hat dies Liedchen erdacht?'[25]

Dreifach heimatlos soll er sich gefühlt haben, 'als Böhme unter den Öster-reichern, als Österreicher unter den Deutschen . . .' usw. usf., aber er wußte – wie mancher andere österreichische Autor – seine Diktion anzupassen. Er hat im Laufe der vielen Jahre, die er als Kapellmeister in Deutschland verbrachte, einzelne nicht in Österreich angesiedelte Vokabeln in seinen persönlichen Sprachschatz aufgenommen wie z.B. 'Junge' anstatt 'Knabe' oder 'Bub', hat aber im wesentlichen an den österreichischen Formen festgehalten.

'Schöne Briefe' und ungeschminkte

'. . . so kann ich mich recht gut erinnern, wie sorgsam ich früher meine Briefe stilisierte und wie sehr ich darauf bedacht war, sogenannte "schöne Briefe" zu schreiben. Aber wahrhaftig, es hing ganz damit zusammen, daß ich mich noch nicht gefunden hatte, und daß mir der, an den ich schrieb, nur eine Gelegenheit war, meine Gedanken anzubringen,' gestand Mahler im Dezember 1895 seiner 'liebsten Anna', nicht ohne die Mahnung anzufügen, sie möge nie eine Pose einnehmen.[26]

Und wirklich finden wir gerade unter Mahlers Freundesbriefen, die rund um 1880 geschrieben wurden, eine große Zahl von solchen sorgsam stilisierten, 'schönen Briefen'. Kurz zuvor hatte er den deutschen Roman-schriftsteller Jean Paul für sich entdeckt, war in dessen ekstatische Empfindungswelt getaucht und hatte sich auch die dazugehörige über-schwängliche Sprache zu eigen gemacht. Die Schreiben an Josef Steiner, an Anton Krisper und auch noch später entstandene an Friedrich Löhr sind arm an Mitteilung; sie sind bloßer Selbstausdruck, zum Teil sogar angelesener: 'O, daß ein Gott den Schleier risse von meinen Augen, daß mein klarer Blick bis an das Mark der Erde dringen könnte!'[27]

Sieht man indes von der weltschmerzlichen Pose ab und lauscht dem Sprachrhythmus dieser Briefe, wird man jenseits der Semantik den Musiker Mahler entdecken. Vor allem die Satzschlüsse verraten ein rhythmisches Empfinden, das gemeinhin nur großen und reifen Prosaschriftstellern eigen ist.

---

24 ebenda.
25 Faksimile in Henry-Louis de La Grange, *Mahler* (Garden City: Doubleday, 1973), Abb. 47.
26 Brief an Anna von Mildenburg, 8.12.1895, GMB: 136f.
27 Brief an Josef Steiner, 17. Juni 1879, GMB: 8.

'. . . an den Schmerz, meinen einzigen Tröster', heißt es da.[28]

[. . —, . . — . . — .]

Ähnlich lautet die Coda in einem der folgenden Sätze:

'. . . diese Welt mit ihrem Trug und Leichtsinn und mit dem ewigen Lachen.'

[. . — . . . — . — . — . . — . . — .]

Hier geht dem Satzende eine Häufung von Betonungen voraus: 'Trug' und 'Leichtsinn' und darauf folgend das zumeist unbetonte, hier aber akzentuierte 'und', das einen Höhepunkt vorwegnimmt, um den Leser festzuhalten – ehe wie im ersten Beispiel der anapästische Rhythmus zum Schlußpunkt führt.

In einem Brief, der nur wenige Tage später geschrieben wurde, stehen die oft zitierten Sätze, die sich auf Mahlers Jugendoper *Herzog Ernst von Schwaben* beziehen, von der nur der Titel erhalten ist.

'Und wir wandeln wieder auf bekannten Gefilden zusammen, und dort steht der Leiermann, und hält in seiner dürren Hand den Hut hin.'

[. . — . — . . . — . . — . . — . , . . — . — . — . , . — . — . — . — . — .]

Man beachte, wie mit dem Leiermann ein trochäisches Versmaß auftritt, das – Zufall? – an Schuberts Lied und damit auch an Leiern erinnert.

'Und in den verstimmten Tönen hör ich den Gruß Ernsts von Schwaben, und er kommt selbst hervor und breitet die Arme nach mir aus und wie ich hinsehe ist's mein armer Bruder.'[29] Nun wird dieses Versmaß aufgegeben, ein frei schwebender Rhythmus setzt ein, der zu einem Cluster betonter Silben – 'Gruß Ernsts von Schwaben' – hinleitet. Nachher bereiten je drei (einmal nur zwei) unbetonte, hastige Silben auf die jeweils betonte vor, bis der Satz mit den Trochäen 'ist's mein armer Bruder' ganz ruhig ausklingt.

Mit zunehmender psychischer Festigung, die durch den Eintritt ins Berufs- leben gefördert wurde, festigt sich auch Mahlers Briefsprache. Man ver gleiche inhaltlich das sehr bekannte anmutige Schreiben, das Mahler aus Olmütz an Friedrich Löhr richtete ('Wagner u. Mozart habe ich standhaft aus dem Repertoire hinausintrigiert . . .'),[30] mit den selbstzentrierten, nur wenige Jahre zuvor entstandenen 'schönen Briefen'. Das heißt nicht, daß Mahler von einem bestimmten Lebensjahr an ohne Pose in seinen Briefen auskam. Wie jeder andere auch nahm er gegenüber einem Vorgesetzten eine andere Haltung ein als gegenüber der Schwester, gegenüber einem Freund eine andere als gegenüber der Geliebten, und wäre diese die angetraute Gattin. Wer Mahlers Briefsprache ein wenig kennt, kann in vielen Fällen

28 GMB: 8.
29 Brief an Josef Steiner, 18. Juni 1879, GMB: 9.
30 Brief an Friedrich Löhr, 12.2.1883, GMB: 21.

zwischen Wahrheit und Schminke, zwischen Gleichgültigkeit und echter Kommunikation unterscheiden, was letztlich ein Zeichen seiner Aufrichtigkeit ist. Sehr häufig finden wir bei ihm einen etwas schulmeisterlichen Ton, in dem oben kurz zitierten selbstkritischen Brief an Anna von Mildenburg, in den Briefen an seine jüngeren Geschwister und sogar in den Briefen an Alma, die die meisten dieser lehrhaften, mahnenden oder gar rügenden Sätze allerdings nicht veröffentlicht hat.

Offen bleibt die Frage, ob auch aus Mahlers Briefen der Reifezeit jene sprachrhythmischen Besonderheiten herauszuhören sind, die in den 'schönen Briefen' der Jünglingszeit mittönen. Nur gesonderte, sehr einfühlsame Untersuchungen könnten hierauf Antwort geben. Ohne an diese Aufgabe zu denken, geschah es mir freilich, daß ich beim Lesen eines Schreibens vom 18. August 1900 an Nina Spiegler,[31] in dem von der Vierten Symphonie die Rede ist, einzelne Motive aus dieser auch zu vernehmen glaubte. Es ist ein Schreiben ganz ohne Pose, an eine Frau gerichtet, mit der Mahler eng befreundet war, die er aber weder als Mann noch als Künstler erobern wollte. Er teilte ihr mit, wie herrlich der Sommer für ihn gewesen sei, weil er ein Werk, die Vierte Symphonie, fertiggestellt habe; er ist glücklich. Es wäre somit kein Wunder, wenn die rhythmischen Figuren der Komposition, und zwar des ersten Satzes, auf den Sprachrhythmus einwirkten.

Bei genauerer Prüfung des Brieftextes glaubte ich zu entdecken, daß es vor allem die mit starken Akzenten versehenen, aus drei Achteln bestehenden Auftakte samt den nachfolgenden noch stärker akzentuierten guten Taktteilen sind, die auch mehrere Sätze des Briefes prägen.

Gleich zu Beginn des Briefs an Nina Spiegler finden wir eine solche Textstelle: 'Innigst gefreut haben mich Deine lieben Zeilen . . .', heißt es da, wobei 'innigst ge' dem Auftakt entspräche und ''freut' das erste Achtel des darauffolgenden Taktes einnähme. Dazu ist zu vermerken, daß Mahlers Wortstellung zwar zulässig und korrekt ist, aber doch etwas ungewöhnlich; man könnte sie sogar als 'gesucht' empfinden. Zu erwarten wäre: 'Meine liebe Nanna! Deine lieben Zeilen haben mich innigst gefreut . . .'

Der Brief enthält noch weitere auftaktige Wortgruppen dieser Art: 'Wenn ich mir das für die Zukunft bewahren kann, [. . .] dann wird auch hier in Wien eine menschliche Existenz für mich möglich sein.' Weiter: 'Mein Werk

---

31 Brief an Nina Spiegler, 18.8.1900, GMB: 247f.

wird heuer im Winter von mir ins Reine gebracht werden . . .', ein Satz, in dem die Passivform dem Werk eine vom Schreiber bereits abgelöste Autonomie zuspricht und dadurch die drei Achtel schafft, denen 'heuer' auf dem guten Taktteil folgt. Die übliche Formulierung würde etwa lauten: 'Heuer im Winter werde ich mein Werk ins Reine bringen.' oder: 'Ich werde mein Werk heuer im Winter ins Reine bringen.' Noch eindeutiger im Rhythmus des ersten Satzes der Vierten Symphonie wirkt, von Mahler besonders hervorgehoben, das folgende jubelnde Bekenntnis: 'Mich ficht nichts an in solchen Tagen . . .' Vier betonte Silben hintereinander, wobei der stärkste Akzent auf 'an' (guter Taktteil) liegt. Auch dies ist eine ungewöhnliche, überhöhte Redeweise, die von der Musik diktiert erscheint und gewiß nicht von dem Bedürfnis, 'schöne Briefe' zu schreiben.

Mahlers Aphoristik

Zuletzt sei noch an Mahlers Vorliebe und Talent zum schlagfertigen Bonmot erinnert. Der Wiener Journalist und Schriftsteller Felix Salten hob diese Gabe in seinem Nachruf hervor: 'Von unvergeßlicher Wirkung war [. . .] die fast naïve Art, Worte von großer Ironie, Aphorismen von schneidender Schärfe, Gedanken von blendendem Glanz wie etwas Harmloses auszusprechen.'[32] Viele seiner Aussprüche machten als 'geflügelte Worte' die Runde, vor allen das berühmte 'Tradition ist Schlamperei'. Dieses Verdikt war kein Witz nach der Freudschen Definition, arbeitete jedoch, obwohl es ernst, bitter ernst, gemeint war, mit einer witzigen, und daher provokanten Verkürzung. 'Tradition' wird als konservativer Wert allgemein anerkannt, besonders, aber keinesweg nur, in Wien; 'Schlamperei' gilt in der ganzen Welt als Fehler. Mahlers Gleichsetzung von Tugend und Laster mußte daher bei den Wahrern einer falschen Tradition Empörung hervorrufen, bei den kritisch Gesinnten ein amüsiertes Lächeln. Alfred Roller hat nach Mahlers Tod eine andere, umständlichere Formulierung als authentisch überliefert: ''Was ihr Theaterleute euere Tradition nennt, das ist nichts anderes als eure Bequemlichkeit und Schlamperei.'[33] Gewiß hat Mahler seine Erkenntnis, die er schon als 25jähriger in Prag gewann,[34] je nach Anlaß unterschiedlich formuliert. Wirksam werden konnte sie nur in ihrer radikalen Verdichtung.

Dem Obersthofmeister Fürst Liechtenstein, der Mahler ermahnte, nicht immer mit dem Kopf durch die Wand zu rennen, antwortete er: 'Ich renne mit dem Kopf durch die Wand, aber da bekommt die Wand ein Loch.'[35] Natalie Bauer-Lechner, die dieses Bonmot überliefert, gibt auch Mahlers

32 Felix Salten, 'Mahler', in *Geister der Zeit, Erlebnisse,* (Wien: Zsolnay, 1924): 74.
33 Ludwig Karpath, *Begegnung mit dem Genius* (Wien: Fiba, 1934): 126.
34 Vgl. Brief Mahlers an die Eltern, Prag 6. September 1885, zitiert nach: Paul Elbogen (Hg.), *Liebste Mutter, Briefe berühmter Deutscher an ihre Mutter* (Berlin: Rowohlt, 1929): 243f.
35 Natalie Bauer-Lechner, a.a.O.: 116.

Kommentar dazu wieder: 'Durch solche Bilder teile ich mich den Leuten überhaupt am leichtesten mit und erreiche dadurch, was ich sonst nicht so bald erlangte.' Absicht war also vorhanden; sie erklärt aber nicht Mahlers Gabe, derartige Metaphern aufzuspüren und sie durch eine unerwartete Wendung zu pointieren. Die Zuspitzung war es nämlich, die im Gedächtnis haftete und ihm Erfolg eintrug. Bestimmt war das Wien der Jahrhundertwende ein guter Boden für Anekdoten, Wortspiele und Scherze aller Art, und Mahler, der das Weitererzählen von bereits geprägten Witzen, insbesondere jüdischen Witzen, ungern ertrug, hatte Sinn für den komischen Vergleich, das spontane Scherzwort, die Sigmund Freud vom eigentlichen Witz scheidet.[36]

Auch ein 'echter' Witz findet sich unter den vielen Anekdoten, ein Witz mit aggressiver Tendenz: Bei einer Abendgesellschaft in Leipzig setzte sich ein junger Mann ans Klavier und spielte eine eigene Komposition im übelsten Salonstil mit dem Titel 'Im stillen Tal'. Nach dem Ende blieb alles stumm vor Verlegenheit. Mahler aber trat an den 'Delinquenten' heran und sagte mit freundlichem Lächeln: 'Ganz, ganz echt! Ich erkenne das Tal, glaube es zu erkennen. Steiermark. Ich danke Ihnen!'[37]

Ein melancholischer Aphorismus ist noch nachzutragen, der in diesem Aufsatz bisher nur fragmentarisch zitiert wurde: 'Ich bin dreifach heimatlos: als Böhme unter den Österreichern, als Österreicher unter den Deutschen und als Jude in der ganzen Welt.'[38]

Mahler war zwar Böhme dem Geburtsort nach, konnte aber nicht Böhmisch, seine Heimat war Österreich, doch wußte er sich den Deutschen sprachlich anzupassen. Als Jude – und auch als Genie – freilich war er ein Fremdling in der ganzen Welt. Zu Hause fühlen konnte er sich nur in den Systemen, in denen er dachte, träumte und sich verständigte, in der Musik und in der Muttersprache.

36 Vgl. Sigmund Freud, *Der Witz und seine Beziehung zum Unbewußten* (Frankfurt: Fischer, 1958), insbes. 171ff.
37 Sikkus [Max Steinitzer], *Porträtskizzen und Momentbilder, Gustav Mahler*, Rheinische Musik- und Theaterzeitung, 31. Juli 1903.
38 AMEB: 135.

3

Mahler and the BBC

ASA BRIGGS

This is a short piece. I know, however, that Donald approves of short talks, which I hope covers short pieces. In his obituary address saluting Hans Keller, which was delivered in 1985, he referred with approval to the short talk on music as one of Keller's 'great innovations'.[1] My own short piece, a birthday tribute, brings together themes that relate closely to both men, friends for almost forty years. The BBC, a different BBC from that of today, provides the context, and the relationship between the BBC and Gustav Mahler, about whom Donald published the first of several books in 1958,[2] the theme. Mahler died in 1911 before the advent of regular broadcasting. Nor were his major works recorded in his lifetime. That they have been broadcast and recorded so many times, particularly since the fiftieth anniversary of his death, is testimony not so much to his survival as to his resurrection, the term that he himself would have preferred.

Keller's role inside the BBC was to serve as its 'musical conscience', and it guided him in the way of helping to shape the BBC's repertoire: Donald's connection with the BBC has often been close too, although he was not a member of the BBC's Central Music Advisory Committee until 1967 and his main role has been that of critic.[3] By 1967 as a scholar of Mahler's music he appreciated how much the BBC had done much to introduce the British public to it:[4] in 1960, for example, it had celebrated the centenary of Mahler's birth with a large number of broadcasts of Mahler's music and with the publication of a pamphlet by Deryck Cooke, introduced by Bruno

---

1 The text 'Hans Keller, 1919–1985' was printed in *Tempo* 156 (March 1986): 2–3, and reprinted in DMCN, 457–60. For early examples of co-operation see *Music Survey*, new series, 1949–1952, reprinted in a single volume (London: Faber and Faber, 1981) and the product of a 1952 symposium, *Benjamin Britten: A Commentary on His Works from a Group of Specialists* (London: Rockliff, 1952).

2 *Gustav Mahler: the Early Years* (London: Rockliff, 1958). A second edition, edited by Paul Banks and David Matthews, appeared in 1980 under the imprint of Faber and Faber.

3 Whatever else the BBC's CMAC had been or was, it was not the musical conscience of the BBC, and Donald left it in 1971.

4 In 1968 Donald enlarged, revised and edited AMML[2] which had first appeared in English in 1946. The paperback edition (AMML[4], 1990) includes on the cover a quote from Keller: 'There isn't a boring line in this racily written book.'

Walter, the conductor who was so close to Mahler that he spoke of 'the enduring bond between us, even though he passed before me across the threshold of a higher existence'.[5]

In his pamphlet Cooke claimed that it was since the end of the Second World War that Mahler's music had 'become more generally available, thanks to the BBC, the recording companies, the growing advocacy of conductors, and the open-minded attitude of a new generation of critics'.[6] Wisely he did not attempt to weigh the various influences against each other. He knew, however, the details of the BBC's contribution which was made in face of scepticism and even opposition from outside and which itself influenced recording policy: 'We [the English] just don't want Mahler here', Eric Blom, editor of the fifth edition of *Grove's Dictionary*, once told Donald.[7] When in 1947 the BBC planned to present 'the complete Mahler symphonies in order',[8] one of the first questions asked by John Lowe, working in its Music Department, was 'which Mahler Symphonies are available in commercial recordings, and what is the standard of performance and recording?'[9]

The idea of broadcasting more of Mahler's music had been prompted by a listener in Bath who got his dates wrong and in April 1946 suggested a programme to commemorate Mahler's death '30 years ago'.[10] In fact the thirtieth anniversary of his death had been celebrated at a concert in the Wigmore Hall on 18 May 1941, sponsored jointly in difficult war-time

5   The foreword by Bruno Walter to Deryck Cooke, *Gustav Mahler, 1860–1911: A Companion to the BBC's Celebrations of the Centenary of His Birth* (London: BBC, 1960): 4. Twenty-five years after Mahler's death Walter had written that Mahler had at last 'triumphed over the resistance of an obtuse world'. The price of the Cooke pamphlet was five shillings. There was no reference to the Mahler anniversary in the *BBC Handbook, 1961* or its Annual Report.
6   Ibid.: 6.
7   Quoted in the introduction to AMML[2]: xiii.
8   John Lowe to George Barnes and Gerald Abraham (not dated, but in 1947); Basil Lam to George Barnes, 4 July 1947. Barnes, later to head BBC television, was then Head of the BBC's recently inaugurated Third Programme.
9   Lowe to Lionel Salter (n.d., but probably early or mid-1947). Lowe suggested that the Second and Sixth Symphonies should 'be recorded for us by 1. Concertgebouw or 2. Vienna Philharmonic'. There had been a longstanding commitment of the Concertgebouw to Mahler's music, and Alma Mahler's reminiscences of her husband were first published in German in Amsterdam in 1940 (AMEB). In a BBC internal note of 4 July 1947 Basil Lam described how much Mahler music the Concertgebouw had performed 'in pre-war days' and how on a visit to London their conductor Van Beinum had said that he would like 'to do one or two symphonies for us'.
10 P. J. Bessell to the BBC, 24 April 1946. In January 1940 Dr Otto Blau, a director of the firm Josef Weinberger, musical publishers, had written to K. A. Wright, then Assistant Director of Music, suggesting that Mahler's *Lieder eines fahrenden Gesellen* should be broadcast that summer, for if Mahler had been alive on 7 July 1940 he would have been eighty years old. (Letter of 30 January 1940.) Wright replied on 8 February 1940, 'I am afraid that we cannot keep pace with birthdays under war-time conditions – let alone hypothetical ones, i.e. birthdays people would have had had they remained alive. But Sir Adrian Boult tells me to say that he, among others, is very fond of these songs and that some time or other we shall certainly be doing them again, but at the moment we cannot say when.'

conditions by the Council of Austrians in Great Britain and the Free German League of Culture in Great Britain; and on that occasion the BBC had shown considerable interest in the programme, which included, as was then most common, excerpts from Mahler's symphonies (2, 3 and 4) as well as songs.[11] 'I am rather sorry', a member of the BBC's music staff, wrote to Sir Adrian Boult, then the BBC's Musical Director, 'that we did not take the opportunity of this anniversary to reintroduce Mahler to programmes, but it is by no means too late, and may I now make a special plea for a discreet but quite frequent representation of his music in programmes.'[12]

The acquisition in war time by Boosey & Hawkes of the world copyright of those of Mahler's works which had been published by Universal Edition, Vienna, meant that Mahler's name would be deleted from the BBC's list of 'copyright music by enemy composers'.[13] And the idea, which was now opened up, of broadcasting more of Mahler's music was greatly appreciated by Boult, who did not need much outside prompting. On the eve of the war in 1939, Bruno Walter, conducting the BBC Symphony Orchestra on 11 January, wrote to Boult to say that it was no exaggeration to say that 'you help to make music history in England . . . Musical culture here in England is rising, by your merits and those of your excellent collaborators . . . Go on as you have done until now.'[14] In November 1938 Boult had conducted Mahler's *Das Lied von der Erde*, sung in English as *The Song of the Earth*, with Walter Widdop and Mary Jarred as soloists.

There was another British conductor, closely involved with the BBC, who long before Boult had helped to make music history by presenting four Mahler symphonies (one of them incomplete) before 1914, the first of them nearly twenty years before the BBC was brought into existence. Sir Henry Wood, knighted in the year that Mahler died, conducted the first Mahler symphony (No. 1) to be heard in England on 21 October 1903.[15] This was probably the first note of any of Mahler's music to be heard here, a

11 The programme began with *Lieder eines fahrenden Gesellen*, sung by Sabine Kalter, and a group of Mahler songs sung by Ernst Urbach. It also included passages from a lecture given by Arnold Schoenberg, *Gustav Mahler – An Appreciation*.
12 Basil Douglas to Boult, 19 May 1941. Boult had criticized the BBC's Music Advisory Committee for its narrow-mindedness and lack of imagination before the Ullswater Committee on the future of broadcasting in 1936. (See Asa Briggs, *The Golden Age of Wireless* (London: Oxford University Press, 1965): 183.) In April 1942 Boult at his own request was replaced as Director of Music by Sir Arthur Bliss: Boult wished to concentrate on his task as Chief Conductor. For the intricate history of the evacuated war-time Music Department of the BBC and the policies it followed see Briggs, *The War of Words* (London: Oxford University Press, 1970): 583–9.
13 J. L. Herbage to R. F. Thatcher, 11 April 1941. For a brief note on the equally intricate publishing history of Mahler, referred to in several places in Alma Mahler's *Memories and Letters*, see AMML⁴: 176, which refers to Mahler's first agreement in 1910 with Universal Edition, headed by Emil Hertzka.
14 Quoted in Nicholas Kenyon, *The BBC Symphony Orchestra* (London: BBC, 1982): 149.
15 Wood conducted Symphony No. 4 in October 1905 and Symphony No. 7 on 18 January 1913. On 31 August 1909 he conducted the *Adagietto* from Symphony No. 5. On 31 January 1914 he conducted the first British performance of *Das Lied von der Erde*.

claim made by Wood in his book *My Life of Music*, published in 1938.[16]

Boult, who was to conduct Wood's seventy-fifth anniversary concert in 1944, wrote to Sir Robert Vansittart, Head of the Foreign Office, on 24 June 1940, after the fall of France, emphasizing the urgency of 'evacuating' Alma Mahler, his widow and of 'the manuscripts she has in her possession'. 'It is very difficult', he told Vansittart,

> to give an accurate pointer in regard to the importance of Mahler as a composer, because, for some reason which it is impossible to explain, there is in England practically no public for his music. The fact remains, however, that I have seen vast audiences deeply moved by performances of his Symphonies, and have myself shared their enthusiasm in places as far apart as Vienna and Amsterdam, and there are critics who will give his work an equal value to that of Brahms, though I admit they are in a minority. These works have, I think, all been published, but as a performer I should like to say that I find examination of an MS of any work, which I may know very well indeed from the printed copy, almost always gives me fresh information and fresh help in preparing a work for performance.

Boult was right to note the lack of a public for Mahler in Britain, although he did not go further and refer to the active hostility to Mahler which some English critics displayed even when they had heard little of his music. In writing his letter to Vansittart he was aware too of Vansittart's own attitudes to Germans (or Austrians) of whatever persuasion, even Jews. The last paragraph of his letter, therefore, was cautious.

> To sum up then: though critics would not agree as to the importance of Mahler's position in the development of symphonic history, the MSS of his works will always have a considerable importance, and their evacuation would therefore be considered a work of great though not perhaps indispensable importance at the present time.[17]

'The present time' was fraught with danger, and Britain was to be cut off from Continental Europe until D-Day, with the BBC as an invaluable communications link.

Boult's was by no means the last word, however. Nor was it the first. The story of Mahler and the BBC which is set out in necessary detail in this short piece – and it is the detail which is most interesting – goes back to 1928, two

16 See the invaluable biography by Arthur Jacobs, *Henry J. Wood: Maker of the Proms* (London: Methuen, 1994): 76. Jacobs points out that the *Monthly Musical Record* in a note on Mahler's death, described him not as a composer but as an 'eminent conductor'. Mahler had never returned to Britain since conducting the first Covent Garden *Ring* in 1892. Wood wrote to Schoenberg, whom he also introduced to the British public, about the 'great success' of *Das Lied von der Erde* (Letter of 2 February 1914, quoted in ibid.: 140–41).
17 Boult to Vansittart, 24 June 1940. Vansittart published his widely read *Black Record* in 1941: it drew no distinction between Nazis and Germans. See also his article 'Vansittartism' in the *Nineteenth Century* (May 1942).

years before a remarkable (delayed) BBC presentation of Mahler's Eighth Symphony, and to Wood, not to Boult. It is based largely on primary sources. Since BBC sources at their richest cover all aspects of musical presentation – publishing; selection; implementation; finance; and performance – they are of special interest and importance. Unfortunately, however, there are often disturbing gaps. They tell continuous stories, including the stories of the BBC Symphony Orchestra and of the Proms, only in short pieces and with irritating breaks.

* * *

The first letter of 1928 preserved in the BBC archives is severely practical in content and tone.[18] Headed 'Mahler's 8th Choral Symphony', the so-called 'symphony of a Thousand', it was a staff note directed to the then Music Executive:

> Will you please note that we shall require, as soon as possible, eight vocal scores for the artists concerned in the above work. Under these circumstances, perhaps it would be as well if we have a dozen copies. I understand that part one is to be in Latin and part two in English, and Sir Henry Wood is very anxious to have the latter as soon as ever possible, as he is already coaching some of the solo singers.[19]

Subsequent correspondence with J. Curwen and Sons suggested that it would take 'ten to twelve days *at least*' to get chorus parts from Vienna.[20] Curwens were also asked to check with Universal Edition in Vienna that the BBC had the right to give a performance of the Symphony, conducted by Wood, in April 1929.[21] The reply was yes: the fee would be fifty pounds which would cover the hire of orchestral material and the purchase of chorus parts.[22]

Wood emphasized from the start how 'intensely difficult' the work was, how many rehearsals were necessary, and how important it was to carry out initial rehearsals of men, women and boys quite separately.[23] And he went on to choose his soloists, who included Walter Widdop (20 guineas) and Muriel Brunskill (30 guineas), before he turned to what was called the 'ticklish' question of the boys' chorus. It proved difficult to find the right boys. Geoffrey Shaw, who was approached first by Stanford Robinson, who had been in charge of a BBC Chorus as early as 1924, had no suggestions to

---

18 Wood and his Queen's Hall players presented the 1928 and 1929 Proms. It was in 1928 that the BBC reached key decisions in relation to the founding of its own Symphony Orchestra. (See Kenyon, op. cit.: 15ff.)
19 Mr Tillett to R. J. F. Howgill, 15 August 1928. Howgill was to become Controller (Music) in 1952.
20 Mr Hook to Stanford Robinson, 19 October 1928.
21 R. J. F. Howgill to Kenneth Curwen, 24 September 1928.
22 H. Joyce to K. A. Wright, 10 October 1928.
23 See Jacobs, op. cit.: 226; Robinson to Pitt, 13 December 1928.

make.[24] There were other difficulties too, and when, for financial reasons, Wood's proposals both for large numbers of rehearsals and for a choir of a hundred boys were judged too ambitious, he appealed to the very top of the BBC to Sir John Reith.[25]

It was not these difficulties, however, which led to the decision being taken in December 1928 to delay the performance of the Eighth Symphony. The reason given was that the BBC Chorus, then part-time and amateur, was being called upon to sing Berlioz's *Damnation of Faust* and Verdi's *Requiem* in 1929. In fact, Wood's first proposals were to prove thoroughly realistic, although the point was not proven until after Percy Pitt, the BBC's Director of Music, had left the BBC at the end of 1929, to be replaced by Boult.[26] Finance came into the reckoning also when the postponement was made. The National Chorus could have tackled the Mahler, Pitt noted, only if the Hallé Chorus had been called upon to sing in Berlioz's *Faust*, and this he had judged to be 'obviously far too expensive an expedient'.[27] Wood, who was in Tunis when over Christmas 1928 Pitt decided to delay the performance, was telegraphed asking for his agreement, to which he telegraphed in reply, 'Agree if London Press informed Postponement due to Chorus and I select April Programme.'[28]

The announcement of the postponement on 14 January 1929, by which time Boult had taken over from Pitt, stated that a different 'attractive orchestral concert' would be offered on 12 April, but added that it was 'the BBC's intention to continue the preparations of the [Mahler] work from now onwards, in order that at its first audition in this country it receives the most adequate performance possible.'[29] Boult himself knew of some of the

24 Robinson to Shaw, 28 December 1928. 'We feel with your great knowledge of church music and choirs in London you will be able to suggest where the best boys are to be found (this means, of course, where the best choirmasters are to be found).' Shaw replied belatedly on 11 January 1929 that he had little knowledge of London church choirs and that 'Choir Masters naturally do not want to have the extra work of preparing things other than the ordinary Church routine.' He suggested an approach to Dr Sydney Nicholson at the College of St Nicolas, Chislehurst, Kent. Nicholson's reply to Robinson (25 January 1929) suggested that he was more interested in getting 'you and the BBC really interested in this place' than in the Mahler. Robinson was a strong supporter throughout of the Mahler venture. One of the key figures in BBC musical organization, he shared offices at Savoy Hill with Jack Payne, the dance band leader. In 1936 he was to become Director of Music Productions.

25 Wood to Reith, 28 November 1928, quoted in Jacobs, op. cit.: 227. Jacobs notes that the latter was annotated by someone inside the BBC 'This is nonsense! and the chorus *can* do it [with fewer rehearsals]. Wood's demands are childish!' Wood had first met Reith in negotiations concerning the Proms in 1926, before the British Broadcasting Company became the British Broadcasting Corporation.

26 According to Kenneth Wright, Pitt read of his own resignation in the *Evening News* (Kenyon, op. cit.: 28). He had joined the BBC in 1923 as part-time music adviser.

27 Pitt to Cecil Graves, then Assistant Controller (Programmes), 28 December 1928. Graves was a future joint Director-General of the BBC from 1942 to 1943.

28 The copy of the telegram survives in the BBC's archives.

29 Note by Howgill, 14 January 1929.

problems. In his previous post as Conductor of the City of Birmingham Orchestra, he had conducted Mahler's Fourth Symphony and the second British performance of *Das Lied von der Erde*.

Preparation began with the recruitment of the boys – Mahler himself had demanded 'a first rate chorus of boys'[30] – and London choirmasters were circularized. The boys were to be offered one shilling for a rehearsal and five shillings for a performance. Leslie Woodgate, who was to conduct many different kinds of music for the BBC, was to be approached to help discover them. He had been a choirboy at Holy Trinity, Sloane Street, where he felt that he could find 'twenty to twenty-five boys', and he also had in mind the Alexandra Orphanage.[31] Other sources suggested by Kenneth Wright were St Stephen's, Wallbrook; St Mark's, North Audley Street; All Saints, Margaret Street, and Southwark Cathedral. 'Don't bother about the question of L.C.C. regulations', Wright added in a note to Robinson, 'as we want the best boys we can get over twelve years of age, and it may be that we can make a test case of this with the L.C.C., or at any rate get special licence for this particular performance.'[32]

A quite different problem was the question of an English text. Universal Edition informed Curwens that a text for the second part of the Symphony had been prepared for a performance in America.[33] Millar Craig thought that it could be used: Woodgate thought not – it was 'impossible to [fit it] satisfactorily both from the point of view of the sense and rhythm'. Wright judged that while the translation was good, 'in other places amusing things occur'; Boult concluded tersely that 'we should have a better translation'.[34] The result was that Millar Craig was asked to prepare a new translation for a fee of five guineas 'on the basis that it represents the same amount of work as a lengthy cantata'.[35] Once more the matter went up the BBC hierarchy to Roger Eckersley, Director of Programmes, who was continuing to express concern about the likely costs of the broadcast, which were now estimated precisely at £1,043 10s.[36] There was a legal snag too about the translation: who should retain the copyright? Universal Edition changed its mind,

30 Ibid.
31 Stanford Robinson to Wright, 21 June 1929. Woodgate was to be appointed BBC Chorus Master in 1934. In the same year he conducted the first Kentucky Minstrels' show.
32 Wright to Robinson, 27 June 1929. He told Robinson in a revealing sentence, 'Don't bother about the question of the permanent Boys' Choir for the time being, but concentrate on raising 120 boys for the Mahler Symphony.'
33 Universal Edition to Curwens, 3 July 1929.
34 Note to Wright, 26 June 1929.
35 Wright to Eckersley, 13 August 1929. The comment 'symphony meets oratorio . . . Symphony meets opera' had been made in 1910 when the first performance took place in Munich with Mahler conducting. There were 500 members of the adult chorus and 350 boys.
36 Graves to Howgill, 6 July 1929. 'Mr. Eckersley is anxious for an estimate of the cost of the Mahler Symphony, which we know will be an expensive work to perform'; Wright to Eckersley, 25 July 1929.

however, on this: 'They now agree not to push the matter of the copyright any further but they hope perhaps later on [that] you will see your way clear to handing it over to them in return for some other compensation they may be able to offer.'[37]

Arrangements were proving so complex that a further postponement was considered,[38] but fortunately Graves, supported by Eckersley, considered that this would be 'disastrous'. The only change made, therefore, was that the concert date was moved four days from 11 April to 15 April 1930. For all the difficulties and the restraints applied to his plans – which had included the idea of understudies for the principal parts – Wood was enthusiastic about the prospects, and in March 1930 he sent a number of detailed points (written in pencil) to Robinson about the score. They included such remarks as 'Pages 56 to 63 require a lot of work: Page 70 Tenors especially. Weak attack at 61.' On page 93 'the Basses were not certain over quavers', on page 204 there were problems about 'sopranos' intonation'. He asked to be forgiven the 'scrawl': he was catching the train to [Manchester?].[39]

Wood was thoroughly vindicated on the issue of the number of rehearsals required and on the number of boys. At the rehearsals they were swamped by the orchestra and chorus. 'It is obviously impossible for such a small number of boys to make any definite impression against such a large number of older voices and instruments', Woodgate pointed out. And Stanford Robinson agreed on this and on other points. 'Sir Henry Wood well knew what he was talking about when he said that it was necessary for the chorus to have 50 rehearsals. The music meeting was rather inclined to pooh-pooh him and I myself thought he was being rather on the extravagant side, but to get a really first-class performance he was quite right – 50 rehearsals would not have been one too many.'[40]

Boult left a handwritten but sadly uninformative note on the same communication. 'Discussed in conversation with Mr Robinson.' Eric Blom was more than informative. The Symphony was 'exactly the sort of music we all dreamed of writing at the age of fifteen, when nothing less than Goethe's *Faust* (part 2) would do'. Mahler was 'a composer of extraordinary artistic imagination, but without a vestige of specifically musical invention that can be called out of the ordinary'.[41] Not everyone inside or outside the BBC was so presumptuous. The BBC's Director of Finance, C. F. Atkinson, wrote to Eckersley two weeks after the performance that he hoped that it would be repeated. 'From my point of view as an outside music lover that performance the other day was something never to be forgotten.'[42]

---

37 Curwens to Eckersley, 11 October 1929.
38 Graves to Eckersley, 25 November 1929. The matter was discussed both at the Music Meeting and the Programme Board.
39 The communication is not dated, but it was sent in March.
40 Woodgate to Robinson, 15 April 1930; Robinson to Woodgate, 24 April 1930.
41 Quoted in Jacobs, op. cit.: 228.
42 C. F. Atkinson to R. H. Eckersley, 30 April 1930. The symphony was not then to be

Boult soon provided his own musical postscript. On 7 February 1934 he directed the first London performance of Mahler's Ninth Symphony.[43] And this time *Musical Opinion* wrote that the Symphony was worth 'all the performances the BBC can give it'.[44]

*　　*　　*

Ten years later in 1944, when Clarence Raybould, then the BBC's Chief Assistant Conductor, offered to conduct Mahler's Fourth Symphony, it was still possible for Julian Herbage, then in charge of musical programming, to reply: 'Certainly, if you think it would be an acceptable programme feature, but I don't think it is important enough to "play" nor to take undue trouble to find a place for.'[45]

By then, however, Benjamin Britten, the great English composer with whom Donald's name will always be associated, had entered the scene, and the BBC had been offered details of a number of arrangements of movements from Mahler's symphonies, four of them by Erwin Stein, who had heard Mahler conducting the Vienna Opera before 1907, and one by Britten himself.[46] The 'brevity and modest orchestral demands' of the arrangements would 'persuade more conductors and concert organizations', Stein and Britten hoped, 'to include them in future programmes, thus providing opportunities for their audiences to hear some wonderful music by a great but neglected composer'.[47]

One musician who responded immediately to the offer of the new arrangements was Lennox Berkeley, who had been given commissions for his own works in 1943 by Bliss. Early in 1944 he wrote to Stein:

Sir Adrian Boult has sent me the second of your arrangements of the second movement of Mahler's Second Symphony, with a view to my placing it in one of my programmes. I am very keen to do this as the music looks delightful, and the chances of doing a whole Mahler symphony are rather remote at the present time.

repeated. Fifty years later on 30 November 1980 Colin Davis conducted a performance of it in the Royal Albert Hall. For other BBC performances see Kenyon, op. cit.

43　The Hallé Orchestra, conducted by Sir Hamilton Harty, had presented the Symphony in Manchester in February 1930. (Kenyon, op. cit.: 95.)

44　Ibid.: 96. Constant Lambert in the *Sunday Referee* (11 February 1934) described Mahler's 'mind' as being of 'remarkable originality'. *The Times*, however, headed a leader, in itself a form of tribute, 'Mahler: The Listener's Ordeal' (8 February 1934).

45　Herbage to Raybould, 21 October 1944.

46　Stein published his eye-witness account of the Vienna Opera in H. Rosenthal (ed.), *The Opera Bedside Book* (London: Gollancz, 1965), which Donald explained 'should be consulted by every interested reader'. At this point, too, through Erwin's daughter Marion, the road to Aldeburgh, so important to Donald, begins to open up. The first performance of Mahler's *Blumine*, the original second movement in the first version of Mahler's First Symphony, performed in Budapest in 1889, was performed at Aldeburgh on 18 June 1967, conducted by Britten.

47　Undated resumé note, probably late summer of 1945.

He also included a letter from Boult and said that he wanted to keep the score 'to read it more thoroughly'.[48]

The arrangements included the *Andante grottesco* [*Feierlich und gemessen, ohne zu schleppen*] from Symphony No. 1, the *Andante pastorale* [*Andante moderato. Sehr gemächlich. Nicht eilen*] from Symphony No. 2, and the *Minuet* from Symphony No. 3, the last of these arranged by Britten. When it was broadcast in February 1944 by the BBC's Scottish Orchestra, along with the *Andante pastorale*, arranged by Stein, it won great praise both in *The Listener* and the *Gramophone*.[49] 'The whole Symphony is recorded', Harcourt Macklin wrote in the *Gramophone*, 'but the above on one record should be a "best seller".' For W. McNaught in *The Listener*, who had already described Mahler's mind as 'one of the most interesting in modern music',[50] this broadcast 'did more to raise Mahler's credit with the public' than the hour-long broadcast of the Fourth Symphony in October 1944.[51]

Bruno Walter, who had conducted Mahler's First Symphony in 1955, was scheduled to conduct the Symphony on 12 May 1957, but fell ill and could not visit England.[52] The Fourth was to be one of the first works conducted by the BBC's new conductor, Antal Dorati, in 1963, by which time Sir William Glock had become the BBC's Controller, Music. Appointed in 1959, Glock, a friend of Donald, was to shape the BBC's music policy throughout the 1960s. He retired in 1972. Along with Donald, he was an invaluable supporter of music at the new University of Sussex, a product of the 1960s. That was where I came in, although I had already been working on BBC history since 1958.

* * *

The last work of Mahler with which the BBC was concerned during the period covered in this article, was his last, the Tenth, which Donald described in 1968 as 'being made known to us as an entity through the brilliant and devoted labours of Deryck Cooke'.[53] The *Adagio* and *purgatorio* had been the only movements hitherto available in a performing edition.

In the BBC archives the first reference to the Tenth Symphony was brief and to the point. When plans were being made in 1948 for the broadcasting of a 'complete cycle of Mahler symphonies', W. R. Collet wrote to Hermann

48 Lennox Berkeley to Stein (c/o Messrs Boosey & Hawkes), 2 February 1944.
49 *The Listener* (17 February 1944); *Gramophone* (October 1945). Of the various arrangements discussed, only these two were published (by Boosey and Hawkes).
50 *The Listener* (28 May 1942).
51 The Fourth Symphony, conducted by Basil Cameron, had been broadcast on 18 October 1944. See also McNaught's comment in the *Listener* (12 July 1945). *Music and Letters* (October 1944), pointed out that while 'pastorale' was not Mahler's own description, it was 'not an inappropriate one, especially when the movement is played as a piece on its own. Nothing is lost of the composer's intentions in the present edition.'
52 Boult had hoped that Walter would be his successor on a three-year contract in 1949.
53 Introduction to AMML[2].

Scherchen in Zurich inviting him to bring over to England at the end of January a steel tape recording that he possessed of the Tenth Symphony. There was no answer, however. Lowe noted also that two movements of the Symphony had been played in Prague in 1924 and that, according to Gerald Abraham, a great deal of 'reconstruction' had subsequently been done.[54] Nothing else happened in 1948, when a recording made by Nordwest Deutscher Rundfunk of the Ninth Symphony was broadcast as part of 'the cycle', and the matter was not raised again until the eve of the Mahler centenary programmes in 1960.[55]

In November 1960 Glock wrote to Frau Alma Mahler, then in New York, seeking her views on a possible talk a few weeks later by Deryck Cooke on the Tenth Symphony: he would then 'play the result' of his own reconstruction ('realization') lasting sixty minutes.[56] Alma Mahler gave 'her blessing' (Glock's phrase) to the talk, but objected strongly later to the fact that the 'realization' had been broadcast.[57] She had been ill in December 1960, she stated, otherwise she would never have 'permitted any additional changes being made to this unfinished work which was protected by copyright until the summer of 1961'.[58] Glock then reassured her that there would be no further performance of the 'reconstructed Tenth Symphony' and the recording was withdrawn from the BBC's Overseas Transcription Service.[59]

Again that was not the end of the affair. The first draft of Cooke's reconstruction, which rendered Mahler's work into as full a score as possible – the whole Symphony except for a quarter of the second movement and a fifth of the fourth – had been studied by the 'experienced Mahlerite' Berthold Goldschmidt, who 'made many valuable improvements to the orchestration'; and Cooke believed that in its fullest form it represented 'Mahler's final comment on life, which after long struggle wins through to a great serenity of spirit'.[60] When the 'reconstruction' was not rebroadcast, Jack Diether, the Vice-President of the American Mahler Society, wrote to Alma Mahler, sending her a copy of a highly favourable English review of the performance by Desmond Shawe-Taylor in *The Sunday Times*.

Diether also wrote to Cooke, telling him that while Alma regarded the

---

54 W. Mann to J. Lowe, 8 January 1948; W. R. Collet to H. Scherchen, 9 January 1948; J. Lowe to K. A. Wright, 19 March 1948.
55 There had been an unfortunate performance of Mahler's Ninth Symphony by the BBC Symphony Orchestra, conducted by Rudolf Schwarz, on 9 December 1959: it was sharply criticized by Donald in the *Daily Telegraph* (10 December 1959). Dorati conducted an effective performance of it with the same orchestra on 1 April 1964. There is a reference in the Britten–Pears Library, Aldeburgh, to a plan, not realized, for Britten to compose a work 'In Memoriam Gustav Mahler' for a BBC Symphony Orchestra concert on 5 April 1961.
56 Glock to Alma Mahler, 30 November 1960.
57 Alma Mahler to Glock, 8 December 1960.
58 Alma Mahler to R. G. Walford, BBC Head of Copyright, 27 January 1961.
59 Glock to Anna Mahler, 20 February 1961.
60 Note by Cooke for the *Radio Times* (December 1960).

Tenth Symphony as 'a private love-letter', attempts had been made earlier to interest other composers, including Britten and Shostakovich, to work on the score.[61] There had, in fact, been earlier 'reconstructions', including one by Joe Wheeler which had been broadcast in South America. Frau Mahler, he believed, would become interested in a broadcast of a 'reconstructed' Symphony only if a 'world-famous conductor' wanted to perform it with 'some leading orchestra'. There had been some suggestion of an international committee of musicians to agree on a definitive 'reconstruction'.[62]

Cooke, who knew nothing of the other 'reconstructions', sent a tape of his own full score both to Diether and to Erwin Ratz, Vice-President of the International Mahler Society, and at last in May 1963 Alma gave the BBC permission to broadcast the version which he and Goldschmidt prepared later in the year.[63] Her own letter is missing. The news came too late for an early broadcast,[64] but – and Wood would have approved – it was included (with the London Symphony Orchestra) in the 1964 Proms. 'I had always wanted it to be a BBC première', Cooke told Glock.[65] This work was later performed by the BBC Symphony Orchestra, with Walter Susskind guest conducting during Dorati's final season as BBC Conductor.[66]

This short piece has a happy ending. In an exuberant letter written in the summer of 1963 Cooke reported that 'Mrs Mahler is extremely enthusiastic that he [Eugene Ormandy] should give the American première in September next year as a "gala opening" to the Philadelphia Orchestra's 1964–5 season.' Plans were afoot also for a German première in February and an Italian performance around the same time. 'Everything seems to have worked out perfectly at last.' May it do also for the subject of this *Festschrift*, who in 1985 dedicated *Gustav Mahler: Songs and Symphonies of Life and Death: Interpretations and Annotations* to Mahler's younger daughter, Anna, born in 1904.

---

61 For a lurid and unconvincing, if gripping account of Alma's attempt to persuade Britten to work on it, see B. W. Wessling, *Alma-Gefährtin von Gustav Mahler, Oskar Kokoschka, Walter Gropius, Franz Werfel* (Düsseldorf, Claasen, 1983): 16–20.
62 J. Diether to D. Cooke, 8 March 1961.
63 Gerald Abraham, then Assistant Controller, Music, to Anna Mahler, 8 May 1963.
64 Cooke to Glock, 6 June 1963.
65 Cooke to Glock, 21 June 1963; 9 August 1963.
66 Kenyon, op. cit.: 329. Dorati had conducted Mahler's Second Symphony on 6 October 1965. There were still reservations about the reconstructed Tenth Symphony in Vienna. Hans Keller told a member of the staff of the Central Office of Information in a letter of 14 August 1964 that 'The International Mahler Society, whose main seat is Vienna, is dead against Deryck Cooke's reconstruction as a matter of principle. They don't know it.'

4

Gustav Mahler: Memories and Translations

PETER FRANKLIN

> And how necessary it is that a person should remain a 'person' and not be
> frozen into a legend, turned into an insufferable plaster-bust.
>
> Alma Mahler-Werfel: *Mein Leben*[1]

Part of the task of historical biography must be to interrogate and scrutinize
the documents on which it relies. In the process they may grow and alter in
appearance, almost like living beings. Questions about their nature and
extent as texts are rarely straightforward. For the biographer who is first in
line, legal and moral problems spring up thornily on all sides, as if to guard
the more intimate sources and the story they could tell. How much may be
revealed while relatives and friends still live? Later generations of biographers have their task of unravelling the 'truth' further complicated when
they find themselves in conflict not only with cherished myths about their
subject, but also with what have become canonical versions of the source
texts which helped to generate those myths and which will have gained the
status of historical documents in their own right.

Mahler biography came of age with the appearance of the first volume of
Henry-Louis de La Grange's mammoth study in 1973.[2] His rich, synoptic
biography of the composer inevitably drew upon all the source memoirs by
Mahler's friends and contemporaries. It also revealed enough about those
texts for their character indeed to begin to change. The discovered sources of
published recollections and letters generated new material, both concrete
and speculative: excised passages could be reinserted in edited versions;
questions could be asked about the reasons for their excision in the first
place. Two texts in particular will occupy me here. In both cases de La
Grange has described what appear to be their primary manuscript sources,
complete scholarly editions of which remain a tantalizing future prospect.
Meanwhile the story of already published editions and translations is worth
telling. Natalie Bauer-Lechner's *Recollections of Gustav Mahler* and Alma

---

1   Alma Mahler Werfel, *Mein Leben* [first published by Fischer in 1960] (Frankfurt a.M.:
    Fischer, 1963): 186.
2   GM(E). It was eventually superseded by the same author's GM¹, GM², GM³.

Mahler's *Gustav Mahler: Memories and Letters* have, thanks not least to the editorial and patronal care of Donald Mitchell, continued to exert a worldwide influence on students of Mahler. Even in advance of any wider accessibility of their complete original sources, the on-going history of these established texts is absorbing.[3] None of my material is unfamiliar in German; fragments of translation (or retranslation) are offered only as provisional suggestions. Perhaps what I have to tell is more in the nature of a cautionary tale for such English and American Mahlerians who either do not read German or do not have access to the relevant German texts. Professional historians should know it all. Or does there exist, perhaps, a special, English readers' Mahler, idiosyncratically marked and defined by textual tradition?

* * *

In 1923 Natalie Bauer-Lechner's engaging and revealing *Erinnerungen an Gustav Mahler* first appeared in book form. This became available in English, translated by Dika Newlin, in 1980.[4] I was then able, in the Foreword, to sketch what was already apparent about the complicated trail of vicissitudes that had attended Bauer-Lechner's original *Mahleriana* manuscript.[5] The material it contained had apparently been extracted from over thirty diaries that had once existed. In these, 'dear, merry old Natalie',[6] as Mahler once called her at a time when her attentions were not proving tiresome, had recorded almost her every meeting and conversation with the man she clearly and yet unrequitedly loved (a possibly comparable manuscript recording conversations with Mahler's long-standing friend Siegfried Lipiner also once existed amongst Natalie's papers).[7] The book's history was extended, and further complicated, by the publication in 1984 of the full German typescript from which the 1923 edition had been made by Johann Killian – a *Gymnasium* professor who was the husband of Natalie's niece. His son, Herbert Killian, was responsible for the new publication and was thus excellently qualified to present fascinating new material about Natalie, not least her outspoken feminism and the 'treasonable' 1918 article on war and the need for female suffrage which led to her arrest and imprisonment.[8] This experience seems to have precipitated the collapse of her health; she died in straitened circumstances in 1921.

---

3 Donald Mitchell has been responsible now for three editions of Alma Mahler's book, each containing more information than the last (for the most recent, see AMML[4]). As head of Faber Music he was responsible for publishing NB-L and, indeed, for allowing the grateful present author to annotate it.
4 NB-L. The source was Natalie Bauer-Lechner, *Erinnerungen an Gustav Mahler* (Leipzig: E. P. Tal, 1923).
5 See NB-L: 9–13.
6 GMB[1]: 145 (letter 108, 1892).
7 See HK: 11.
8 HK: 12.

She had previously entrusted the *Mahleriana* manuscript (having been dissuaded from publishing it 'by earnest friends')[9] not to Johann Killian, as I suggested in 1980, but to her friend Erika Spann-Rheinisch, who was charged with its publication in Natalie's last will and testament (dated 5 August 1920).[10] In the event Frau Spann-Rheinisch declined the task in favour of Johann Killian, but she had played an important role. She it was who appears to have persuaded Natalie, in 1920, not to demand, after all, a hundred-year delay before the Mahler material might be published; she appears briefly to have been on the point of signing a contract for publication that year.

Extracts from the manuscript *were* published in 1920, in the *Musikblätter des Anbruch*,[11] adding to those which first appeared anonymously in the Mahler edition of *Der Merker* 1912.[12] A further element in the story now contributed by Herbert Killian was that Natalie's will described the relevant *Mahleriana* manuscript as 'recently revised, modified and extended in 1916'.[13] The version published in 1984, while much longer than the 1923 edition, is not the complete manuscript owned and described by de La Grange.[14] What is clear, however, is that although that more complete version exists, as the most important references to it in de La Grange's *Mahler* indicate, the new Killian edition replaces innumerable excisions and further adds sixty complete new headed sections (of varying length) to the original one hundred and forty-nine, representing an expansion by over one-third. They include most of the material presented in Constantin Floros's 1977 publication of hitherto unknown extracts from Bauer-Lechner's 'complete manuscript' (in an Appendix to the first volume of his Mahler study).[15] The new material is far more extensive than indicated by Norman Lebrecht in his *Mahler Remembered* (1987); significantly a large portion of the extract from the full manuscript text which he prints 'for the first time' was already to be found in the new Killian edition).[16] My comments here arise specifically from comparisons between the 1923 and 1984 published texts.

Material reinserted in otherwise familiar sections often concerns Natalie's personal feelings towards Mahler: it extends rather than radically alters the impression gained of their relationship from the edited version. Some of the new matter is interesting for other reasons too, as where it exemplifies the writer's own response to Mahler's works. In 1896 (at the Berlin concert

---

9 HK: 12.
10 HK: 12–14.
11 *Musikblätter des Anbruch* 7–8 (April 1920): 305–9.
12 *Der Merker* (March 1912): 184–8. (The edition is wrongly ascribed to 1913 on p. 12 of the English edition [see n. 4].)
13 HK: 14.
14 See GM(E): 700.
15 See Constantin Floros, *Gustav Mahler*, Vol. I, 'Die geistige Welt Gustav Mahlers in systematischer Darstellung' (Wiesbaden: Breitkopf and Härtel, 1977): 190–201. All but the last ('Platonische Dialoge', 15 November 1901) appear in HK.
16 See NL: 7.

including the Fourth Symphony, the *Lieder eines fahrenden Gesellen* and the first movement of the Second Symphony) Natalie watched Mahler's 'beloved form' on the podium and heard the struggles and experiences of his inner life 'painfully actualized' in the 'gigantic sounds' of his music.[17] Other sections reveal more details of Mahler's notorious regime at the Vienna Court Opera, as in this recorded statement of 1898:

> ... when I have a moment to spare ... I run into the rehearsal room where repetiteurs and conductor are working with chorus-members or soloists. With the first, when they are making a mess of things, I break in right away and show them how to do it. With the illustrious conductors that is not possible, so I summon the singers to me directly after the rehearsal and go through more or less everything again from both musical and dramatic aspects.[18]

Complete new sections add much in the way of material quoted quasi-verbatim from Mahler on his works, his conducting and his artistic philosophy. Even Mahler's elsewhere discreetly mentioned bowel troubles play a more prominent role in this less severely censored version of Bauer-Lechner's narrative. In the summer of 1899 we see him rushing off in delight as a laxative pill finally takes effect in the middle of a conversation about artistic creativity; he returns with 'Revelge' sketched in his notebook ...[19] Later, at the November 1900 performance of the First Symphony in Vienna, Natalie is found considering with amusement the extent to which Mahler's music disturbed the standard Viennese concert audience – particularly its fashionable, high-society members in the most expensive seats. The real listeners and enthusiasts, she tells us, were to be found amongst the students, musicians and eager young women 'in the galleries and particularly the standing-places'.[20] Natalie saw and understood a great deal and demonstrates strength and shrewdness as much as gushing adoration in the newly printed material. This concludes, as de La Grange had described in 1973, with her sad private farewell to the recently married Mahler, whose fate she can only entrust to the 'highest, eternal Master'.[21]

Particularly touching is the reinstated description of Natalie's last spring and summer days with Mahler in 1901, first in Abbazia and then at his newly built house on the Wörthersee, familiar to us from Alma Mahler's later memoirs. Fleetingly, perhaps for want of anyone else, he seems to have drawn closer to his sister Justine's friend. In April he shared with Natalie the recollection of two remarkable childhood dreams.[22] One was an apocalyptic nightmare, involving his mother and brother Ernst (the shock of whose early

---

17 HK: 46.
18 HK: 114.
19 Summer 1899. See HK: 135, and GM(E): 522–3.
20 HK: 177.
21 1902. See HK: 204; also GM(E): 699.
22 See HK: 185–6.

death has figured in many psychological analyses of Mahler's personality): at its climax he was summoned by the Eternal Jew, who handed him a staff surmounted by a golden cross. In the other dream, Death had come to claim him in a room full of people. Natalie later describes a musical house party at Maiernigg made up, as it were, of two unmarried couples: Justine (the composer's eldest surviving sister) and Arnold Rosé, Mahler and herself. The evening ended in idyllic fashion for Natalie:

> Excited by the music and struck by the most beautiful moonlit night, Mahler and I walked to the lakeside while the others began to settle down. We looked for the extended walk along the shore and the various new paths in the adjoining woodland – this Mahler had acquired as far as the 'spring', over whose good, clear water he never ceased to delight. Mahler was happier, more relaxed in himself than for a long time. 'Look, once again the truth of the saying is proved: What one longs for in youth one has in plenty in old age. Would you have believed that we could ever call such a divine place our own?'
> In childish delight we ran to all the lovely spots, the upward-curving paths slowly emerging to our gaze amongst the thickly grown woodland. Coming back out of the mysterious darkness of the trees, we climbed up to Mahler's little lamplit room, the most magnificent of lofty dens that he has ever had. When we walked out on to the balcony the night sky's myriad points of light were mirrored in the lake with such miraculous splendour that we put out the lamp and quietly talked and dreamed for a long time.[23]

The whole scene could have been a cinematic gift to Ken Russell, not least its conclusion, when the calm was strangely broken, shortly after they had parted for the night, by the cries of an unknown man who had fallen into the water and had to be rescued by Mahler.

Eventually the day arrived for the latter to return to Vienna. Natalie joined him in the carriage taking him to Klagenfurt and the station, on a night so cold that they huddled together for warmth. She notes that as a sign of their 'besten Übereinstimmung' that summer (literally 'time of closest mutual harmony'), Mahler sent her the sketches of all the songs he had composed during the course of it.[24]

* * *

Almost within weeks, he had met the brilliant young woman who would become his wife and the last, and perhaps most significant of his 'source' biographers. Chronologically, the *Memories and Letters* of 1940 had been preceded by her 1924 edition of Mahler's letters[25] and, more recently, by

23 HK: 191–2.
24 See HK: 195.
25 AMWB.

other first-hand accounts of his life. Bruno Walter's little book was first published in 1936, the twenty-fifth anniversary of Mahler's death.[26] It was, however, an oddly studied and formal expression of his affection for Mahler and in many respects highly derivative; it was certainly modelled in form and even content upon Richard Specht's *Gustav Mahler* of 1913.[27] In a sense much closer to Alma, in both attitude and even probable date of writing, was the remarkable, if often bitter memoir (first published in 1973) by the critic and composer Ferdinand Pfohl who had known, admired and been exasperated by Mahler during his Hamburg period.[28] Pfohl, no less than Alma, was fascinated by the enigmatic contradictions and charismatic power of Mahler's personality and had been similarly ambivalent in his evaluation of them. Behind that ambivalence lay the personal hurt of being 'dropped' by Mahler after the latter had moved to Vienna. Pfohl's portrait of the composer nevertheless demonstrates, no less than Walter's, a significant investment in the neo-romantic image of the Genius that was still supported by traditional musical culture between the wars. With Alma we encounter a newer, more iconoclastic kind of intelligence.

She has been vilified as a faddish Nietzschean modernist, her memoirs scorned for the 'all too feminine vision' they manifest (this in *The Times Literary Supplement*'s review of the English translation of the *Memories and Letters* in 1946).[29] We are now in a position to see that hers was altogether a more modern approach, while anticipating from the start the potentially sensationalist fascination for irrational phenomena that would characterize the popular intellectual culture of post-Second-World-War America (she ended her days there, in New York, in 1964). Of course her attitudes had to do with the fact that she was a woman, but so too that she was a highly articulate and thinking woman: one who confronted head on matters that few of her contemporaries, men or women, cared to discuss or question. (Mahler himself, whom she married in 1902, seems to have been no exception in this.)

In its way, the 1946 *TLS* review of *Memories and Letters* initiated the long-running debate about Alma's two widely read autobiographical works which was joined around 1970 by both Donald Mitchell and Henry-Louis de La Grange, the latter observing that 'the most serious distortions of the truth . . . are those which were deliberately introduced and fostered by [Mahler's] wife . . .'[30] In his 1969 Foreword to the American version of his

---

26 Bruno Walter, *Gustav Mahler*, tr. James Galston, with a biographical essay by Ernst Krenek (New York: Vienna House, 1973 [originally Vienna: Herbert Reichner, 1936; new edition Berlin: S. Fischer, 1957]).

27 Richard Specht, *Gustav Mahler* (Berlin: Schuster and Loeffler, 1913).

28 Ferdinand Pfohl, *Gustav Mahler: Eindrücke und Erinnerungen aus den Hamburger Jahren* (Hamburg: Karl Dieter Wagner, 1973). A quotation will be found in NL: 92–4. Further quotations and commentary on Pfohl's book will be found in Peter Franklin, 'Mahleriana', *Musical Times* 126 (April 1985): 208–11.

29 *The Times Literary Supplement* (10 August 1946).

30 Henry-Louis de La Grange, 'Mistakes about Mahler', *Music and Musicians* (October

revised edition of Basil Creighton's English translation, Mitchell more generously maintained that 'Alma Mahler's recollections . . . are exceptionally well founded and accurate, even though she may have erred in detail . . .'[31] The 1946 *TLS* review had nevertheless concluded as follows: 'A more detached and more expert writer would not have achieved the paradox of turning an apologia and an encomium into an indictment.'

Never was there a more revealing statement bearing on the vexed issue of truth and falsehood in biographical writing. Was it not inevitable that there should be ambivalence in Alma's record of coming to terms with a husband twice her age whom she discovered to be at once a genius, a hypochondriac, a frenetic hill-walker, a tyrant and a sometimes childlike, sometimes insensitive intellectual who would read Kant aloud to take her mind off her labour pains? Is not Alma's complex assessment of the same man, with essentially the same self-image, as had been described by the earlier biographers a function of both age and cultural difference, rather than of a deliberate attempt at denigration? It now seems far less clear that we need read her account as an 'indictment'.

*　*　*

The reader of Alma Mahler does, however, need to be aware of textual problems not unlike those affecting Natalie Bauer-Lechner's recollections. Once again there exist behind the published texts one or more 'source' manuscripts. In 1972 de La Grange was to describe these as including

> the complete and unpublished manuscript of . . . *Ein Leben mit Mahler*, the personal diary she kept when she was engaged to him, a few later passages from the same diary and many unpublished letters which Mahler wrote to her . . . [in which] occasional passages have been crossed out by Alma herself to conceal some awkward truth.[32]

The three-volume edition of de La Grange's biography includes further details about this manuscript material;[33] vital parts of it, like the remarkable 'ultimatum' letter that Mahler wrote to Alma, setting out the terms of their marriage in December 1901, are quoted there.[34] The notes to the new, 1990 edition of *Memories and Letters* by Donald Mitchell and Knud Martner are also rich in quotations both from *Ein Leben mit Mahler* and Alma's diary.[35] Three works drawing upon all this material were in fact published during Alma's lifetime (accusations of selectivity and suppression might be

   1972): 20 (a longer version of a similarly titled article which had appeared in the *Saturday Review* in 1969).
31 AMML⁴: xxxvi–xxxvii.
32 Henry-Louis de La Grange, op. cit.: 21.
33 See GM³: 767, n. 246.
34 See GM(E): 684–90.
35 AMML⁴. Knud Martner's redating of many of the letters makes this edition doubly valuable.

countered by the clear indication that she wanted to publish more in 1960 than the German editor of *Mein Leben* thought advisable).[36] Although they overlap in content, the three books are distinct from each other in important ways. They can be listed chronologically by publication date as follows: 1940: *Gustav Mahler: Erinnerungen und Briefe*[37] (translated in 1946 as *Gustav Mahler: Memories and Letters*); 1959: *And the Bridge is Love* (in English, compiled and translated with Alma's collaboration by E. B. Ashton);[38] 1960: *Mein Leben*.

The last of these is frequently described as a German 'version' of *And the Bridge is Love*,[39] but this is true only to a very limited extent. Both books represent complete autobiographies based on her diaries, but *And the Bridge is Love* covers the full span of her life and is mostly narrative. It includes a drastically shortened (47 as opposed to 198 pp.) and 'newly translated'[40] version of the Mahler-period material that comprises the narrative sections of the *Erinnerungen und Briefe*. In *Mein Leben*, the Mahler section is further reduced to fewer than 16 pages, largely consisting of direct quotations from her diary, however, and thus complementing her other accounts in an interesting way. The text of *Mein Leben* is a chain of direct quotations from diary material, linked by, but not fully absorbed into short sections of narrative. While the *Erinnerungen und Briefe* text represents the fullest published version of *Ein Leben mit Gustav Mahler*, non-German readers are to be warned that Basil Creighton's 1946 English version, although incorporating material that was apparently added at that time and is not found in the German original, is often characterized by a cavalier tendency to abridge and 'revise' (particularly where the original was direct about sexual matters). In later printings of his splendidly informative edition of 1968, Donald Mitchell has clearly been obliged to use the same truncated and inadequately translated Creighton text. In 1973 he nevertheless included a valuable list of the omissions from the 'Letters' section and additional footnotes by Knud Martner, much extended in 1990. He had already begun, in his Introduction to the 1969 American Edition, to draw attention to other material omitted by Creighton, like the the account of Mahler's and Alma's experience in Warsaw on the way back from the 'honeymoon' trip to Russia.[41] It is characteristic of the uncertain relationship between published versions of Alma's memoirs that that story is found (told more briefly) in *And the Bridge is Love*,[42] the English style of which, if in certain material respects more faithful to comparable sections in the German originals, tends nevertheless

36 See Willy Haas's introduction to Alma Mahler, *Mein Leben*, op. cit.: 10.
37 AMEB.
38 ABL.
39 See Susan Filler, *Gustav and Alma Mahler: A Guide to Research* (New York: Garland, 1989): 147, entry 504.
40 It is so described in a footnote in ABL: 19, n. 38.
41 See AMML³: xxxiv–xxxv.
42 ABL: 27, n. 38.

to coarsen and sensationalize Alma's own German style (to what extent professional 'ghost writers' were involved in all cases must remain a matter for conjecture).

Given that the *Memories and Letters* remain widely read and influential, it is worth reconsidering the extent of the omissions from the still standard English text. The opening section, 'First Meeting' [Begegnung/1901], is not uncharacteristic of the whole. The first, fateful words that Zuckerkandl utters to Alma on the Ringstrasse are recorded by Creighton as 'We've got Mahler coming in tonight – won't you come?'[43] A more faithful and complete rendering might be 'Mahler will be coming to us today. Don't you want to be there too? – I know you are interested in him.' The omissions are minor but they indicate why one might be disinclined to trust this translator. Some pages later, after the biographical digression, Creighton's decision not to translate Mahler's anonymous love poem compounds the problem of his rendering (p. 5) of Mahler's parting words to Alma after that first meeting at the Zuckerkandls'. She had promised to accept his invitation to the dress rehearsal of *Tales of Hoffmann* only if she had previously completed some useful work (for Alexander Zemlinsky, with whom she was studying composition). He responds, according to Creighton, 'Then that's a promise?'[44] The German is 'Ein Mann – ein Wort' ('A man's as good as his word' comes close enough); this, of course, is the phrase Mahler works into the last stanza of his poem, with its deliberate musical imagery:

> It happened over night.
> I shouldn't have believed
> That counterpoint and form
> Could give me a heavy heart again.

> In just one night
> It overwhelmed me;
> All the parts just converge
> Homophonically into a single line.

> It happened over night
> – I stayed awake throughout –
> That now I find myself, at every knock,
> Turning my eyes towards the door.

> I hear it: a man's as good as his word!
> Continually it plays –
> A sort of canon:
> I look at the door – and wait.[45]

---

43 Creighton version (all edns): 3. The German text I have used is the second edition (1949) of AMEB. Here compare p. 9.

44 Creighton: 5; German text: 12, n. 43.

45 Creighton: 16. An alternative translation is provided in Françoise Giroud, *Alma Mahler, or The Art of Being Loved*, tr. R. M. Stock (Oxford: Oxford University Press, 1991): 26. Questions about the date of receipt of this anonymous poem are raised in a new note in AMML⁴ (see n. 35); textual questions must, of course, include one about Alma's

In the section 'Marriage and Life Together' (p. 33), Creighton's Mahler catches 'a severe feverish chill' on the train to St Petersburg; Alma comments that he 'suffered all his life from these infections and his fatal illness was partly due to one of them'. In the German text Mahler has a 'terrible migraine [*furchtbare Migräne*]' and Alma describes it as 'one of those auto-intoxications [*Autointoxicationen*] from which he suffered all his life and which contributed to his fatal illness'.[46] Quite what she means by auto-intoxication, is not entirely clear, but thus it should remain. By the same token, passages that might once have been omitted as reasonable economies deserve to be reinstated – like the short paragraph in 'Sorrow and Dread'[47] which described how the great physicist Ludwig Boltzman (1844–1906) had written to Mahler, suggesting that 'two such people' as they, living in the same city, should surely become acquainted. Alma could not recall how Mahler had responded, but notes that Boltzman died soon after (he committed suicide) and that they never met. Textual losses of a more humorous nature include Mahler's private names for Schoenberg and Zemlinsky, whom he liked to call 'Eisele und Beisele' (literally: 'small ice' and 'pub' or 'tavern').[48]

Most regrettable of the many omissions from the Creighton version, how-ever, are surely the letters, poems and notes of 1910 in which Mahler found expression for his painfully reawakened passion for Alma after the long-developing breakdown of their marriage. His love, and his pain, were to be inflamed by Alma's infidelity with the infatuated young Walter Gropius. In his 1968 comments about these omitted effusions, Donald Mitchell rightly described them as 'highly personal documents' which are 'wellnigh impossible to translate'.[49] Perhaps, however, if we construe translation as part of an on-going process of comprehension, the attempt must be made as our under-standing of the rest of the text is examined and revised.[50] We can hardly now draw back from them as we might from the private documents of a living acquaintance. These undeniably painful and moving revelations of an emotional storm afford striking insight into one of the major crises of Mahler's life. Some commentators have explored the links between them and the Tenth Symphony.[51] Even the most restrictively 'objective' observers

---

attribution of this phrase to Mahler in her account of their first meeting. Did she recall it exactly, or did she make the link with the poem retrospectively by putting that phrase into Mahler's mouth?

46 See Creighton: 33; German text: 45.

47 Compare Creighton: 119, with German text: 151.

48 German text: 102 (cf. Creighton: 78).

49 AMML[2]: 332 (note). GM[3]: 1296–1300.

50 Many other problems with the Creighton version could be cited: it consistently obliterates Alma's satirical dialect-rendering of the coarse speech of Richard and Pauline Strauss (and others) and frequently omits qualifying descriptions of people mentioned; the account of Mahler's death includes two small but annoying inaccuracies (compare Creighton version: 200–201, with the German text: 251–2): Mahler's last word there was not 'Mozart' but the diminutive 'Mozartl' and the storm was quite not the mythical Beethovenian 'thunderstorm' but a 'hurricane-like' [*orkanartig*] wind storm.

51 See for example, Jan Jongbloed, 'Mahler's Tenth Symphony: The Order of Composition of

would accept that the music is what most matters; consistently, perhaps, some of them would apparently wish to suppress the Tenth Symphony itself, as if in the nervous suspicion that Mahler's poetic and musical rhetorics might indeed have run in close parallel with each other. The highly charged annotations in the manuscript of the Tenth (often, as Alma herself noted, precisely aligned against corresponding musical events)[52] darkly complement the more persuasive language of both despair and sensuality employed in poems such as this, of 17 August 1910:

> Sweet hand which binds me!
> O lovely bond to have found!
> Voluptuously I feel myself imprisoned;
> Eternal slavery is my desire!
>
> O blissful death in hours of pain!
> O Life – spring from my wounds![53]

The following extract is from another, longer, poem to Alma of the same day:

> I would draw together all the thrilling of my joy,
> of the eternity of holy bliss upon your breast,
> into a single melody that, as the sun's bow the
> heavens, would boldly span your sweetness.[54]

We need not crudely link the image of the 'Sonnenbogen' (not the more usual Regenbogen) with the solo flute melody in the final movement of the Tenth Symphony[55] to see how Mahler's poetry might contribute to our understanding of that incomparable, uncompleted work. Never was a 'foreboding of premature death'[56] so urgently and passionately filled with life. How we read and even translate Alma's vexing text might be conditioned by ways in

its Movements', in Paul Op de Coul (ed.), *Fragment or Completion? Proceeedings of the Mahler X Symposium Utrecht 1986* (The Hague: Universitaire Pers Rotterdam, 1991): 151–3.

52 Similarly aligned manuscript annotations are found in the Ninth Symphony, where Mahler seems to have revived the practice, otherwise apparently dropped since the Third Symphony of 1896.

53 German text: 461 (see n. 43). Alma discovered this on her bedside table.

54 Ibid.: 462.

55 As Jongbloed does, see n. 51 above.

56 Richard Specht; see 'The History of Mahler's Tenth Symphony', in Deryck Cooke (and others), *Gustav Mahler: A Performing Version of the Draft for the Tenth Symphony* (London: Faber Music, 1976): x. Alma herself described the fundamental mood or content of the Tenth as 'Todesgewissheit, Todesleid, Todeshohn!' (literally: 'certainty of death, grief at death, scorn at death') in her introductory note to the facsimile of the sketches which she published as *Gustav Mahler: Zehnte Symphonie* (Berlin/Vienna/Leipzig: Zsolnay, 1924). Alma's comment about the precisely repeated alignment of the last annotations in the Finale appeared in a footnote to her transcription of the manuscript annotations in the second edition of AMEB: 479.

which we wish to read the music of the man who loved her. The reverse may also be true; certainly their respective measures of both revelation and concealment are inextricably locked together in the larger, composite text in whose creation we too may unwittingly play the games of selection, emphasis and even censorship.

5

Mahler and the New York Philharmonic: The Truth Behind the Legend

HENRY-LOUIS DE LA GRANGE

Before coming to Mahler the musician, let me say a word or two about Mahler the man. My view, acquired in the course of forty years of intensive research, while reading several thousand books, letters, reports, reminiscences, articles, reviews, after writing some three or four thousand pages of biography, is that Mahler was not the morbid, tormented neurotic he is so often depicted to have been. True, Freud believed that artistic creation was always in some way connected with neurosis. The great composers of the past could all have been considered as neurotic, in some way or other, but Mahler was no more so than Beethoven, Chopin, Schumann or Brahms for instance, certainly far less than Bruckner or Tchaikovsky.

A knowledge of Mahler's personality and behaviour in everyday life, of his courage in the face of adversity, of the dignity, the reserve he displayed when fate struck hardest, all these traits of character make nonsense of the traditional image. The origin of the legend can easily be detected: Alma survived Mahler by some fifty years. Whereas he never wrote or spoke about his relationship to Alma, she later published two books which describe Mahler as an 'ascetic', a sickly man for whom all pleasures were suspect, to whom, furthermore, his daughter's death and the heart specialist's diagnosis were deadly blows. The sombre nature of some of Mahler's most popular works, such as the *Kindertotenlieder* and *Das Lied von der Erde*, helped propagate a legend that appealed to the preference most of us secretly harbour for the easy and simplistic image rather than the more complicated but less romantic reality. Thus Mahler became known as a typical *fin-de-siècle* artist, morbid, tormented, forever obsessed with the sad realities of human destiny and tortured by the demon of introspection.

The real Mahler did indeed suffer all his life from two chronic ailments, haemorrhoids and inflamed tonsils, but they in no way prevented him from leading an intensely active life. The real Mahler had more than a normal person's ration of vigour and stamina. The real Mahler enjoyed putting his physical strength and endurance to the test: he loved to swim long distances, climb mountains, take endless walks and go on strenuous bicycle tours. He of course resembles no other composer in that he led three different and simultaneous lives, and pursued three different careers – that of virtuoso conductor, that of theatre director, and that of composer. And what is more, his inflexible idealism, his practice of music as a religion, did not allow him to consider any of them as a minor activity on which he could permit himself to husband his resources. Mahler was incapable of sparing himself, of not seeking perfection in every realm. But that surely is the normal state of mind of all great creative artists.

The man who led the Vienna Opera for ten years during a critical epoch of transition cannot have been a neurotic. Anyone who has witnessed the difficulties, material and psychological, encountered by all Viennese opera directors since Mahler – Weingartner and Strauss, more recently Karajan, Maazel, Abbado – knows the amount of tact, diplomacy, self-control, as well as talent, will-power, idealism, required to run such a house in a city where everyone was only too ready to believe the worst, where evil gossip, a spirit of intrigue and maliciousness tended to blow up every incident into a 'scandal'. When Mahler left Vienna for New York, he was not the physical and mental wreck he has been depicted as being. He had faced the death of his beloved daughter; he had grieved in silence and with his usual stoicism. He was indeed worried about his heart condition because the doctors had deliberately led him to believe that his life was in danger. Their gloomy diagnosis hung over him for several months, almost a year, until, during the summer of 1908, he realized how exaggerated his fears had been, and started once again to lead his normal life.

I don't know whether to laugh or throw up my hands in exasperation, when I read descriptions of Mahler's 'desperate' condition in 1908 and 1909, while composing the Ninth Symphony and *Das Lied von der Erde*, when I see that these works have become in most people's eyes Requiems for his own death. (I am perhaps better able to speak on this subject than many, for I myself was informed, at a time when I was about to complete the last volume of my biography, that I myself had a valvular insufficiency. May I add that it has not prevented me from taking endless walks in the mountains and going on scuba-diving tours.)

Recently, an eminent Viennese specialist in such matters as depression and suicidal tendencies, the late psychoanalyst Erwin Ringel, has led the way towards a different and less simplistic view. Looking back to Mahler's childhood, Ringel regarded his 'knowledge of death', acquired in losing seven of his brothers and sisters, as an experience that few human beings have had to live through. Mahler's frequent encounters with death, combined with an intense will to live and an insatiable love of life, Ringel regards as his greatest strength in a world in which most human beings find solace only in putting thoughts of death out of their minds. Mahler, in his view, was a constant 'discoverer of the present', 'a man of powerful feelings', a man 'who radiated truth', 'who set all people afire', a 'man of passion and a man of love'. Depression and despair truly came to him only during those dreadful summer months of 1910 when he realized that Alma had been unfaithful to him, that she had ceased to love him and had even considered leaving him.

But was that not an understandable reaction in the face of such a tragic revelation? However, as late as 1910, Mahler was still making plans for his old age: he was searching for a house in the country in which to live and compose and had already put aside the volumes of Goethe's letters which he looked forward to reading.[1] During the winter of 1910–11, he was still happily making plans for the construction and interior decoration of his house-to-be in the Semmering mountains.[2]

When, in 1907, Mahler accepted the post offered him at the Metropolitan Opera, his eldest daughter was still alive. However, by the time he left for the United States six months later, he had indeed suffered three blows: his child's death, the doctors' diagnosis of his weak heart, and the attitude of the Viennese administration, which had done little or nothing to keep him at the head of the Opera. At that time America had a bad reputation among German and Austrian musicians. The United States had surely been described to him, in terms of the European cliché, as 'the land of the almighty dollar'. Richard Strauss, who had earlier conducted a symphony concert in Wanamaker's, the large New York department store, during shopping hours, could not take Mahler seriously when he spoke of his fears that he would not be understood in America. He had merely replied: 'But my dear Mahler, you are and will always remain a child! Over there, all one does is climb on to the podium, do this [gestures of a conductor], and then this [gesture of counting money].'

Assuredly, Mahler was a realist as well as an idealist, and his decision to leave for New York was not only motivated by his desire to turn his back on Vienna and Europe. He was anxious to earn money for his family and to curtail his professional activities, so as to have more time to compose. Although he had, before leaving the Vienna Opera, received offers from other European institutions, the disappointments he had experienced there were such that he longed to start anew on another continent.

Mahler's first experience of American musical life was not exactly calculated to give him a favourable picture. Heinrich Conried, who had engaged him, was an astute business man, a clever operatic entrepreneur, rather than an artistic director. Furthermore, the Metropolitan Opera at that time had a predominantly social function. Some of Edith Wharton's great novels – *The House of Mirth, The Age of Innocence,* and *The Custom of the Country* – show that attendance at the Metropolitan Opera, and in one's own box moreover, was not so much a declaration of interest in music or the well-being of that venerable institution as the most tangible evidence they could offer of their ranking in New York society. Thus the scenes, the jewels and the dresses, and human interplay in the boxes often attracted more attention than the performance on the stage, where star singers such as Caruso and

1 Alfred Roller, *Die Bildnisse von Gustav Mahler* (Leipzig: Tal, 1922): 19ff.
2 Maurice Baumfeld, 'Erinnerungen an Gustav Mahler', *New York Staatszeitung* (21 May 1911).

Marcella Sembrich were the main attraction. It is much to Mahler's credit therefore that he was able to earn his greatest operatic triumphs in New York with 'difficult' works such as *Fidelio, The Marriage of Figaro, Don Giovanni* and the Wagnerian dramas.

However, Mahler's career at the Metropolitan Opera is not part of my subject in this essay. What matters is that he earned his greatest and most unanimous triumph there on 20 March 1908 with *Fidelio*, a work more admired than loved, which had never been popular anywhere in the world. There was a tremendous outburst of applause after the *Leonore* Overture No. 3: Henry Taylor Parker, of the *Boston Evening Transcript*, thought that 'more than rediscovered', *Fidelio* had been 'born anew' after having 'fallen in musty disrepute at the Met'.[3] The *New York Evening Sun* wrote: 'Tremendous, nothing less, was the rapt attention . . . The house went crazy in the dark. The riot over Mahler equalled that over Caruso in *Il Trovatore*.'[4] The next day, Mahler was praised by the overwhelming majority of critics, more enthusiastically, perhaps, than he had ever been in Europe.

Conried's resignation as manager had already been announced at the time of the memorable performance of *Fidelio*. Mahler was asked by the Board of Directors of the Metropolitan Opera to take his place. But he was unwilling to accept the administrative burden that the post implied and Gatti-Casazza was engaged, together with his star conductor Arturo Toscanini. The Mahler–Toscanini 'quarrel' has aroused endless comments, many of them unfounded. The simple fact is that there was no room in any opera house for two conductors of such calibre and that Mahler would not relinquish the production of *Tristan* he had prepared the year before to his younger colleague. Unknown to Mahler, Gatti had promised Toscanini that he would make his Wagnerian début in New York in *Tristan*. Mahler had his way for one season before leaving the way free for Toscanini. He left the Metropolitan Opera without ill feelings, while Toscanini harboured resentment for the rest of his life.

Despite the Met's shortcomings at the time, Mahler enjoyed his first months in New York. In a letter to Alma's stepfather, Carl Moll, he wrote:

> All the stories which circulate at home on America originate from this *sickening kind of Germans* whom you know as well as I do . . . The scum of our society who blame 'circumstances' for all the failures caused by their own insufficiency and indolence, they complicate matters for all those who come after them, by provoking an increasing mistrust of foreigners.[5]

3 *Boston Evening Transcript* (3 August 1908).
4 *New York Evening Sun* (21 March 1908).
5 Letter to Carl Moll, 16 February 1908, Pierpont Morgan Library, New York. 'Alle Erzählungen, die bei uns über Amerika im Umlauf sind, rühren von dieser *ekelhaften Sorte von Deutschen* her, die Du ebenso kennst, wie ich. Der Abhub unserer Gesellschaft, die allen Misserfolg, der aus ihren eigenen Unfähigkeit und Indolenz herrührt, den "Verhältnissen" in die Schuhe schieben [schiebt] und zugleich allen Nachkommen die Sache dadurch erschweren [erschwert], dass sie das Misstrauen gegen die Fremden immer höher anwachsen machen.'

Mahler was delighted 'after the Viennese wasteland, to find everywhere goodwill and gratitude for the little I am able to accomplish'.[6] 'The climate, the people here and the universal broadmindedness suit me exceptionally well'[7] . . . 'Next winter I shall come back. We both have much enjoyed this country. The freshness, healthiness, and honesty of the human relationships hold great attraction for us.'[8] I have deliberately selected passages from Mahler's letters to his family and friends because he was expressing his true feelings and cannot be suspected of having been merely tactful in the presence of American journalists.

He was delighted therefore when, towards the end of his second season at the Met, new plans for his future in New York developed as an aftermath of the memorable performance of *Fidelio*, and particularly of the third *Leonore* Overture. Mrs George Sheldon, the wife of a New York banker who was closely associated with J. P. Morgan, had been so impressed that she decided that 'Mr Mahler's influence was deeply felt at the Metropolitan Opera House this winter and it would be a pity if he should not have a chance to conduct purely orchestral music with an orchestra of his own.'[9] The original plan was to create a Mahler orchestra, but eventually it was found wiser to reorganize the oldest New York orchestral society, the Philharmonic.

Since he had left the Vienna Philharmonic in 1901, Mahler had conducted many orchestras as a guest but he had not had one entirely in his hands. In any case, a symphonic vehicle such as the Boston Symphony, which gave 'more concerts in one season than the typical European orchestra in five years',[10] 'was something European conductors could only dream of'. After a whole life spent in the 'penitentiary' of opera houses, Mahler was of course delighted by Mrs Sheldon's unexpected proposal. However, when it was made to him, he had already been negotiating for some time with Walter Damrosch, who planned to engage him to conduct three concerts with the New York Symphony Orchestra.

The short period of time during which Mahler negotiated with both Damrosch and Mrs Sheldon was to have unforeseeable and highly negative consequences for Mahler's New York career. Henry Krehbiel later wrote in his vicious obituary of Mahler: 'While still under contract to the Symphony Orchestra he entered into an arrangement with a committee of women to give three concerts with the orchestra of the Philharmonic Society.' The truth

6   Ibid. 'Ganz neu ist es mir – nach der Wiener Wüstenei – überall Wohlwollen und Dankbarkeit vorzufinden für das Wenige, was ich zu leisten im Stande bin.'
7   Undated letter to Paul Hammerschlag (17 February 1908), AMWB: 373. 'Das Klima, die Menschen hier und die überaus grosszügigen Verhältnisse behagen mir ausserordentlich.'
8   'Im nächsten Winter gehe ich wieder zurück. Wir beide haben sehr grosses Gefallen an diesem Land gefunden; die Frische, Gesundheit, und Geradheit aller Verhältnisse ziehen uns stark an.' (AMWB: No. 401, to Zemlinsky.)
9   *New York Times* (19 April 1908).
10 Howard Shanet, *Philharmonic: A History of New York's Orchestra* (New York: Doubleday, 1975): 220.

is that, at the time when the Philharmonic's proposal were made, during the last two weeks of March 1908, Mahler was not 'under contract'. He had merely accepted to conduct some concerts with Damrosch's orchestra at the beginning of the next season. On 22 or 23 March, he asked Damrosch for a ten days' respite before signing his contract with the Symphony, but did not reveal the cause of this delay, and for a very obvious reason: Mrs Sheldon had sworn him to secrecy as long as nothing was settled. But Damrosch did not even have to wait for ten days. A week later, on 1 April, he received a letter from the Ladies' Committee's lawyer asking him whether Mahler could accept their offer to conduct three 'tryout' concerts with the Philharmonic in the autumn. Damrosch quite naturally refused, and an agreement was reached by which Mahler would conduct three concerts with the Symphony Orchestra in the Autumn of 1908, and two Philharmonic concerts in the spring of 1909. Although Krehbiel later accused Mahler of having 'neglected his legal and moral obligations', Mahler's correspondence with Damrosch does not provide the slightest evidence that his behaviour had at any time or in any way been dishonest or in any way unethical. Be that as it may, subsequent events were to show that Damrosch never forgave him for having delayed the negotiations without informing him of Mrs Sheldon's offer.

Damrosch proceeded to do everything in his power to make sure that Mahler's three concerts with the Symphony in the autumn failed miserably. Reginald de Koven (*World*) wrote in the *New York World*, the day after the performance of the Second Symphony: 'Herr Mahler, as I hear, was reported to have said that his conducting yesterday was something of a farce, as the members of the orchestra neither came nor stayed at rehearsals, as he wished them to.'[11] No effort of any kind was made to advertise the three concerts, Damrosch's intention obviously being to prove that Mahler's presence on the podium would not attract the public. Thus the hall was half empty for the first concert. Max Smith recalled how liberal the Damrosch brothers had always been with free tickets for their concerts whenever the sales had not been adequate. 'Why shouldn't a Sunday concert with Mahler draw at least as big a crowd as a Sunday concert with Damrosch?' he asked. 'Are we to believe that a man of Damrosch's social friendships can fill Carnegie Hall more readily by waving a baton than a man of Mahler's musical greatness? . . . Is it established that his [Damrosch's] pretty graces as conductor exert a greater attraction on a New York public than Mahler's genius?' Worse still, according to Max Smith, the orchestra's 'ragged playing' made it 'obvious that the men playing for him had not learned their task properly in the time allotted for rehearsing'. They had been only partially able to 'respond to demands so highly wrought and so quietly suggested . . . To play smoothly, precisely and euphoniously under the guidance of a man who beats time like a metronome is far different than answering with equal exactness and beauty

11 *New York World* (30 November 1908).

the demands of a conductor whose interpretations are impregnated with significant detail.' Henry Krehbiel was the only critic to claim that the orchestra performed well in spite of Mahler's conducting.

Walter Damrosch's father, Leopold, had founded the New York Symphony in 1878 and conducted it until his death in 1885. Walter had succeeded his father at the age of twenty-three and had very soon revealed a remarkable talent as an organizer, a lecturer and a money-raiser, if not as a conductor. He had married the daughter of James Blaine, one of America's most famous – if most controversial – politicians. Blaine was an intimate friend of Andrew Carnegie, and Damrosch had persuaded the millionaire-philanthropist to build the concert hall that bore his name. For the New York Symphony's twenty-eight concerts per year, it was Damrosch's policy to engage famous soloists and to introduce a great number of new works. However, although the orchestra had been 'reorganized' in 1907 and now gave thirty-four concerts a season in New York, its level of performance was low because the musicians were engaged only for a seven-month season and a long tour; substitutes often played for them at rehearsals and concerts; these were insufficiently rehearsed; and, most important of all, Damrosch himself was neither a very demanding nor a very talented conductor. His habit of making introductory speeches on the podium had exasperated some of the orchestra's most generous patrons such as J. P. Morgan. Arthur Judson, the concert magnate and head of Columbia Concerts, once told me in the 1950s that that was the reason why the famous banker and collector was so easily persuaded to switch allegiance from the Symphony to the Philharmonic when Mrs Sheldon asked him for his support.

The Philharmonic and the Symphony were longtime rivals and competitors. Both orchestras played in the same hall and often recruited the same extra musicians. It was obvious from the start that Walter Damrosch had everything to lose from the reorganization of the Philharmonic, from the increase in the number of concerts it would give per year, and from the presence on the podium of a conductor of Mahler's stature. Damrosch himself had earlier attempted and failed to raise the necessary funds for the Philharmonic's reorganization, and he resented the Guarantors' Committee's initiative all the more since several members, such as J. P. Morgan, E. Francis Hyde and Mrs Sheldon herself, had formerly supported his own orchestra. Furthermore, Mrs Sheldon had persuaded Andrew Carnegie to stop making the Hall available to Damrosch for his Sunday afternoon popular concerts. In a letter to Carnegie, Damrosch called the Philharmonic 'an unfair competitor into a field that I have hitherto developed and occupied alone'. What had previously been mere rivalry now became animosity, hostility, a 'fight to the death' between the two institutions. From then on, it became obvious that most of the reviewers were partisans of one side or the other. Furthermore, the supporters and officials of the Symphony were now firmly convinced that the aim of the Ladies' Committee was to eliminate Damrosch from the New York musical scene. To prove once again that Mahler's presence on the podium was no asset, Damrosch divulged the financial results of his three concerts given in the autumn with the Symphony in an interview that was published early in 1909 in *Musical America*: they had cost $10,000 and brought in only $4,300.[12] Three years later, in his obituary, Krehbiel followed suit: 'Mr Mahler was an expensive and unprofitable proposition', and 'a case of large outlay and small income'. Without perhaps realizing it, Mahler was entering a true battlefield, the survival of the two societies being at stake.

The first two Philharmonic concerts, which took place in March/April 1909, augured well for the future. The performance of Beethoven's Ninth Symphony was well received, but it convinced Mahler that changes in personnel were indispensable in the ranks of the orchestra. Unfortunately, he then discovered that the search for new players was going to prove a more delicate proposition than he had anticipated. Major Higginson, the sponsor of the Boston Symphony, had been careful to create a non-union orchestra, unlike the Philharmonic, which had to observe the rules laid down by the New York unions which required all players to be hired from their rosters. Thus, no foreigner could play in a union orchestra, except as soloist, until elected a member after six months' residence in the country. In spite of this regulation, nearly 50 per cent of the musicians were replaced before Mahler's first season began. The plans for the reorganization of the orchestra were ambitious, too ambitious perhaps. The number of Philharmonic concerts per season was to be raised from eighteen to forty-six, the orchestra was to travel regularly to Brooklyn and Philadelphia and to tour New England. The eight Thursday evening subscription concerts were to be repeated on Friday afternoons. Three cycles (six historical concerts, five Beethoven concerts, five Sunday popular concerts) brought the total number of New York concerts to thirty-five. David Ewen, the author of a pioneering book published in 1947[13] called *Music Comes to America*, describes the New York of forty years earlier as ill-prepared for such an avalanche of symphonic music. Despite its old tradition for opera, the city had never had a permanent orchestra comparable to those of Boston (1881), Chicago (1891), Pittsburgh and Cincinnati (both 1895), Philadelphia (1902), Minneapolis (1903). The musical public in New York favoured mainly virtuoso soloists and star singers. The two American String Quartets (Kneisel, 1885, and Flonzaley, 1904) often played to empty halls.[14] Now the Philharmonic's avowed aim was to provide the city with an orchestra comparable in quality to the Boston Symphony, and an orchestral institution as respected as the Met. This was the main reason for Mahler's engagement as musical director. Theodore Spiering, the concertmaster whom Mahler had engaged on Fritz Kreisler's recommendation, recalled the tremendous enthusiasm with which he started to rehearse in the autumn of 1909.

---

12 *Musical America* (20 February 1909): 4.
13 David Ewen, *Music Comes to America* (New York: Allen, Town and Heathe, 1947): 87.
14 Ibid.: 83ff.

The first concert, on 4 November, was very well received by the audience and the reviews were mostly favourable. Even Mahler's enemies agreed that his orchestra was becoming 'a joyful, responsive and flexible instrument'.[15] However, on 16/17 December 1909, Mahler made a hazardous decision in including his own First Symphony in the programme of the regular subscription concerts. New York was no more prepared than Europe had been for an 'ironic' Funeral March, for the innocence of the first movement and the hurricanes in the Finale, and the majority of reviews were scathing. Furthermore, this performance was to transform the already hostile Krehbiel into a mortal enemy. He was in charge of the programme notes for the Philharmonic concerts, and he asked Mahler for permission to reprint a letter of his which Ernst Otto Nodnagel, Mahler's self-appointed analyst, had quoted some years earlier in Germany in a text concerning the First Symphony. Mahler, whose hostility to 'programme music' had increased with the years and was by now firmly established, denied having ever written such a letter and would not allow any programme notes at all to be published. Krehbiel's answer came in the form of two articles. One of them filled a whole page of the *New York World*. It was a bitter assault on Mahler as a 'programme musician' ashamed of being so. From then on until Mahler's last concert in New York Krehbiel's attacks never ceased.

Mahler's daily life during the first and second Philharmonic season can be described as far more relaxed and sociable than it ever had been in Europe. He and Alma went to dinner parties, attended large gatherings in several millionaires' mansions and made a great number of new friends and acquaintances. Mahler was undoubtedly working much harder than he had during the two previous seasons, yet he wrote optimistic letters to his family and friends informing them that he had never felt better and that he enjoyed his work. The Mahler whom an anonymous journalist interviewed at the end of March 1910, at the end of a long and trying season of concerts, was neither exhausted nor depressed:

> The energy that inspires Mr Mahler was manifest last week, when a *Tribune* representative visited him in his apartment in the Hotel Savoy. Mr Mahler was alone at the time, and he was forced to answer his doorbell a dozen times during the course of the interview. A father arrived who wished the conductor to hear his son play the cello; packages kept coming; telephone calls galore regarding rehearsals, and from persons who wanted interviews – yet, though he answered them all, he never seemed out of patience . . . 'Excuse me but this afternoon I must be my own servant.'

The journalist summed up Mahler's character as that of 'a sceptical enthusiast. He sees the transitory nature of all things. He feels that nothing really endures. Yet he admires, he admires enthusiastically all genuine self-expression.'

---

15 *New York Sun* (5 November 1909).

On 6 and 7 January 1910, Mahler scored one of the greatest triumphs in his entire career with a concert featuring Busoni as soloist. The programme, on each of the two evenings, included Berlioz's *Symphonie fantastique*, Beethoven's Fifth Piano Concerto and the *Meistersinger* Prelude. The editors of *Musical America* were so overwhelmed that they reprinted all the reviews *in extenso*, thus filling no fewer than five large pages of their second January issue. Busoni records in a letter that one of the Committee ladies expressed her disapproval of the performance at a rehearsal, but Mahler does not appear to have taken her criticisms seriously.

A more embarrassing incident occurred at the end of January. Mahler had invited as soloist for the Schumann Piano Concerto a gifted, but eccentric German pianist of Hungarian origin named Josef Weiss. During the dress rehearsal, it seems that Mahler congratulated him with more politeness than conviction at the beginning of the second movement (according to one of the versions of the incident reported in the *New York America*). Weiss took offence, flew into a rage, threw his score to the floor and left the stage. A cartoon depicting the scene appeared the next day in the press and one can sense the Committee ladies' disapproval between the lines of the newspaper reports. It is clear that they found such an incident incompatible with the dignity of the institution. A phrase in Edith Wharton's portrait of New York society in *The Age of Innocence* comes to mind: 'people who dreaded scandal more than disease, who placed decency higher than courage, and who considered nothing more ill-bred than "scenes", except the behaviour of those who gave rise to them'. In his *History of the New York Philharmonic* Howard Shanet calls the Weiss affair 'a typical Mahlerian contretemps',[16] yet it would be difficult to find another incident remotely like it in the whole of Mahler's career. His only mistake was apparently to have underestimated Weiss's explosive temperament.

The first Philharmonic season ended with an epoch-making performance of Beethoven's Ninth Symphony. This was infinitely superior to the performance of the previous year, and proved conclusively how much the orchestra had improved under Mahler's 'iron rule'. This was acknowledged by the immense majority of critics, except of course Krehbiel, who chose not to review – and probably not to attend – the concert at all. Unfortunately, the financial results of the season were disappointing. The Hall had often been less than half full for many of the concerts. Walter Rothwell, the conductor of the Saint-Paul Symphony Orchestra, commented as follows about the New York musical public:

> There is only one city in America which I cannot understand, and that is New York. I cannot believe it possible that I have seen correctly the audiences at the three Philharmonic concerts I attended. In Europe, people would have travelled miles, yes hundreds of miles, to hear Mahler conduct the Ninth Symphony . . . That he should be here and that his concerts

16 Howard Shanet, op. cit.: 217.

should not be of more importance to people supposed to care for music, shows that you have not the audience in New York that I thought you had because to manifest an indifference when Mahler gives something of himself, is not possible to people who really appreciate and understand music for itself.[17]

Ernst Jokl, a Berlin journalist who attended several of Mahler's concerts in the closing weeks of the season, also complained of the audience, 'the majority of whom arrived late and left before the end of the performance'. Yet Jokl had been struck by the way in which Mahler 'identified with the works'. 'He was resigned [to such indifference]', but 'his temperament and his strength were unaffected, indeed perhaps all the more concentrated and intensified'.[18]

Clearly, the Philharmonic concerts had not yet become an essential part of New York's musical life. This is perhaps hardly surprising after only one season and the steep increase in the number of concerts. It was then rumoured in the press that Mahler would perhaps not renew his contract. The deficit had practically wiped out the entire amount of the Guarantee Fund ($90,000). However, the Guarantors felt it would take more time for a new public to develop, and persuaded three generous sponsors, Joseph Pulitzer, J. P. Morgan and Andrew Carnegie, to make further large contributions for the following season. A number of important new measures were taken. The first, which had been strongly recommended by Mahler, was the hiring of a professional business manager named Loudon Charlton. The second was the engagement of a number of new players (18 per cent of the personnel was thus renewed). The third was another large increase in the number of concerts, which tends to prove that neither the Committee nor Mahler had been disheartened by the results of the preceding season. Both knew they were engaged in a pioneering venture which could not be expected to succeed in so short a time. In a letter to his sister Justi, Mahler made the following comment about the first Philharmonic season: 'For me, everything went remarkably well this year and I myself am amazed how well I bore all the exertions. I am definitely more capable of work – and happier than I have been in the last ten years.'[19]

During the summer of 1910, Mahler suffered in his personal life one of the most brutal blows that fate had yet inflicted on him. He suddenly discovered that his wife had been unfaithful to him. Far from repenting, she blamed him in large part for her conduct, and confronted him with a catalogue of the innumerable grievances she had borne against him over the years. Those painful summer months have sometimes been called unproductive by people

17 *Musical Leader* (14 April 1910).
18 Ernst Jokl, 'Mahler in Amerika', *Musikblätter des Anbruch*, Mahler issue, 2/7–8 (April 1920). 'Das Publikum dessen grösseren Hälfte zu spät kam und vor Schluss des Konzertes davonlief.' 'Er identifiziert sich mit dem Werke . . . Mahler war resigniert aber sein Temperament und seine Kraft waren unberührt – ja vielleicht noch konzentrierter und gesteigert.'
19 Undated letter to Justine Rosé (March 1910), University of Western Ontario Library.

who forget that during them Mahler composed the entire Tenth Symphony (what he left uncompleted would have been finished in a matter of days, excluding of course the orchestration). He also learnt seventy-three new scores by seventeen composers all of which he was to conduct during the following season. After crossing half of Europe to consult Freud about his relationship with Alma, he spent the first half of September in Munich, rehearsing and conducting the huge forces required for the first performance of the Eighth Symphony. A full schedule for a man who has so often been described as close to death! Although his relationship with Alma took on an obsessive, pathological intensity, he was very soon just as active professionally as before.

During the same summer of 1910, Mahler found out that the Philharmonic's new manager, Loudon Charlton, had persuaded the Committee to increase the number of concerts even further, from forty-five to sixty-five. He was understandably angry not to have been consulted or informed, and asked for an increased salary of $25,000 instead of the $20,000 earlier planned. After six months' negotiations, the Guarantors eventually granted him an increase of only $3,000. The prolonged negotiations certainly did nothing to improve the Committee's relations with Mahler. Another source of tension developed at the end of the year, when Mahler befriended a second violinist by the name of Th. E. Johner. One of Mahler's true weaknesses was – and had always been – to believe all too easily that people disliked him. In Vienna, his brother-in-law, Arnold Rosé, had often briefed him about the intrigues devised by hostile members of the Philharmonic. Johner was soon suspected of being Mahler's spy and was nicknamed by his colleagues 'the Judas of the orchestra'. In the 1950s, Hermann Reinshagen, a double-bass player under Mahler, informed me of the official reason for his eviction: Johner had pleaded illness and had been allowed to stay home while the rest of the orchestra went on tour to Pittsburgh, Buffalo, etc. When the manager heard that he had nevertheless participated in a concert in New York, he immediately dismissed him. One task which Mahler had perhaps assigned to him could well have been that of identifying the player or players who took care to inform Krehbiel before each concert of every alteration he introduced in classical scores.

Alma Mahler states that 'Mahler had become rude with the orchestra, irritable and intolerant. He believed Jonas [Johner] to be his only true friend, and was sure that all the rest of the orchestra hated him.'[20] However, Alma seldom attended rehearsals and there are serious reasons to doubt her statement. In the 1960s William Malloch interviewed the surviving members of Mahler's Philharmonic, and none of these invaluable first-hand interviews substantiates her claims.

---

20 Alma Mahler, *Erinnerungen und Briefe* (Frankfurt: Propyläen Verlag, 1971): 213. 'Mahler wurde ausfallend gegen das Orchester, gereizt und unduldsam ... Das ganze übrige Orchester hasse ihn. So weit war es gekommen.'

At the beginning of Mahler's second Philharmonic season, a serious effort was made to appeal to a new and larger public. The price of seats and especially that of subscriptions was lowered, the number of out-of-town concerts increased and a new attempt made to render the programmes more appealing. Thus, the number of works by Tchaikovsky, New York's most popular composer, was more than doubled. Mahler's first performances of the *Pathétique* had been poorly reviewed. The next ones, however, proved that he had done his best to identify with New York's most popular modern symphony as he had before with the same composer's operas. Although the programme of the first concert, Mahler's arrangement from Bach Suites, Schubert's C major Symphony and Strauss's *Zarathustra*, was anything but popular, it was loudly applauded by a full house, and well reviewed by a large majority of critics (except of course Krehbiel).

Later on, the success of the orchestra's big tour, which included Cleveland, Pittsburgh and four cities of upper New York State, can only be described as triumphant. The unanimously favourable reviews contain a number of perceptive remarks about the orchestral performances and Mahler's interpretation which prove that these cities had a high level of music criticism. Mahler himself was praised as he had rarely been. The *Buffalo Evening News* spoke of his 'dash, verve and brilliancy', 'his vitality that pulsated with life and energy', his 'masterly, commanding authority'; the *Pittsburgh Gazette Times* his 'temperament', 'personal magnetism' and 'intellectual grasp'; the *Utica Observer* spoke of that 'mysterious hypnotic force more important still than his gestures'. The *Cleveland Leader* called him 'a man with mind in every muscle'[21] and the *Cleveland Plain Dealer*'s reviewer, Miriam Russell, waxed lyrical:

Little Mahler with the big brain! Little Mahler endowed with the strength of a giant! Little Mahler with a great musical imagination! Little Mahler with the mighty force that makes other conductors look like pygmies . . . It was all splendid. Mr Mahler has come once this year. May he come three times next year, and just as often thereafter as we can get him![22]

In January 1911, Mahler had not quite made up his mind to return to New York for another Philharmonic season. The salary he demanded ($30,000) had been found too high by the Guarantors who were negotiating with other conductors. Shortly after the orchestra's big tour, a genuine dispute developed concerning Mahler's programmes. It seems that he had once let himself be persuaded – imprudently no doubt – to relinquish part of the responsibility for programme making and to declare himself willing to conduct any works the Guarantors found necessary to attract the public. The press even claimed that his programmes had already been altered more than

21 *Buffalo Evening News* (8 December 1910); *Pittsburgh Gazette Times* (6 December 1910); *Utica Observer* (9 December 1910); *Cleveland Leader* (7 December 1910).
22 *Cleveland Plain Dealer* (7 August 1910).

once by the Committee. His readiness to make concessions was proved at the end of the year, when he conducted twice in New York and once in Brooklyn an all-Tchaikovsky programme made up of unfamiliar works (including Symphony No. 2 and Suite No. 1). But further concessions were no doubt being required from him.

At the end of January, measures were taken by the Guarantors to reduce Mahler's powers, and two sub-committees were formed, one in charge of finance, another of programmes. The unpleasant scene described by Alma, when a lawyer who had been taking notes of what Mahler said appeared from behind a curtain, surely occurred at a session of the programme committee and in the absence of Mrs Untermeyer, who had from the start been Mahler's friend and loyal supporter among the Guarantors. Although he must have been exasperated and hurt by this painful scene, Mahler was certainly aware that his power in New York was still considerable. The fact that he was already doing the job, his international reputation, his past accomplishments and the progress achieved with the orchestra were all strong arguments in his favour. Furthermore, no first-rate conductor was apparently willing or able at this time to replace him. In the first dissertation about 'Mahler in New York', written in 1973, Marvin von Deck pertinently remarks that the meeting in Mrs Sheldon's house suffices to prove that the Guarantors' committee had decided to re-engage him as music director, other-wise they would only have needed not to renew his contract. Unfortunately, we have no evidence from a key witness of Mahler's dealings with the Guarantors' Committee, Mrs Sheldon herself. Since my mother in her youth had known both Mrs Sheldon and her daughters, I made several attempts, during the 1950s, to find out whether she had left any papers or statements, but none of my efforts ever bore fruit.

The letters Mahler wrote to Europe at the end of January prove that he had practically made up his mind to return to New York for at least another year: 'As the dice here seem to have fallen,' he writes to the young Swiss writer William Ritter, 'I may well become my own successor next season. With their love and willingness, the people here are making it virtually impossible for me to leave them in the lurch. And thus I am half decided to return here next winter.'[23] To the Munich impresario Emil Gutmann, who had recently organized the première of the Eighth Symphony and had further proposals to make, his answer was: 'As concerns next year, it is, as I had foreseen, difficult to leave here. The people are making every effort, and will probably capture me again. I think that eventually I shall have to abscond in secret, otherwise I shall never get away from here.'[24] One of

23 Undated letter to William Ritter poststamped 27 January 1911, GMUB: 153. 'Wie die Würfel hier zu fallen scheinen, werde ich wol zunächst in der nächsten Saison mein eigener Nachfolger sein. – Die Leute hier machen es mir wirklich durch ihre Liebe und Willigkeit unmöglich, sie in Stiche zu lassen. Und so bin ich denn halb entschlossen im nächsten Winter wieder herzukommen.'
24 Letter to Emil Gutmann, 21 January 1911, GMUB: 85. 'Was das nächste Jahr betrifft

Mahler's close friends, Maurice Baumfeld, the critic of New York's main German newspaper, the *Staatszeitung*, recalled that 'when he began to feel that the public was starting to warm up to his truly sacred seriousness, he had decided to come back and complete his task here'.[25] In fact, Baumfeld adds, he was starting to feel at home in New York. He sometimes sat for hours at the window of his apartment watching the busy to-and-fro of the city. He 'had a real passion' for its sunny climate and often said 'Wherever I am, I feel homesick for this blue sky, for this sun and this throbbing activity.'[26]

The New Year had begun at the Philharmonic with two all-Wagner programmes, one of which was also given in Brooklyn, Philadelphia and Washington. In the *Evening Sun*, Henry T. Finck describes how 'Mahler was recalled again and again with the same expressions of frenzied enthusiasm'.[27] In the *Evening World*, Sylvester Rawling called the first of these evenings 'the most inspired and inspiring concert of the season'.[28] Shortly thereafter, Mahler included his own Fourth Symphony in a programme, and it was misunderstood in New York just as it had been in Germany and Austria. Once again, according to Reginald de Koven, Mahler had shown, 'his predilection for folksongs and somewhat archaic formulas'. Then, 'he suddenly seems to say to himself: "Ha! I have forgot, I must be modern", and proceeds forthwith to shake out the whole bag of tricks of the modern musical juggler.'[29] Unbeknown to them, the New York critics were only repeating the tired old clichés of their German counterparts. How surprised they would have been if told that, fifty years later, New York would be ahead of the rest of the world in the rediscovery of Mahler's symphonies!

Despite the failure of the Fourth Symphony, a comprehensive examination of the season's reviews reveals that they were much more favourable than those of the preceding season. Even critics such as William Henderson (*Sun*) and Arthur Farwell (*Musical America*), whose previous articles had been mostly negative, now acknowledged the progress accomplished by the orchestra and the general high level of the performances. Looking back on the whole season, Henderson found that more than three-quarters of his own reviews had been favourable.[30] Needless to say, the critics who had

---

so ist es, wie ich vorausgesehen, schwer, hier wegzukommen. Die Leute mache alle Anstrengungen, und wahrscheinlich fangen sie mich wieder ein. Ich glaube, ich muss einmal heimlich durchgehen, sonst komme ich hier nicht weg.'

25 Maurice Baumfeld, 'Erinnerungen an Gustav Mahler', *New Yorker Staatszeitung* (21 May 1911). 'Als er aber zu fühlen begann, wie sich das Publikum für seinen wahrhaft heilgen Ernst zu erwärmen begann, war er entschlossen wiederzukommen und sein Werk hier zu vollenden.'

26 Ibid. 'Ganz verzückt konnte er stundenlang sitzen und auf das webende Leben vor sich hinauszustarren. "Wo immer ich bin, die Sehnsucht nach diesem blauen Himmel, nach dieser Sonne, diesem pulsierenden Treiben geht mit mir."'

27 *Evening Sun* (16 January 1911).

28 *Evening World* (16 January 1911).

29 *New York World* (21 January 1911).

30 William J. Henderson, 'Novelties of the Season', *New York Sun* (23 April 1911).

been well disposed towards Mahler from the start, for instance Richard Aldrich (*Times*), Henry T. Finck (*Evening Post*) and Max Smith (*Press*) maintained their support. Needless to say also, Krehbiel's hostility reached new heights. He did not miss a single occasion to disparage Mahler, whether or not he was specifically writing about the Philharmonic. By 21 February, Mahler had conducted forty-six concerts, nearly three-quarters of those scheduled (sixty-three).

On 4 February, after rumours had leaked out in the press of tensions between Mahler and the Guarantors, Mrs Sheldon was interviewed by *Musical America*:

> Personally I feel that Mr Mahler is the greatest conductor today, either in Europe or in America, and I feel further that we have been most fortunate in keeping him as long as we have. While it is not settled absolutely, I believe that he will remain with us at least another year. Of course, we have not been entirely fortunate in the attitude of the critics towards the orchestra. Certain of the critics are entirely free, that is they have no other interests which prevent them from writing what they think and can criticize a programme favourably, or adversely, merely upon the music's merit. On the other hand, there are critics in this city whose interests in other institutions and organizations are so great that they cannot afford to write as they must feel concerning the magnificent work of the orchestra.

Everyone must have known whom she was referring to, for it was public knowledge that both Krehbiel and Henderson held teaching posts in the Institute of Musical Art, the school founded and directed by the Damrosch brothers.

Shortly after the onset of Mahler's illness, his re-engagement was officially announced by several newspapers. As we shall see, this announcement was premature, for no decision had as yet been reached. When it appeared, Mahler had already taken to his bed. Coming so soon after the rumours of his dispute with the Guarantors' Committee, his illness was inevitably interpreted as feigned or 'diplomatic'. He was reported to be 'sulking against the powers of the Philharmonic', while in fact, on 8 March, in an official letter addressed to the Guarantors' committee, he again, but this time in writing, declared himself willing to conduct ninety to one hundred concerts during the following season for a salary of $30,000. Once more, the Executive Committee found his demands excessive and decided to sign him up only if Felix Weingartner were not available. Had Mahler recovered, the outcome of this negotiation could easily be predicted. Since Weingartner was either unable or unwilling to leave Germany, Mahler would have remained the obvious and necessary choice and would no doubt have accepted a small reduction of his salary. That he did not plan to leave New York is clear from the fact that twice, during his last illness, when his condition briefly improved, he immediately arranged to hold an orchestra rehearsal the next day and started discussing the programme with which he would take leave of New York for the season.[31]

31 Maurice Baumfeld, op. cit.

In early May, while Mahler was being treated for endocarditis in a French sanatorium near Paris, Alma granted to Charles Henry Meltzer, of the *New York American*, an interview which was immediately reproduced in many German and American newspapers and magazines, and which has often been quoted since then:

> You cannot imagine what Mr Mahler has suffered. In Vienna my husband was all powerful. Even the Emperor did not dictate to him, but in New York, to his amazement, he had ten ladies ordering him about like a puppet. He hoped, however, by hard work and success to rid himself of his tormentors . . . [32]

This sounds dramatic enough and casts the ladies of the Guarantors' Committee as villains in the eyes of posterity. Yet it must be remembered that, as her memoirs were later to prove, Alma always spoke of Mahler as a sickly man, whose constant overwork never ceased to undermine an already weak physical constitution. Furthermore, at this time, she had every reason to feel secretly guilty after the cruel blows she had inflicted upon him during the preceding summer. The letters first published in Reginald Isaacs's Gropius biography[33] of 1983 also revealed new and painful truths about her affair with Gropius, the first one being that she had no intention of giving him up. Mahler must have had strong suspicions, to say the least, and some kind of *modus vivendi* must have been reached whereby she would keep Gropius but would remain his wife and the mother of his children. Be that as it may, Alma's interview with Meltzer contributed a great deal to the legend. It was generally assumed from then on that Mahler's illness was the result of overwork and nervous stress caused by his conflict with the Guarantors' Committee. Yet, a few days before Alma made these dramatic and much publicized statements to Meltzer, Mahler, in what was probably his last interview, had spoken to a Viennese journalist and said:

> I have worked really hard for decades and have born the exertion wonderfully well. I have never worked as little as I did in America. I was not subjected to an excess of either physical or intellectual work there.[34]

It has been hinted that the course of a fatal illness, even when it is caused by an infection, can be hastened by psychological factors. Such an assertion is of course hard to prove scientifically, but if any psychological factor can be claimed to have lowered Mahler's resistance to disease, it is more likely to have been Alma's infidelity, the thought of having henceforth, so to speak, to share her with her lover, and the idea that only his own death would set her free to marry him. However that may be, all medical experts today agree

32 *Musical America* (13 May 1911).
33 *Walter Gropius: der Mensch und sein Werk* (Berlin: Mann, 1983–4), 2 vols.
34 *Neue Freie Presse* (11 April 1911), quoted in Kurt Blaukopf and Zoltan Roman (eds.), *Mahler: sein Leben, sein Werk und seine Welt in zeitgenössischen Bildern und Texten* (Vienna: Universal Edition, 1976): 279.

that, thirty years before the miracle drug – penicillin – was discovered, Mahler's illness (Osler's disease) was invariably fatal.

Thus Mahler was killed, not by the hectic pace of American life, nor by overwork at the Philharmonic, nor by sadistic New York committee women, but by slow endocarditis, which is not a heart disease in the usual sense of the word, but a serious infection – incurable at that time – whose seat is in the heart. Had he lived, he would have most likely found a way of dealing with the domineering, troublesome, and surely tactless, ladies, to whom moreover he had many reasons to be grateful. Despite tensions, misunderstandings and painful conflicts, he would certainly have acknowledged the deep feeling of happiness and fulfilment which the Philharmonic post had brought to him. To a Viennese journalist who came to interview him just before he left America, he spoke of the Johner affair as 'insignificant in itself', but admitted having hesitated before signing his new contract because of it.[35] Most likely, he would have settled his dispute concerning programmes as he had many others in his life before. Deadly enemies such as Walter Damrosch, hostile critics such as Henry Krehbiel, were nothing new in his life. He would have gone on ignoring them and his only reaction would have been, as before, to work hard and to strive for the steady improvement in his orchestra and in the high quality of its performances. Ten years earlier he had written to his bride-to-be: 'The important thing is never to let oneself be guided by the opinion of one's contemporaries and, in both one's life and one's work, to continue steadfastly on one's way without letting oneself be either defeated by failure or diverted by applause.' In all likelihood, Mahler would have gone on to conduct one or more further seasons in New York. And his influence on the musical life of the city would certainly have been deeper and more lasting, now that the first two pioneering years were behind him.

Many traits of Mahler's character were attributed in New York to his 'nervousness', but they were in fact inherent in his genius. His ardent wish to improve and reform, to strive always for the best, his intransigence and obstinacy in all artistic matters, his conception of music as a religion, his lack of concern for social amenities, his impatience in the face of mediocrity, all these were strengths rather than weaknesses. However, it can be argued that Walter Damrosch's gifts as a pedagogue and musical educator, his desire to 'bring great music to the masses' rather than to 'educate the public', were perhaps better suited to New York at this time. New York in the early 1900s clearly had a strong taste for virtuosos and 'stars', and while it is true that Mahler was a virtuoso conductor if ever there was one, he was the very opposite of a star. His behaviour on the podium deliberately avoided any hint of theatricality. Toscanini of course resembled him in this respect, but his fiery Italian temperament, his technical feats, his legendary memory, surely lent itself better to creating a public 'image' than Mahler's *Sachlichkeit*

35 *Neues Wiener Tagblatt* (11 April 1911).

[pragmatism]. Had Mahler perhaps come too soon? It is worth noting at this point that Toscanini, despite his early New York triumphs at the Met, returned to Europe before the Second World War and conquered the city as conductor of the Philharmonic only many years later.

The legend of Mahler's 'failure' spread abroad, and was even amplified over the years. Krehbiel's had written, in his notorious obituary:

> He was looked upon as a great artist, and possibly he was one, but he failed to convince the people of New York of the fact, and therefore his American career was not a success. His influence was not helpful, but prejudicial to good taste ... It was not long before the local musical authorities, those of the operatic and concert field, found that Mr Mahler was an expensive and unprofitable proposition ...

In another article published a week later, the same Krehbiel added:

> The artistic failure of the Philharmonic scheme was so complete as its disappointment from a popular point of view. Thousands of dollars were lost to show how little demand for the enterprise of the Society existed in this city ...

The friend of the Damrosches and the faithful supporter of the New York Symphony is of course speaking. Yet the Philharmonic not only endured, it flourished and proved without a shadow of a doubt that a strong demand for such an enterprise indeed existed in New York. In the autumn following Mahler's death, the society was to receive half a million dollars' legacy from Joseph Pulitzer. Far from being defeated by the Symphony, as Krehbiel hints, it was the Philharmonic which later absorbed the rival Society and became New York's leading orchestra.

In his obituary, Krehbiel made the following remarks about the retouches Mahler introduced in classical scores:

> He never knew, or if he knew he was never willing to acknowledge, that the Philharmonic audience would be as quick to resent an outrage on the musical classics as a corruption of the Bible or Shakespeare. He did not know that he was doing it, or if he did he was willing wantonly to insult their intelligence and taste ...

Only Krehbiel, in fact, had considered Mahler's alterations in repertory scores an 'outrage'. Most of the other critics had hardly mentioned them.

Such was the tone and contents of Krehbiel's obituary that a large number of professionals and music-lovers were deeply shocked. In the *New York Press*, Max Smith wrote:

> Gustav Mahler is dead; but even death has not silenced the tongue of one of his most relentless persecutors in New York. We have been informed that the objectionable comments, which have been characterized as one of the most 'savage attacks on a dead man's memory' ever printed in this city, and have outraged the feelings of every reader possessed of a grain of

common decency, were inspired by 'a sense of duty', by an irresistible desire to tell the 'truth'. Coming from a man, however, most of whose utterances concerning Mahler from the day that [this] conductor was engaged by the Philharmonic Society, breathed the venom of animosity, the explanation is far from convincing. No explanation, in fact; no manner of reasoning will serve as an excuse in the minds of Americans for so un-warranted an assault, immediately after his death, on the memory of a musician who, whatever his faults as an artist, was a master of his craft; whatever his sins as a man, he suffered cruelly and died in agony.[36]

Yet, for many years to come, Krehbiel's resentful remarks, as well as Alma's dramatic statements, were still colouring all the descriptions of Mahler's last two years in America. In 1947, David Ewen wrote in *Music Comes to America*:

> In New York as in Vienna, Mahler was hated. He refused to inject a popu-lar note in his programmes – which prejudiced his audiences against his concerts . . . As a result, Mahler was continually hounded on all sides. The musicians who played under him in the Philharmonic resented him (why did he have to drive them like slaves?). The women who employed him were impatient with him (why did he have to be so obstinate in the matter of programmes, even to the point of excluding Tchaikovsky's beloved music?). The critics who reviewed his concerts annihilated him . . . The public would not take to him. Without a doubt, he was a failure as conductor of the Philharmonic . . . He broke down under the impact of continual friction.[37]

Less than twenty years later, when New York was leading the way for the whole world towards a Mahler revival, Theodore Cron's and Burt Goldblatt's *Portrait of Carnegie Hall* added new details to this by now traditional tale of woe: Mahler was now reported to have 'finished his Symphony of a Thousand while in New York, and its gigantic canvas repelled the ladies'. His retouches to classical scores 'further enraged' them; thus, 'he grew to hate them and their pretentious city' and went to rehearsals in the morning 'like an old steer making up his mind to go to the slaughter house', so much so that 'these cruel conflicts exhausted his heart' until he 'collapsed'.[38] It is obvious that these two authors knew little about Mahler's life and were not interested in finding out more.

By 1990 I thought the truth had at last prevailed and that such exaggera-tions, falsifications and inventions were a thing of the past. I also thought that Krehbiel's obituary had at long last been forgotten or disregarded as a piece of insidious, evil-minded polemic, rendered all the more distasteful for

---

36 *New York Press*, reprinted in *Musical America* (10 June 1911).
37 David Ewen, op. cit.: 99.
38 Theodore O. Cron and Burt Goldblatt, *Portrait of Carnegie Hall* (New York: Macmillan, 1966): 22.

its pretence of objectivity and for its having appeared so soon after Mahler's death. One day, I opened my new issue of the excellent *Opera Quarterly* magazine and read a lengthy review of my colleague Zoltan Roman's useful and informative book, *Gustav Mahler's American Years*.[39] I could hardly believe my eyes! Of the countless reviews favourable to Mahler and his Philharmonic concerts, the reviewer did not quote a single line, but selected instead a few venomous phrases from the pens of Mahler's two bitterest opponents, Henry Krehbiel and William Henderson. In any case, according to him, Mahler, after 1907, was a man 'racked by misfortune and sorrow . . . unable to find a balance between enthusiasm and despair'. In 1911, the Philharmonic 'was eager to get rid him' but 'he seems not to have understood he was being pushed out'. The ending of the *Opera Quarterly*'s review is worth quoting *in extenso*:

> The reorganization of the Philharmonic was a nest of intrigues . . . Why did Mahler . . . think that he . . . was going to be able to command events? Most of us, I suspect, as Mahler sails from these shores to die in Vienna, will weep for him. Yet I confess that I tempered my tears with the thought that he, more than anyone else, had shaped his fate in New York, largely by his foolishness and naïveté. In his naïveté he seems very arrogant. Also foolish [once again]. What happened to his desire for a light work load, to favour his weak heart and allow time for composition? Offered an orchestra, as in his vanity he seems to have thought he had been, the sensible desire evaporated, and he rushed to the same extreme of work that he had fled in Vienna.[40]

Need anyone be reminded that Mahler never attempted to 'command events' at the Philharmonic, but merely attempted to build up a first-rate orchestra comparable to the Boston Symphony? That 'vanity' was perhaps not his principal motive in accepting to conduct the reorganized Philharmonic. That he did not 'rush to an extreme of overwork' but that his schedule was in fact a good deal less strenuous that that of later Philharmonic conductors, such as Dimitri Mitropoulos for instance. The viciousness of this review and its deliberate falsification puzzled me, all the more since it appeared nearly eighty years after Mahler's death. Its writer, George Martin, I knew as the author of a number of serious books on music and politics. Suddenly the title of one of these, which I had examined when it was published ten years ago, sprang to my mind: *The Damrosch Dynasty*. And I began to wonder whether the ghosts of Walter Damrosch (and his spokesman Henry Krehbiel) were not influencing the judgement of their erstwhile chronicler, thus causing him to transform Mahler's New York career into the disaster it was not.

---

39 Zoltan Roman, *Gustav Mahler's American Years, 1907–1911: A Documentary History* (New York: Pendragon Press, 1989).
40 *Opera Quarterly* 7/1 (Spring 1990): 176.

Yet, if Mahler had survived, I have no doubt that he would have brought further changes to the musical life in New York, if only by improving the general level of orchestral playing, and that of the Philharmonic in particular. That level deteriorated quickly after his death, when the conscientious but uninspiring Josef Stransky was chosen to replace him. Stransky has been called a 'society conductor',[41] for he was better able to please the ladies of the Committee and knew how to cater to the tastes of the public. Like all reformers, Mahler, it is true, had sometimes been too demanding and too loath to compromise, but this had surely been his main asset as renovator of the Philharmonic. Yet fate, not he himself, nor the critics, nor the Philharmonic's Guarantors, was responsible for the sudden interruption of his activity as musical director. His real mistake was to die too soon.

41 Interview with the bassoonist Benjamin Kohon, in William Malloch's 'Mahlerton' broadcast.

6

Mahler on Stamps

GILBERT KAPLAN

Mahler's contribution to music has been recognized over the years in many ways. There have been recurring festivals focusing on his music, several museums have been created, prizes have been established in his honour, and Mahler societies to champion his work have sprung up in more than ten countries.

Five countries and a group of islands have recognized Mahler by issuing stamps in his honour. The first stamp was offered by Austria in 1960 on the occasion of the 100th anniversary of Mahler's birth. This was followed by Cuba in 1976, Hungary in 1985, and Grenada in 1986. In addition, Bernera, a small group of islands off the west coast of Scotland, issued a 'stamp' in the late 1970s. The circumstances surrounding the issue of this stamp are described in the caption to the stamp itself, which follows. In addition, in 1990 France issued a pre-paid telephone card picturing Mahler.

In March 1995, the Netherlands issued a Mahler stamp on the occasion of *Mahler-Feest*, an event organized by the Concertgebouw in Amsterdam from 1 to 17 May, featuring performances of all Mahler's music as well as a symposium, *Gustav Mahler: The World Listens*. The Dutch stamp also has a special connection to Donald Mitchell who served as the principal adviser for the *Mahler-Feest* from its inception.

*   *   *

I am grateful to Herbert Moore, one of the foremost authorities on musical images on stamps, for his contribution to this article.

Austria

Value: 1.50 schilling
Issued: 4 July 1960, for Mahler's
birth centenary
First day of use: 7 July 1960
Colour: deep reddish brown
3,000,000 issued in sheets of 50
Designed by Professor Robert Fuchs
Executed: Georg Wimmer
Scott catalogue #654

Cuba

Value: .30 centavo
Issued: November 1976, for the
5th International Ballet Festival
in Havana
Ballet is entitled *Vital Song* and is
danced to music based on Mahler's
Fifth Symphony, the *Scherzo* move-
ment. It was choreographed by Azari
Plisetski and first performed by the
National Ballet of Cuba in 1976.
Scott catalogue #2099

Hungary

Value: 5 forint
Issued: 10 July 1985
Six stamps picturing composers
and instruments were issued for
the European Music Year. Europa
stamps were first issued in 1956 by
the six members of the European
Coal and Steel Community.
Gradually, other countries, including
non-member nations in Eastern
Europe, as well as non-European
postal administrations, began to
issue Europa stamps. Mahler's black
and white bust is combined with the
instruments in colour.
Scott catalogue #2942

Grenada

Value: 5 dollars
Issued: 6 January 1986
A set of four stamps and one souvenir sheet were issued for the centenary of the Statue of Liberty. The $5.00 souvenir sheet pictures the following famous 'immigrants' superimposed on the skyline of New York City: Gustav Mahler, Bertrand Russell, Carl Schurz and Dr Stephen Wise. (Mahler, of course, never emigrated to the United States.)
Scott catalogue #1351

Bernera

A small group of islands off the west coast of Scotland issued these labels in the late 1970s. They were produced perforated and imperforate, as singles and in souvenir sheets. They picture various composers. In 1985 a US Circuit Court ruled in a tax case that 'These islands are privately owned and not independent political jurisdictions; two of them are uninhabited and another has only two residents . . . The stamps produced from the plates are not really postage stamps since they are not valid for the transmission of mail.'

The Mahler stamp, a 2p value, is inscribed with his name and dates and the words 'Sixth Symphony'.

France

Telecom phone card picturing Mahler
Issued: January–June 1990
Value: 50 units
Issued by La Poste, the government agency that also controls post,
telephone and telegraph (PTT).
Front has the word 'Arsenal'.
Rear contains the amusing 'letter' reproduced below.

Metz, le 27 Janvier 1990

Alma Chérie!

J'arrive à Metz. Voyage très agréable grâce au confort de la XM. La ville est
superbe! J'ai apprécié, dans Le Républicain Lorrain, les analyses pénétrantes
de H. L. de la Grange.
    J'ai commencé les répétitions de la Vᵉ avec le Royal Philharmonique de
Flandre. Excellent! La Grande Salle de L'Arsenal est magnifique et sonne
merveilleusement. Téléphone-moi ce soir à l'Arsenal (87749598). Je t'aime.

[signed Gustav Mahler]

Translation:

Metz, 27 January 1990

Alma darling,

I have arrived in Metz. Very pleasant trip due to the comfort of the [Citroen]
XM. The town is wonderful! I very much enjoyed the perceptive reviews by
H. L. de La Grange in *Le Républicain Lorrain*.
    I have started the rehearsals of the Fifth with the Royal Philharmonique de
Flandre. Excellent! The big hall of the Arsenal is magnificent and the sound
is wonderful. Call me tonight at the Arsenal (87749598). I love you.

[signed Gustav Mahler]

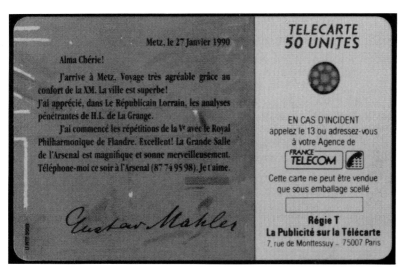

Netherlands

Value: 80 cents
First day of use: 21 March 1995
Number of stamps issued: 8 million
Colour: black photograph, with typography both in white and in black
and musical notation in white on a blue background
Designed by: W. H. Crouwel
Issued on the occasion of *Mahler-Feest*, 1–17 May 1995
at the Concertgebouw in Amsterdam

The image is a photograph of Mahler, taken in March 1906 by H. de Booy,
when Mahler was in Amsterdam to perform his own works – Symphony
No. 5; *Kindertotenlieder*; 'Ich bin der Welt abhanden gekommen' and
Das klagende Lied – with the Concertgebouw Orchestra. The background
of the image is the autograph manuscript of Mahler's Seventh Symphony.

7

Mahler and Self-Renewal

COLIN MATTHEWS

Not so many years ago the pairing of Bruckner and Mahler was a musical cliché that was taken for granted (up until the 1960s they even shared a volume in the 'Master Musicians' series). Yet their common roots in the Austro-German symphonic tradition are practically all that ever brought them together. To take a single example, virtually the only formal problem Bruckner had to solve when tackling a new symphony was whether to put the slow movement or the scherzo second (a radical over-simplification, of course, but in context not unjustified) whereas for Mahler every symphony meant a new beginning, a new 'world', as he described it to Sibelius. Bruckner's symphonies might, again taking the naïve view, be thought of as nine ways of looking at the same thing; each one of Mahler's symphonies explores new ground, musically and emotionally. Can there be any other composer who has produced a coherent body of work with so little reliance on revisiting familiar territory, so little repetition of the tried and tested?

Such a suggestion may surprise and antagonize those whose dislike of Mahler has always stemmed from their antipathy towards the intensely personal nature of his music. It's certainly fair to say that Mahler's emotional world, with its morbid fascination with death, love of the grotesque and banal, the way in which he so often wears his heart on his sleeve, gives the music a uniformity of expression – tending towards the extreme – which some have found, and will always find, distasteful. From such a viewpoint, Mahler's music will inevitably seem to be repetitive, if not long-winded, and too concerned with self-expression to have much variety of mood. Though that is probably a minority view, even the majority who have no problems with Mahler may well overlook his remarkable ability to renew himself.

That this ability was hard won becomes clear when one looks at Mahler's almost painful progress towards becoming a symphonist. If he had died or ceased composing early in his career, like his close friends and contemporaries, Hugo Wolf and Hans Rott, there would have been very little indication of what he would go on to achieve. By the beginning of 1893, at the age of thirty-two, he had composed several chamber works, the large-scale cantata *Das klagende Lied*, around twenty songs with piano or orchestral accompaniment (including the *Lieder eines fahrenden Gesellen*), a five-movement 'Symphonic Poem in two parts', and the first movement of a

Symphony in C minor, possibly another symphonic poem, to which he had given the name *Todtenfeier* ('Funeral Rites'). As far as the outside world was concerned, he was a rising young conductor who also dabbled in composition: the 'Symphonic Poem' had a single performance, as had a handful of songs.

That particular year, 1893, was a watershed for Mahler. He was beginning his third successful season at the Hamburg Opera House, having already made a name for himself as director of the Royal Budapest Opera, and, after five years in which he had virtually no time for composing, he was at last able to think again of his own music. He revised *Das klagende Lied*, began to work on the other movements of the C minor symphony (eventually, of course, to become the Second), and, most importantly, made a comprehensive revision of the 'Symphonic Poem', which now became a programmatic symphony in four movements (although the second movement, 'Blumine', was not discarded until 1894).

Mahler's first four symphonies were all subject to indecision as to their final format – the Third and Fourth were inextricably intertwined from the beginning, and still retain much material in common. Not until the Fifth Symphony, with Mahler benefiting from the security his post at the Vienna Opera gave him, was he able to establish a regular composing regime (though this remained confined to his summer holidays). His creativity reached perhaps its peak in the summer of 1904, when he composed the finale of the Sixth, completed the *Kindertotenlieder*, and began work on the Seventh Symphony, composing the second and fourth movements – the two nocturnes (*Nachtmusik*). In the midst of all this his younger daughter Anna was born!

Nor should it be overlooked that frequently Mahler was preparing the performance of an earlier symphony shortly before embarking on a new one. Thus the Sixth Symphony's first performance in May 1906 immediately preceded the composition of the Eighth (or rather, not immediately, since Mahler first made substantial revisions to the already printed score of the Sixth); while the Tenth was sketched more or less simultaneously with the hectic preparations for the first performance of the Eighth in the summer of 1910. Three more contrasting symphonies than the Sixth, Eighth and Tenth would be hard to imagine.

Yet this non-stop schedule reflects only one aspect of Mahler's creativity, and makes it all the more remarkable that the symphonies themselves, and their internal structure, are so extraordinarily diverse. Not only is there no repetition of overall formal plan from symphony to symphony – in fact, quite the opposite, almost as if Mahler were each time trying to put the maximum distance between himself and his previous symphony – but there is virtually no repeated model for any individual movement. Each of the fifty-one movements (including *Das Lied von der Erde*) that comprise Mahler's symphonic output is original and self-referential in a way that is unparalleled in the symphonic tradition, before or since.

The chart below attempts to set this out schematically: but it cannot but be tentative, since there is no way to codify many of the individual movements. For instance, although the Eighth Symphony's form is relatively classical, it is so on Mahler's own terms: the second movement's combination of slow movement, scherzo and finale, all of them, of course, vocal and choral, should not really come under the classification 'choral finale' which is shared here with the Second Symphony. For the sake of simplicity it has been classified as such, with a modifying number. Similarly the rather unsatisfactory classification of the second movement of the Fifth Symphony as 'song form' in no way implies any relationship to the opening movement of the First Symphony, which is itself too free in structure to be described as 'classical first movement' (a term that is, in turn, deliberately used so as not to straitjacket its respective movements into 'sonata form': 'extended sonata form' being a further avoidance of typecasting). This attempt to establish some relative unity is irrevocably deficient, since ideally there would be no alternative but to give each movement a separate classification. As it is, I suggest seventeen different archetypes, with no attempt at being definitive, and with several movements (there should be more) falling into two categories. The classification is, obviously, subjective and could be argued over and rearranged endlessly.

Symphony No. 1*	A1	B1	C1	D1	E1	
Symphony No. 2	F1	C2	G1	H1	I1	
Symphony No. 3	F2	J1	G2	H2	H3	K1
Symphony No. 4	L1	D2/C3	M1	H4		
Symphony No. 5	N1	A2	G3	B2	O1	
Symphony No. 6§	L2	M2	G4	E2		
Symphony No. 7	L3	D3/J2	G5	J3	O2	
Symphony No. 8	P	I2				
Das Lied von der Erde	A3	M3	J4	G6	H5	N2/K2
Symphony No. 9	Q1/F3	C4/D4	D5	K3		
Symphony No. 10	Q2	G7	B3	G8/D6	E3	

*   Including 'Blumine'
§   Scherzo as third movement

Key

A   Song form (I.i, V.ii, *DL*.i)
B   Intermezzo (I.ii, V.iv, X.iii)
C   Dance [scherzo] (I.iii, II.ii, IV.ii, IX.ii)
D   Parody (I.iv, IV.ii, VII.ii, IX.ii, IX.iii, X.iv)
E   Classical finale (I.v, VI.iv, X.v)
F   Extended sonata (II.i, III.i, IX.i)
G   Scherzo (II.iii, III.iii, V.iii, VI.iii, VII.iii, *DL*.iv, X.ii, I.iv)
H   Song (II.iv, III.iv, III.v, IV.iv, *DL*.v)
I   Choral finale (II.v, VIII.ii)
J   Pastorale (III.ii, VII.ii, VII.iv, *DL*.iii)
K   Slow finale (III.vi, *DL*.vi, IX.iv)
L   Classical first movement (IV.i, VI.i, VII.i)

M   Slow movement (IV.iii, VI.ii, *DL*.ii)
N   Funeral march (V.i, *DL*.vi)
O   Rondo finale (V.v, VII.v)
P   Choral first movement (VIII.i)
Q   Slow first movement (IX.i, X.i)

A glance at the chart shows an astonishing lack of symmetry, both horizontally and vertically, with the single exception of the five scherzo third movements. But a moment's recollection of the character of each one of these scherzos should suffice to rule out any accusation of repetitiveness. The one example of (surely deliberate) repetition is that of the first movements of the Sixth and Seventh Symphonies, where Mahler is explicitly revisiting the same world; the two scherzos, though formally and musically different, are also similar in character (both are grotesque and scary). Yet the respective finales of these two works are almost blatantly opposed to each other (the hollowness of the Seventh's optimism seeming clearly to result from Mahler's attempt to turn round the bleakness of the Sixth).

This schematic outline of the symphonies ignores, of course – except in the broadest terms – their musical content. It is all very well to describe the first movement of the Third Symphony as 'extended sonata', but the extraordinary richness of invention in this great and hugely loveable shaggy dog of a movement deserves something better. Mahler, of all composers, cannot be reduced to statistics. Yet without an analysis of how the symphonies are put together, starting at the very basics of construction, it is all too easy to underrate the capacity for self-renewal which I believe Mahler demonstrates more than any other composer.

8

In Search of Mahler's Childhood

DAVID MATTHEWS

I first visited what was then Czechoslovakia in October 1984, accompanying the Nash Ensemble who were including my Clarinet Quartet on a short tour of the country. The tour began in Brno, and as I had a free day there I decided to go to Jihlava – Iglau – by train and find the houses where Mahler was brought up. The train was old, dirty and slow and the fifty-mile journey took several hours. At Jihlava I discovered that I had only an hour and a half before my train back to Brno, and that the station was over a mile away from the town square, near which I knew the Mahler houses were located. I set off on foot and eventually found my way to the square (the largest town square in Europe) and located Malinovského – old Pirnitzergasse – a little street running off its southern end. The Mahlers lived at No. 4 from 1860 until 1872 and then moved next door to No. 6. On the front of No. 4 is a plaque with a bas-relief of Mahler's head in profile. I took photographs and hurried back to the station. On the journey back, equally slow, peasants got in at almost every station with full baskets of mushrooms they had collected from the forest.

In January 1986 I was in Brno again. I had been asked by Roger Scruton, a founder and trustee of the Jan Hus Educational Foundation, to give an unofficial seminar in Brno on Mahler and on my own music. The Jan Hus Foundation at that time operated as an underground university in Brno, Prague and Bratislava. It had begun in 1980 with a request from the philosopher Julius Tomin at the Charles University in Prague to Oxford University for help with their philosophy course. This had been severely depleted after the Russian invasion in 1968, when most of the staff had been purged and forced to take menial jobs, such as street-sweeping or boiler-minding. The Foundation's work had rapidly spread to other disciplines, and eventually to music. In Brno, the seminars were organized by Petr Oslzlý, dramaturge and unofficial leader of the Brno experimental theatre company Theatre on a String, and Miroslav (Mikin) Pospíšil, an English lecturer at the university. These seminars took place in Petr's flat, and like all such potentially subversive meetings under the communist regime were illegal, though the secret police, whom I imagine must have been aware of what was going on, caused us no trouble (the only visitor ever to be arrested was the French philosopher Jacques Derrida, who was released after the personal intervention of President Mitterrand; perhaps the secret police got cold feet after that).

In Petr's seminar I introduced and played a recording of Mahler's Tenth Symphony in Deryck Cooke's performing version, on which my brother Colin and I had collaborated. The choice of Mahler was important to Petr: for him, Mahler was a true representative of that Central European culture which the state, with its narrow emphasis on nationalism and its distaste for 'cosmopolitanism' (a thinly disguised anti-Semitism), was suppressing by neglect. It was also moving for me to be talking about Mahler, my favourite composer while I was growing up, in the country of his birth. Many of the immediate emotions I had had when young, but which have since receded, came back to me as I spoke, and listened to this marvellous, poignant music.

The following day, Petr and Mikin offered to take me to the village of Kaliště to see the house where Mahler had been born. Kaliště is an isolated village on the border of Bohemia and Moravia, about seventy miles north-west of Brno and five miles from the town of Humpolec. It looks much as it must have done in Mahler's time: a little red-roofed church and a cluster of houses around a village green with a pond, and opposite the church, the pub (*zájezdní hostinec* – roadside inn) that Bernhard Mahler kept when Gustav was born. The original building was burnt down in 1937 after being struck by lightning and a new one, similar in design, erected on its foundations. This unpretentious pub was looked after by a rosy-cheeked *babička* in her seventies, Mrs Kratochvílová. She showed us her visitors' book, photographs and sheaves of press cuttings, and kept up a constant, high-pitched mono-logue in which (as I learned later) her random thoughts about Mahler ('poor man, he died so young') were interspersed with complaints about her health and her own hard life. It was a bitterly cold day, with a thick layer of snow on the ground. We took photographs – there is another plaque on the out-side wall of the pub, similar to the one in Jihlava – and drove to the Jewish cemetery in Humpolec to see if we could find the grave of Mahler's elder brother Isidor, who had died in infancy in Kaliště, but almost all the graves had inscriptions in Hebrew only and we soon gave up.

That October I was in Brno again. The Foundation had asked me to arrange a series of seminars by British composers. The first one was by Nigel Osborne, and I was there too, primarily to attend the Brno International Music Festival. That year there was also, for the first time, a simultaneous festival of contemporary music. On my January visit I had already been impressed with some of the contemporary Czech music I had heard, parti-cularly from the younger Brno composers, which still seemed infused with the lively spirit of Janáček, and I had conceived the idea of trying to get some of it played in Britain. I had some success in doing this over the next few years, but that is another story.

During my visit Mikin Pospíšil took me to Kaliště again and we also visited the new Mahler museum in Humpolec. This was the brainchild of a local headmaster, Jiří Rychetský, who had single-handedly set it up, with some generous state funding, on the theme of Mahler as a Czech. Rychetský, a tremendous enthusiast, knew all the Mahler associations of the local country-side and took us to Želiv (Seelau), a few miles to the west of Humpolec. On the way we passed an 800-year-old lime tree, under which Hussite sermons had been preached in the fifteenth century and which, Rychetský assured us, was the very tree under which the hero of the *Lieder eines fahrenden Gesellen* lies down to sink into Romantic oblivion at the end of the cycle. A nice story, and at least Mahler would have almost certainly known this famous tree. Mahler visited his friend Emil Freund and stayed with him at his parents' house in Seelau on holidays between 1878 and 1881. He also briefly fell in love with one of Emil Freund's cousins, an affair that had a tragic consequence, for in 1880 she committed suicide by throwing herself in the river which runs through the village. There is a splendid monastery beside the Želivka river designed by the baroque architect Santini, the Czech Hawksmoor, as Nikolaus Pevsner called him.

My next visit to Czechoslovakia, in August 1987, was a holiday with Maggie Hemingway, who wrote her extraordinary novel *The Postmen's House* out of her experiences that month. We stayed with Petr Oslzlý, his wife Eva and their two daughters in their summer house in another village called Kaliště (the name means 'muddy pool'), south-west of Jihlava. Petr told us with relish of how some Japanese Mahlerians came to his village by mistake, asked where Mahler's house was, and were innocently directed to a house near his which by coincidence happened to be owned by some people called Mahler. He believed that a photograph of the wrong house had sub-sequently appeared in a Japanese book on Mahler.

The countryside around Petr's Kaliště is unspoiled and beautiful, a high hill country with woods, old-fashioned farms and small lakes. My first venture into the pine forest was revelatory: I heard the opening of Mahler's First Symphony. The wind whistling through the trees produced a sound uncannily like that six-octave A on string harmonics. The whole opening, with its bird calls and distant fanfares, derives from Mahler's childhood memories of being alone in the forests near Iglau. It took him a long time before he found the precise sound he had in his memory, for originally the strings played their A normally, without harmonics, a sound, as Mahler later told his friend Natalie Bauer-Lechner, that was 'far too substantial for the shimmering and glimmering of the air that I had in mind'. For the work's second performance in 1893 he hit on the idea of harmonics.

I had another revelation when Petr played me a tape of a village band who specialized in performing old-fashioned band music. Here was the source of the trio of the First Symphony's Funeral March: clarinets and trumpets in thirds playing sentimental melodies, pizzicato bass, and a bass drum with cymbals attached. I had not realized before to what extent the music that Mahler heard as a child must have affected him. Mahler told Bauer-Lechner, in connection with the 'Fischpredigt' from the *Wunderhorn* songs, that 'the Bohemian music of my childhood home has found its way into many of my compositions'. How much so is probably not yet fully understood.

We made another expedition to Mahler's Kaliště and met Jiří Rychetský who took us this time to Lipnice (Lipnitz), the home of Mahler's paternal grandmother and the probable birthplace of Mahler's father. Jaroslav Hašek, the author of *The Good Soldier Schweik*, ended his short and dissolute life there and we saw his house. Lipnice is dominated by a ruined medieval castle, and I thought of the opening line of the second part of *Das klagende Lied*, 'Vom hohen Felsen erglänzt das Schloss'. No wonder Mahler was attracted to *Des Knaben Wunderhorn*: his childhood landscape was a Romantic world of forests, lakes and castles identical to the one in which the poems are set.

Exactly two years later I was once again in Mahler country with Petr, Mikin, and a cameraman, Aleš Záboj. Petr wanted to film Kaliště, the pub and Mrs Kratochvílová; I suggested that he should also try to film all the nearby places associated with Mahler's childhood. With copies of Donald Mitchell's *Gustav Mahler: The Early Years* and Henry-Louis de La Grange's biography in my bag and with my memories of Jiří Rychetský's guided tours, we went from place to place with our video camera: the linden tree; Emil Freund's house at Želiv; Lipnice; finally Jihlava.

Jihlava is a historic town and has been mostly well preserved, though in the 1960s a communist party boss, disregarding preservation orders, managed to demolish a group of medieval houses in the main square and erect a hideous supermarket in their place. Most of the handsome Renaissance buildings lining the square, however, are intact. We knocked on the door of No. 6 Malinovského and introduced ourselves to the Navrátils, the present owners, who remembered Knud Martner's visit some years back. They were a friendly couple and allowed us to film inside and out. In the back yard were the dilapidated remains of Bernhard Mahler's Schnaps distillery. They were about to be demolished, so our filming was timely. Rummaging in the piles of broken glass and other rubbish that was strewn around the brick buildings, Mikin found an intact spirit flask which he gave to me as a souvenir. From its appearance, it could have dated from Bernhard Mahler's time, and I was certainly willing to believe it.

We filmed Mahler's primary school, and the Gymnasium to which he was sent at the age of nine. We retraced his walk to school, across the square and down a side street. The building now houses the town archives, and the staff readily produced Mahler's school reports and essays for us and, with remarkable casualness, left us alone so we could film them. We went on to the theatre where Mahler heard his first operas, still in its original state but unfortunately about to be modernized and its nineteenth-century interior destroyed; then to the Dělnicky Dům ('Workers' House' – a social club), once the Hotel Czap where Mahler played in a concert on 12 September 1876 which included his violin sonata – since lost. The salon where the concert took place was still intact, but this too was going to be demolished as the building was to be turned into a new post office. Our last destination was the Jewish cemetery. We were not certain if Mahler's parents were buried there, though we strongly suspected they must be; but the cemetery was a forlorn place, with many graves destroyed by the Nazis and most of the others overgrown by bushes and trees. We could find no trace of Mahlers. It was a chilling reminder of the fate of the Jews in this largely German-speaking town.

During those August days none of us had any idea that in a few months' time there would be a revolution that would overturn the communist government. So much has changed since then. Mrs Kratochvílová has died and the pub in Kaliště is for sale: what will happen to it is uncertain. Petr Oslzlý, after two years as an adviser to President Havel, is back in Brno as director of the new, splendidly equipped Theatre on a String. Mikin Pospíšil is head of the now official, Brno-based Jan Hus Foundation, which acts as an agent for further education in both the Czech Republic and Slovakia. Brno is once again a neighbouring city of Vienna; Prague is no longer, as Milan Kundera once wrote, 'gradually fading away into the mists of Eastern Europe, to which it never really belonged'. The idea of a unified Central European culture is being reborn: those who cherished it during the long years of cultural oppression will not, I hope, lightly give it up. Mahler's part in that culture is crucial, and within it he cannot any more be regarded as the thrice homeless figure he once called himself, but equally at home as a Bohemian and an Austrian, and as the greatest of Jewish composers.

Bernhard Mahler's Schnaps
distillery, Jihlava, 1989

9

Vestdijk on Mahler, 1924–69: A Symphony in Words

EVELINE NIKKELS

I got to know Gustav Mahler when I was little more than a child. Under Mengelberg as conductor, of course. I can't quite remember whether it was the First or the Fourth I heard that first time; but I do remember that I instantly felt, as ever since every true admirer, be he young or old, well grounded or not, must have felt: this is *the* music and strictly speaking there is *nothing else*. That may be a terribly one-sided view but doesn't take away the fact that 'competitors' haven't got the slightest chance against Mahler.

Simon Vestdijk, 1969

In his last essay, 'The Fishes and Mahler', Simon Vestdijk stresses yet again that to him only one composer really mattered in the end and that composer was Mahler. In this essay, which can be viewed as a coda to the 'symphony in words' entitled 'Vestdijk on Mahler', he points out as well that no one should be allowed to dislike Mahler's music and that any person so doing shows his inability to react to music as music. This kind of provocative declaration led to many a conflict with the press during Vestdijk's lifetime, which is the reason why in this article I shall concentrate on the impact of Vestdijk's musical essays on his fellow writers.

The first written reaction to listening to Mahler's music dates from November 1924, when Vestdijk wrote an article for the magazine *Urania* under the title 'Astrological Reflections on Gustav Mahler', a title that speaks for itself. Though sometimes difficult to understand for a non-astrologer (zodiac signs and planets make frequent appearances), it forms the beginning of what will be, for the next forty-five years, Vestdijk's vision of the symphonic *oeuvre* of Mahler; that there is a 'secular' and a 'celestial' side to Mahler (later to be replaced by concepts such as 'natural' and 'sacral–demonic' or 'diastolic' and 'systolic'). The two highlights within this *oeuvre* are the last movement of the Sixth Symphony, 'which in itself is a world within a creation that Mahler hardly ever surpassed', and his Ninth, 'to me the most gripping music ever written'. The last words of this essay sound like a prophecy:

Mahler's music has been written for the future, for the forthcoming age of Aquarius; people aren't yet ready for it. A higher life, in communion both with our fellow human beings and with the cosmos, will also bring Mahler's symphonies closer to people's hearts and imbue them with an understanding of many things intellect and science will never be able to reach.

Right now we are at the brink of 'the age of Aquarius' and if the signs are not misleading us we no longer have to wait and Mahler's time, as he himself prophesied ('Meine Zeit wird kommen'), has come. Now, what about Vestdijk's reflections on Mahler? Has Vestdijk's time come too? This essay will try to discover an answer to this question, based on the changing critical attitude of Vestdijk's fellow writers and musicologists. But let us first listen to the words of the writer himself in his big essay, 'The Condemnable Emotion', which served as a raw sketch for the book he subsequently published on the structure of Mahler's symphonies.

1 Vestdijk on Mahler, 'heftig bewegt'

In 'The Condemnable Emotion', a title that itself poses quite a few questions – what does Vestdijk mean by a 'condemnable emotion'? Are we to judge this in a positive or a negative way? – Vestdijk launches a few negative criteria with which to judge/condemn Mahler's *oeuvre*. Vestdijk – as other Mahler enthusiasts from the earliest days – is astonished that after the big Mahler festival of 1920 a public silence descended on the composer lasting in effect until the end of the 1950s. Was it caused by the anxiety of listeners unable to cope with this overwhelmingly emotional music or did the accusations of plagiarism condemn the composer to the sidelines? Or, as Vestdijk proposed in his *Urania* article, was it that mankind wasn't yet ready for 'by far the most emotional composer' we know? To enable us to get to the core of the art and the essence of Mahler himself, Vestdijk in 'The Condemnable Emotion' offers us some assistance, primarily by illustrating the religious aspect, not from a clergyman's point of view, but from a pantheistic or nature-elevating philosophical stance. This explains why Vestdijk labels Mahler's religious music 'sacral–demonic'. There exists true 'religious' music, such as the final choral passage in the Second Symphony; however, the 'sacral–demonic' encompasses more than the 'religious'. It is built up of the primitive component of the 'demonic' combined with the 'sacral', the higher spiritual aspiration. The demonic element is indispensable because Mahler's music speaks of destruction and total annihilation. The climax of this alliance between God and demon is the Ninth Symphony.

As to the charge of plagiarism, Vestdijk is very outspoken, citing *quod licet Iovi non licet bovi*: 'The issue is that apparently Bach is allowed to steal but Mahler not.' The extent of Mahler's melodic constructions (another cause for criticism) is explained by Vestdijk as essential to Mahler's art, which is based on 'insatiability', while the triviality and banality identified by Mahler's detractors are the consequence mainly of the romantic character of Mahler's lyrical themes. All of these negative 'points' are completely outweighed for Vestdijk by the only thing that really matters to him: the emotion the composer puts into the music and evokes in the listener. And this emotion, formless in itself, is perfectly controlled by Mahler (e.g. in sonata form). The effect resembles a lava stream revealing features of temples and palaces – in short, solidified matter.

In a word, the conclusion of this essay is brilliant, and in itself a 'condemnable emotion' for the true Mahler fan:

> In my opinion, Mahler will have a great future when the insight that it is better to steal a melody than systematically to create melodies that are no melodies has materialized in those people that can still admire musical emotions . . .

This quotation ends with more prophetical words: 'We'll live to see another Mahler festival.' Noted!

As a kind of elaboration, followed by reprise and coda, Vestdijk's *pièce de resistance*, 'Gustav Mahler: On the Structure of his Symphonic *Oeuvre*', relates to 'The Condemnable Emotion'. Here as well Vestdijk is open to criticism, which however should be mitigated by a positive attitude: it is essential to be instinctively receptive to his ideas. Once this condition has been met Vestdijk gives us a guided tour round Mahler's symphonies in fascinating, albeit controversial, style, dividing them into either 'systolic' or 'diastolic' works.

The first thing that strikes us here is that Vestdijk has chosen medical terms for his two categories; he claims to have found the distinction in Goethe. I think it is more likely to be a remnant of his time spent practising as a doctor. A psychologically interesting feature is that both terms are related to the heart ('systole' is the contraction of the heart; 'diastole' the period in between two contractions), and that, as we know, Mahler was suffering from a heart condition!

Vestdijk applies this distinction because he disagrees with the traditional three-way division chosen by most Mahler commentators: the 'Wunderhorn' symphonies (Nos. 1, 2, 3 and 4); the middle symphonies (Nos. 5, 6, 7 and 8) and the 'Spätwerk' (*Das Lied von der Erde*, No. 9 and the unfinished Tenth). He sees, rather, a distinction between symphonies alternately concerned with 'tension' and 'relaxation'. 'Systole' (tension) is the masculine, 'diastole' (relaxation) the feminine element. The 'systolic' element is dominant in the 'even-number' symphonies, Nos. 2, 4, 6, 8 and 9=10 (Vestdijk's formulation). So, to Vestdijk, the Ninth Symphony becomes the Tenth with regard to its quality of tension; that accords astonishingly well with Mahler's own way of counting his symphonies, because in order to avoid the death-laden figure 9 Mahler called his *Das Lied von der Erde* a symphony, thereby effectively making his Ninth into his Tenth. But one cannot escape fate: from a purely symphonic point of view No. 9 was the *finalis* for Mahler, his Tenth remaining unfinished. In itself this is a clearly argued and – from Vestdijk's point of view – acceptable order. It becomes more difficult, and certainly less user-friendly, when the different symphonies each get their own characteristic and are labelled with a number. Being a great authority on Mahler himself (I don't think a single bar from Mahler's symphonic *oeuvre* held any secrets for Vestdijk – structurally or emotionally) he expects the reader to have a quick, knowledgeable mind, leaping effortlessly from one symphony to another (preferably with the score in his mind or in front of him). Does this make Vestdijk challengingly opaque to the reader? On the contrary. However, he does place great demands on his musical reader, as he does on his literary reader. Both categories should rejoice: the literary reader will delight in the expressive language whereas the musicologist will read with mounting astonishment how Mahler's ornate musical ideas can be expressed so eloquently in words. What, for example, should one make of 'It has to be a roaring and blaring finale, a flood of undeniable joy of living' to describe the finale of the Seventh Symphony, or the expression 'warehouse' finale.

It is striking and significant that Vestdijk spends most pages on the symphonies he likes best. His essay on the Sixth surpasses all else, not only in length (twenty-four pages) but in profoundity and depth of analysis as well. In this essay Vestdijk offers the reader his great knowledge of Nietzsche and of the relationship between Mahler and Nietzsche. Vestdijk's image of Mahler is severely prejudiced by his own 'philosophical–literary' reading matter: Goethe, Dostoevsky and Nietzsche, who – *mirabile dictu* – were Mahler's favourites as well. A logical conclusion therefore could be that there is something to be said for Vestdijk's ideas. He is one of very few Mahler authorities not to consider Mahler's 'Tragic' Symphony as the most tragic music written by the composer. Finding evidence to support this thesis should certainly challenge musicologists. Another striking thing is Vestdijk's resistance to the finale of the Second Symphony and its 'warehouse' finale. His biggest problem is that (too) much material from the first movement is reused in the finale, which is thereby shockingly devalued. Or could it be related to Vestdijk's ambivalent attitude towards life after death ('He doesn't believe in it', is written in the *Beaker of Love*), subject of the *Auferstehungs-hymne*. Here Vestdijk raises the topic of Mahler's problems with 'weak' finales (as he does equally cogently in his essay 'Tempo Problems with Mahler'). The only finale really to deserve its title as the culmination of a symphony is the finale of the Sixth. Alone with this finale as the *non plus ultra* (as we've seen before) stands the first movement of the Ninth: isn't that sacral–demonic music *per se*, where the transcendental is the central idea in the sense that here one can't speak of the relationship between man and death (which is almost uniquely the content of Mahler's creations) but rather of the relationship between God and death? It doesn't surprise Vestdijk that the Ninth Symphony wasn't followed by a complete Tenth, since 'music such as 9–1 has never been written before and will never be written again: Mahler himself would not have been able to cope with it. People die time and time again, a god dies only once.'

2 Scherzo, *Vestdijk as Critic*

Besides his inner reflections on Mahler, specifically based on the Mahler
literature and music scores known to him (he possessed several symphonies
in a piano extract for four hands as well, in which he carefully notated the
instrumentation) Vestdijk also wrote a few critiques on so-called 'music in
tin' (i.e. cylinder recordings) and music 'live' of which 'Tempo Problems in
Mahler' is one of the most interesting. Most important, Vestdijk lacks
Mahler's own metronome timings in order to arrive at an informed opinion,
because relative speed is either *schnell* or *nicht eilen*. He is annoyed by what
he calls the killing of Mahler's music by the wrong choice of tempi, e.g. by
playing a funeral march when it starts *nicht eilen*: 'In what can only be
judged as a slight alteration the metronome timing shoots up or down.'
Performances of the Seventh, the Fourth, the Fifth (later the subject of its
own short essay), the Sixth and of course the Ninth successively are critically
considered in an ironic or satirical manner. The only remark I find
astonishing is one with regard to a highly praised performance of the
Seventh Symphony by the Concertgebouw Orchestra under Van Beinum: 'As
one knows, the Concertgebouw Orchestra isn't exactly overflowing with
love for Mahler.' How could he have forgotten the past so quickly? On the
other hand he greatly admires Eduard Flipse, a disciple of Mengelberg, who
was at that time especially esteemed for his interpretation of the Sixth. The
last section – a comparison between a recording 'in tin' by Horenstein and
Kletzki and a 'live' recording by Kubelik – brings another set of wonderfully
vivid *aperçus*. For example: 'Horenstein paints in oils with thick daubs,
Kubelik shows a preference for pastel and Kletzki is an etcher'; or: 'It isn't
really necessary to meet Mahler's Ninth Symphony broken, ploughed and in
tears.' With his remark about the finale, painted as 'a series of destructive
blows, which causes naked creatures, pitiful slaves, to crawl around in blood
and filthy lucre', Vestdijk is off on his favourite topic again: this work is not
only a 'conveyor of sorrow'.

The Ninth under Kubelik is at the centre of 'Mahler's Two Poles', where it
is linked to a preview of a performance of the Third Symphony. This time he
doesn't use the terms 'diastolic' and 'systolic' as opposing poles but 'secular'
and 'celestial' – but what's in a name? In essence it's all about the same thing:
the blessed relaxation of the Third Symphony as opposed to the heavenly
tension of the Ninth.

'Mahler's Fifth' to some extent continues from where 'Tempo Problems
with Mahler' left off. The success of the Fifth, this time judged from a live
performance under Haitink, depends to a great extent on the right choice of
tempi. It is fascinating to read that Vestdijk was at that time already disputing
the meaning of the *Adagietto*. Since then, with the publication and reporting
of Gilbert Kaplan's views, a lot of discussion has been generated on this
subject. Kaplan suggests eight minutes only (basing himself on Mengelberg),
whereas Haitink requires thirteen. Vestdijk belongs to the 'slow' school in
view of his statement that 'the *Adagietto* is sometimes being played too

quickly', whereas the score clearly states *sehr langsam*, which makes him believe *Adagietto* means 'little adagio' rather than 'slightly quicker than adagio'.

The last essay from this anthology dates from 1964 and deals with *Das Lied von der Erde* (= No. 9 in Vestdijk's terminology). It contains a comparison between two recordings by Bruno Walter, who was conductor at the world première (as Mahler himself had died). From the title 'last but one' it shows once more – and Vestdijk states so quite explicitly – that one had better leave out the Tenth Symphony (which would be No. 11). The monumentality applies to the two corner pieces in which death plays the leading role, once as a pendant to life and once as a farewell 'auf ewig'. By eliminating the two 'weaker' movements (the fourth and fifth), Vestdijk aims to create a symphony almost as 'strong' as the Sixth or the Ninth. He explains in a nutshell the quintessence of the last movement of *Das Lied von der Erde* by quoting Mahler: 'Allüberall blauen licht die Fernen.' This may be unacceptable for such an authority in literature, but, as he states: 'This song symphony not having a perfect last movement guarantees the musically perfect escape where more meaningful words would have lost their meaning.'

3 Rondo burlesque: *The Critics on Mahler's Essays on Music*

Rondo burlesque: hidden in that title is a criticism of Vestdijk. 'Rondo' stands for a constantly returning theme; 'burlesque', according to the dictionary, is 'the playful imitation of the great and sublime'. This is because Vestdijk in everything he writes on music always talks about the 'great and sublime' of his beloved art form, everything of course being expressed in his own unique way. And it is this uniqueness that, in the eyes of the critics, makes him into nothing more than a dilettante whose amateurish writing and pseudo-scientific reflections should be promptly curtailed. For a long time the critics kept on discussing this same subject; for a long time Vestdijk defended himself in burlesque. Yet how do we, more than thirty years later, regard Vestdijk's essays? Are they of any importance to, for example, a music study? The answer to this, most certainly in the case of the Mahler essays, is yes. Too little has been written in Dutch on Mahler and never on the literary and musical quality of Vestdijk's work. Probably the critics have felt the same as Vestdijk felt on reading Adorno's book on Mahler: 'It's a difficult book to read.' I would like to quote his own words as my critique of Vestdijk: 'It is the testimony of a highly gifted writer, and experience tells us that he who writes best will always in the end win.'

4 Misterioso: *Vestdijk about Mahler, Mahler and Vestdijk*

'More so than by Vestdijk's reflections on his personal preference for a few bars and fragments in the masterpieces of music . . . I was struck by what he seemed to reveal about himself in that way,' wrote Helle S. Haasse. Add to this Vestdijk's own words that in his personal life music from early childhood had always played a more important role than any kind of literature, that he wanted to be a musician, and the inference is quite clear. In everything Vestdijk says about Mahler he bares his soul, in other words: in Mahler's music he sees himself reflected as 'nicht zustanden gekommene Musiker'. In this context it is interesting to know that Vestdijk stopped composing when he heard Mahler's music for the first time.

There are more similarities. It would be overstating it to call Mahler a 'nicht zustanden gekommene Dichter'. However, the fact remains that he did write a series of more than amateurish poems and that many of his (youthful) letters show a *flux de plume*. Where Mahler and Vestdijk have most in common, in my opinion, is in their mutual quest for the ultimate truth on Life and Death, about the relationship between mankind and God. A guideline in this respect to both were the thoughts of Friedrich Nietzsche, as expressed *Also sprach Zarathustra*, as elsewhere. 'Vergiss nicht Mensch, du bist der Stein, die Wüste, bist der Tod', Vestdijk quotes the philosopher; 'O Mensch! Gib Acht!' Mahler sings – with Zarathustra–Nietzsche – in his Third Symphony. It is exactly in this quest for a religion, which is non-Christian, that Mahler and Vestdijk could have been two souls with one mind. Maybe Vestdijk's Mahler essays are in fact 'a message from the hereafter'!

10

A New Transition: Some Pages from the Third Movement of Mahler's Ninth Symphony

EDWARD R. REILLY

Friends of Donald Mitchell who had the pleasure in earlier years of visiting him at his apartment in London will almost certainly also have had the pleasure of examining the rare autograph leaf from the third movement of Mahler's Ninth Symphony, a gift from the composer's daughter Anna. That manuscript, illustrated on pp. 102–3, is now at the British Library.[1]

In this brief study I would like to describe the contents of this leaf and draw attention to a whole group of further pages connected with the third movement of the Ninth Symphony which thus far seem little known.[2] Through the kindness of Albi Rosenthal, I was able to see a number of them in 1976, when he was serving as their custodian for Anna Mahler. Sadly, since her death they have been dispersed. One of them was sold as lot 315 at an auction at Sotheby's in London, 16–17 May 1991. The recto of the leaf, which contains a draft orchestral score of bars 508–17 is reproduced in the catalogue. Thus it can be identified as leaf VII of the pages formerly belonging to Anna Mahler listed below. Another was sold as lot 578 at Sotheby's London auction of 28–9 May 1992. The verso of this leaf, showing a version of the material from bars 471 to 483, is reproduced in the catalogue. It corresponds to I verso listed below. The names of the purchasers of these autographs remain unknown. Happily, all of the pages that I saw had been at some point photographed, and copies are found in the archive of the Internationale Gustav Mahler Gesellschaft in Vienna. At an earlier stage, however, at least two more leaves had been acquired by American collectors.[3]

1   *GB–Lbl* part of Deposit 9353.
2   They are mentioned but not discussed in detail by Colin Matthews in his volume *Mahler at Work: Aspects of the Creative Process*, in the series *Outstanding Dissertations in Music from British Universities* (New York: Garland Publishing, Inc., 1989): 164–5, and by Peter Andraschke, *Gustav Mahlers IX. Symphonie: Kompositionsprozess und Analyse*, in the series *Beihefte zum Archiv für Musikwissenschaft*, Vol. XIV (Wiesbaden: Franz Steiner Verlag, 1976): 72.
3   An important group of sketches that belong to a much earlier stage in the development of the Symphony are found in a sketchbook for the Ninth that formerly belonged to Mrs F. Charles Adler and is now in the Österreichische Nationalbibliothek. They are transcribed and discussed by Colin Matthews, op. cit.: 112–16.

Above and facing: Two pages from the *Rondo burleske* of
Mahler's Ninth Symphony (*GB–Lbl* part of Deposit 9353).
By permission of the British Library

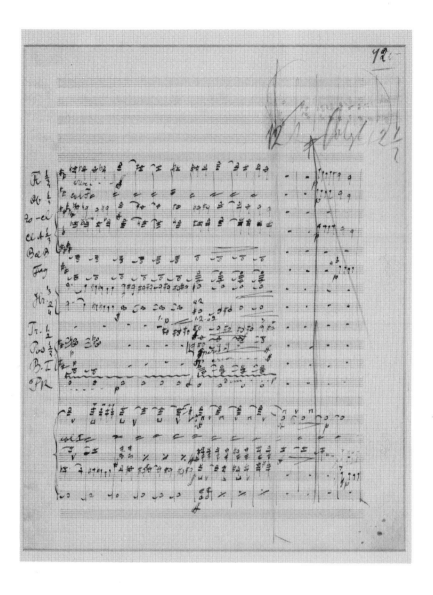

Donald Mitchell's manuscript, the seven leaves that formerly belonged to Anna Mahler and two further leaves in private hands, are all connected with the transition from the middle section of the movement back to its opening material at Tempo I. *subito* in bar 522. Bars 412–521 encompass the larger part of the music found in these manuscripts. Both preliminary sketches on two to four staves and nearly full-page draft full scores appear, in some cases on the same page. Before undertaking a further investigation of this material, however, it is important to note that at the time that Mahler completed the draft orchestral score of this movement, now in the Österreichisches National-bibliothek in Vienna, this transition passage differed significantly from its final form.[4] Bars 471–81 are not found in the draft, and were added between the draft and the completion of the fair copy. On the other hand a nineteen-bar section that appears in the draft immediately before Tempo I. *subito* (bar 522), was later crossed out in the fair copy, now in the Pierpont Morgan Library in New York, thus drastically modifying the transition.[5]

The nature of the preliminary sketches found in these pages varies con-siderably. With at least one important exception, it is difficult to determine whether they belong to the period prior to the draft orchestral score in the Nationalbibliothek, or were written in conjunction with the modifications found in the new pages of score. The latter much more clearly reflect an interim stage, or series of explorations, between the Nationalbibliothek draft score and the Pierpont Morgan fair copy. I suspect that at least some of the sketches belong to an earlier stage, and that Mahler was simply using up the remaining available space on the manuscript paper when he wrote the pages in score.

Donald Mitchell's leaf consists primarily of two pages of full score that approach the quality of a fair copy. The recto of the page numbered 12 also contains a pencil sketch that is related to the material found in bars 462–7, a passage to which Mahler repeatedly returns in the other sketches. The music in full score corresponds to bars 412–25 of the published movement. The last two bars appear to be cancelled and carry the notation 'folgt 12½', which clearly refers to a sketch on page IV among the manuscripts described below. The entire verso of the leaf, which contains bars 426–42 of the final form of the movement, is also cancelled with a diagonal stroke. The words 'bleibt Alles' [everything remains] have been added at the top of the leaf, to indicate that the entire page, and probably the two measures from the recto, have been restored. Contrabassoons and first and third horn parts have been

4   Gustav Mahler, *IX. Symphonie: Partiturentwurf der ersten drei Sätze: Faksimile nach der Handschrift*, ed. Erwin Ratz (Vienna: Universal Edition, 1971). The pertinent pages are those numbered III/30 to III/35 in the facsimile.

5   The manuscript is part of the Robert Owen Lehman Collection, on deposit at the library. See J. Rigbie Turner, *Nineteenth-Century Autograph Music Manuscripts in The Pierpont Morgan Library: A Check List* (New York: The Pierpont Morgan Library, 1982): 33. The passage that was cut is found in bifolio 14, pp. 1 and 2 of the third movement.

added at the top of the score, timpani and harp at the bottom. The tempo marking 'Etwas zurückhaltend', has also been added, reversing 'Sempre l'istesso tempo' found in the earlier Nationalbibliothek draft score. Neither marking found its way into the published version. Above the final bar Mahler has also added circle with a line through it (∅) and a question mark. The composer often used this sign to indicate a connection with another page similarly marked, suggesting a new or different continuation of the original passage. Another such sign does in fact appear in one of the pages discussed below (VI recto), but we cannot be entirely sure that it is actually connected with the present page. Other pertinent pages may well be lost. What is found on the two sides of this leaf clearly suggests that Mahler was working on transforming his earlier orchestral draft into a fair copy, and became dissatisfied with the shape of the transition from this point to the return of the opening material of the first section. At that time he explored several alternative possibilities. The first seems to have been to cut the last two measures of the recto and the entire verso and move directly to the new passage found sketched in the leaf numbered 12½, which shows the preliminary form of bars 471–83 and indicates their continuity with the remaining numbered pages. Mahler also seems to have considered another alternative, restoring all of the music on this leaf, and introducing another, still uncertain, alternative cut, possibly to some modified form of the passage in bars 480–92. This possibility, however, is a very uncertain one. (I am inclined to believe that we lack a page that matches the cut sign and question mark found on the verso of this leaf.) Ultimately Mahler kept the material found in this leaf and inserted his new passage at a different point, following bar 470, and introduced a different cut in his fair copy, the 19 bars before Tempo I. *subito*.

As indicated above, in 1976 seven further leaves connected with this passage still belonged to Anna Mahler, and at least two more were in other collections. Whether the order in which they were found at that time goes back to an earlier sequence is unknown, but some patterns in their arrangement suggest that this may be the case. With the exception of I verso, pages I to IV contain sketches of varying length. Pages V, VI, and VII, on the other hand, are primarily draft full scores, with a single sketch at the top of VII recto and several more on its verso. The order in which I found them at that time, however, does not correspond to that in the catalogued copies, listed under the number Ph 104, in the archive of the Internationale Gustav Mahler Gesellschaft. Thus in the following descriptions of the contents of these pages the order in which I discovered them is reproduced together with the equivalent numbers in the listings in the archive.

I recto (= IGMG 15)[6]
Sketches in ink roughly corresponding to bars 508–15, with numerous differences in relation to the final form of this passage.

6   These numbers are for the individual pages within Ph 104.

I verso (= IGMG 1)
Draft full score of bars 471–83, the passage added to the movement after the completion of the draft full score at the Nationalbibliothek. In ink, with the last four bars in lead pencil. See IV recto for a preliminary sketch of the passage, and V verso for another orchestral draft.

II recto (= IGMG 2)
Sketches in ink. Not ultimately used. Connected with the development of the opening motives of the movement.

II verso
Blank.

III recto (= IGMG 3)
Three different sketches: A approximates bars 462–72, with a continuation from 473 to 483 on a single stave. Lower on the page a variant of bars 462–9 appears. B presents a form of bars 394–407 at a different pitch level. C shows a sketch for bars 508–17, with an alternative version of bars 511–17. In ink and red pencil.

III verso
Blank.

IV recto (= IGMG 6)
(No explanation is given for the break in numbering.)
Page numbered 12½. Sketch of bars 471–83. Used as the beginning of a kind of continuity sheet, with blank bars following the notated material numbered 13, 14, 15, and 16, and below them the comment 'Hierauf Reprise' [the reprise follows]. The remaining numbers clearly refer to the corresponding pages of draft score noted below. And the musical material sketched here is found in score in I verso and V verso. The version in V probably followed that in I. In ink and blue pencil.

IV verso
Blank.

V recto (= IGMG 7)
Draft full score, cancelled, roughly equivalent to bars 458–65, with a pair of bars preceding them not found in the finished work. The heading at bar 462 is 'Nur schattenhaft!' [just shadowy]. In ink, blue and red pencil.

V verso (= IGMG 6b)
Draft orchestral score of the same passage found in IV recto, corresponding to bars 471–9, with the last two bars crossed out. Also related to another orchestral draft of these bars on I verso. In ink, blue and red pencil.

VI recto (= IGMG 8a)
Draft full score of eighteen bars, numbered 13, with the first three bars, equivalent to bars 466–8, cancelled. The continuation is comparable to bars 480–92. A circle with a slash through it, such as that found in Donald Mitchell's leaf, appears at the beginning of the passage that remains, and indicates a connection with another part of the work so marked, but not necessarily the one in the Mitchell page. In ink, blue and red pencil.

VI verso (= IGMG 8b)
Draft full score, numbered 14 in blue pencil. Corresponds to bars 493–507, with 507 partly cancelled. In the upper right corner Mahler has written 'H-moll' and 'Schattenhaft/Etwas gemessener' in ink above bars 506–7. In ink, blue and red pencil.

VII recto (= IGMG 11)
Draft full score, cancelled, of bars 508–17 (thus a continuation of VI verso), with two further sketches, in lead pencil, of the passage similar to that beginning at bar 462. The first corresponds to bars 462–7; the second, more elaborate, is roughly equivalent to bars 462–71. In ink, lead and red pencil.

VII verso (= IGMG 7b)
Four sketches in lead pencil. The first, third, and fourth (7 bars, 5 with the first cancelled, and 12 respectively), all explore uses of the opening motives of the movement, and suggest early attempts at finding a way to the return of the opening section. None was finally used, but the last bar of the fourth is marked 'Pos[aune]' and shows the pick-up to bar 522 (Tempo I. *subito*) at the correct pitch level. Bars 3–6 of this sketch also show the inverted form of the theme used in bars 462–5, while in the finished movement the upright form of the theme appears in the horns in the four bars immediately before the return of the opening material. The linking of the theme and the opening motives may explain the presence in the second sketch of yet another version of the theme combined with its inversion. In this case it roughly approximates bars 462–7.

Leaf 1 in a private collection (current location unknown)
No copy in the IGMG Archive.[7] The recto, marked 15, corresponds approximately to bars 508–17, in draft full score, and is thus a replacement for VII recto above. Ten bars in pencil appear above the ink score, two of which are circled as an insert. The verso, marked 16, departs radically from the completed score after two bars similar to 518–19. The continuation is probably similar to that found in the Nationalbibliothek draft score, the last six bars of page III/34 of the facsimile, and the first 2 of page III/35,

---

7 I do not have a copy of this leaf. I saw it briefly many years ago and was able to take only cursory notes on it at the time. Thus gaps exist in my information.

immediately preceding the material on the leaf described below. These eight bars are cancelled in blue pencil. Seven further bars, not identified, in lead pencil appear above the ink score, with the last two cancelled in blue pencil. The notation 'bleibt' [remains] has been added in the upper left corner of this side of the leaf.

Leaf 2 in a private collection
One side of the leaf is reproduced in the third edition of Donald Jay Grout's *A History of Western Music* (New York: W. W. Norton, 1980): 640. (It is not included in the most recent edition of the work.) The recto shows a more advanced but cancelled draft full score of the passage in bars 3–13 on page III/35 of the facsimile of the Nationalbibliothek draft score. The verso contains the remaining three bars, the second two cancelled, found on III/35. Most surprisingly, four additional bars follow, also cancelled, that show Mahler returning to the opening four bars of the movement at their original pitch level. Although not so labelled, these might well be the *Einlage*, also of four bars, indicated in the right-hand margin of page III/35 of the orchestral draft. The exclusion of these bars here may in turn have some bearing on Mahler's ultimate decision to preserve them at the beginning of the movement. In the fair copy of the full score at the Pierpoint Morgan Library, they were at one point crossed out, then restored with Mahler's customary notation 'bleibt' [remains]. The final bar on the leaf, which is not cancelled, corresponds to 522 of the completed work, the beginning of that section, later marked Tempo I. *subito*, which was the musical goal of all of Mahler's revised versions of his transition.

From the information found through study of these manuscripts, which may well be only a portion of what was originally a larger group, at least some conclusions can be reached. All of the passages in orchestral score among these pages represent an intermediate stage between the Nationalbibliothek draft score and the fair copy in the Pierpont Morgan Library. It seems clear that Mahler was dissatisfied with his original handling of this portion of the third movement. The numbered sequence of pages of draft full score represents one or more attempts to improve the passage, and one aspect of these explorations was the addition of the new passage in bars 471–81. The cancellation of the pages containing the 19 bars that originally led to the return of the movement's opening motives suggests that, although he finally eliminated them only after completing his fair copy, he may have had doubts about them at an earlier stage. Alternatively, he may have cancelled most of these pages after he had completed his fair copy.

The sketches are more problematic. A surprisingly large number are connected with the passage beginning in bar 462 and extending to about 469, and reflect many versions of the music found in them, some of which are at different pitch levels. The appearance of these sketches, in which the theme that first appears in bars 311–18 is combined contrapuntally with its inversion, suggests at least two possible explanations. They may in fact go back to a considerably earlier stage in the composition of the movement, and Mahler later simply used the blank portions of the pages to map out changes in his orchestral draft. Or Mahler may have been considering further uses of this configuration of the motives. Since the passage beginning at bar 462 is already well developed in the draft score in the Nationalbibliothek (see page III/32 of the facsimile), further use of the material seems less likely at a later stage, and the first of these explanations seems the more probable. The remaining sketches include one for the new passage (bars 471–81), and preserve some possible motivic developments that remained unused.

Donald Mitchell's leaf can now be seen as the first of an important group of pages that preserve elements of a significant intermediate stage in the evolution of the third movement of the Ninth Symphony. The developments preserved in these pages are of special interest and importance because they led to the emergence of one of the most striking and beautiful passages in the movement. Problematic as the material may be at times, I hope that this preliminary study of the known material may lead to a search for additional leaves that belong to this group, and to further detailed study of their contents.

11

The Song of the Earth: Some Personal Thoughts

PETER SCULTHORPE

The very first concerts that I ever heard were of Chinese folksongs. Almost every week, when I was six or seven, my father bought vegetables from a Chinese market garden. He would always take me with him. There, just outside Launceston, in Tasmania, open-air performances would be mounted for our benefit. I was captivated by the nasal singing and the twanging and thudding of the stringed instruments. I must confess that when my mother took me to symphonic concerts a few years later, I found the music somewhat pallid by comparison. All the same, I did embrace most Western European music written after the turn of the century.

* * *

During the Second World War, Neville Cardus, the music critic and cricket enthusiast, presented a weekly programme, *The Enjoyment of Music*, on the ABC. It was on this programme that I first heard such works as *Verklärte Nacht*, *Sea Drift* and *La Mer*, works that became very important to me. Most important of all, though, was *The Song of the Earth*. I was in my early teens, and if any work helped me decide to commit my life to musical composition, it was this. The old recording, with Kerstin Thorborg and Charles Kullmann, and the Vienna Philharmonic Orchestra conducted by Bruno Walter, still lingers in corners of my mind.

* * *

In talking of Mahler as a composer, Cardus said that he saw him and thought of him as 'a shell left on the shore of his century's romanticism, a shell in which we can hear the sound of a withdrawing sea'.[1] I liked this, for I loved listening to the sounds of the sea in seashells. Indeed, the sea is in my blood: several generations of ancestors on my father's side had been seafarers.

* * *

1   Neville Cardus, ABC radio broadcast, early 1940s; subsequently published in Cardus's *Ten Composers* (Sydney/Auckland: Collins Bros, 1945): 88.

Late in 1942, my mother took my brother and me to Melbourne, crossing Bass Strait on the ageing SS *Taroona*. During the night, all passengers were summoned to stand by the lifeboats. An unidentified submarine, believed to be Japanese, had been sighted. My brother and I were thrilled, unable to understand our mother's concern. We arrived safely, and my mother led me to Hall's Book Store in Bourke street, Melbourne, where we bought the vocal score of *The Song of the Earth*.[2]

*   *   *

Books and scores are at the centre of my life. For this, I shall be ever grateful to my mother. All the same, my mother's uncle, Frederick Moorhouse, often warned me never to build a library: 'If you do,' he exclaimed, 'you will be like me, forever tied to your books, and if you move away from them, you will forever pine for them.' I made my choice at an early age. My mother, then, gave me all she knew of English literature, especially Joseph Conrad. She found many first editions, and she even found a copy of the magazine *Scrutiny*, with an article on Mahler by Wilfrid Mellers.[3] Little did I realize then that Wilfrid would one day become one of my closest friends, that more than fifty years later I would be with him in Dartington for his eightieth birthday celebrations.

*   *   *

Of all the music in my early collection, the Mahler vocal score was my favourite. As time passed, however, I began to lose interest in its first five parts. On the other hand, the sixth part, 'The Farewell', became more and more important to me. For almost a year, if a day passed without my playing it through on the piano, I believed that I would be the victim of some terrible misfortune.

*   *   *

Looking back, I regard myself as uncommonly fortunate. It seems not unreasonable to assume that, without knowing it, I embraced in my own music many aspects of 'The Farewell'. Certainly, impassioned appoggiaturas appeared early in my work, as did long-held funereal pedal-points. Even today, in my orchestral music, there is a dependence upon tam-tam punctuation, and the singing of birds in lonely places, *come veduta a volo d'uccello*. There is also the importance of C major, for Mahler the embrace of the

2   Gustav Mahler, *The Song of the Earth*, vocal score (London: Boosey & Hawkes, 1942). (The English translation used in this text is by Steuart Wilson, and the piano reduction by Erwin Stein.)

3   Wilfrid Mellers, 'Mahler as key-figure', *Scrutiny* (1941): 343–51; subsequently published in Wilfrid Mellers, *Studies in Contemporary Music* (London: Dobson, 1947): 109–19.

earth, for me the warmth of the comfort of God. Often, too, in my music there are echoes of an aching for lost beauty:

O Beauty, O life of endless loving.
Wild delirious world.

* * *

Of course, it is possible that in hindsight I am being somewhat fanciful. Certainly the use of the pentatonic scale in much of my *oeuvre* is unrelated to 'The Farewell'. Similarly, I doubt that I ever related Mahler's settings of translations of Chinese poetry to the Chinese folksongs of my boyhood. On the other hand, what seems to me to be fundamental to Mahler's music did become fundamental to my own. This is the use of two-part counterpoint. I believe that whatever else may be fanciful, 'The Farewell' provided me with this particular means of musical expression.

* * *

When I was at Oxford in the late 1950s I never thought of myself as being anything but Australian. Upon my return, I was not sure how I regarded myself. I was torn between the New World and the Old. Many Australians still feel like this in similar circumstances. Furthermore, as a Tasmanian, I believe that I inherit a particularly strong sense of dualism:

That small stretch of water, Bass Strait, causes a many-layered feeling of separation between mainland Australians and us. I suspect that this separation shaped a number of beliefs held by . . . me. I take joy in the fact that my music would have been very much less without it.[4]

* * *

I first incorporated this separation, this notion of duality, into my music through the use of two-part counterpoint. In Mahler, the two lines are usually in conflict. In my own music they simply co-exist.

* * *

Many of my works are founded entirely upon dualism. Every aspect of my theatre work *Rites of Passage* (1974) is made up of opposites. Through this idea, I was able to create building blocks upon which to construct music on a large scale. At the end of the work, thesis and antithesis are brought together in synthesis:

4   Peter Sculthorpe, *The 1993 Stuart Challenger Memorial Lecture* (Sydney: NSW Ministry for the Arts and Australian Broadcasting Corporation, 1993): 2.

> How happy mortals were,
> If that pure love did guide their minds
> Which heavenly spheres doth guide![5]

*   *   *

Some years before composition began upon *Rites of Passage*, I became interested in the once-held belief that the planets made music as they moved through the heavens. In the early part of the seventeenth century, the astronomer Kepler, a contemporary of Shakespeare, computed what he believed to be the Music of the Spheres. His music for planet Earth is G to A♭, and then back to G, a tiny dolorous palindrome. A♭ being adjacent to, and dissonant with G, the two are dualities. These pitches have permeated almost all my music since that time. Many of the works are like extended songs, both sorrowful and joyful, songs for this earth, for the survival of this planet.

*   *   *

I still treasure my vocal score of *The Song of the Earth*, even though it belongs to my youth, to my beginnings as a composer. I must confess that after these beginnings, the work receded in its importance to me. Upon reading about Kepler, however, I suddenly recalled, in delight, the opening of 'The Farewell'. The extraordinary sound of the C pedal is followed by an introduction in two-part counterpoint. The lower part, in thirds, is the sound of planet Earth: G to A♭ returning to G. In the course of the movement, the heart-wounding appogiatura, A♭ to G, grows into perhaps the most inspired music, and the most forward-looking, that Mahler ever wrote.

*   *   *

6. The Farewell
6. Der Abschied

*   *   *

5   Boethius, *The Consolation of Philosophy*, ed. William Anderson (London: Centaur Press, 1963): 59.

The above thoughts and ideas were written as a tribute to Donald Mitchell, upon his seventieth birthday. Donald and his wife, Kathleen, have been friends of mine for almost thirty years. Donald was also the first publisher to show true commitment to my music, and the first work of mine that he published was my String Quartet No. 6 (1965).[6] Written long before I knew about the Kepler premise, this music is dominated by the pitches A♭ and G. I imagine that Mahler, too, was unaware of the premise when he wrote 'The Farewell'. I find it comforting that one's life is made up of such happy coincidences, if they are coincident.

*   *   *

We all need comfort at times. Several days before I finished writing down these thoughts and ideas, and after some weeks of caring for her, my mother died. She was ninety-three. She knew Kathleen and Donald well; and she sustained my love of *The Song of the Earth*. I thank her for her part in my life's journey.

> The lovely earth, all, everywhere,
> Revives in spring and blooms anew,
> All, everywhere and ever, ever,
> Shines the blue horizon,
> Ever . . . ever . . .

6   Published by Faber Music in 1966.

12

Mahler the Factual

ERWIN STEIN[1]

What, in my youth, fascinated me at once in Mahler's music was its total lack of academicism. It all sounded like an exciting novel which again and again took a new and unexpected and surprising turn. At the same time, the expressive power of this music was so convincing, and its artistic effect so deep, that all the talk about banality, formless pot-pourris and claptrap could not disconcert me. The case of Mahler was the first to teach me how

---

1 Erwin Stein (1885–1958) wrote this article in 1930 for the Viennese periodical *Anbruch*. In the years following Mahler's death, Stein was one of those fervent admirers of Mahler's *oeuvre* who gathered around the leading figure of the new music, Arnold Schoenberg. Stein was responsible for a chamber ensemble arrangement of Mahler's Fourth Symphony, first heard at a concert promoted by Schoenberg's Society for Musical Private Performances in 1921. Following the *Anschluss* in 1938 and his consequent emigration to England, Stein became a key figure in the relatively small band of Mahler devotees in the UK which included among its number Benjamin Britten, Henry Boys and Berthold Goldschmidt (like Stein, a refugee from Europe). At the music publishers Boosey & Hawkes, by whom he was employed as an editor and adviser until his untimely death in 1958, Stein continued to promote Mahler's cause. For example, in the 1940s both he and Britten made reduced orchestrations of selected movements from Mahler's symphonies (see p. 40).

Later in the 1940s Stein's association with Mahler and Britten brought him into direct contact with two young critics, Donald Mitchell and Hans Keller (another refugee from Vienna), then beginning to make names for themselves through *Music Survey*, the polemical quarterly journal which they edited. In 1952 Mitchell and Keller jointly edited a Britten symposium published by Rockliff. Stein made significant contributions to this volume, and it was through this closer encounter that Mitchell and Keller put forward the suggestion that their older colleague should compile a collection of his own writings for publication; the result, Stein's *Orpheus in New Guises*, was published by Rockliff in 1953. For that volume Keller translated most of the articles which had originally appeared, pre-war, in German, including 'Mahler the Factual'.

It was Marion Thorpe (Stein's daughter) who suggested the inclusion of 'Mahler the Factual' in the present tribute volume to DM. Although Stein did not live to see the remarkable growth in Mahler's reputation through performances, recordings and scholarship, the extraordinary popularity of the composer – today such an accepted aspect of Western musical life – is in no small measure due to Stein's torch-bearing activities from the 1920s onwards. In a sense that flame passed directly to DM (and others) in the 1950s: DM's first Mahler volume (*Gustav Mahler: The Early Years*) appeared in 1958. If Stein were alive today, how gratified he would be by the results of his efforts on behalf of Mahler, and how pleased he would be to be able to join us in saluting DM. [PR]

in the end a single mind could prove right against a crowd of detractors.

Now that the temporal distance has widened, our picture of Mahler is becoming clearer and the contours of his artistic personality are emerging more distinctly. His music has retained its direct and immediate effect, and we have come to realize that the lasting validity of his work transcends the Romantic era. We are aware that his intense expressive urge has created new musical forms. This urge may have had its Romantic roots, but Mahler's symphonies are amongst our musical literature's most beautiful examples of how expression may divide into form without a remainder as it were, how art objectifies the subjective.

It is not, however, their amplitude alone which makes these forms difficult to survey. Their equipoise depends only in part on the rhythmic laws of symmetry and on the harmonic laws of the cadence. Well balanced as the separate parts are against each other, and exactly 'right' as everything appears to a developed formal sense, closer listening soon reveals amazingly asymmetrical goings-on in this music: an introduction will expose the motifs in what seem quite irrational rhythmic relationships (Third Symphony); with each new entry a counter-melody will 'counter' the theme at a different point; and the different periods will be almost invariably extended by repetitions of motifs or insertions, making a rule of irregularity. All such devices are methods of loosening the form where necessary.

Nor are the themes themselves unalterable building-stones; despite their solid structures, they are yet sufficiently pliable to provide ever-new building material. Mahler's motivic and thematic work is perhaps the most original aspect of his technique and has also proved most fruitful for the future. But perhaps it is not quite accurate to talk of 'work' in this connection. For in the uninterrupted flow of his imagination these themes assume ever-new forms. To be sure, the thematic material endows the movements with their palpable homogeneity. But the first shape in which any theme appears is by no means the last: it is far less binding than a first statement had hitherto been. Unmodified repetition of a theme is no longer the rule: almost as a matter of principle, repetition means variation. And the type of Mahler's variations is novel too. The *Poco adagio* of his Fourth Symphony is the only real example of that well-known kind of modified recapitulation which is closely akin to the lyrical species 'Variations on a Theme . . .' In some respects, the movement may indeed have been modelled on the *Adagio* from Beethoven's Ninth. In this type of lyrical variation, the theme retains its original structure and it is its motifs that are modified. But elsewhere, Mahler's variation technique works the other way round. Out of new combinations of the motivic material, out of a different order, different repetitions and a different development of the motifs, ever-new melodic shapes arise kaleidoscopically which have nothing in common with the original structure of the theme, though they remain intimately related to it through their motifs and, in fact, assume the proper symphonic functions of a theme when they appear in the development, recapitulation or coda. These variations themselves bear developmental character and show developmental function.

Sequential models, indeed sequences altogether, make no more than rudimentary appearances in Mahler's music, e.g. in the Sixth's first movement, or in the second movement of the Fifth, where they figure as introduction to the development section and give rise to that chain of free variations which forms the development proper.

The technical import of Mahler's methods of variation is inestimable. It is not only that they bring about an untold wealth of melodic shapes which retain their homogeneity and remain comprehensible by dint of their motivic characterization and pithiness. From the technical point of view, there are two possibilities of continuing a theme (or music in general), namely, repetition and contrast. The sequence, varied or no, is but a sub-species of repetition. Mahler's variations, too, have to be considered as a sub-species which, however, is immeasurably richer in prospects. They enable the composer to keep to his 'subject' for a longer time on end – to say more things, and more comprehensive things, about it. Thus the range and size of Mahler's symphonic movements is determined by his variation technique. His themes are laid out in wide measurements and will be misunderstood by those who search in them for the kind of unalterable ideas which make suitable music examples for programme notes. And it was no doubt the flow of melodic events with its surprising thematic transformations, a flow produced by Mahler's variations, which seemed so unacademic to me as a young man, so novelistic, adventurous and thrilling.

But the sound of this music, too, was thoroughly unacademic. What struck me in the first place were the new colours – muted trumpet, clarinet in Eb, *col legno* in the strings, and the percussion. It was only later that I realized that Mahler's sounds are simply a function of his textures which are eminently economical and factual: there are no embellishments. In point of fact, Mahler furnished the first reaction to the overloaded orchestral textures of neo-Romanticism – see his thin wind-writing with its linear parts, or his two- and three- (and more) part textures on the *forte* level, whose contrapuntal and rhythmic clashes are not mitigated by additional, filled-in, notes. Where Mahler does employ supplementary parts or fillings, they are composed rather than scored, a means of characterization rather than of sonority. At this early stage in the development of new music, his structures were already alive to economy's demand for what one might call 'thorough-thematicism'. And his instrumentation – the term is out of place – merely realizes his ideas through the registers of the gigantic organ that was his orchestra. His need for such a giant organ was no doubt determined by the dimensions of his movements which required great dynamic contrasts – i.e. again by factual reasons. At the same time, we must not forget that he was the first to use a chamber orchestra (in his songs) and to insist on clean colours in the full orchestra too. Mixed sonorities and tutti sounds are comparatively rare in Mahler. The chief reason why he avoids them is that they tend to blur the part-writing. For he is not concerned with 'beautiful' sonorities but with clear sound: hear his exposed string parts. Even where, at first sight, a passage looks 'orchestrated', closer inspection will unearth its

117

factual reasons rather than any aesthetic determinants. After the first exposi-tion (oboe) of the theme in the Third Symphony's minuet, for instance, the melody is divided between strings and woodwind in order that its motivic build-up be made plain. The paling of the concluding note, however, is a subtly orchestrated diminuendo in which the flutes suddenly replace the oboe. The essence of Mahler's instrumentation is structural clarification in general and transparence of part-writing in particular. It is as if he wanted to ensure himself against the elusiveness of the notes and the ambiguities of notation: this is how we have to interpret his orchestrated accents, his differentiated dynamics, his sudden increases of tone and abrupt crescendos.

Mahler has had an essential influence on the sound-ideal of the succeeding generation of musicians up to our own days, even though some of them do not know who made their ears. The factual spirit that informs his structures and textures with their transparent sonorities is exemplary. The widely held opinion that his work has not been of any consequence is therefore erroneous. Not the externals of his diction, to be sure, but the essentials of his technique have remained fruitful in the minds of the best composers of our time.

13

Mahler and Pfitzner: A Parallel Development

JOHN WILLIAMSON

The relationship between Gustav Mahler and Hans Pfitzner was one of the most historically charged of the early twentieth century. It was a meeting between men of remarkably similar outlook. Two commanding personalities with the most intransigent artistic ideals confronted each other, but from positions of potential distrust. Crudely expressed, it was a meeting of a conservative nationalist Germany with the spirit of modernism that found a congenial home for a time in central Europe. When Pfitzner conducted Mahler in Strasburg, the symbolism was inescapable; conservatism met modernism in one of the great cities of the Middle Kingdom. But the meeting did not imply understanding. The music of Pfitzner was accepted, perhaps somewhat slowly and grudgingly, by Mahler, and was conducted by him with his customary devotion to any score which he respected. But when Pfitzner conducted Mahler, the act was one of gratitude to a great man and conductor, but not in any sense a homage to an outstanding creative talent.

What renders the situation even more complex are the recognizable points of musical contact between the two. It is legitimate to ask whether this was in fact a major source of misunderstanding. Two composers whose music fed off folk sources, whose concepts of orchestration were remarkably similar, and whose radical treatment of counterpoint came to maturity almost simultaneously, had perhaps too much in common for either to feel comfortable in the other's company. The well-known photographs of Mahler and Pfitzner in the garden of Carl Moll's villa seem almost to emphasize the ideological distance between the two men.[1] Mahler stands in one gazing at Pfitzner's back, as both smoke cigars. In another they gaze out in parallel directions at an oblique angle to the camera; their eyes do not meet. But the same photographs stress one important fact. The company that they kept was the same, embracing Alfred Roller, Josef Hofmann, Gustav Klimt, and Max Reinhardt. It may be objected that here Pfitzner was on Mahler's territory, a kind of fish out of water, as indeed he is often depicted in social gatherings.

---

1 These photographs have been reproduced in several publications, e.g. Kurt Blaukopf, *Mahler: A Documentary Study*, tr. Paul Baker et al. (London: Thames & Hudson, 1976), Plates 232–3.

But Reinhardt at least collaborated in a major undertaking with Pfitzner (the production of *Das Käthchen von Heilbronn* that saw the creation of Pfitzner's incidental music and its overture which Mahler later conducted in America). For all Pfitzner's apparent ideological apartness from Mahler, at the beginning of the twentieth century they moved for a time in a complex culture in which the dividing line between nationalist conservatism and artistic modernism was as yet far from firmly drawn.

Whether Mahler and Pfitzner would have come together at all is doubtful were it not for the roles played by Bruno Walter and Alma Mahler. Walter's historical role as an interpreter of Mahler's music is well known. His part in the championing of Pfitzner's music is best known in connection with the first performance of *Palestrina* in Munich on 12 June 1917. But there were numerous other occasions, both earlier and later, when Walter worked on Pfitzner's behalf. In the season of 1900–1901, he conducted Pfitzner's first opera *Der arme Heinrich* in Berlin with a cast that came close to the composer's ideal. Within a year, Pfitzner's second opera, *Die Rose vom Liebesgarten*, had appeared at Elberfeld, while Walter had moved from the Hofoper in Berlin to be Mahler's assistant in Vienna. A letter from Walter to Pfitzner of 15 November 1901 congratulated Pfitzner on the triumph of the new work and expressed the hope that its success might be of some help to his own efforts on the opera's behalf in Vienna.[2] An indication of what Walter had to overcome is given in a letter to his father of 20 November 1901 with its reference to Mahler's 'overwhelming antipathy' to *Die Rose*, a matter that Walter amplified and qualified in a letter to Pfitzner of 6 March 1902:

> . . . we have already clashed very seriously over *Die Rose*; you must not believe that it has been treated *en passant*. On the contrary, [Mahler] has been busy with it again and again. In spite of his passionate distaste I still hope to make a performance possible here precisely because it depends on Mahler. Whoever knows (and loves) him, as I do, knows that each motion with him is an explosion; and it is not out of the question that, if I find the opportunity at a favourable moment to show him something from *Die Rose* whose beauty then becomes obvious to him, he will suddenly insist upon a performance with the same passion with which he currently refuses it.[3]

Walter's efforts included working on Mahler's friends as well as the composer himself. The letter shows how vital the matter was for Pfitzner. *Die Rose vom Liebesgarten* was not going to remain in the permanent repertory in the theatre at Elberfeld, which Walter thought no home for the work in any case. Pfitzner needed a big triumph to enable the work to make its way

---

2   Bruno Walter, *Briefe 1894–1962*, ed. Lotte Walter Lindt (Frankfurt a.M.: S. Fischer, 1969): 45.

3   Ibid.: 46 and 57. That Walter complains bitterly to his father of Viennese anti-Semitism at the same time as rejoicing in the success of *Die Rose* in Elberfeld is a measure of his generosity to Pfitzner whose anti-Semitism cannot have been unknown to him; it is also a yardstick of the extent and variety of the anti-Semitic problem itself.

in the world, especially since even Walter was aware of 'a certain lack of clarity and confusion in the text'. It was his suggestion that Pfitzner write a short essay on the work, which may be seen as the starting-point for the slightly disingenuous little piece on 'Die "Symbolik" in *der Rose vom Liebesgarten*'.[4]

The work that created the circumstances suitable for Mahler's about-turn on *Die Rose* was Pfitzner's String Quartet No. 1 in D major. The description of Mahler's encounter with Pfitzner is provided in one of the most memorable pages of Alma's recollections. The meeting took place at Crefeld in June 1902 when Mahler was preparing the first performance of his Third Symphony. Her story is well known. To Pfitzner's pleading on the opera's behalf, Mahler drew attention to the familiar charges against the work: ' . . . libretto too bad – whole symbolism incomprehensible, too long, far too long'.

> And at intervals the pleading voice broke in. One trial – last hope – Mahler the only musician who could understand him – otherwise, despair. The two voices rose higher as the door was reached. I could not hold myself in any longer. I jumped up, pulled the curtains apart, ran to Pfitzner and squeezed his hand to show how deeply I sympathized. I shall never forget the look he gave me. Then he went out. Mahler was not angry. To my astonishment, he was not angry![5]

A year later Pfitzner asked Alma if he might send her the Quartet in D, which according to her marked the beginning of their friendship. The manuscript arrived in Maiernigg as Mahler worked on 'the first sketches of the Sixth Symphony'. He broke off to inspect the Quartet and announced two hours later that it was a masterpiece.[6]

The researches of Henry-Louis de La Grange have shown that Alma's tale is a somewhat romanticized account of Mahler's encounters with Pfitzner's music. What she received was a copy of the first edition of 1903, with its dedication of the work to her (though she probably knew the manuscript from the time of the first performance in January 1903).[7] Furthermore, Mahler had already recommended Pfitzner's String Quartet to Arnold Rosé in December 1902 (and was by now viewing the libretto of *Die Rose*, not its music, as the principal stumbling block to a performance in Vienna). Walter, for that matter, had already written to Pfitzner in December 1902 of his efforts to convert Mahler and his wife to the Quartet. It was in some ways a contradictory experience for him, since he loved three of the movements but found the slow third movement's 'sphere of feeling' difficult to penetrate. But Mahler preferred this movement, and Walter found himself in the position of

4   Ibid.: 58.
5   AMML⁴: 41–2.
6   AMML⁴: 59–60.
7   GM²: 363–4; for a somewhat fuller possible dedication of the quartet to Alma, see John Williamson, *The Music of Hans Pfitzner* (Oxford: Oxford University Press, 1992): 69.

121

advocating Pfitzner's music to Mahler and then coming round to the latter's opinion.[8] Walter had no doubt as to the extent to which Alma had become Pfitzner's main advocate by the time of the first performance of the Quartet in Vienna in January 1903. From autumn 1903 onwards, according to her own account with its somewhat cavalier chronology, she pressed the piano score of *Die Rose vom Liebesgarten* on Mahler. There was still much work to be done. When Mahler saw *Die Rose* in Mannheim in January 1904, he was still assailed by doubts. Pfitzner for his part reacted badly to Mahler's attitude. The opening of 1904 was the occasion of his well-known contretemps with Anton Webern and Josef Polnauer in Berlin. Sent by Guido Adler to Pfitzner as a potential teacher, Webern and Polnauer returned to Vienna on hearing Pfitzner's derogatory remarks about Mahler. To convert the latter to *Die Rose vom Liebesgarten* required what de La Grange has termed 'an underground but methodical campaign' in which Alma and Walter were the ring-leaders.[9] But there was no such campaign to convert Pfitzner to Mahler's music.

The experience of April 1905, when Mahler finally conducted *Die Rose vom Liebesgarten* in Vienna, was a revelation to Pfitzner.

> It was the first time in my life that a great, esteemed conductor had given himself up to the rehearsal of a work from my pen with all his soul and every conceivable effort.

The feelings Mahler's efforts aroused in him are famously expressed in the words, 'in ihm ist Liebe'. Almost certainly this was a reflection of the care that Mahler took to interpret Pfitzner's wishes correctly. For a man as committed to the notion of *Werktreue* as Pfitzner, Mahler's consideration must have been gratifying. An incident at rehearsal shows how Mahler bowed to Pfitzner's easily offended feelings. Pfitzner asked him,

> 'May I sit quietly somewhere in the stalls with a little writing-pad and make a note of where I might perhaps have a request.' He retorted quite sharply, 'No, no, sit behind me in the front row of the stalls, nudge me at a tempo that doesn't seem right to you, and give me the correct one. Do you imagine that I should feel degraded before the orchestra? After all you know it better, you composed it.'[10]

What is more, Pfitzner noted, Mahler was as good as his word. Since a great deal of Pfitzner's comments about distinguished conductors concerned their offences against works of music and their unwillingness to be corrected, his praise of Mahler in rehearsal obviously comes from the heart.

---

8   Walter, op. cit.: 58–9.
9   GM²: 431 and 630.
10 Pfitzner's most comprehensive account of his relationship with Mahler is given in 'Eindrücke und Bilder meines Lebens', recently reprinted in Hans Pfitzner, *Sämtliche Schriften*, Vol. 4 (Tutzing: Hans Schneider, 1987); see in particular the section 'Wien' on pp. 688–92 from which the above quotations are taken.

Concerning their personal relations, Pfitzner grew quite heated. He was aware that there were those who claimed that he had slandered Mahler; the story of Webern and Polnauer in Berlin in 1904 suggests that there was something to this at a time when their relationship was tense over Mahler's reaction to *Die Rose vom Liebesgarten*. Years later, when writing his memoirs, Pfitzner branded such claims as 'malicious vulgarity and addiction to calumny'. But it was a different matter where Mahler the composer was concerned. Here Pfitzner was quite outspoken.

> Judgement on him as a creative artist, as a composer is something quite different and belongs on a different plateau. Naturally here I have had to pass a refined judgement, such as would not be done in a pure eulogy. I have formulated my judgement on Mahler as composer in the following way: he is subjectively sincere [*echt*] and objectively dishonest [*unecht*], that is, what he writes is always filled with the most perfect devotion, is always written with his heart's blood, but he cannot do anything beyond his nature. When he resorts to old German texts in his symphonies, for instance (like 'Es sungen drei Engel'), he has (so one feels) a warm love for this world, but what stands on the music paper is by no means an adequate expression of the intended feeling. With this I believe that I have clarified what I meant by 'subjectively sincere, objectively dishonest'.[11]

The example of the 'old German text' is a revealing one since Alma's reminiscences make it clear that Mahler and Pfitzner were furthest apart when it came to national, German matters. There is the example of Wagner, whose Germanness was to Pfitzner his 'deepest and truest thing', while Mahler felt that 'the greater an artist was, the further he left nationality behind'. Then there was their deliberate disagreement over the hallowed closing lines of Goethe's *Faust*. Finally there is another well-known story retold by Alma of Pfitzner's disgust at the 'proletarian faces' of a workers' procession; Mahler on the other hand recognized them as his brothers.[12]

Too much can be made of Mahler's socialism, perhaps, though de La Grange's estimate of Mahler as a socialist in spite of limits and contradictions seems quite ungainsayable.[13] In their relationships with the musicians in their charge, Mahler and Pfitzner were remarkably similar. Both were autocratic and intolerant in their approaches though seldom authoritarian. What seemed dangerously like egoism to others was to them a form of sacrifice to the spirit of the work. In other matters, their dedication could be equally extreme. Thus Pfitzner's belief in 'the Platonic idea of Germany' survived catastrophes that would have shattered the faith of a less single-minded man.[14] For him, music and Germany were twin stars; indeed in Pfitzner's nationalism, Germany could almost be defined by its music.

11 Ibid.: 691.
12 AMML⁴: 81–2.
13 GM²: 637–43.
14 Hans Pfitzner, *Reden, Schriften, Briefe*, ed. Walter Abendroth (Berlin: H. Luchterhand, 1955): 324.

Mahler never made quite so explicit an equation between music and ideas, yet there can be little doubt that the music was the man. Mahler's socialism may have been a matter of emotion, a feeling of solidarity with the downtrodden, rather than a conscious ideological outlook, but it has always seemed to many commentators to be of a piece with his art. The sincerity with which Pfitzner and Mahler held their convictions merely served to make contact between them the more difficult. The problem of their emotional ties to Alma obviously exacerbated the differences. As a result, we must interpret very carefully Pfitzner's services for Mahler's music in Strasburg.

Pfitzner's principal biographer, Walter Abendroth, is fairly explicit that the Strasburg performance of the Second Symphony on 11 November 1908 was 'an act of gratitude'.

> For he found it impossible to approach this, to him, deeply alien type of art and spirit from inner preference; also the work did not seem to him indispensable for the programmes of his concerts. How much effort it cost him to tackle the symphonic colossus is betrayed by the laconic line in a letter (to Levin, undated, November 1908): 'I still haven't mastered the Mahler symphony, it will rise on the 11th.' [15]

Equally the later performance of the Fourth Symphony in Strasburg on 25 October 1911 was, in Abendroth's account, almost entirely a posthumous tribute to Mahler the man; there is no mention of Pfitzner's response to the work.[16] At no time did Pfitzner make any overtures to Mahler the composer; rather he was quite forthright in expressing his distance from the work. The exact significance of Abendroth's account is gauged by the reference to 'deeply alien type of art and spirit'. There is nothing overtly anti-Semitic in the choice of words. Equally it is impossible not to remember that Pfitzner's abstract anti-Semitism derived from Otto Weininger made great play with the notions of spirit and ideal; the Jewish spirit in this account was defined in terms of opposition to 'the Platonic idea of Germany' rather than by biology or vulgar racism, which explains how Pfitzner was capable of sustaining friendships with highly assimilated Jews such as Willy Levin and Paul Nikolaus Cossmann; they were at once Jewish by race and German by cultural disposition. In the case of Pfitzner's relationship with Mahler, the situation was rendered even more complex by Pfitzner's sympathy for Mahler's ideals as a conductor; on at least one occasion (in his book *Werk und Wiedergabe*), Pfitzner noted that Mahler's greatness as a conductor might have had much to do with the fact that he was also a composer; he could sympathize with other creators.[17] But in spite of this, and for all the personal contact between Mahler and Pfitzner, there can be little doubt that anti-Semitism of the Weininger kind played a part in Pfitzner's judgement of

15 Walter Abendroth, *Hans Pfitzner* (Munich: Langen-Müller, 1934): 156.
16 Ibid.: 176.
17 Hans Pfitzner, *Werk und Wiedergabe*, 2nd edn (Tutzing: Hans Schneider 1969): 240.

Mahler's music, which he and his friends (always more numerous than Pfitzner liked to claim) quite simply regarded as un-German. His distinction between 'echt' and 'unecht' is also found in the extensive documentation which de La Grange provides of the attitude of Rudolf Louis, who went on to make the distinction explicit in terms of Mahler's position as a Jew within German music.[18] Pfitzner never made his own position so explicit, but the parallel still exists.

This broad classification, which is not without certain peculiar resonances in the way we think of Mahler today, served to obscure the very real parallels between the music of the two composers. This is not simply a matter of genres. An often repeated question in Mahler studies is why did Mahler write no operas. In Pfitzner studies, the parallel question might be why did Pfitzner write no symphonies. Of course he did write three symphonies, but all were late works written well after the period of his acquaintance with Mahler; one is an arrangement of a string quartet, another stands in relation to the symphony as a sonatina does to the sonata, while the third, seemingly the most authentic, is a curious piece that seems more about its genre than in it. Pfitzner needed to explain this curious gap himself, and did so by reference to Wagner's view that the symphony had really been perfected by Beethoven and its legacy transferred to music drama.[19] In the relationship Mahler–Pfitzner, the symphonist, conscious that he is innovating in the genre, confronts the music dramatist. Nor is there an equivalent in Mahler's output to Pfitzner's ambitious series of chamber works. The most imposing work by Pfitzner apart from *Palestrina*, the 'Romantic Cantata' *Von deutscher Seele*, is in a genre that Mahler abandoned after *Das klagende Lied*. Only in the field of song do their composing careers overlap.

The parallels of course may be traced to common antecedents, most notably Wagner. Both regularly conducted Wagner, though Pfitzner never had the resources of a great opera house to enable him to mount a challenge to Mahler as a Wagner interpreter. Yet neither was in any sense a follower pure and simple. This is obvious in Mahler's music. Donald Mitchell has suggested that it was influenced not by the mature Wagner but by *Tannhäuser* and *Lohengrin*.[20] Where Mahler in his symphonies evokes the later Wagner (the reminiscences of *Die Meistersinger* in the finale of the Seventh Symphony for instance), the listener is always made conscious of the citation by its incongruity in context. Pfitzner clearly had Wagnerian phases as a young man. *Der arme Heinrich* was a self-confessed product of an infatuation with *Tristan*.[21] The names of the characters in *Die Rose vom Liebesgarten* boast of their association with the Wagnerian past. But even in these works, there is an echo of a different kind of music drama. The shades

18 GM²: 384–5.
19 Pfitzner, *Sämtliche Schriften*: 131.
20 Donald Mitchell, *Gustav Mahler: The Early Years*, revised and ed. Paul Banks and David Matthews (London: Faber and Faber, 1980): 52–3.
21 Pfitzner, *Sämtliche Schriften*: 623.

of Weber, Marschner, and Lortzing are also present, reminding us that for Pfitzner, being an admirer of Wagner and being a Wagnerian were two quite different things. To love the works was not to accept their ideological apparatus; there was a different kind of German opera which had also to be cultivated. So critical an attitude to the past is also apparent in their guarded appraisal of Brahms, and even in their approach to Schumann. Pfitzner, it is true, was inclined to defend Schumann's orchestration (by pointing out that criticism of it was the product of a later period that had known Wagner).[22] Mahler on the other hand felt that it needed his expert hand. But Pfitzner in turn sinned against *Werktreue* by improvising interludes between the songs of Schumann's cycles, even in public. Mahler and Pfitzner were true to their own idiosyncratic images of Schumann, for whom one might as well substitute the whole tradition of the nineteenth century. Pfitzner quite explicitly agreed with Mahler (in *Werk und Wiedergabe*) that tradition could in certain circumstances be *Schlamperei*.[23]

Such generalities do not explain more striking particulars in the realm of style. Here much invaluable work has been done on the relationship by Egon Wellesz and Wolfgang Osthoff.[24] The striking parallels that they have revealed between Mahler's instrumental symphonies and *Die Rose vom Liebesgarten* are now an accepted part of musicological wisdom. These are partly orchestral. The fantastic noises Mahler's orchestra produces in the introduction to the finale of the Sixth Symphony have their parallel in the opening of Act II of Pfitzner's opera, right down to the tolling percussion and cavernous tuba-writing. The company of dwarfs and grotesques that then flood on to the stage in *Die Rose vom Liebesgarten* sing in a brittle polyphony that is obviously akin to things in Mahler's symphony. And to seal the comparison, there is Mahler's quotation of a motif from the opera, almost note-for-note; it is no random occurrence, either, since both men make the motif an essential part of the fabric of their respective works. Clearly *Die Rose vom Liebesgarten* could not have been influenced by the Sixth Symphony, but the chronology of the years 1903–4, when Mahler wrote the work and heard the opera in Mannheim, allow the possibility of Pfitzner's influence on Mahler. There is a catch which Osthoff, with the scrupulousness of a great scholar, has noted.[25] The motif depends on motion within the first three scale degrees of the minor mode. So obsessed was early Mahler scholarship by the role of the fourth in Mahler's melodic and motivic writing that the importance of this minor third has perhaps been somewhat underplayed; it is, however, one of the most important thematic building blocks in

22   Ibid.: 131.
23   Pfitzner, *Werk und Wiedergabe*: 234.
24   Egon and Emmy Wellesz, *Egon Wellesz: Leben und Werk*, ed. Franz Endler (Vienna: Zsolnay, 1981): 27–9; Wolfgang Osthoff, 'Hans Pfitzners *Rose vom Liebesgarten*, Gustav Mahler und die Wiener Schule', *Festschrift Martin Ruhnke: zum 65. Geburtstag*, ed. Institut für Musikwissenschaft, University of Erlangen-Nürnberg (Neuhausen-Stuttgart: Hänssler 1986): 265–93.
25   Osthoff, op. cit.: 275, 278, and 286.

the Sixth and Seventh Symphonies, and also has a very prominent role to play in the second movement of the Fifth. The form taken in the Fifth is present in Pfitzner's opera at the words 'Heil, Wunderer!', and here chronology does not permit talk of citation. Rather, one should speak of a parallel trend in the two composers' works, in which several aspects combine: an obsession with march material, a brittle orchestration, and a preference for contrapuntal tension over the blended harmonies of Wagner.

How to explain this parallel is not simply a matter of invoking the *Zeitgeist*. There are uncanny similarities between other works of the composers. When Pfitzner lamented Mahler's use of old German texts, he cited 'Es sungen drei Engel' from the Third Symphony, but not the more interesting case of 'Das himmlische Leben'. If we search for further parallels in the composers' careers, the case of the Symphony with which that song ends springs to mind. Composed in 1899–1900, it does not predate Pfitzner's String Quartet in D major from 1902 by much. When Mahler came to know that work, perhaps he recognized a kindred spirit. In his excitement over the Quartet, he described Pfitzner approvingly as 'a "sharp fellow" [*ein herber Kerl*], not austere à la Schillings'. [26] But what we most know of his reaction is his particular liking for the powerful slow movement. The latter was a kind of test piece for Pfitzner, an exploration of counterpoint on a scale unknown at that time in his music. The counterpoint is severe; in a fugal context, Pfitzner exploits augmentation, diminution, and stretto without compromising a harmonic style that is fully of its age. Such writing is not really similar to the counterpoint of Act II of *Die Rose vom Liebesgarten*. Pfitzner seems to master the past before going on to create his own style. There are other such 'studies' in Pfitzner's output, notably the Petrarch sonnet, 'Voll jener Süsse', which was a self-confessed preparation for *Palestrina*. For Mahler, the Quartet movement may have struck a very specific chord. As recently as the summer of 1901, he had been extolling to Natalie Bauer-Lechner the genius of Bach, and particularly his polyphony, as 'a marvel beyond belief, not only for his own, but for all times'. [27] In Pfitzner's slow movement, he was confronted by a monument to polyphony that survived the transplantation to the harmonic climate of his own time. But there was another aspect which may not have struck him immediately. The whole of Pfitzner's Quartet is a kind of self-overcoming. Whereas the major chamber work of Pfitzner's earlier years had been a Piano Trio that wrestled violently to create a Beethovenian drama from ambitious, perhaps intractable material, the Quartet tames all excess into an almost classical form. In places, the scherzo and finale in particular, it is tempting to speak of a neoclassical approach. In his Fourth Symphony, Mahler had performed a similar act of retrenchment. In drawing back from the fantastic complexities of the Third Symphony, Mahler found a clarity of form and spirit that encouraged the new directions

26 Walter, op. cit.: 63.
27 NB-L: 169.

of the instrumental symphonies. To have formed an exact appraisal of the comparable character of Pfitzner's Quartet, Mahler needed to have been aware of his earlier music and its general development, and for this no documentation seems to exist (though it is unlikely that Walter would have been slow to point out the virtues of Pfitzner's music in general as part of his campaign for *Die Rose*). Nevertheless, the formal clarity of the Quartet was a starting-point that Mahler could appreciate.

There are more specific aspects of the Quartet which suggest parallels with Mahler's Fourth Symphony. Mahler's key scheme is a facet of his Symphony which gives the lie to its apparent classical regularity. The work is far from being simply in G. Rather it 'resolves' by stages into E major, a procedure that may be explained according to various structural models, but that serves to undermine the principle of monotonality, the principle that a work should finish in the key in which it begins. Only the finale, 'Das himmlische Leben', among the movements actually subverts the rule, but that effectively unbalances the whole work, leaving us to explain musically a procedure that has its origin in Mahler's response to the song text. Pfitzner's first movement similarly veers between D major and B minor before finally closing in the latter. In this case, three movements remain in which D can be recovered, but the procedure is still surprising, given the formal regularity of the movement in other respects.

Both works have scherzos which feature obbligato instruments. In Mahler's Symphony, the scherzo is led by the *scordatura* violin, the embodiment of that macabre strain of humour found in all periods of Mahler's work. The image of Death the fiddle-player is at once humorous and uncanny, a combination evoked by the edgy tone of the mistuned violin. In Pfitzner's scherzo, placed second like Mahler's, the obbligato instrument is the viola. Part of the muted colouring which emanates from so much of Pfitzner's music is a reflection of his love of viola sonorities. The instrument is also a featured soloist in the later Piano Quintet, notably in the slow movement. The first act of *Palestrina* relies on many different aspects of viola tone including the viola d'amore briefly included for the music of the angels who sing songs of praise. The beginning of this side to Pfitzner's music may be the prelude to Act I of *Der arme Heinrich* which opens with four solo muted violas in an evocation of a spiritual sickness that runs through the whole work. In the Quartet's scherzo, a more robust side to the viola's personality is seen in its presentation of various humorous motifs that eventually grow into a comic cadenza on the last page of the movement. Pfitzner's humour, however, is unlike Mahler's. At least one writer on Pfitzner has spoken of a Hoffmannesque aspect to this movement, but this description seems more suited perhaps to Mahler. What Pfitzner seems to be attempting is a re-creation of the spirit of the Viennese classics, with its comic treatment of rhythm, bar-line, and motif. It has been rightly pointed out that Pfitzner frequently sought to recapture something of the spirit of Haydn in his instrumental works, particularly in those movements and sections where an unabashed diatonicism takes over.[28] The 'linear ascetic' of the Quartet's slow movement imitates an eighteenth-century rusticity that seems not to be aware even of Mozart (whose symphonies Pfitzner held in lower regard than those of Haydn). By comparison, the naivety of Mahler's Fourth Symphony seems a matter of greater complexity, a humour shadowed by something malevolent.

The finales of the two works present a rather different picture, if only because specific verbal associations come into play. In the case of the Symphony, this is a matter of the text chosen, a naive folk poem that describes a child's view of heaven expressed in crudely material terms but with a surprising twist: the final music of heaven which causes the movement to drift to inaudibility in E major. Pfitzner's finale at first sight resembles Mahler's mainly in that it uses a pre-existing source. Whereas Mahler moved a complete song into his finale, Pfitzner used merely a theme composed in his childhood. The movement is a rondo, intended to be played 'Im heiteren Reigen-tempo'. Once again the spirit of Haydn is present, nowhere more so than in the closing bars. The fragmentation of the theme recalls similar strategies in Haydn, notably at the end of the finale of Symphony No. 102 in B♭. The opening gesture of the movement becomes its closing bow. Semantics enter into the discussion only because Pfitzner was not content to rest here. The theme reappears in 1906 as the closing sequence of Pfitzner's incidental music to Ilse von Stach's *Das Christ-Elflein* (and survived to fulfil a similar function in the *Spieloper* that Pfitzner created from the incidental music in 1917). The Haydnesque humour becomes part of a tableau of cherubs in heaven. Both Mahler and Pfitzner seem to interpret Haydnesque humour as part of a musical never-land, in which material that is consciously folk-like acquires a sentimental gloss.

This conclusion, however, is slightly misleading, if only because Haydnesque humour in Pfitzner is remarkably persistent, and angelic associations do not always spring so conveniently to hand as in the finale of the Quartet. This in turn points to one of Pfitzner's goals as a composer. In Haydn's music, folk-like melodic inflexions and high art of a harmonic sophistication and contrapuntal ingenuity exist in a remarkable symbiosis that suggests a continuum of experience. Few of Haydn's rondos fail to evoke deeper currents, as in the minor mode episode amidst the peasant dances of the 'London' Symphony's finale. To re-create such a symbiosis is a more long-term goal in Pfitzner than merely evoking an angelic choir. It is arguable that this is the great unattainable goal of his career. The writings of the early Pfitznerians certainly suggest this in the emphasis that they constantly throw on the Germanic folk inspiration of his music. And here is the true problem of his relationship with Mahler. Songs such as 'Das himmlische Leben' and 'Es sungen drei Engel' suggest that there is more than one way of absorbing folk influences. By their very existence within the sophisticated

---

28 Reinhard Seebohm, 'Pfitzners Verhältnis zu Joseph Haydn', *Mitteilungen der Hans Pfitzner-Gesellschaft* 34 (October 1975): 34–54.

confines of a Mahler symphony they suggest a diversification of the musical experience that is sometimes unresolved, and may even be unresolvable. What Pfitzner wished to integrate, Mahler chose to embrace as one of many different varieties of experience. Even if one accepts that after the Fourth Symphony there were no more such movements in Mahler, something of their heterogeneity survives into isolated moments of later works.

The works by Pfitzner that best capture a folk tone are his songs which from time to time encapsulate a scene with the same kind of snapshot vividness that we associate with Mahler's 'Wunderhorn' settings. These sometimes have a humour which reinforces the parallel. 'Gretel', a song of 1901 (and thus nearly contemporary with the Quartet), is a good example of such a comic vignette that captures the atmosphere of a folk poem; the underlying harmonies tell us that a more sophisticated musical imagination is controlling the process, but apart from that the imprint of Pfitzner's personality is light. His musical style seems to retreat before what is appropriate to the text. Elsewhere, folk tone in Pfitzner acquires a more exalted character that suggests a sentimentality of a quite different kind from anything in Mahler. This is often associated with a hymnal tone, seen at its most convincing in a song such as 'Der Gartner' from the mid-1890s. In 'Untreu und Trost', a song of 1903, this tone reminds the listener perhaps of the Schubert of 'Der Lindenbaum' (there is a linden in the text), though an equally valid comparison might be the folksongs of Brahms. With Pfitzner, the square cut of the folk poem is captured in the simple crotchet movement of the music and the slightly sanctimonious four-part harmony. Contrapuntal complexities appear as something extraneous to the basic tone. True counterpoint in Pfitzner tends to stand apart from the folk-like. By contrast in Mahler's 'Wunderhorn' settings, counterpoint is frequently the agent of comic effect. The original bass motion in 'Wer hat dies Liedlein erdacht' is an example in an apparently artless context; the interplay of instruments and voice in 'Des Antonius von Padua Fischpredigt' is a somewhat more intricate instance; 'Lied des Verfolgten im Turm' is a special case where the interweaving of lines serves as a substitute for the clarity of melody that folk settings traditionally demand.

This is not to say that humour and counterpoint remain irreconcilable in Pfitzner's songs. 'Tragische Geschichte', a Chamisso setting from 1907, most notably combines a counterpoint of comparable complexity to the Quartet's slow movement with a humorous tone; a simple two-part texture explodes into a web of contrapuntal complexities to depict the perplexities of someone who doesn't like the fact that his pigtail always hangs behind him. The twisting and turning of the vexed simpleton naturally evokes a complex of inversion, cancrizans, augmentation, and stretto. At such moments Pfitzner achieves a satirical bite that is one of the most recognizable traits of his songwriting. This tone, however, was not easily carried into his instrumental works, whereas a central aspect of Mahler's instrumental work is a parodistic tone forged in the creation of the 'Wunderhorn' settings. The critical tone that Adorno and others have described in Mahler's music is dependent upon this tension between the sophisticated claims of his symphonies to high art and the vulgarity which breaks through from march, fanfare, and the voices of an underclass not represented in the traditional symphony. There is no comparable critical tone in Pfitzner, rather a capacity for sharp satirical vignettes which remain illustrative in technique; there is no comparable critical tone in his instrumental music, where the goal is rather that Haydnesque symbiosis described above. The curious situation arises that our modern perception of Mahler resembles in a distorted fashion that of the early Pfitznerians. To them, Mahler stood apart from the tradition of German music on grounds that could be explained by his race, even if that was interpreted as an abstraction. Nowadays Mahler is frequently read as if he injected the poison of a modern critical consciousness into the same tradition. In both approaches, his otherness is stressed. In point of technique, Mahler and Pfitzner stand remarkably close. But Pfitzner's profound suspicion of Mahler the creative artist is impossible to wish away. The paradox of their situation can be seen in the reproaches that men such as Louis cast at Mahler. The charge of musical 'impotence' is repeatedly directed at him, as though his foreignness to the German tradition sapped his music of its vitality. Nowadays, Pfitzner's music seems at its most problematic precisely at the point where he seems to stand closest to the past, in those Haydnesque movements which seem underpowered beside the contrapuntal complexities of his best scores. It is significant that his masterpiece *Palestrina*, for all its hymns to tradition, adopts a folk tone only incidentally. The burden of tradition which Mahler ceaselessly questioned rested uneasily on the shoulders of Pfitzner, who became more of a modernist than he would perhaps have acknowledged.

II

On Britten

14

From Nō to Nebuchadnezzar

MERVYN COOKE

'Just done Curlew River here . . . Got a good idea for another opera in the same style – so be prepared!!' So wrote Britten to his librettist William Plomer on a postcard from Amsterdam dated 9 July 1964,[1] less than one month after the première of the first church parable. Two months later Britten was more specific about the subject matter he had in mind for the new work: 'I think alot about Church Parable II – and long to discuss Shadrach, etc. . . . or possibly Tobias and the angel. Do you have any feelings?'[2] When Britten had 'Christianized' the Nō play *Sumidagawa*, abandoning its Buddhist content in order to convert the Japanese source into what became *Curlew River*, he had opened up possibilities for the treatment of biblical stories. The second parable seems to have been intended as an Old Testament story from the outset: a New Testament parable, *The Prodigal Son*, would complete the trilogy in 1968.

On 16 October 1964 Plomer sent Britten a carefully considered letter in which he discusses the relative merits of the two stories for the follow-up piece initially suggested by the composer:

> I warmed at once to your suggestion about Tobias and the Angel, a story I'm very fond of, but the problems of making it presentable in the Nō convention of Church Parable I seem, at first sight, rather daunting. Shadrach and company would be surely much more manageable (though much less impressive, lighter, slighter), as being nearer to the Nō tradition of a single magical episode or situation. I see Tobias as almost like a novel or (Western) play, with a story, a variety of characters, and two different places that have to be journeyed between.

Clearly the requirements of the dramatic conventions established by *Curlew*

---

1 All quotations from Plomer's letters and libretto drafts appear by kind permission of Sir Rupert Hart-Davis; all those from Britten's correspondence are © 1995 The Trustees of the Britten–Pears Foundation and not to be further reproduced without written permission.
2 Unpublished letter from Britten to Plomer, 8 September 1964. The story of 'Shadrach, etc.' is recounted in the first three chapters of the Book of Daniel: the tale of Tobias and the Angel is found in the Book of Tobit, which forms part of the *Apocrypha*.

River were to be the fundamental consideration in the choice of the new story, and it is significant that the subsequent correspondence makes repeated reference to the Nō theatre in spite of the biblical subject matter.

The two men must have spent part of Christmas together in order to discuss the project, since on 10 January 1965 Plomer wrote to Britten:

> It was very exciting to feel . . . the New Nō beginning to come into focus, and as you can imagine, I begin to hear the beginnings of utterances and to think I hear with them the first stirrings of 'the cornet, flute, harp, sackbut, psaltery, and dulcimer, and all' (well, not quite *all*) 'kinds of music'.

Their meeting had obviously resulted in the decision to take the story of 'Shadrach and company' as the basis for the new libretto, and Plomer confirms this in a letter dated 18 April ('I have indeed thought about the Boys in the Fire, and could almost pass an exam on the Book of Daniel . . . I have made notes but have nothing really shaped or demonstrable yet'). On 24 May Plomer wrote that 'The Jew Boys now begin to be visible and almost audible', and on 30 May Britten informed his librettist that Colin Graham was arriving in order to go through the synopsis of the new work. The producer was called in at a much earlier stage than he had been during the composition of *Curlew River*, a clear acknowledgement of the role he had played in shaping the dramatic style of the parable genre. Graham later recalled that the story of the 'Boys in the Fire' was originally suggested to Britten by a sculpture of Nebuchadnezzar he saw in Chartres Cathedral, where the impressive stained-glass windows were also to inspire the work's colourful and vivid stage presentation.[3]

On 13 July Plomer began what was to become a lengthy debate on possible titles for the new piece (see below, p. 138) and three days later sent Britten the first draft libretto for comment. Before the composer left the country for a holiday in Armenia with Rostropovich he found time to look in detail at this document and wrote to Plomer on 28 July to suggest the removal of the character of Arioch (whose lines were to be reallocated to a Herald played by a chorus member) and to confirm that the Soothsayer would be portrayed by the Abbot:

> I think we agreed that it did not matter the Abbot impersonating a sinister character. Would you perhaps like him to make a passing reference to this in his first address to the congregation – it could either be in general or particular?
>
> . . . (Colin has nice ideas of the Acolytes singing and tumbling, which may need some words, but we can leave that for the moment. I hope you know some nice Babylonian folk songs.)
>
> . . . The plan for the musicians' procession at the moment is like this: they leave their seats, process as far round the church as possible, to be joined

3 Colin Graham, 'Staging First Productions 3', in HOBB: 49.

by the chorus, Abbot and Soothsayer at various points, they arrive back on
the plate [i.e. the raised circle on the Nō-inspired stage platform] where
Nebuchadnezzar meets them, at which point the image rises in the background. Could we have a few sentences for the singers to chant as they
follow the procession?

. . . The Song of the Three, eventually Four, may need a little musical
adjustment. Certainly they must all sing the Benedicite, and if we decide the
Abbot and Chorus should join in with the latter, I feel they should do it
quietly, almost subconsciously. But I am not clear in my mind yet about the
end of the whole opera; whether this is the musical climax, or after
Nebuchadnezzar's change of religious heart . . .

The desire for a single climactic moment reflects the continuing influence of
the Nō aesthetic emulated in the dramatic structure of *Curlew River*.

Two days after receiving this long letter Plomer wrote to Britten to say
that his detailed suggestions would be 'duly pondered'. In September, Plomer
sent him a typescript of a new libretto version and on 27 October Britten
declared: 'I have got down to the Burning Fiery Furnace and although I am
enjoying it can't be really said to have caught fire yet.' In this same letter
Britten suggested further alterations to the text which Plomer supplied on
three handwritten pages in a letter dated 1 November. On 6 December
Britten told Plomer that 'about half the music is sketched out' and finally
informed him on 2 February 1966 that the composition sketch (*GB–ALb*
2–9500543) was completed. In spite of an operation for diverticulitis, Britten
completed the full score (*GB–ALb* 2–9500544) on 5 April and *The Burning
Fiery Furnace* went into rehearsal on 16 May, the first performance taking
place in Orford Church on 9 June as part of the 19th Aldeburgh Festival.
The work was dedicated to Donald and Kathleen Mitchell.[4]

Many of the source materials for the libretto survive and may easily be
fitted into the chronology established from the correspondence examined
above. Plomer began by making a rough draft of the work in an exercise
book which contains a preliminary attempt to establish a working title:

---

4   DM recalled the endearing circumstances of this act of dedication in a note to accompany the Kent Opera performances of the *Furnace* at the 1989 Aldeburgh Festival: 'It
was while the Decca recording of *The Burning Fiery Furnace* was being made in Orford
Church in 1967 that Britten told me the work was to be dedicated to Kathleen and me.
Actually, that was not quite how it went. He took me off in the lunch break for a drink
and a sandwich to a nearby pub and said something like this: "I want to dedicate the
Furnace to you both, but I want to be *absolutely* sure you like the idea." And before I
had had a chance even to respond, he was continuing, "Please, if you *don't* like the idea,
say so – I shall *perfectly* understand," and he looked at me anxiously and repeated this
assurance at least two times more, as if there were indeed a serious possibility that the
offer might not be accepted. It was an exchange altogether characteristic of the composer.
Characteristically generous, too; and twenty-three years on, I need hardly add, the association of our names with the second church parable brings us special joy' (*Aldeburgh
Festival Programme Book* (1989): 79).

- ? Something about Babylon –
STRANGERS IN BABYLON
GOLD IN THE FIRE
THE FOURTH MAN

The first manuscript draft[5] is entitled 'Strangers in Babylon' and is close to the final libretto in all important respects. (It is presumably this document to which Plomer alludes as a 'basic rough draft' in his letter of 13 July.) The fact that little reshaping of the text proved necessary is an indication not only of the suitability of the story for the parable medium but also of the increased confidence of composer and librettist after the success of *Curlew River*. The initial eight years of gestation which had led to the creation of the new idiom (Britten had first conceived the idea of reworking *Sumidagawa* soon after his return from Japan in 1956) allowed the rest of the trilogy to be conceived and executed at a far greater speed.

At the beginning and end of the first draft Plomer made provision for an 'Entrance Hymn' and a 'Terminal Hymn' in an obvious response to the precedent of *Curlew River*, Britten proceeding to select an appropriate plainsong before beginning the composition of the music. The most significant difference between this initial draft and the final libretto is the complete absence of the entertainment later to be provided by the Acolytes at the feast, which Plomer wryly came to call the 'cabaret'. This was a modification first mentioned by Britten in his letter of 28 July (see above, p. 136). The strong element of comedy in the new work is vividly present in a line given to Nebuchadnezzar: when confronted by the Jews' abstinence, he exclaims, 'Are you all on a diet?' This amusing stylistic lapse on Plomer's part was removed in subsequent versions of the text.

A typescript top copy of the first draft survives at the Britten–Pears Library (2–9500545) with a number of pencilled annotations added by Britten. The Herald is added to the cast list to replace Arioch and the Chorus Leader (originally intended to have portrayed the Abbot as in *Curlew River*) is deleted, the Abbot doubling as Soothsayer instead. The opening speech formerly given to Arioch is heavily cut and reassigned to the Herald, who announces the impending royal feast. This pruning is significant, as Arioch's longer passage had been a self-introduction in exactly the same spirit as the Ferryman's *nanori*[6] borrowed from *Sumidagawa* in *Curlew River*. Already the text of *The Burning Fiery Furnace* was being modified to depart from a Nō convention it had originally been the intention to retain. When Nebuchadnezzar decrees a general monotheism as a result of the miracle he

---

5 Now in the Plomer Collection at Durham University Library. Three draft scenarios in Britten's hand, pre-dating Plomer's first manuscript draft, survive at the Britten–Pears Library (2–9500557) inscribed in one of the composer's old school exercise books.

6 Literally 'name-saying'; see Kunio Komparu, *The Noh Theatre: principles and perspectives* (Kyoto: Tankosha, 1980; English translation, New York: John Weatherhill, 1983): 283.

has witnessed in the Furnace, a pencilled note reads 'Latin Hymn for all'. This later became the setting of the Benedicite, which was conceived as a parallel to the hymn 'Custodes hominum' in *Curlew River*: once again, the concept of a structural convention appears to have been uppermost in the composer's mind.

A carbon copy of this typescript (*GB–ALb* 2–9500546) bears further annotations and additional material in Plomer's hand. The title is now finalized, and Plomer added the lines for the Abbot requested by Britten (in his letter of 28 July quoted above) on a slip of paper sellotaped to the bottom of a page:

> We all shall play our parts
> And I, your Abbot, must appear
> A heathen, and an evil man:
> It is all for the glory of God.

The first line of this insert was an afterthought added in black ballpoint, the remaining three lines having been written in blue ballpoint. A new page in Plomer's hand bears the Herald's revised *nanori* which begins with the phrase 'I am the Herald' in a direct allusion to the convention established by the Ferryman's parallel passage in *Curlew River* (Fig. 8). Even this modestly Nō-inspired line was later to be removed to make the Herald's proclamation still less like that of the Ferryman's. A first version of the Acolytes' 'cabaret' was also inserted into this copy of the text.

A new typescript was compiled from this revised version[7] and contains annotations dated 5 January 1966, mainly minor corrections such as the standardization of the spellings for the three Jews' names. A significant departure is the rewriting of the Herald's proclamation prior to the instrumentalists' march so that the phraseology corresponds directly to that of his announcement at the opening of the work. This enabled Britten to incorporate a logical and structurally effective recapitulation of the music from the Herald's first passage at this, the turning point of the drama (cf. Figs 7 and 52). The line 'Lord, help us in our loneliness' is now included as a refrain to the words sung by the Jews as they anxiously await the return of Nebuchadnezzar. During the invocations of 'Merodak!' Britten marks the long 'o' with a stress mark: Plomer had drawn his attention to this accentuation in a 'Note on pronunciations, which I have looked up' included in the first libretto draft. Especially noteworthy in Britten's musical setting of these invocations is the spine-chilling adaptation of a style of vocal *portamento* which in *Curlew River* had been directly inspired by Nō vocal techniques.

The third version of the text was retyped[8] to include the words of the

---

7 Two carbon copies survive at the Britten–Pears Library, one annotated by Britten (2–9500547) and the other by Britten and Colin Graham (2–9500548). An incomplete, unmarked carbon copy of this version (pp. 1–16 only) also survives (2–9500549).

8 Copies are preserved at both Durham University Library and the Britten–Pears Library (2–9500550): the latter is annotated by Britten and Colin Graham.

entrance plainsong (the hymn *Salus aeterna*) and to incorporate a major re-allocation of lines in the Benedicite ensemble. A carbon copy of this document was corrected by Plomer, Colin Graham and Rosamund Strode on 2 February (*GB–ALb* 2–9500555). Many of the annotations refer to the version of the text Britten had included in his composition sketch, and a felicitous addition at this late stage is the provision for the instrumentalists to 'warm up' on their parts for the processional march during the final prayer of the three Jews (Figs 56–8). A definitive typescript was then prepared from this version, differing only in the correction of minor errors in punctuation (*GB–ALb* 2–9500556).

Plomer's opinion of *The Burning Fiery Furnace* was high, as shown by his remarks in a letter to Britten dated 26 March:

> I'm only a precursor of many who will be filled with fascinated admiration at the richness of invention and effect you've achieved within the strict limits laid down by what is now the precedent of *Curlew River*.

Once again these remarks reveal the importance of the 'precedent', but in several significant respects the new work constituted a departure from the dramatic conventions established by the first church parable.

Both dramatically and musically, the *Furnace* is considerably more extrovert than the austere Nō-inspired idiom of its predecessor: this is simply a necessary shift in dramatic emphasis which prevents the work from becoming a pale imitation of its model. There is a strong vein of humour in the work (cf. the deleted line 'Are you all on a diet?'), not only in much of the phraseology but also in the characterizations of Nebuchadnezzar and the Astrologer which border on the satirical and can have had no source in Nō drama. It seems likely, in fact, that the inspiration behind the treatment of these characters lay in the medieval mystery play (a European genre contemporaneous with Nō) on which Britten and Plomer had already drawn during the creation of *Curlew River*. Britten's copy of Karl Young's two-volume study *The Drama of the Medieval Church* (Oxford: Clarendon Press, 1933; 1951 reprint) contains many passages highlighted by the composer with marginal pencil strokes, among them a passage recounting an *imago* ceremony at Bamberg similar to the treatment of the Image of Merodak (volume 1, p. 484), and a detailed account of the comic portrayal in the Freising *Magi* play of King Herod (volume 2, p. 99) whose impulsiveness, naïvety and arrogance are unmistakably reflected in Britten's Nebuchadnezzar.[9]

If any Japanese dramatic source may be said to lie behind the extrovert

9 A similar portrayal of Herod appears in the draft libretto prepared from medieval sources by the composer for the final 'opera', *The Innocents*, from his so-called 'Christmas Sequence', in preparation in 1974–5. (The work was intended for Pimlico School, the Inner London Education Authority's specialist music school where Kathleen Mitchell was headmistress.) Although no music was composed for this work apart from a few tiny sketches, it seems possible that Britten's portrayal of Herod might have drawn on the musical characterization of Nebuchadnezzar in the *Furnace*. [PR]

idiom of *The Burning Fiery Furnace* it must surely be Kabuki, which made a strong impact on Britten's tour party in Tokyo when they visited a Kabuki theatre on 17 February 1956. Peter Pears confessed to having been 'knocked sideways' by the medium[10] and his interpretation of the role of Nebuchadnezzar would not be entirely out of place on the Kabuki stage. As Donald Mitchell recalled, the impersonation

> included the splendid miming of P.P. in the Babylonian feast, which the small boys later satirize. He brought to a very fine art indeed his simulated munching and drinking, above all the plucking of the imagined grapes from the imagined bunches, each grape held fastidiously between finger and thumb, appraised and fastidiously gobbled.
>
> This scene was astonishingly evoked one night in New York (an improbable setting), when B.B., P.P., Sue [Phipps], Kathleen [Mitchell] and I were taken off to a Japanese restaurant by our generous New York friend, Laton Holmgren . . .
>
> We had here of course a special combination of circumstances: an explicit link with Japan (shades of the Nō-play!), a feast of no less than Babylonian proportions, and a compulsory silence [Pears had lost his voice] which made mime a convenient substitute for speech. At any rate, the next time I looked across at P.P. I was amazed to find that he had vanished and Nebuchadnezzar sat in his place, going through his Babylonian gobbling routine with inimitable verve, plucking food out of the air, and consuming it with evident satisfaction, much to the mystification of the New Yorkers by whom we were surrounded. It was not a long display but I think we were all transported back to Suffolk and Orford Church in a matter of seconds; and I remember it struck me at the time that this brilliant bit of impromptu stage business only went to show how P.P. carries the art of impersonation around with him at his very fingertips.[11]

The Acolytes' cabaret may also owe a debt to Kabuki, particularly since Colin Graham calls in his production notes for it to be performed in a 'slightly grotesque' fashion. In a Japanese production of the *Furnace* televised in Tokyo during March 1979 the entertainers used the main aisle of the building as a Kabuki *hanamichi*,[12] as did Nebuchadnezzar and the Astrologer when they receded down it at the centrepoint of the work. In *The Prodigal Son*, too, the *hanamichi* is clearly emulated in the unexpected first appearance of the Tempter at the back of the church.

In spite of this fundamental divergence in spirit, the dramatic shape of the *Furnace* libretto is very close to the Nō-derived structure of *Curlew River*. A tripartite shape (reflecting the *jo–ha–kyū* organization of Nō

---

10 Personal communication.
11 Donald Mitchell, 'Double Portrait: Some Personal Recollections', in Ronald Blythe (ed.), *Aldeburgh Anthology* (London: Faber and Faber, 1972): 435; reprinted in DMCN: 486–7.
12 Literally 'flower-way', a raised aisle allowing Kabuki actors to move into the heart of the audience space.

plays)[13] conditions the overall action. The *jo* section begins with the Herald's *nanori*, which leads to Nebuchadnezzar's entrance music (recalling the *shidai*[14] convention emulated in *Curlew River*). The beginning of the central section (*jo-of-ha*) is marked by the name-giving ceremony and includes the 'cabaret'. The Jews' abstention begins the central part of the central section (*ha-of-ha*) and their prayer when Nebuchadnezzar has withdrawn forms a static centrepoint related to the river crossing in the earlier parable. Nebuchadnezzar's absence may be paralleled with the Nō convention by which the principal actor (*shite*) withdraws in the middle of the play leaving the secondary character (*waki*, in this case a composite character comprising the three Jews) to provide quasi-interludial comment. The identification of Nebuchadnezzar as *shite* and the Jews as a composite *waki* is reinforced by the fact that, as invariably in Nō, the latter is present to evoke a specific response from the former: in this case, a spiritual revelation. The closing part of the central section (*kyū-of-ha*) is represented by the raising of the Image and the worshipping of Merodak, a moment directly corresponding to the revealing of the tomb in *Curlew River*. The third and final part of the work (*kyū*) comprises the miracle in the Furnace and Nebuchadnezzar's subsequent conversion. The appearance of the Angel is an obvious parallel to the vision of the child's spirit in *Curlew River* (both are played by boys after the Nō convention of *kokata*),[15] and Nebuchadnezzar's conversion corresponds to the cathartic effect of the boy's spirit on his mother's madness in the earlier work. The strongest connection between the two parables is this concept of new (or renewed) faith. It is crucial to note that this is entirely unrelated to Nō philosophy and was the one significant addition which had to be made to the *Sumidagawa* story when it was transformed into *Curlew River*.

The actors and instrumentalists take a much more active part in the dramatic presentation of *The Burning Fiery Furnace* than they had in *Curlew River*. The instrumentalists' procession maintains Britten's fascination with the orient in its likely derivation from the ritual procession of a gamelan he had witnessed during a temple ceremony in Bali in January 1956:

> Beneath the roof of the meeting place, in front of the entrance to a complex and highly ornate temple, sits a gamelan . . . There are about twenty metallophones, gongs, drums. [The musicians] play beautiful, complicated music without looking at each other – they have the confidence of sleepwalkers, smoking cigarettes. The gamelan gradually gets to its feet and moves off in a small procession around the area. An old priest mumbles nasally from a high bamboo stall in front of the temple. He plays skilfully with his fingers, spraying water from stalks of flowers and ringing a small handbell here and there.[16]

---

13 See Komparu, op. cit.: 24–9. The central *ha* section is itself subdivided into a tripartite pattern: *jo-of-ha*, *ha-of-ha* and *kyū-of-ha*.
14 Literally 'next in order', the generic term for entrance music in Nō.
15 *Kokata* are child actors in Nō used to portray the sanctity of emperors and other revered characters.
16 Prince Ludwig of Hesse and the Rhine, *Ausflug Ost* (Darmstadt: privately published,

The religious context of this incident strengthens the assumption that it provided the stimulus for Britten's comparable 'temple ceremony' in the *Furnace*.

In *Curlew River* Britten had been aware that he was departing from the conventions of Nō by making the chorus portray a band of pilgrims taking part in the river crossing.[17] In Nō, the chorus (*ji-utai*) remains sitting on its special side stage (*waki-za*) for the duration of the play and never takes part in the action. The *Furnace* represents a further step away from the Nō model: the chorus forms a band of subservient courtiers who mindlessly echo the King's words (and therefore neatly retain the Nō convention of voicing the *shite*'s thoughts) but also take an active part in the feasting and idolatry. In *The Prodigal Son*, Britten was to move still further away from the Nō model by making the chorus represent contrasting groups of characters in successive 'scenes'.

The stage used for the first production of the *Furnace* was identical to that created for *Curlew River*, thus preserving the important visual link with the Nō theatre. The props for the new parable also continued to reflect the Nō influence, with the Image of Merodak corresponding directly to that of the tomb in the earlier work (the Image raised on the same simple pole which had been used to support the ferryboat's sail). The coloured silk screen devised to represent the Furnace itself was close to Nō in its extreme stylization and in the fact that two on-stage attendants (called *kōken* in Nō) were required to operate it. The costumes were generally more opulent than those in *Curlew River*, a departure fully in keeping with the process of revitalization which characterizes the work, and masks were retained for Nebuchadnezzar and the Astrologer but not for the three Jews. This is another indication that Nebuchadnezzar corresponds to the Nō *shite*, since the *shite* is the only masked character in Nō plays.[18] Stylized acting gestures (e.g. those for Power, Authority and Refusal) continued to reflect the Nō influence: the gesture for Prayer, for instance, borrows a Nō gesture (*kata*) called *ogamu*.

Britten was clearly as concerned with furthering the musical conventions he had created in *Curlew River* as with reworking its dramatic formulae. Several external influences which had appeared in the earlier work under the direct influence of Nō and Gagaku (Japanese court music) were retained, including the concept of entrance music. The Herald's opening

---

1956): 43–4 (14 January 1956). Quoted by permission of HRH Princess Margaret of Hesse and the Rhine; translation by Mervyn Cooke.

17 On 4 January 1964, while working on *Curlew River*, Britten had written to Plomer that 'the Chorus, seated at one side [in emulation of the Nō *waki-za*], is going eventually to give the appearance of being *in* the boat'.

18 In *Curlew River* all the main characters were masked. In this respect the *Furnace* is therefore closer to Nō conventions, perhaps reflecting the fact that Colin Graham undertook a detailed study of Japanese theatre only after he had finished work on the first parable (personal communication). This may also account for the greater use of specific Nō gestures in the *Furnace*.

proclamation, conceived in the dramatic style of the Ferryman's *nanori*, owes an additional debt to the Ferryman in its instrumentation, the stark horn Ds in the earlier work now being replaced by alto trombone (Fig. 7). The trombone supersedes the flute as the principal instrumental sonority throughout the work, although its function in terms of characterization is not as clearly established as the flute/Madwoman association. Flute and drums remain prominent in the score in a continuing souvenir of the Nō instrumental ensemble,[19] and the flautist doubles piccolo towards the end of the work in a clear parallel with *Curlew River*. The other percussion instruments are more specialized, and it is possible that the 'multiple whip' reflects Britten's awareness of the Japanese *shakubyōshi*, a whip-like instrument employed in Gagaku.[20] The *Furnace* contains a single instrumental set-piece as *Curlew River* had before it: the march prior to the raising of the Image (*Furnace* Fig. 58) corresponds in terms of its dramatic juncture to the instrumental fantasy accompanying the hoisting of the ferryboat's sail (*Curlew River* Fig. 55).

The closest musical similarity between the two works lies in the Abbot's prologue and epilogue and in the ceremonial robing music. It is the framework set up by these symmetrically placed events which most firmly establishes the parables as a distinct and unique genre, and the original Japanese influences are most acute in these portions of the scores. Britten's first sketch for the opening of the Abbot's address in the *Furnace* is much closer to the corresponding moment in *Curlew River* than his final version, in which the accelerating drum roll (borrowed from Nō and Gagaku drumming techniques such as *nagashi* and *katarai*) was replaced by a decelerating pattern in an attempt to make the parallel less exact. The organ begins with the same ascending flourish it had been given in *Curlew River* under the influence of the Gagaku mouth-organ known as the *shō*, and the blurred ligatures between each chord in the subsequent progression remain indebted to the *shō* idiom without utilizing specifically Japanese harmonies as had been the case in the earlier parable.[21] Little needs to be said about the new robing music: the heterophonic treatment of the plainsong is virtually identical to that in the earlier piece even down to the retention of precisely the same chromatic deviations.

In his review of the *Furnace* in the *Guardian* on 10 June 1966, Edward Greenfield wrote:

---

19 A bamboo flute (*nōkan*) and two or three drums – shoulder drum (*ko-tsuzumi*), hip drum (*ō-tsuzumi*) and an optional stick drum (*taiko*) – are the only instruments employed in Nō music.
20 For information on the other unique percussion instruments created for the church parables, see James Blades, *Percussion Instruments and Their History*, revised edn (London: Faber and Faber, 1975): 424.
21 Britten bought a *shō* for himself while in Japan in 1956 and learnt how to play it. For a full discussion of the influence of *shō* techniques on the organ part in *Curlew River*, see Mervyn Cooke, 'Britten and the *shō*', *Musical Times* 129 (May 1988): 231–3.

Britten has attempted a cross-fertilization from Oriental music more striking than in *Curlew River*. No doubt the avant-garde will condemn the experiment for its 'reactionary' qualities, but in some ways Britten is here as close as any of the avant-garde . . . to achieving the new 'complex of sounds' which is the confessed ideal of Pierre Boulez.

Michael Kennedy also declared of the instrumentalists' march that 'the resulting sonorities are more oriental, appropriately enough, than any in *Curlew River*',[22] and it is ironic that a passage in which the specific debt to oriental music is actually negligible should have led both critics to speak of a greater debt to Asian music in the second parable. It may well be that the lyra glockenspiel, small cymbal and 'Babylonian' drum create an exotic atmosphere far more colourful than anything in *Curlew River*, but this superficial resemblance to an imaginary 'gamelan' is certainly not indicative of a 'cross-fertilization from Oriental music more striking' than in the earlier work. The depth of Britten's debt to Far Eastern music is rather to be found in the completely natural manner in which the techniques of heterophony and superimposition are deployed throughout the entire score in continuing development of the novel procedures established by the musical idiom of *Curlew River*.[23]

The creation of an extrovert and colourful work within the confines of the austere conventions established by the introvert and starkly monochrome *Curlew River* is in itself no mean achievement, and has often been overlooked by those who find the second parable a 'weakening' of the impulse which had fired the earlier work. We may well agree with Robin Holloway that *The Burning Fiery Furnace* is, in conscious contrast to *Curlew River*, 'clearly something of a fun piece'.[24] Britten's increased use in the *Furnace* of 'realistic' dramatic procedures derived from his own, Western, operatic experience (of which the enhanced activity of the chorus is a prime example) represents a move away from Nō conventions inevitably resulting in a general decrease in importance of the original Japanese stimulus. Yet the trilogy as a whole would scarcely have been possible without that famous encounter with Japanese theatre in 1956; and the developmental course of the three church parables demonstrates how Britten could make an external influence his own and progress beyond it by a process of gradual assimilation to create a varied triptych in which contrast and innovation are found alongside the idiosyncratic musical and dramatic formulae that uniquely characterize the church parable genre.

22 Michael Kennedy, *Britten*, 2nd edn (London: Dent, 1993): 220.
23 There is, however, tantalizing evidence to suggest that Britten may have contemplated using Indian musical material in the *Furnace*. A 'Toda welcome song' from southern India appears among the fragmentary sketches for the second parable, presumably originating from the composer's trip to the Indian subcontinent in the spring of 1965. This was discarded, but in 1968 Britten went on to base his alto flute melody in *The Prodigal Son* on a recording of an Indian *raga*. See also Philip Reed (ed.), *The Travel Diaries of Peter Pears, 1936–1978* (Woodbridge: The Boydell Press/The Britten–Pears Library, 1995): 95, n. 18.
24 Robin Holloway, 'The Church Parables II: Limits and Renewals', in BC: 221.

15

Britten and His Fellow Composers: Six Footnotes for a Seventieth Birthday

DAVID DREW

Not only for critical and scholarly purposes but also for those of concert planning, the study of Britten's links with other major composers – as with lesser ones – had proved its worth long before comparable pairings became a cliché of concert promotion on both sides of the Atlantic. Hans Keller's pioneering thesis on Britten and Mozart was written in 1946 and first published two years later, but was not to achieve fame and notoriety until its reappearance in *Benjamin Britten: A Commentary on His Works From A Group of Specialists* (1952). By then, Donald Mitchell, Paul Hamburger and Keller himself had greatly extended the field of reference in their writings for *Music Survey* and the *Music Review*.

In its historical context – that is, in the context of a musical culture whose inborn insularity had become in the war years a necessary defence mechanism – the collocation of Britten and Mozart was provocative in the highest degree. The liberating force of Britten's cosmopolitanism had been resisted from the start by opponents of his similarly outward-listening teacher Frank Bridge. For them, the Mozartian parallel was so gross an impiety that they were ready to applaud Martin Cooper's brilliantly subversive suggestion that the true analogy was not with Mozart but with Saint Saëns.

At a time when the reputation of that immensely accomplished and widely enjoyed composer was somewhat tarnished, comparisons with Britten had a polemical thrust that is almost unimaginable today. In *Phaëton*, in *Le Rouet d'Omphale*, even in the *Carnival of the Animals*, today's listeners may hear without embarrassment something of what Britten himself must once have heard. That it was not of signal importance to him, and could never have been, is self-evident. Mozart is quite another matter. Even Poulenc may be.

The 1994 October Festival at Aldeburgh and Snape featured the music of Britten and Poulenc, with a prolonged sideways glance at Milhaud, with whom Britten's connections may have seemed tenuous. Even more to the surprise of some ears, its predecessor of 1992 had featured Britten and Weill.

From the Aldeburgh Festival itself there has flowed in recent years a stream of performances and productions illustrative of Britten's manifold links with the composers of his day, whether purely musical, or personal as well. Among many other voices, those of Stravinsky, Henze, and Lutoslawski have been representative of that polyphonic programme-planning which reflected Britten's creative dialogues with his contemporaries no less than with such mighty forebears as Purcell, Mozart, Schubert, and Mahler.

Invertible counterpoints in the art of creative programme-planning, all such juxtapositions are implicit in the critical and scholarly work of the present volume's dedicatee, and have become manifest in his entrepreneurial activities in England and abroad. In that context, the following notes are the merest embellishments – from which, however, a flourish of trumpets appropriate to the present celebrations could easily be extracted. If they have a further use, it will be as memoranda for future research.

1 Britten and Weill

The only encounters that are known of, and probably the only ones ever, were over a brief holiday period in August 1940, at the Owl's Head Inn in Maine. Britten refers to the meetings in his letter of 22 August to Elizabeth Mayer:

> We came in to dinner the other evening & heard some pretty sophisticated talk going on & recognised Kurt Weil [sic]! He was spending a few days here with Mr. & Mrs. Maxwell Anderson (Key Largo fame – or infame!).[1] We saw quite alot of him & he really was awfully nice & sympathetic, and it was remarkable how many friends we had in common, both in Europe & here. He tells me that Werfel was not shot & may be coming here, & that Golaud [sic] Mann apparently has been contacted with – other news not so good.[2]

Without overt connection but also without paragraph break, Britten goes on to say 'I'm terribly relieved to be in contact with Wulff'. Whether or not Wulff's father Hermann Scherchen was one of the 'friends' or erstwhile friends Britten and Weill had spoken about, the continuity of Britten's paragraph is evident.

The question of precisely which friends or acquaintances he and Weill had in common merits scholarly investigation, at least to the extent that it may shed light on the life and work of either composer or both – limited though that extent is likely to be, especially in Britten's case. Guesswork alone could produce a long list of possibilities, beginning chronologically with those

---

1   Maxwell Anderson (1888–1959) was one of the leading American playwrights of his day, regarded by some as heir to the mantle of Eugene O'Neill. *Key Largo* (1939) is a typically Andersonian thesis-play whose notoriety derived from its political overtones (*vis à vis* Roosevelt and fascism) and some incidental but not gratuitous violence. It is remembered today in the classic film version (1948) directed by John Huston.
2   All quotations from Britten's letters and diaries are © 1995 the Trustees of the Britten-Pears Foundation and not to be further reproduced without written permission.

figures who had been members of, or tangential to, the Busoni circle, and were still prominent in the International Society for Contemporary Music in the 1930s: for instance, E. J. Dent, Edward Clark, and indeed Scherchen. From there it would have been a short step to the topic of Universal Edition, and Boosey & Hawkes's post-*Anschluss* absorption of such notable UE executives as Alfred Kalmus, Hans Heinsheimer, and Erwin Stein, all of whom had been closely associated with Weill in his European years.

A larger topic might have been the entire nexus of human and intellectual relationships arising from Germany's, and especially Berlin's, cultural influence on British musicians, writers and artists during the period from 1928 (and the première of *Die Dreigroschenoper*) to 1933 (and Hitler's seizure of power). There, the central importance of W. H. Auden is obvious, not because of any known contacts between him and Weill – circumstantial evidence suggests that there were none – but because the theatres of Brecht and Piscator, with which Weill was directly connected, and of Ernst Toller, to which in principle he remained sympathetic until the end of the 1930s, were crucial to the Auden–Isherwood collaboration. Long before his meeting with Britten, Weill had been actively interested in the fruits of that collaboration.

However cordial their discussions in the summer of 1940, the grounds for continuing them on some later occasion were clearly insufficient. Within days of their Owl's Head meeting, Weill was back in New York, immersed in the orchestration of *Lady in the Dark*, and in the practical preparations for its opening in Boston in December. The New York opening in January 1941 marks the crucial change in Weill's fortunes in America: on the one hand a Broadway hit of the first order, on the other, his final disgrace in the eyes of those musicians, writers, and intellectuals who had welcomed him to America primarily if not exclusively on the strength of two or three of his collaborations with Brecht.

Either in the columns of *Modern Music* – where Weill was famously attacked by the critic and theatre-composer Samuel Barlow[3] – or in the corridors of 7 Middagh Street, Brooklyn (where Britten and Pears had settled in November, and where the landlord was Lotte Lenya's future husband, George Davis), Britten would surely have heard something of the *Lady in the Dark* controversy. How much and how little he would have cared about it may best be read in the score of *Paul Bunyan*, for which the first sketches were made towards the end of 1939.

With *Lady in the Dark* or its representative public, *Paul Bunyan* has no connections whatsoever. With its predecessor, *Knickerbocker Holiday*, it has a slender one, in the sense that there is some basis for arguing – though none as yet for demonstrating – that Auden had read the published version of Maxwell Anderson's 'book'.

Potentially more significant, however, and certainly more probable, would be some subterranean link between the Owl's Head discussions and Britten's

---

3   Samuel L. M. Barlow, 'In the theatre', Modern Music 18/3 (March–April 1941): 189–93.

next major work, *Paul Bunyan*. Britten says nothing of talks with Maxwell Anderson, who was old enough to be his father, and culturally from quite another world. Yet Anderson cared for music and respected composers and their craft. Weill, who was only twelve years his junior, seems to have liked and admired Anderson more than he liked or admired most of his work. But he valued his theatrical craftsmanship and Broadway know-how, appreciated his decency, his courage, and his political integrity, and was much endebted to his knowledge of American history, literature, and folklore.

Literature and folklore: Washington Irving's *The History of New York by Diedrich Knickerbocker* had been the basis of Weill's first successful collaboration with Anderson, *Knickerbocker Holiday*[4] – half European operetta (with strong overtones of Gilbert and Sullivan) and half Broadway musical (in the satirical tradition of Gershwin's *Strike Up The Band*). The setting is seventeenth-century Manhattan, the hero a penniless knife-grinder, the villain, an historically authentic tyrant figure.

Anderson's gloss on Irving's spoof history and invented folklore was eminently suited to the late stages of the New Deal era, just as the eponymous hero of Weill's and Paul Green's *Johnny Johnson* had been appropriate to the purposes of a 'democratic' anti-war musical for New York's Group Theatre in 1937.

Nineteen thirty-seven had been the year of Weill's first formal step towards acquiring American citizenship – another possible topic for discussion with Britten. From then until the end of his life, his search for new and indigenous forms of musical theatre was often inseparable from his search for versions of American myth that would be adaptable to musical purposes. Immediately prior to *Knickerbocker Holiday*, he and H. R. Hays were working intensively on *The Ballad of Davy Crockett*. (Hoffmann Reynolds Hays was a left-wing author, playwright, and translator with whom Auden, together with Brecht, was to collaborate in 1943 on a version of *The Duchess of Malfi* which George Rylands directed three years later in Boston and New York, and furnished with recorded excerpts from Britten's *Serenade*).

Hays's original play had been produced in 1937 first by the Columbia University Players and then by the Federal Theatre. In that form it had attracted the attention of Burgess Meredith (the already celebrated actor), and the writer and dramaturge Charles Alan. (It was from Alan that Weill borrowed a copy of *The Ascent of F6* which was never to be returned.) Meredith was a close friend of Weill's, and was primarily responsible for recommending the Hays play to him and organizing the basis for a Federal Theatre production of his musical version. After Weill had composed twenty numbers in vocal score, he abandoned the project in favour of *Knickerbocker Holiday*.

'Most myths are poetical history – that is to say, they are not pure fantasy,

---

4   Maxwell Anderson, *Knickerbocker Holiday* (New York, 1939).

but have a basis in actual events.' The words with which Auden began his essay on *Paul Bunyan* apply equally to the figure of Davy Crockett (1786–1836), a real-life Congressman before his election to mythology's supreme chamber. Crockett was not the first and was by no means the last of the legendary American heroes investigated severally or together by Weill, Meredith, Charles Alan, and Maxwell Anderson (a friend and neighbour of Meredith as of Weill in Rockland County). As potential protagonists of musical plays or even operas, many of these mythic heroes are mentioned in Weill's correspondence or noted in his *aides mémoires*. Although the name of Paul Bunyan does not appear in any of the known documents, it would surely have cropped up during at least one of countless discussions between Weill and his friends in the years 1937–40. But the absence of any written reference to it virtually rules out the possibility that any such discussion was significant.

If, as seems likely, Britten mentioned to Weill the newly begun *Paul Bunyan*, Weill would surely not have hesitated to mention *The Ballad of Davy Crockett*, given that the project had long since been abandoned. Some reference to the ballad and vaudeville forms Weill had had in mind for *Crockett* would naturally have followed.

Even in the unlikely event that the sole topics of conversation were personal ones of the kind Britten identifies in his letter to Elizabeth Mayer, the tone of Britten's account is such that he would have been sure to tell Hans Heinsheimer of his surprise meeting. Now in charge of the newly established Boosey & Hawkes office in New York, Heinsheimer was an exact contemporary of Weill, and in Universal Edition had been his confidant and closest ally for the five critical years before the political events in Germany caused UE to 'release' their Jewish composers, Weill included.

Soon after his arrival in New York, Heinsheimer resumed his contacts with Weill. Although their relationship would never again be as close or as cordial as it had been in the UE days, it was amicable enough to ensure that he was always more or less up to date with Weill's thoughts, plans, and activities. Since no one was better placed than he to elaborate upon, and provide a background for, any impressions left upon Britten by his meeting with Weill, anything he would have said was likely to have some bearing upon the gestation of *Paul Bunyan* during the year that remained before its première.

Beyond that, any search in *Bunyan* itself for signs of Weill's musical influence is likely to prove unrewarding. Were there the slightest evidence that Britten might somehow have chanced to peruse a stray copy of the unpublished score of Weill's *Mahagonny* 'Songspiel' after its solitary but notorious London performance in 1933, there might be some excuse for suggesting that there is more than mere coincidence in what sounds like a fleeting and distant echo in *Paul Bunyan* of the Songspiel's mendaciously moonstruck conclusion. No such evidence having come to light, nor being at all likely to, further speculation seems pointless.

In the music of each composer, but more often and more especially in the case of Britten, the passages that most clearly, though always briefly, call the other to mind are those where the source of the supposed reflection was either unobtainable or not yet in existence. As for the jazz, blues and cabaret idioms which Britten made his own in the Group Theatre and GPO Film Unit days (and their radio-music offshoots), the apparent 'influences' of Weill are often no more than loose generic affinities, though occasionally heightened by direct contacts with the music of composers such as Copland or even Virgil Thomson, who were themselves influenced, however marginally, by Weill's example.

Britten's diary entry of 8 February 1935 regarding that evening's concert performance of *Die Dreigroschenoper* – which Edward Clark had promoted and himself conducted as part of his exceptionally important Contemporary Music series for the BBC – is blankly negative about the music and the performance. (Most of the London music critics, including Ernest Newman, were vituperative.) Had Weill been free to supervise the rehearsals, the performance might have been better. But the very nature of the music would still have been alien to the Britten of 1935, leaning as he already did towards Vienna.

More than a decade later, Weill's reaction to a preview of the New York première of *The Rape of Lucretia* (28 December 1948) – in a letter sent the next day to his lifelong friend Maurice Abravanel – was in essence equally negative, but in its implications much more complex. Having demeaned himself with a comment unbecoming to a composer whose trusted friends, colleagues and librettists included numerous homosexual or bisexual men and women, and whose European stageworks were by no means without conscious or unconscious homoerotic elements, he then told Abravanel that there was 'no music' in *Lucretia*, just 'orchestra effects'; and he ended by rejoicing that 'your friend' Virgil Thomson had 'roasted' *Lucretia* in his *Herald Tribune* review, and that the audience was 'bored stiff'.

Weill had fallen out with Virgil Thomson – an old admirer – after his negative review of *Lady in the Dark*, and, since that turning-point in his American career, had kept his distance from the *Modern Music* world on the East Coast (while preserving his old links with the erstwhile modernist George Antheil, now reborn as a Hollywood columnist, a successful film-music composer, and an occasional symphonist in the Soviet manner). On distant if amicable terms even with Copland, Weill had swiftly sensed the challenge represented by the young Leonard Bernstein. Bernstein had got to know a few of Weill's German works through Marc Blitzstein, who passionately admired them, but was highly ambivalent about Weill's American career. Some while after the première of *Lady in the Dark* Bernstein – or so the legend has it – encounted Weill at a fashionable New York party, and pointedly cut him dead.

The première of *Peter Grimes* under Bernstein at Tanglewood in August 1946 is unlikely to have passed unnoticed by Weill at a time when he was completing *Street Scene* and telling people abroad – presumably on Heinsheimer's authority – that Boosey & Hawkes might be publishing it. In *Street Scene* there are two brief passages which for Weill were stylistically almost inconceivable without the example of Bernstein's *Fancy Free,* a ballet Weill had dismissed as 'phony' *(sic)* in a letter to Lenya of 12 August 1944. Though perhaps conditioned to some extent by the public snub from a much younger composer, Weill's repressed hostility is being bought off in the coinage of his unconscious recognition of Bernstein's talent.

A similar compensation process is discernible on a much larger scale with regard to *The Rape of Lucretia* and its composer. In the immediate post-war era, when Weill had deliberately and joyfully removed himself from all contact with classical modernism and the neoclassical reactions to it, the sudden emergence of a Menotti, let alone a Britten, represented a clear threat to his carefully planned future as a composer of 'opera in the vernacular', as he called it. The Britten of *Peter Grimes* was no longer the diffident-seeming figure he had met at Owl's Head.

It is not so much his gleeful response to the failure of *The Rape of Lucretia* in New York that reveals Weill's awareness of the challenge represented by such a composer, as the comparative ease with which he found a way of neutralizing the challenge by meeting it on his own terms in his own territory. In the spring or early summer of 1949 – just a few months after the New York première of *The Rape of Lucretia* – Weill quite suddenly broke with Broadway's long-established orchestral traditions. For *Lost in the Stars* – his and Maxwell Anderson's forthcoming version of Alan Paton's *Cry the Beloved Country* – he invented a Broadway version of Britten's English Opera Group chamber orchestra: a reed section of three players, plus trumpet, piano, harp, percussion, two violas, two cellos, and solo bass – twelve players in all. With thanks, perhaps, to Brahms's example, violins are omitted; with no thanks to Britten, a 'Greek' commenting chorus is introduced, for the first time in any work of Weill's since 1933. *Lost in the Stars* was to be Weill's last completed work.

In the *Saturday Review of Literature* of 31 December 1949 the distinguished theatre director and critic Harold Clurman – a close friend of Copland's since the early 1930s, but one who in 1937 had hailed Weill as 'the finest living theatre-composer' – published an essay entitled 'Lost in the Stars of Broadway'. Characterizing Weill as a chameleon-like figure, he views his American career as one of steady decline from the relatively high point of *Johnny Johnson* to the nadir of *Lost in the Stars.* With singular injustice, he writes of the latter that it is 'as slickly impressive and as basically void as the architecture of our giant movie emporia'.

Asked for his own view of the work, Weill's good friend Darius Milhaud replied with a benevolent inversion of Weill's judgement on *The Rape of Lucretia,* an inversion so precise that one can only wonder whether their mutual friend Abravanel had shown him Weill's letter. Too kind by far to say that there was 'no music' in *Lost in the Stars* (or rather, none or not much that suited his own taste), he avoids mentioning the music altogether, and turns, as Weill did in Britten's case, to the orchestration. So far from suggesting, as Weill did, that the orchestration is just a bundle of effects, he calls it a work of genius. Which indeed it is; though not without a small debt to the large genius of Britten.

2   Britten and Milhaud

The only documented meeting, and probably the only extended one, was in July 1964, on the occasion of Britten's visit to the Aspen Festival to receive the First Aspen Award in the Humanities, and to deliver his celebrated address. A photograph shows Britten standing in front of Milhaud's wheel-chair, smiling affectionately at the seventy-two-year-old composer, who had been a much-loved teacher and guest-of-honour at Aspen since the early 1950s. At the performance of *Albert Herring* mounted by the Opera Department of the Aspen Music School, Britten sat next to Milhaud and his wife.

Milhaud's letter to Britten of October 1964 is warmly appreciative of his visit, and enquires with more than polite interest about *Curlew River*, telling him how often he has thought of what Britten had told him about it, and remembering that is to be published by Faber. He requests a copy 'when it comes out'.

'I . . . ask myself', he remarks earlier in the same letter, 'how it is that for so many years we have hardly ever seen each other'.

Thanks to the initiatives of Edward Clark, Milhaud had often been invited to conduct his works for the BBC during the 1930s (a tradition that was to continue after the war). On 14 March 1932 the nineteen-year-old Britten noted in his diary that he had listened to a BBC concert conducted by Milhaud himself. Among the works were *La création du monde*, the First Violin Concerto, and the *Saudades do Brasil*. Britten thought the music 'poor'.

On 26 June 1935 Britten attended a Milhaud concert at the BBC, again conducted by the composer. There is no mention of their having met, though one of Britten's companions at the concert was Antonio Brosa, who had been the soloist in Milhaud's 1932 concert. Of the four works in the programme, Britten found 'the most striking' to be the Jewish Songs (presumably the *Poèmes juifs* of 1916). On 16 January 1937 he listened to *Christophe Colomb*, and was 'very interested' despite the distractions.

'[It] has been suggested', wrote Scott Goddard in 1946, '[that] the immediate urge [to compose *Les Illuminations*] came from hearing Milhaud's cantata *Pan et Syrinx*'.[5] The cantata (1934) is one of the gems in that unique set of works for vocal ensemble with chamber orchestra which Milhaud inaugurated with his sixth chamber symphony of 1923, it soon vanished, like so much else, into the growing mass of Milhaud's output. Goddard's allusion may therefore have struck all but a handful of his readers as absurdly arcane and far-fetched. But in fact *Pan et Syrinx* happens to have have been one of the four works featured in the Milhaud concert of 1935 which Britten had attended; and the soprano soloist on that occasion was none other than Sophie Wyss, soloist five years later in the première of

---

5   Scott Goddard, 'Benjamin Britten', in A. L. Bacharach (ed.), *British Music of Our Time* (Harmondsworth: Penguin, 1946): 213–14.

Les Illuminations.[6] What more likely source for Goddard's allusion? To consider the actual or coincidental relationship between *Pan et Syrinx* and *Les Illuminations* is a task beyond the scope of the present notes, for it would entail some detailed preliminary assessment of Britten's astonishing *Quatre chansons françaises* of 1928, coupled with at least a general survey of Milhaud's numerous accompanied cycles and cantatas for vocal ensemble since 1921. Meanwhile, the first British performance of *Pan et Syrinx* for (probably) sixty years would be a disservice to no one.

Specific influences between composers are likely to prove a didactic rather than a spontaneously musical basis for programme-making. Affinities, which call for less information and insight but more intuition and in-hearing, tend to be an altogether sounder guide. It is hard to imagine, for instance, that Milhaud could have failed to sense a deep affinity with *Albert Herring*, irrespective of Maupassant, though incidentally mindful of polytonal procedures akin to his own in principle, however different in practice.

Albert Herring epitomizes two long-term aims and long-range visions that were characteristic of both composers: on the one hand, the universalization of a lovingly defined local context (the Suffolk of Britten, the Provence of Milhaud); on the other, the localization of the universal – the Suffolk of *Grimes* and all its successors, the Provence of *Les Malheurs d'Orphée, Esther de Carpentras,* and all theirs.

As for *Curlew River*, which flows into the same North Sea as *Albert Herring* but now from the furthermost point on Britten's globe, it is clear from Milhaud's letter of October 1964 that his insatiable interest in technical problems and their musical solution had been stimulated by whatever Britten had told him about it in Aspen that summer. One wonders what he for his part had had to say in Aspen about his own recent work: about, for instance, the 'Etude de hasard dirigé' which forms the second movement of the string septet he had finished in Paris three months earlier; about the choral symphony *Pacem in terris* which he had composed in Aspen the previous year (to an excerpt from the April 1963 Encyclical of Pope John XXIII); or about the *Cantate de la croix de charité,* composed in 1960 to a commission

---

6   Milhaud's *Pan et Syrinx* is scored for soprano and baritone soloists, vocal quartet (SATB), flute, oboe, alto saxophone, bassoon and piano. Three instrumental 'Nocturnes' (with wordless vocal quartet) frame two extended solo numbers; the final 'Danse de Pan' unites all the forces. Sixty-one years after the successful première, publication of the score is still awaited. (The author is grateful to Mme Milhaud and Editions Salabert for enabling him to examine an inspection copy.) At first sight, Milhaud's cantata has no connection with *Les Illuminations* apart from its occasional resort to a type of declamation which Britten, in his letters to Sophie Wyss about his Rimbaud cycle, was to describe as 'heraldic'. Otherwise, the Britten-oriented reader has no surprises in store until the second nocturnal interlude, and even there, the link – a harmonic one – is with the Britten of *Peter Grimes*, and surely coincidental. It is the finale which will astonish ears attuned to Britten – not because of any specific 'influence', but because the tritone relationships (tonal as well as harmonic) confirm the music's Panic intuition of a path between the world of (say) Debussy's *Rondes de printemps* and that of Britten's vernal music for children.

from the International Red Cross which three years later received the *Cantata misericordium* from Britten.

No composer active in the second half of our century has been closer in spirit to the Britten of *Ballad of Heroes* and *War Requiem*, and their numerous tributaries, than the Milhaud of the *Cortege funèbre* (from Malraux's own film of his *Espoir*), the *Cantate de la Guerre*, the *Ode pour les morts*, and his late masterpiece *Le château de feu*, perhaps the only musical commentary on the Holocaust that speaks of the unspeakable in tones adequate to the task of complementing those of Schoenberg's *Survivor from Warsaw*.

There remain the children, as survivors or otherwise in the bad times, as friends and companions in the better times, and as beggars, alas, at all times (for they, we learn, are 'always with us' – just as Milhaud's highly characteristic 1937 version of *The Beggar's Opera* will be 'always with' Britten's of 1948, not because it is likely ever to stand beside it, but because Milhaud was the first modern composer of any note to use Gay's and Pepusch's original material).

With Milhaud as with Britten, the place reserved for children in his music is no nursery or kindergarten, but it is unusually well appointed, and generally sunlit. The darker side is revealed only when children appear as witnesses of the incomprehensible or victims of atrocity, as they do in *Le château de feu* and the Elie Wiesel cantata *Ani maamin*. In 1932, the year in which he also composed the prophetic *La Mort du Tyran*, Milhaud tried by his own example to encourage other French composers to establish a literature for children's music-theatre: first with the 'musical play' *A propos des Bottes*, then with the 'game' *Un petit peu de musique*, both accompanied by an ensemble of violins and cellos (or by piano).

His chosen model was *Wir bauen eine Stadt* by Hindemith, with whom the Milhauds had been friendly since the early 1920s.

3   Britten and Hindemith

The British première of *Wir bauen eine Stadt* – 'Let's make a town' rather than an opera, for it is in fact a play or 'game' – was given at the ISCM Festival at Oxford in July 1931, and was widely commented upon.

Thanks to his phenomenal all-round musicianship, Hindemith had long been a respected figure in the British musical world. His reputation as the *enfant terrible* of German music had preceded him, but Sir Donald Tovey's unequivocal endorsement of his music had unlocked many doors in the more enlightened wings of the British colleges and conservatories. No less important (in that respect) than the warmth of Tovey's enthusiasm was the bond between Hindemith and William Walton. Established in the 1920s, it was cemented when Hindemith was persuaded by Edward Clark to stand in for the indisposed William Primrose, as soloist in the première of Walton's Viola Concerto.

Frank Bridge, being a string-player as well as an eminently broad-minded composer, would surely have been well disposed towards Hindemith and his music. Among Britten's closer contemporaries, Walter Leigh had begun his studies with Hindemith in Berlin in 1927, and Arnold Cooke had followed two years later.

Leigh was to have many links with Britten in the film-music world – via Basil Wright and their work for the GPO Film Unit – and Cooke and Britten were to see a lot of each other at music festivals in the 1930s.

In the circumstances, it is remarkable how resistant to Hindemith's influence Britten remained. Although there are traces of it in some of the music left unpublished at his death, they are transient and superficial compared to the strong Hindemith influence in so much of Michael Tippett's music from 1939 until the completion of his Piano Concerto in 1955.

Hindemith for his part was fully aware of Britten. It was at his instigation that the *Cantata Academica* was commissioned for the quincentenary at Basle University; and the tributes he paid in public to Britten's operatic achievements were backed up by his practice in the classroom, where Britten was one of his chosen models, and held up to his students as exemplary with regard to word-setting, dramatic declamation, and clarity of voice-and-orchestra texture.

4 Britten and Markevich

Among the innumerable 'students' of Hindemith who never actually studied with him, by far the most celebrated in the 1930s was Igor Markevich. As the prodigious and much-admired pupil of Nadia Boulanger at the Ecole Normale de Musique in Paris – from which he obtained his diploma in 1928 – Markevich had been perhaps the first in her analysis class to grasp the true signifance of her (now generally forgotten) advocacy of Hindemith. While Stravinsky was always to remain her exemplar among the moderns, she found in Hindemith some necessary and complementary virtues, to which, perhaps, she could relate her experience of Fauré. For the young Markevich, Hindemith provided among other things a coherent means of circumventing the challenge of Stravinsky until by 1932 he was ready to take his own path.

In his diary entry of 31 March 1931, Britten records his first encounter with Markevich's music:

> Go to Waterloo Studio (B.B.C.) to hear contemporary concert, with Bridges. He [i.e. Frank Bridge] conducts B.B.C. orch "Enter Spring" & "Willow aslant a Brook" (Bridge) rather badly played, but magnificent, inspired works. Brosa St. quart. plays with orch concerto by Conrad Beck. Interesting, but that's all, incredibly played. And to end up with an absurd Concerto Grosso by Igor Markievitch. Intolerably difficult, & consequently only mod. played by the orch. This *must* have been written with the composer's tongue in his cheek.

Hailed by Milhaud and others as a revelation when Roger Desormière conducted the world première in Paris in 1930, the *Concerto Grosso* is by no means absurd, and certainly written in deadly earnest. The French critics were struck by the precocious originality of the piece, but failed to notice (as Milhaud can hardly have done) the Hindemith influence that would be immediately apparent to any informed listener today – the influence, indeed, of a specific work, namely the Concerto for Orchestra of 1925. Only in the slow movement, and in the Gogolesque episodes in the Finale, do Markevich's Russian origins betray themselves – in terms that the young Shostakovich might have recognized more readily than the young Britten.

Britten's next encounter with Markevich was at the 1934 ISCM Festival in Florence, where on 4 April he noted in his diary that Markevich's *Psaume* had caused 'a bit of a scene' (in fact an uproar, as Slonimsky notes in *Music since 1900*). Britten found the work 'interesting and original in spots', but 'not really so important'.

In his diary entries about contemporary music, the epithet 'interesting' is always the next-to-highest form of response, and never a word that is used lightly or academically. For Britten, its connotations may be objective in the sense of perceived quality, but are intensely subjective in the sense that the music must at some level speak to *him* (to 'interest' the critics and the cognoscenti was never his concern). Seldom if ever does the music so described fail to measure up to his minimum criteria; and *Psaume* is no exception. But the least rewarding, and certainly the least original, passage in the work is no mere 'spot', but a protracted recitative at the very centre of the structure. The rest of *Psaume* is anything but patchy; on the contrary, it is so stridently and obsessively single-minded that the furore it created in Florence is understandable to this day.

What Britten might have found especially 'interesting and original' in *Psaume* is the rejection of (neo)classical and European models in favour of South-east Asian ones – not in order to creat 'exotic' effects, but rather to explore purely technical and structural possibilities.

At the International Colonial Exhibition held in Paris in 1931, the so-called *'spectacles exotiques'* included theatre from Annam (Central Vietnam, as it became in 1946), and traditional music and dance from Cambodia, Thailand and, last but not least, Bali. In one sense the exhibition harked back to the historic World Exhibition of 1889, where the revelatory effect of the Annamite Theatre upon Claude Debussy had been typical of the long-term influences that stemmed from so many of its non-European exhibits. By definition more concentrated, the 1931 Exhibition offered a new range of resources for the performing and decorative arts, and creative artists in general. Now that Modernism had won its early battles, the re-appraisal of non-Western arts in all their forms was both possible and timely.

Stravinsky being fully preoccupied with his neoclassical adventures, it was too late for him to stand in for Debussy, but not too early for his devoted admirer Francis Poulenc. In the surreal *montage* of Poulenc's Concerto for Two Pianos and Orchestra of 1932, blocks of artificial Balinese temple music are brilliantly incorporated. Together with Jacques Février, Poulenc played one of the two solo parts in the Concerto's première on 5 September 1932. Two or three months earlier, Markevich – whose work Poulenc continued vociferously to praise in his music reviews – had begun the composition of *L'Envol d'Icare*, while recovering in the South of France from the rigours of an unsupervised and unmedicated self-cure of a recent opium addiction.

Whereas the 'gamelan' episodes in the Poulenc Concerto were fugitive impressions even within the work itself, and as such, unlikely to recur once they had been captured, the impact upon Markevich of the Balinese orchestras is felt throughout *L'Envol d'Icare*, and far beyond it. On the polyrhythmic and modal levels, and to some extent on the textural ones, that impact can already be sensed from the recent CD recording[7] of a version of *L'Envol d'Icare* for two pianos and four percussion; but it is through the heterophonies and the microtonal tunings of the original orchestral version that the non-Western orientations of the score are ultimately defined.

On 16 January 1955, and just a few weeks before he began work on *The Prince of the Pagodas*, Britten was co-soloist with Poulenc in a Royal Festival Hall performance of Poulenc's Concerto for Two Pianos. Had Markevich been been in London at the time (he had a home there) and free to attend, he would surely have been delighted to do so, as an old friend of Poulenc and a more recent one of Britten and Pears. Only in such a context might Poulenc have been reminded of the sensation caused by the Paris première of *L'Envol d'Icare* – an event unprecedented, it was claimed, since the première of *The Rite of Spring*. On that evening, the now long-forgotten legend of 'the two Igors' was born. But *L'Envol* was not heard in England until 1938, when Constant Lambert conducted it in one of the BBC's Contemporary Music concerts. As far as is known, Britten was not present.

In the final section of *L'Envol*, the 'Balinese' transfiguration of the fallen Icarus is already looking forward to the *tranquillo* coda of *Psaume*, which celebrates 'l'espoir de toutes les extremités lointaines de la terre et de l'Océan'. That 'hope' is to be reborn in the gamelan-influenced passages of the oratorio *Le Paradis perdu*, before it finally dissolves in the tumults of *Le Nouvel age*, a *sinfonia concertante* completed in January 1938 and performed in London at the ISCM Festival in June of that year.

If the experimental and unpublished *Hymnes* for orchestra (1933) is included in the list – which it should be – Markevich responded to the Balinese allurements of 1931 and the narcoses of early 1932 by composing one substantial score per year for five years, in each of which there are significant gamelan elements (though only in *L'Envol d'Icare* are they microtonal).

In his diary entry of 20 December 1935, Britten records his attendance (with Basil Wright among others) at the BBC Contemporary Music concert in the Queen's Hall. Substituting at the last moment for Hermann Scherchen, Markevich had conducted the world première of *Le Paradis perdu*. Given

7 Igor Markevich, *L'Envoi d'Icare* (with *Galop, Noces, and Serenade*) on LARGO 5127.

that the work is in every respect, including negative ones, a consolidation of *Psaume*, it is curious that Britten avoids commenting on the work itself, and instead comments on its composer, whom he appears to have met at the 'very nice' post-concert party:

> very capable brilliant young man – but with rather a stereotyped and conventional mind – as strict as Cherubini and people.

Ten days later, in a letter to Marjorie Fass, Britten mentions the 'brilliant young man' again (Markevich – born in Kiev on 17 July 1912 – was Britten's senior by sixteen months):

> The real musicians are so few & far between, arn't they? Apart from the Bergs, Stravinsksys, Schönbergs & Bridges one is a bit stumped for names, isn't one? Markievitch may be – but personally I feel that he's not got there yet. Shostakovitch – perhaps – possibly.

In Britten's sense, Markevich's arrival might have been signalled by the *Cantique d'amour* of October–December 1936, a work inspired by Markevich's union with and marriage to Nijinsky's daughter Kyra. Its proposed London première under the auspices of the BBC was blocked after internal memos regarding the personality and morality of the composer had once again left Edward Clark in an isolated position. (The work had its world première in Rome, under Mario Rossi, in May 1937. It has yet to be heard in the UK.)

The *Cantique d'amour* heralded the 'late' Markevich of *La Taille de l'homme*, *Lorenzo il magnifico*, and the *Variations and Fugue on a theme of Handel*. Well below the surface of each of these works, small traces of sublimated gamelan can still be detected. There are none, however, in the final page of the Handel Variations – a coda to the Fugue which unforgettably distils what sounds like a lifetime's experience, though in fact the composer was still in his thirtieth year. Forty years later, that page was given the title '*Envoi*'; for it had in fact marked Markevich's unpremeditated withdrawal from composition, at the very point where his achievement promised most for the future.

Markevich spent most of the war years in Florence, where his wife Kyra was teaching dancing. After their separation and a prolonged and nearly fatal illness, he was befriended by Bernard Berenson, who gave him the use of a gardener's cottage. After a period in the Italian Resistance, Markevich began the conducting career which brought him international fame in the immediate aftermath of the war. By then he was married to Topazia Caetani.

It was from the Markevich's London home at 10 Netherton Grove, Chelsea, that Topazia's first extant letter to Britten was addressed – on 4 May 1955, just over three months after the Britten–Poulenc concerto performance. Apart from a passing reference to Dallapiccola – with whom Markevich had been on friendly terms since the time of the *Psaume* scandal – that letter and the subsequent correspondence with Britten reveals Markevich in his sole and now all-exclusive role as conductor.

True, Boosey & Hawkes were now publishing a 1943 revision of *L'Envol d'Icare*, together with a version of *The Musical Offering*. But these were purely expedient transactions, without regard to future composition. Retitled *Icare*, the new version was typically the work of the nascent conductor, who for all his insights and expertise, is prepared to sacrifice the non-European character and much of the rough-and-ready originality of the original score, in the interests of producing an effective concert item. Having done so, he turned to other arrangements – Johann Strauss, Musorgsky, and so forth. Before long, he had safely lost sight of his own compositions, and so had the musical world.

On 6 December 1960, Markevich wrote to Britten from his native city of Kiev to report among other things that he had just seen Rostropovich:

> He asked me to tell you his great joy for the concerto [*recte*: sonata] that you write for him.

It was Markevich's first visit to Russia since his parents took him to Switzerland in 1914. His music had never been heard there, but now that he was appearing exclusively in the guise of conductor and teacher, he was soon a celebrity. Until his eventual and inevitable clash with the authorities, he was an important influence on musical life in Moscow, where he stayed for several lengthy periods.

It was in Moscow that Britten and Pears visited Markevich during their tour in 1963. Markevich later recalled (in conversation with the author, 1980) taking them deep into the countryside to visit a remarkable painter who had fallen foul of the arbiters of Socialist Realism.

His correspondence with Britten ends in 1965. By then, his international career as a conductor had been crippled by the deafness that had struck him, without warning, while rehearsing in Weimar in 1960. For the one-time composer whose phenomenal powers of hearing had been legendary since his early days in the Boulanger class, such a blow might have been supportable; for the conductor whose fame was acquired at the expense of the composer's, it determined a prolonged involvement with Beethoven, and finally – just a year or so after the death of Britten – the rediscovery and acknowledgement of his own music.

As a conductor of his own music, Markevich had had extensive studies in the 1930s with one of his own principal advocates – Hermann Scherchen. As a full-time conductor, he remained endebted to Scherchen, but seldom followed in his footsteps with regard to twentieth-century music. If his choice of repertory reflected his origins as a composer, it was only in the negative sense that his commitment to congenial composers such as Dallapiccola, Messiaen, and Britten – whose international fame, in each case, post-dated the fame he himself had renounced – was strictly limited.

Moreover, and perhaps conclusively, he ignored as a conductor the exceptional insights which as a composer had led him to discover the genius of

Schoenberg in the mid-1930s. That discovery had been another bond with Britten, and it was all the stronger because it was equally foreign to the prevailing climate of opinion (but also, in his case though not in Britten's, to the passionate convictions of his teacher).

It was not in Schoenberg that the post-war Markevich found common ground with Britten, but in Berg – above all, the Icarian Berg (or so he imagined) of the Violin Concerto.

5 Britten and Gerhard

The première of Berg's Violin Concerto, with Louis Krasner as soloist, was given at the ISCM Festival in Barcelona on 19 April 1936, with Hermann Scherchen conducting. The first half of the programme had opened with a *Prelude and Fugue* by Edmund von Borck, continued with the first (and to date the last) performance of Roberto Gerhard's *Ariel*, and ended with the three pieces from Krenek's first twelve-note opera, *Karl V.* All this, wrote Britten, was 'completely swamped' by the second half:

> Berg's last work Violin Concerto (just shattering – very simple, & touching) & the Wozzeck pieces – which always leave me like a wet rag.

Britten and Lennox Berkeley were the two British composers represented at the festival – Britten by his Suite, Op. 6, for violin and piano, in which the soloist was Antonio Brosa, with the composer at the piano. Three months to the day after the première of the Berg concerto, Franco's North African troops landed in Spain, and the Civil War began.

The prime mover of the Barcelona ISCM Festival had been Roberto Gerhard. Since his return in 1929 to his native Catalonia after four years of study with Schoenberg, Gerhard had thrown himself into the task of rescuing Barcelona's contemporary music movement from a provincialism wholly at odds with the cultural life of a city which otherwise vied with Paris, Berlin, and London as an international centre – the city of Gaudí, Picasso, Miró, and many other major figures in the modern movement. Schoenberg's acceptance of Gerhard's invitation to Barcelona in 1931 had at one stroke transformed the nature of Gerhard's campaign – and the six or seven months Schoenberg spent so happily and so creatively as a guest of Gerhard and his Viennese wife Poldi were more than merely symbolic of the regeneration and modernization of musical life in Catalonia.

At the ISCM Festival in Vienna in June 1932, the performance, conducted by Webern, of Gerhard's *Six Catalan Songs* had been one of the few notable successes – so notable, indeed, that Henry Wood included the work in his 1933 Promenade Season. His soloist was Sophie Wyss.[8] With the outbreak

8 Part 1 of Henry Wood's Promenade Concert on 5 October 1933 began with the *Bartered Bride* Overture, continued with the Gerhard Folk Songs and the Elgar Violin Concerto

of Civil War, Gerhard became Adviser to the Catalan Ministry of Fine Arts, and a member of the Republican Government's Central Music Council.

Thanks to the success of the Prom performance of the *Catalan Songs*, the BBC – probably on the advice of Edward Dent and J. B. Trend – commissioned a short orchestral work from Gerhard for a series of programmes about the life and culture of embattled Spain. Entitled *Albada, Interludi i Dansa*, it was furnished with an anonymous programme note which – like the BBC series in general – was required to dissemble its pro-Republican sympathies, since any overt expression of them might have compromised the Corporation's Reithian impartiality. Gerhard himself conducted the première, with the BBC Symphony Orchestra, on 27 October 1937. Two months later, Britten and Berkeley completed *Mont Juic*, the orchestral suite they based on the Catalan folksongs they had collected in Barcelona the year before.

In 1939, shortly before Barcelona fell to Franco's troops, Gerhard and his wife fled to Paris. From there they moved to Cambridge, at the invitation of Professors Dent and Trend. Without either a teaching post or a publisher, let alone private means of support, Gerhard survived the war years and their aftermath chiefly by undertaking precisely the kind of radio and film work that remained one of Britten's mainstays until the success of *Grimes*.

Had Gerhard needed more moral support than his own strength of character afforded him, it would have been available from several quarters – first and foremost from his compatriot Antonio Brosa, who as early as 1940 asked him for a violin concerto, then from Sophie Wyss, who asked him for more and yet more folksong arrangements, and from Constant Lambert, who in 1942 took up the cause of his unperformed *Don Quixote* ballet. Through his zarzuela arrangements and fantasies for the Spanish service of the BBC, Gerhard also established a friendly professional relationship with the conductor Stanford Robinson, who in 1949 was to conduct a BBC studio broadcast and recording of the first performance of his three-act opera *The Duenna*, with the leading tenor role sung by Peter Pears.

There is strong but not incontrovertible evidence that after the broadcast of *The Duenna*, Gerhard received from Britten, via a third party, a request for a souvenir in the form of an autograph copy of the Act III Wedding March.

Among the many passages in *The Duenna* which might have struck the Britten of 1949 as 'interesting and original', perhaps even inspired, the Wedding March is prominent enough to lend credence to reports of such a request. If, however, Gerhard complied with it, the autograph has not come to light since Britten's death. If he did not, it was probably because of Gerhard's ill-health, which was soon to culminate in the first of his numerous cardiac crises.

(soloist: Albert Sammons), and ended with the 'Unfinished' Symphony. Part 2 began with Frank Bridge's *Dance Poem*, conducted by the composer.

Britten attended the morning rehearsal as well as the concert itself (at the Queen's Hall). In his diary that same evening he notes having heard '6 attractive, yet flimsy, Catalan Folk Songs', and also, *inter alia*, 'Elgar's Impossible Vln concerto'.

Not long after the *Duenna* broadcast, and certainly well within a year of it, Britten and Pears – with support from George Harewood on the one side and Erwin Stein on the other – readily agreed to invite Gerhard to write a work for the Aldeburgh Festival. The result was the Concerto for Piano and Strings, whose composition followed immediately upon that of the three *Impromptus* (written as a wedding present for George Harewood and Marion Stein). The Concerto was completed in good time for its appointed première at the 1951 Festival, but owing to some clerical oversight, it seems that Gerhard received no notification of the rehearsal schedule, nor any invitation to the performance itself. With the proudness of a Spaniard who knew his own worth at a time when the British musical world was largely ignorant of it and Franco's Spain was in effect closed to him, Gerhard was disinclined to attend the première, or in any way to solicit the invitation which materialized only at the last moment.

The rehearsals, with Noel Mewton-Wood as soloist and Norman Del Mar conducting, seem to have been more than usually fraught, not only because of the (at that time) considerable complexity of the string-writing – and consequent problems, perhaps, with regard to orchestral parts extracted without the editorial intermediacy of a publisher – but also because of the very nature of the idiom. Unfortunately, word reached the composer in Cambridge to the effect that at the first rehearsal a section leader had raised the usual questions about 'wrong notes', only for someone to call out, amidst general hilarity, 'Who knows, and who cares?'

In the name of musical and professional integrity, no one apart from the composer himself would have cared more than Britten. Even so, the Concerto was far removed from anything that might have been expected two years earlier from the composer of *The Duenna*. Strictly serial and dodeca-phonic, though not in the old textbook sense, it excluded the entire range of expanded diatonic and bitonal harmony which Gerhard had first made his own in the *Catalan Songs* of 1929, and then continued to explore thoughout the next two decades. Especially in such vocal works as the *Cantata* of 1931, the Spanish and French folksong cycles for Sophie Wyss (including the now famous *Cancionero de Pedrell*) and above all *The Duenna*, it was surely a harmony that Britten would have found congenial. From 1951 onwards, it was no longer to be heard, except in Gerhard's incidental music, and even then with decreasing frequency.

Perhaps at some level Gerhard felt that the death of Schoenberg in 1951 had finally released him from further self-affirmative obligations towards a highly distinctive harmonic idiom that owed much to his Viennese training, but little or nothing to the Schoenbergian principles he had already begun to discard in his final apprentice work, the Wind Quintet of 1928. Having respectfully recalled them, from a great distance, in the Violin Concerto he wrote for Antonio Brosa (completed in 1945, and first performed under Scherchen in Florence in 1950) he returned to them, or rather, to his own version of them, at precisely the point where he and Britten in effect parted company – in the Concerto for Piano and Strings.

6 Britten and Leopold Spinner

Throughout the last thirty-five years of Britten's life, and then for a further four years, the only composer active in the United Kingdom who stood in direct line of succession from Schoenberg, Webern and Berg, was the Austrian-born Leopold Spinner (1906–1980). Unrecognized to this day in his adopted country, and virtually unknown even in Austria, Spinner is one of the very few twentieth-century composers who has fulfilled an historic role without finding even the humblest of places in the histories and guidebooks.

As for the music itself, it would be hard to conceive of something so remote from the representative needs and requirements of cyberspace and the weekend culture supplements – not the obscurest of fifteenth-century Flemish contrapuntists, not the driest of Mannheim symphonists, not the palest of *fin-de-siècle* operetta hacks; and certainly not the magic pipings of some endangered tribe from the Guyanan rainforest.

Yet Spinner was a master – more than a *petit maître*, and in the moral dimensions of his craft and calling, as exigent and incorruptible as the greatest of the classical masters who were his gods. Arriving almost penniless in England in 1939, he spent most of the war years in the Midlands – where he worked for a while in a locomotive factory – but settled in London when the war was over. Through Erwin Stein he was introduced to Boosey & Hawkes as a freelance copyist and editor, and before long he joined the editorial department on a full-time basis, with particular responsibility for Stravinsky, but also (via Stein) for Britten.

On 5 April 1934 the chamber music concert at the Florence ISCM Festival began with Britten's Phantasy Quartet:

> Goossens and the Grillers really play my Phant. very beautifully & it's quite well received. Other works – Trio by Neugeboren (apparently v. conventional – I didn't hear it) – Sturznegger a Cantata for various instruments rather colourless – an interesting quartet by Spinner . . .

Spinner's *Kleines Quartett* – or *Quartettino* as it was called in Florence – was played by the Kolisch Quartet, three of whom had given the exceptionally well-received première of his String Trio at the 1932 ISCM Festival. Neither score has come to light, though Louis Krasner stated in 1987 that the manuscript of the *Kleines Quartett* was in his possession, but temporarily mislaid – unlike his other Spinner manuscript of 1934, the Two Pieces for violin and piano.[9] Copies of the Two Pieces are in the Spinner Archives (Music Division of the National Library in Vienna) and confirm the impressions which Spinner's 'sehr persönliches' (Paul Stefan) 'in Schönberg–

9 See Regina Busch, *Leopold Spinner* (Bonn: Boosey & Hawkes, 1987): 55.

Bahnen' (E. Steinhard) *Kleines Quartett* had left on two influential and discerning critics.

'Interesting' as the two violin pieces should likewise have been to the Britten of 1934, two of the large-scale Spinner works from exactly the same period would by their very nature have made an even stronger impression. One of them, the *Passacaglia* for wind ensemble, violin, cello, and piano, might indeed have registered (consciously or otherwise) as 'fascinating'; for the twelve-note passacaglia theme is saturated with fourths and quartal implications whose harmonic and formal consequences are such that the future composer of *The Turn of the Screw* would unerringly have grasped their significance. (Awarded the Henri-Le-Boeuf prize and performed in Brussels on 29 April 1936 by an ensemble under the direction of Hermann Scherchen, the *Passacaglia* was not heard again until the spring of 1992, when the Ensemble Modern under Friedrich Cerha performed it in the Queen Elizabeth Hall.)

While the *Passacaglia* suggests affinities with Alban Berg and in particular with his Chamber Concerto of 1925, Spinner's four-movement String Quartet of 1934–5 is, after his own fashion, as Schoenbergian as the violin pieces, but still, like the *Passacaglia*, governed by a tone row rich in quartal implications. To the best of our knowledge, this masterly work was the last that Spinner composed before clairvoyantly taking the unique step (for a mature composer at that time) of aligning himself with, and apprenticing himself to, Anton von Webern.

'Interesting & very beautiful in parts': thus Britten again, reacting to a performance of Webern's *Five Pieces*, Op. 5, for string quartet, played by the Kolisch Quartet on 1 December 1933.

Unlike Schoenberg, Webern composed no mature tonal music. Unlike Webern, Spinner made one solitary exception, subdivided into three phases: the first two date from 1960–61, when he turned to the same Herbert Hughes collection of *Irish Country Songs* that Britten had drawn upon in the late 1950s, and composed *Six Canons on Irish Folksongs* for mixed chorus *a cappella*, followed by four more (but only two new ones) for mixed orchestra and string orchestra; and finally in 1964 came another set of *a cappella* canons. Even for a composer whose art, like Webern's, was now rooted in canonic procedures, these were no exercises. Nor was Ireland an escapade, or folksong a commercially determined choice. The canons were a family matter, in a tradition that Bach would have recognized.

From time to time – when the need arose or when the production department had nothing better or more urgent to do – the Managing Director of Boosey & Hawkes, Dr Ernst Roth (another arrival from Universal Edition after the Nazi annexation of Austria) would authorize production and limited publication of a Spinner score. Aware as he was that his music was being published out of kindness and collegial respect rather than out any belief in its future, Spinner must also have recognized that the very acceptance of such kindness was, by his own uncompromising standards, a kind of compromise.

If among those who knew Spinner there was anyone who would have grasped what such a compromise might have cost him, it was surely Benjamin Britten, a composer and musician who in his own very different way was as intransigent as he.

for Donald
London, 9–15 January 1995

16

Donald Mitchell as Publisher:
A Personal Recollection

PETER DU SAUTOY

Donald Mitchell achieved something that may not have been equalled by any other music scholar and critic of similar standing: he became the publisher of one of the contemporary composers whose work he had conspicuously admired and championed – Benjamin Britten. As I played a small part in this process, perhaps I may explain briefly how it came about.

I had been a director of the publishing company Faber and Faber Limited since 1946. I was not an editor, more of an administrator or manager, but all directors were encouraged to take part in editorial work and attended the weekly meeting of the 'Book Committee' that dealt with manuscripts received, projects for consideration and many other subjects of general interest to the Board. Faber had published Constant Lambert's *Music Ho!* in 1934 and it occurred to me that there might be a place for a fresh survey of contemporary music some thirty years later. I received the approval of my colleagues for taking this idea further. I wrote to Frank Howes, music critic of *The Times*, to ask his advice and received a reply from his assistant, William Mann, who said that the author I must go after was Donald Mitchell, at that time assistant music critic on the *Daily Telegraph*. I got in touch with Donald who promised a book which later turned out to be *The Language of Modern Music*, eventually published in 1963. A fourth edition was published in 1993, evidence of the book's continuing importance. The book dealt mainly with two composers not directly involved in this *Festschrift* – Schoenberg and Stravinsky: proof of Donald's wide and expert knowledge.

However, there was a more important development that has to be recorded, quite separate from the publication of one book. Donald had established himself, largely through *Music Survey* (1947–52) which he edited, latterly with Hans Keller, as a champion of Benjamin Britten's music. In fact his association with Britten and with what went on at Aldeburgh was widely known. Britten's music was published by Boosey & Hawkes and for a short time Donald acted as an adviser to that firm. He maintained a connection with Faber, as Music Books Editor, which had a surprising consequence. Britten wanted to move to a new publisher and confided in Donald that he

had Faber in mind, though they had never yet published music. Urgent
negotiations took place and Faber agreed to become a music publisher, first
by establishing a Music Department with Donald in charge but very soon by
creating a new company, Faber Music Limited, with Donald as Managing
Director. So Faber became Britten's publisher. Britten became a director of
the new company, though I cannot recall his attendance at more than one
board meeting. He was always much interested in the work of the company.
When he died his place on the Board was taken by Peter Pears.

The birth and progress of Faber Music are chronicled in its publication
Faber Music: The First 25 Years, 1965–1990, by David Wright; Donald's
contribution to this remarkable development is fully described. I cannot do
more than offer some personal recollections to add to this account.

One of Donald's most valuable assets was knowing where to turn to for
advice and help. This is one of the most important qualifications for a publisher to have. He cannot know everything, or everyone, but he must know
where to turn for information. Publishing Britten's music gave Faber Music a
head start and would no doubt attract young composers to the list, but
expansion was urgent and Donald set about securing this with great energy
and originality. He obtained an option to publish Raymond Leppard's
realization of *L'Incoronazione di Poppea* (Monteverdi), which led to other
performer editions. Contact with Imogen Holst at Aldeburgh led to the
publication of some Holst pieces; and works by Malcolm Arnold, Humphrey
Searle, Peter Sculthorpe and Roger Smalley appear in the early lists.

An important part of the early activities of Faber Music was its educational
list: in particular the Waterman–Harewood Piano Series which was
announced in the Faber Music Catalogue of 1967 and is still selling strongly.
It was at Britten's suggestion that the series was offered to Faber Music.

While the building of Faber Music's list proceeded, Donald continued to
advise on music books for publication by Faber and Faber. A cursory glance
at my own bookshelves reveals the extent and importance of the books in
the field of music that the firm published during the 1960s and 1970s. The
list is too long to reproduce here, but there are two books I would especially
like to mention.

The first is *Arnold Schoenberg Letters*, selected and edited by Erwin Stein,
translated by Eithne Wilkins and Ernst Kaiser (the two outstanding trans-
lators from the German of that period), published in 1964. I think it was the
publication of this book that first led me to an appreciation of Donald's
potentiality as a publisher of books on musical subjects. There were also
personal rewards for my wife and myself. We got to meet Erwin Stein and
his wife Sophie (everyone loved her!) and their daughter Marion. Through
them I met Mrs Gertrud Schoenberg, the composer's second wife, when I
went to the annual Frankfurt Book Fair. (Her first question was always:
'How is Marion?') Marion Harewood, now Mrs Jeremy Thorpe, became not
only a Faber author, as already mentioned, but a valuable supporter of
Benjamin Britten, and later of the Britten Estate and the Britten–Pears School
for Advanced Musical Studies.

In addition to the personal consequence of publishing the Schoenberg letters, there came an appreciation of Donald's knowledge of the contemporary music of Europe – and later of the contemporary culture of Japan and the Far East. All of which marked him out as well qualified to undertake a career as a publisher.

The second book I want to mention is *All What Jazz* by Philip Larkin (1970). I don't think any further comment is needed. The range of interest and enthusiasm is clear.

17

The Key to the Parade

OLIVER KNUSSEN

THE KEY TO THE PARADE   Oliver Knussen

A personal observation about the Fanfare which opens Britten's Les Illuminations, shared with Donald Mitchell a few years ago and published here in honour of his 70th birthday.

THE KEY TO THE PARADE

VII
BEING
BEAUTEOUS ♩=40   un È-tre de beau-té de hau-te tai-lle

VIII
PARADE ♩=96-100   O - - le . . plus violent . . .

[NB cf also IIIa. PHRASE]

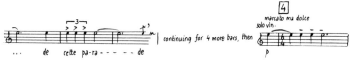

alternating B♭ (beauté) + E (violent) arpeggios for 4 bars, then:-

Largamente (alla breve)
ff declamato

[3]

J'ai   seul la clef. . . .

E maj   B♭ maj

[NB cf also XI. INTERLUDE]

... de   cette pa-ra - - - - - de

continuing for 4 more bars, then

marcato ma dolce
solo vln.
[4]

IX.
DÉPART ♩=72 As-sez vu.   La vi-sion s'est re - con-trée a   tous les airs

Thus the FANFARE can serve as a mnemonic for the whole cycle and, within this context, the identification of the composer, his text and the musical structure is complete.

26th November 1994.

171

18

Notes on a Theme from *Peter Grimes*

LUDMILA KOVNATSKAYA

One can make endless reflections about an artistic text. They can reflect the accumulated cultural experience of the age, or they might dig deep into history. For a piece of music, no less than any work of art, represents to a significant degree a transformation of its own musical past. Its 'then', i.e. its past life, and its existence 'here and now', form the co-ordinate points which help to establish more clearly the work's significance and trace the path of its destiny.

This is applicable to a work of art both in its entirety and to any one part. Thus I should like to turn my attention to one musical theme which functions as a leitmotif in the opera *Peter Grimes*.[1] I have in mind the theme that brings to a close the first scene of Act I. It expresses a lonely man's dream of finding refuge and spiritual calm ('What harbour shelters peace?') in the face of the violence and hatred of public gossip ('there'll be no quarrels'), and his hope of living in a world where 'night is turned to day'. In a word this is the theme of Grimes's dreaming.[2]

The 'dream' theme clearly stands out amidst that multitude of beautiful melodies so abundantly strewn throughout the opera, whether full of tender lyricism or dramatic tension, whether refined or ungainly dance tunes, whether ironic or energetic. It towers above them and enters the consciousness immediately and powerfully. Moreover it works upon one's aural memory in such a way as to make one compare and relate all other themes in the opera to it.

Britten prepares the theme's appearance rather as an experienced dramatist prepares the entry of his hero(ine). Its appearance will be an event of major significance and everything will be done to emphasize this fact.

Two bars before the first note of the theme (Act I scene 1), the composer

---

1 In Russian Britten studies, analysis of the system of leitmotifs in *Peter Grimes* has been made by Adeodatas Tauragis, '*Peter Grimes*: the Opera by Benjamin Britten', in S. Pitina (ed.), *Iz Istorii Zarubezhnoi Muzyki* (Moscow: Muzyka Publishers, 1971): 203–9. See also Ludmila Kovnatskaya, *Benjamin Britten* (Moscow: Sovietski Kompozitor Publishers, 1974): 81–4.
2 In the given context the notions of 'leitmotif' and 'Leit-theme' are structurally differentiated.

interrupts the energetic pulse of the rhythmic figuration, which has become faster and faster as the conflict's thermometer level has risen; by tightening the emotional tension he creates in the listener a sensation of impending disaster. And suddenly we feel as if this dynamic wave has struck an invisible barrier;[3] having raised it up, Britten halts it with a gesture worthy of Prospero, and it is at this moment that we hear the theme. It flows out on the crest of a new wave and everything about it contrasts with what has gone before. This is a different kind of movement and a different measure as the 6/8 *Vivace* gives way to the 2/2 *Largamente* in minims. After the nervous and agitated babble comes an expansive and arioso-like melody. External movement and action is replaced by inward contemplation (mirroring the dialogue/internal monologue relationship). Against the warm colouring of the strings in A major and the deep breath of the dominant pedal we hear the tonic and dominant alternating every three bars. Its upwards motion and wide open character is confirmed by the final V–VI progression, thrice repeated. Neither the marcato vocal phrase ('Away from tidal waves', 'Terrors and tragedies'), nor the syncopated instrumental figure, which try to attack the theme, are able to reach it. It floats high above all day-to-day cares and worries. It would be hard to imagine a more perfectly formed image!

Ex. 1

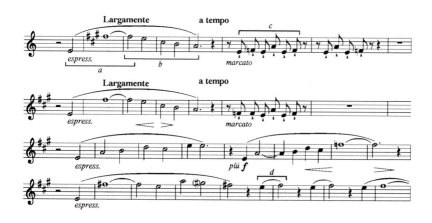

---

3   In *Peter Grimes* Britten demonstrates his mastery by creating the crowd scenes using the effect of a growing dynamic wave with an ever-developing inner structure.

The complete exposition of the 'dream' theme takes up 36 bars; virtually an entire arioso for Grimes. It possesses certain semantically significant elements: its A major tonality, as we well know, represents for Britten the realm of the purest feelings and thoughts, the most passionate romantic lyricism, an Apollonian perfection; the anhemitonal passage in the major is a simple and versatile song-like phrase (cf. the fishermen's chorus); the fourth-plus-tritone chord is that storm chord of spiritual turmoil whose significance in Britten's music has already been established; last but not least we should note the intervallic leap a major ninth upwards as the soaring voice seems to float beyond time.

All those elements of the theme which have been mentioned are lexemes which live their own active and independent life within the texture of the score, developing their own intonational plot, enriching their own meaning as well as the whole spectrum of meanings contained within the theme. Each element emerges in the opera as a polysemantic symbol. Thus the 'dream' theme can be seen as the end result of an interesting piece of thematic development.

None the less the biography of this theme is determined not only by the behaviour of its component parts. It has its own story line within the opera itself. The stages of this story line are, briefly, as follows:

1 The Prologue. The humiliation of the court is behind. Peter and Ellen are alone; two lonely people, an unabating sense of indignation and tender consolation. The voices of these two lonely people are woven into a lyrical and expressive dialogue. Finally, in silence, the two melodies become one in the unison rising minor ninth ('My/your voice out of the pain').

Ex. 2

The beauty of this melody is to be found in any one of its elements: the juxtaposition of the major triads (E–C–Db–E), the undulating melodic line, the mirror-like interrelationship of the leading notes (in the iambic second and third sections of the sequence), the choice of intervals in the theme (both those which remain constant in the sequence and those transformed by it), the rhythmic expansion which slows down the movement, the contraction of the melodic range which occurs at the end, thus resolving the conflict between registers. This is where our intuition and sense of logic first tell us that the composer will surely not be able to abandon this melody: it is a leit-motif. Let us call it the theme of 'hope'.[4]

2 Act I scene 1. Among the inhabitants of the Borough there is virtually no one to sympathize with Grimes. Only the old sailor Balstrode is prepared to take a friendly interest. He understands Grimes ('you're a lonely soul'). The storm approaches. It is easier to confess when confronted by the elements, and Grimes remembers 'that evil day', when his apprentice boy died. The rising minor ninth announces the appearance of the leitmotif.

In this A minor arioso it is heard six times, and on each occasion the composer varies it as though he were searching for its ideal form.

Ex. 3

Without losing any of its expressiveness, he simplifies the melody and brings out both its inner structure – the rising ninth (motif *a*), the anhemi-tonic section (motif *b*), the small intervals of the recitative passage (motif *c*) –

4   The semantics of the E major/C major juxtaposition within the same theme (leitmotif) can be examined in the wider operatic context, from the 'love' leitmotif in Verdi's *Otello* (finale of Act I) to Britten's *Death in Venice*. See R. Leites, *Dramaturgicheskie Osobennosti Opery Verdi 'Otello'* (Moscow: Muzyka Publishers, 1968): 36–9 and *passim*; and Eric Roseberry, 'Tonal Ambiguity in *Death in Venice*: A Symphonic View', in Donald Mitchell (ed.), *Benjamin Britten: Death in Venice*, Cambridge Opera Handbook (Cambridge: Cambridge University Press, 1987): 89–98.

and its optimum rhythmic shape (extending the first motif), and confirms the combination of anhemitonality with the semitonal attraction of leading note to tonic, as well as reaffirming the basic tonality of A minor/major.

In this arioso ('Grimes's narration') Montagu Slater gives the so-called 'key-word' to the last appearance of the theme ('Alone, alone, alone with a childish death'). The word 'alone' is given added importance by being repeated three times, by its unusual syntax, and by the new melodic height here reached (the interval of the eleventh straightens out the melodic arc). This version of the theme should be called the theme of Grimes's loneliness.

3   The 'dream' theme is the third version of the leitmotif. It emerges as the result not only of micro-motival work but also of thematic and variational development. This development tends towards greater simplicity. The theme differs qualitatively from its two previous versions. This one, in the major, is broad, expansive and luminous. The initial motif here is particularly emphatic. The major ninth is perceived here as a consonance, being a resolution of the dissonant minor ninth. The theme is not completed but left open – the arc is again straightened – as it is extended by the upwardly striving melodic V–VI progression (motif *d*), which represents a reduced form of the initial motif *a*.

One cannot fail to be struck by Britten's consummate mastery in creating this genuinely romantic 'secondary theme' which leads one to search out and discover in *Peter Grimes* a whole layer of symphonic techniques and sonata-form principles.

4   From this point onwards the 'dream' theme is perceived as a reminiscence. Its ecstatic (A major) appearance is the culmination of the Storm Interlude – where the tempest and Grimes's fits of passion are in complete harmony, mutually reflecting and dissolving in each other. '. . . This universe is but the discharge of passions,/long stored in the human heart' (Boris Pasternak). Grimes's appearance at the pub (Act I, scene 2) calls forth a truncated and distorted version of the theme (a bitonal A/A♭ four-bar phrase), a sombre precursor of its forthcoming final metamorphosis.

Ex. 4a

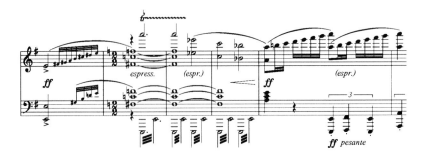

In the vast tragic monologue (Act III, scene 3) the theme returns as a symbol of dreaming, but broken, weakened and crawling and wilting.[5]

Ex. 4b

What striking capacity for imagery does Britten's melodic invention possess! One never tires of listening to the theme.

Its mode, harmony and melodic shape draw on diverse historical strata without self-contradiction. It presents a harmonious co-existence of the major–minor duo-tonality with the pentatonic scale, an 'old-fashioned' alternation of simple harmonic progressions (dominant–tonic), as well as the fourth-plus-tritone (or fifth-plus-tritone) chord signalling the most complex non-triadic modal process in contemporary music.[6] In Britten's idiosyncratic style, as in the work of any creative genius, the 'past' turns out to be an inherent part of the 'present', with which it forms an organic synthesis. I intend to discuss only one of the many subject-matters which could serve as a source for this, one of Britten's most splendid musical themes. It is connected with the names of two composers extraordinarily dear to Britten – Mahler and Shostakovich. When referring the reader to critical works of comparative analysis dealing with the music of any two of the above named composers, one must remember that Russian Shostakovich studies devote no less an important place to the Shostakovich–Mahler digression than Britten scholars in England lend to the Britten–Mahler parallel.[7] It would hardly be

5   The bi-directional tendency is reflected in the mode: both sharpened (A♭ major moves to Lydian A♭), and flattened (A♭ minor with flattened second and fourth degrees).
6   The structural modal phenomenon of this chord, with its horizontal and vertical versions, has been investigated in detail by Yuri Kudriashov based on both musical theory and individual composers' works. See his magnum opus *Ladovye sistemy yevropeiskoi muzyki XX veka* (Leningrad, 1991, ms).
7   See L. -W. Hesse 'Schostakowitsch und Mahler', *Bericht über das Internationale Dmitri-Schostakowitsch-Symposion*, Köln, 1985 (Regensburg: Niemöller and Zaderackij, 1986); K. Meyer, 'Mahler und Schostakowitsch', in *Gustav Mahler: Sinfonie und*

possible to list here all those books, articles and essays which would provide one with a great number of interesting and thought-provoking reflections.

Let us avoid discussing the question of what music the composer was listening to immediately before the composition of the opera. Such indications are relevant but can be misleading; after all, Britten, if we are to go by the evidence of his diaries and letters, was an indefatigable listener.[8] So we will rather leave this area at least partially open for others to analyse the great amount of available evidence and fruitful comparisons. Our concern here is with another matter: choosing and selecting the intonational models and carriers of the integral meaning, irrespective of whether this process was carried out consciously or not.

The extent to which Shostakovich and Britten – two musical geniuses of our century – were spiritually attached to Mahler, is well known. Should we be surprised at the various links and cross-links between their works, whether direct or indirect?! There is room here for those thematic reminiscences in the form of quasi-quotations, stylistic imitations, paraphrases, veiled hints and allusions. These 'moments of pre-existing significance' appear in the fabric of the works as 'alien words', thus creating a meaningful counterpoint, dialogue and polylogue.[9] At the same time they are assimilated, transformed beyond recognition and become germane to the individual style. Recognizing and searching for its pre-supposed original source (the Ur-significance), the procedure of making attributions, discovering a secret meaning – these perspectives offered by research work are fascinating in that the music itself dictates and prefigures the channels of its interpretation. This is one of the mechanisms of cultural memory about which Osip Mandelstam wrote in terms of genetic continuity:

> We are all, even without realizing it, carriers of an enormous embryological experience; after all, the whole process of recognition, which culminates in the memory's triumphant effort, is amazingly similar to the phenomenon of growth. In both cases – whether the first bud or embryo, whether a tiny

Wirklichkeit (Graz: Kolleritsch, 1977); D. Redepenning, 'Mahler und Schostakowitsch', *Das Gustav-Mahler-Fest* (Hamburg, 1989), *Bericht über den Internationalen Gustav-Mahler-Congress* (Kassel: Matthias Theodor Vogt/Bärenreiter, 1991); Donald Mitchell, 'What do we know about Britten now?', in BC: 21–45; Ludmila Kovnatskaya, 'Britten i Shostakovich', paper given at the International Conference *Ars Britannica II: Anglo-Russian Cultural Interactions* (Leningrad, 11 December 1989) ms; Eric Roseberry, 'A Debt Repaid? Some observations on Shostakovich and his late period of recognition of Britten', paper given at the International Symposium *Shostakovich in a Changing World* (Saint Petersburg, 17 May 1994), ms.

8 See DMPR.
9 The questions of the relationship of text and system, of internal textual multi-significance, of the movement of semantic units within the dimension of all meanings, and of the artistic function of 'alien words' are addressed by Mikhail Bakhtin (Problemy poetiki Dostoevskogo (Moscow: Sovietski Pisatel' Publishers, 1963)) and Yuri Lotman (*Analiz poeticheskogo teksta* (Leningrad: Prosveschenie Publishers, 1972)). See also Elena Popova, 'Poetika zaimstvovannykh smyslov v khudozhestvennoi sisteme Bramsa', in Ada Shnittke (ed.), *I. Brams. Cherty stilya* (Saint Petersburg: RIO Conservatoire, 1992).

facial feature or half-formed character trait, or a whisper of sound . . . – this all develops not of its own accord, but merely as a response to an invitation, as a reaching out in justification of all expectation.[10]

The intonational world of the 'dream' theme in *Peter Grimes* joins together and fuses the typical characteristics of Mahler's lyrical thematicism, which also found a realization in Shostakovich's music. The expressive lyricism of the rising minor ninth and the exultant major ninth (motif *a*) form a key element of Mahler's instrumental declamatory style and its 'deep melodic breathing', its tragedy and its apotheosis. The relationship of the major and minor ninths is no less a recognizable hallmark of his style as is the shimmering vacillation of the major/minor third in Schubert's music. The anhemitonic scale (motif *b*) is linked to Mahler's poetics of the inner world of contemplation and the external world of Nature. The interval of the second in motif *d* is perceived as an inversion (in every sense of the word) of the Mahlerian 'Ewig' from *Das Lied von der Erde*. Just as the two-note motif 'Ewig' (III–II progression), it is repeated three times and is left open-ended.

The step of a rising ninth, i.e. a second transposed up an octave, is structurally identifiable (albeit abstractly) with a second: in terms of the actual sound, it has to overcome a tremendous resistance in time and space. Therefore it carries within itself a double semantic load, both as *passus duriusculus* and as *saltus*. The semantic role of the *saltus duriusculus* is determined by the extraordinary force of the enormous intervallic step, which goes beyond the octave barrier. This intonational 'sub-plot' is one of the most predominant features in the melodic world of Mahler, Britten and Shostakovich. It also establishes and makes inventive play with the stability of the octave as a function of the clearly defined melodic field.[11] Quite often the melody seems to be struggling within an octave cage, which is undermined by sevenths and diminished octaves. And then the augmented octave and the minor and major ninths sweep away the upper limit of the octave, thus freeing the melody. A revealing example is to be found in Grimes's 'dream' theme (Act I, scene 1; 3, 6 and 9 bars after Fig. 50), where the upper line moves from octave to major ninth in semitones (E–F–F♯).

An even more typical situation is where the melodic spread of an octave or

---

10 Osip Mandelstam, 'Puteshestvie v Armeniyu', in *Stikhotvoreniya. Perevody. Ocherki. Stat'yi* (Tbilisi: Merani Publishers, 1990): 336.

11 For the sake of brevity, I shall limit myself to examples from Britten: 'Now the Great Bear and Pleiades' (*Grimes*, Act I scene 2) – the scalic descent to the octave; 'O when you pray, you shut your eyes' (Chorus, Prologue) – scalic ascent combined with accentual jump; the fishermen's chorus (Act I scene 1, and Act III scene 2) – sung on the triadic notes; 'Nothing to tell me' (Ellen, Act II scene 1) – the emphasis of leading note to octave; 'Loud man, I never did have time' (Auntie, Act I scene 2) – chromaticized melody within the octave; 'Until the Borough hate' (Peter, Ellen, Prologue) – the gentle, rhythmic playing with thirds and sixths within the octave; Interlude III ('Sunday Morning') – the horizontal splicing of two fifths; 'God have mercy upon me' and 'Grimes is at his exercise' (Act II scene 1) – the spring-like twist-and-turn of the melodic phrase; etc.

more is achieved after several attempts, as the interval is ever increased. Inna Barsova has written of this technique as a typical feature of Mahler's melodic variations.[12] In this light we only have to compare Ellen's arioso (B minor, Act III scene 1) with Katerina Lvovna's aria (F♯ minor, *Lady Macbeth of the Mtsensk District*, Act I scene 3, Nos. 153–4), in order to be convinced how typical this device is for Britten and Shostakovich in their arioso writing.

Intonational fluidity is an art that combines both the energy of the broad gesture and the refined 'mime-like' expression of movement in seconds, and so carries significance. For Mahler this is a lexeme, and the same is true for Shostakovich and Britten. The interval of the ninth responds to the impulse for self-confession which demands utmost expressiveness. It appears at the critical moment of the confessions of Peter Grimes and Katerina Lvovna.

The sharp feeling (sometimes almost painfully so) of the semitone as a nuance has been described by Boris Asafiev in his book *Musical Form as Process*.[13] The poet's ear is not deaf to this feeling:

> Car nous voulons la Nuance encor,
> Pas la Couleur, rien que la nuance!
> Oh! la nuance seule fiance
> Le rêve au rêve et la flûte au cor![14]
> (Paul Verlaine, *Art Poétique*)

How revealing it is that Boris Pasternak, when translating these lines, used the Russian word for 'semitone' to convey the French 'nuance'.

The Lithuanian musicologist Adeodatas Tauragis has noted the similarity of the 'dream' theme from *Grimes* to the pesante motif given to six unison horns in the final part (bars 7–8 of Fig. 30) of the second movement of Mahler's Fifth Symphony.[15] In actual fact evidence and examples of such a close relationship are countless in as much as the ninth is a seminal figure in the intonational world of the Fifth. Here it is smelted in the crucible of the *Trauermarsch* and forged by the main intonation of the following movement, that most tense stage in the symphonic drama, the very 'heart of the symphony, which provides the other movements with life and is fed by fibres from the entire organism'.[16] In what Mahler marks 'Stürmisch bewegt, mit

---

12 Inna Barsova, *Simfonii Gustava Malera* (Moscow: Sovietski Kompozitor Publishers, 1975): 408. There is a vivid example in *Peter Grimes* – 'We live and let live and look/ We keep our hands to ourselves' (Act I scene 2).

13 Boris Asafiev, *Muzykal'naya forma kak protsess* (Leningrad: Muzyka Publishers, 1971): 229 and 242.

14 [For we ever desire nuance,
    Not colour – nothing but nuance!
    Oh! nuance alone may join
    Dream to dream and flute to horn!]
    In *Zarubezhnaya Poezia v perevodakh B.L. Pasternaka* (Moscow: Raduga Publishers, 1990): 454–5.

15 Adeodatas Tauragis, op. cit.: 203. This was also noted independently by Hans Keller.

16 Inna Barsova, op. cit.: 179.

grösster Vehemenz', we hear, within the rich succession of motifs, the flight upwards by a ninth and the descent to the tonic via the very notes of the scale found in Britten's theme. This motif rushes by, rhythmicized by small note values. The domain of the semitone is extended to such an extent that there is created the impression of the composer's having used non-tempered and natural tuning, and having specified third- and quarter-tones in the orchestral parts. Then the motif of the ninth is transformed rhythmically, is compressed, straightened out, stretched and, finally, given that form which allows us to call Britten's 'dream' theme in *Grimes* a quasi-quotation. Britten's theme is related to the countless versions of the Mahler motifs in the Fifth Symphony in a variety of guises: hints, allusions and paraphrases, etc.

In Mahler's music the biography of the musical phrase or motif based on the ninth goes far beyond the Fifth Symphony. We hear its apotheosis in the third movement (Fig. 12) of the Fourth Symphony, where it is given to the flute and the first violins in 'unthinkable augmentation', and signals the most decisive and dramatically crucial turning-point. (Let us also pay attention to the counterpoint of the timpani and the double-basses and note the proto-type of motif *c* from Britten's theme.) In the first movement of *Das Lied von der Erde* (in the transition to the recapitulation and the recapitulation itself) the rising minor and major ninths ('dieser Erde!', 'Sehr dort hinab!') prefigure the expressionistic flight up to the peak and the tragic headlong fall (glissando, 'Lebens!'). One only has to open the score of the Ninth Symphony, which Britten confessed to being able to listen to for hours on end (see his diary entry for 27 January 1935), to discover the familiar outline of these motifs and musical phrases with the ninth (for example the first movement).

There are plenty of motifs based on the ninth in Mahler's symphonies. One of their roles is dynamic. They enrich the musical texture by throwing into sharp relief the chromatic notes of the scale; quite often the motif's rising tension is underlined by a glissando. Another role is static. At moments of ecstatic culmination or states of deep contemplation Mahler seeks to arrest the passing moment by expanding the motif rhythmically.

The motif based on the ninth is predominantly found in Mahler's music in the sphere of the 'sublime' (in the sphere of 'Trivialmusik' it aids the grotesque transformation of dance- and song-like themes). In the context of the romantic style it is truly universal in the way it is drawn to a polarized expressiveness and ambivalence of meaning: it is both dynamic and static; nervously explosive but also calmly narrative and nobly restrained; it expresses open action and secret, hidden emotion; it contrasts terrestrial pain and passions with heavenly beauty and spiritual ecstasy.

Many composers have felt the fascinating influence of this Mahlerian intona-tion, no less than other aspects of his melodic style.[17] Shostakovich and Britten

17 It would be only just and appropriate to note that the motif called Mahlerian in this article
  is a lexeme common to the 'intonational vocabulary of the age' (Asafiev's concept) – the

are no exception. With Britten, these motifs are not confined within any one single work; the motif of the ninth traces its 'crusade' from *Our Hunting Fathers* and the *Seven Sonnets of Michelangelo* through to *War Requiem*. The semantic significance of the movement upwards, either as a sudden leap or as gradually increasing energy, followed by a sharp fall or smooth, sliding descent, has enormously expressive potential. Both Britten and Shostakovich, following Mahler's example, have drawn copiously at this source.

In his Fourteenth Symphony, which is dedicated to Britten, Shostakovich makes use of the expressive qualities of the ninth both as an intervallic motif and as the outer limits of a melodic phrase. If we open the score at the third movement, 'Lorelei', we find on two occasions a phrase, very similar to the one already mentioned from *Katerina Izmailova*; a dreamy rising ninth, this is the main and representational intonation of the 'dream' theme from *Peter Grimes*. In the 'Lorelei' movement the minor ninth (E–F) is replaced by the major ninth (E–F♯), using the very same notes which appear in *Grimes*'s themes of loneliness and dreaming (from three bars after Fig. 40 to Fig. 48 in the Shostakovich). In Apollinaire's poem the Lorelei dreams of seeing her castle (Fig. 41) and imagines her beloved's voice calling to her as he sails past (from three bars after Fig. 40 to Fig. 41). The soloist's voice is answered by the celesta.

Ex. 5

post-and post-post-Wagnerian age, of Richard Strauss, Alexander Zemlinsky, Alban Berg and others. However, the model for Britten and Shostakovich was undoubtedly Mahler.

The timbre of the celesta plays an exceptionally important role in Britten's sound world. The semantics of this timbre (for Britten!) took shape in the *Kindertotenlieder* and were consolidated in *Das Lied von der Erde*,[18] where the celesta takes up the singer's 'Ewig' (fourth bar after Fig. 61). Britten and Shostakovich were both to remember *Das Lied von der Erde*, 'Der Abschied', 'Ewig' and the other worldly celesta's farewell. Britten wrote, 'I cannot understand it – it passes over me like a tidal wave – and that matters not a jot either, because it goes on for ever, even if it is never performed again – that final chord is printed on the atmosphere.'[19] 'I remember how he (Shostakovich) said . . . that the final movement of *Das Lied von der Erde* is the greatest thing of genius ever created in music.'[20] Shostakovich himself said, 'If I only had one hour left to live, and if I were able to listen to one record only, then I should choose the finale of *Das Lied von der Erde*.'[21]

The celesta's inherent capacity to give the impression of arrested time, its crystal translucency and its icy impersonality and isolation create a sonority which leads us into another sound dimension, to quote Stefan George's line, 'Ich fühle Luft von anderem Planeten'.

According to Edison Denisov, Shostakovich, for all his admiration for the score and its composer, once expressed gentle irony at the thought that 'Eternity in Mahler is presented by the celesta.'[22] In *Lady Macbeth of the Mtsensk District*, Shostakovich used the celesta in a different way. It is heard in the third scene of Act I after Katerina Lvovna's monologue and before Sergei's appearance in her bedroom (Fig. 160). Surely, its mundane context cannot detract from the fact that this celesta chord, with its C major tonality and the movement of its middle voice from E, via E♭, to D, and back to E (without the tonic C), represents a 'terrestrial' version of 'Ewig'? Shostakovich was actually writing *Lady Macbeth* just at the time (1930–32) when his closest friend Ivan Sollertinsky was working on a book about Mahler (1932); we should not underestimate the role Sollertinsky played in Shostakovich's enthusiasm for Mahler.

Shostakovich once again has recourse to the celesta in his next substantial work, that most Mahlerian of all his symphonies, the Fourth. And, needless to say, it appears in the coda of the final movement (Fig. 255). It is scored in Mahlerian fashion for ensemble (celesta with harp, timpani, double-bass, double-bassoon and strings); as in the coda of 'Der Abschied', the other instruments fall silent one by one, leaving the celesta alone with the strings. The celesta's final motif, a rising fourth A–D, whose open intonation has been interpreted by Marina Sabinina as an unanswered question,[23] enters

18 See SSLD: 129 (nn. 11–12), 139 (n. 31), 415, 496–7 (nn. 152–3) and 614 (n. 61).
19 Letter to Henry Boys (29 June 1937), in DMPR: 493.
20 Quoted in D. Gojowy, *Dmitri Schostakowitsch* (Reinbek: Gojowi, 1983): 64.
21 Quoted in: K. Meyer, op. cit.: 118.
22 Quoted in: D. Redepenning, 'Maler i Shostakovich' *Muzykal'naya Akademiya* 1 (1994): 169.
23 Marina Sabinina, *Shostakovich-simfonist* (Moscow: Muzyka Publishers, 1976): 114.

into dialogue with the concluding pages of *Das Lied*, as indeed does the Symphony's closing C minor tonality.

Very relevant here are the memoirs of Isaak Glikman, as well as Shostakovich's own highly emotive reflections on *Das Lied* in his letters to his friend.[24] For example, on 7 July 1963, while holidaying in Dilijan in Armenia (where Britten was to stay two years later), Dmitri Dmitrievich writes, 'I think constantly of Mahler's *Das Lied von der Erde*. My own *Lied von der Erde* is coming to fruition.'[25] Shostakovich was working at the time on his Thirteenth Symphony, although Glikman does not make any attempt to relate these words to it. For us, it is important that out of all the occasions when the celesta is used in the score of the Thirteenth Symphony, only once does it appear in a farewell context (the first movement, 'Babi Yar', in the fragment 'It seems to me I'm Anna Frank', Fig. 14). Here again Shostakovich comes close to Mahler.

The Fourteenth Symphony became his 'Symphony in Songs'. Its score reveals many clear allusions to *Das Lied von der Erde* and 'Der Abschied'. And here, in this world of associations, Shostakovich deftly drops in a reminiscence not so much of Katerina's heartfelt cry as of Grimes's dreamy impulse (cf. 'Lorelei', *Adagio*, 'He calls me', 'My soul is calm'). And although the music of the celesta is highly distinct from its figuration in *Peter Grimes* (end of Act II), none the less we feel the spirit of Britten's music. The addition of the vibraphone to the celesta points us even more firmly to Britten, who had used this timbre combination to such telling effect in Tadzio's leitmotif in *Death in Venice*. The Fifteenth Symphony confirms this associative link. Was this perhaps a (subconscious?) farewell from Shostakovich to one of his dearest and closest contemporary composers?

Looking at these reflecting mirrors and prisms of Britten, Mahler and Shostakovich, many new details come into focus, thus confirming the basic and well-known supposition: if in the 1930s and 1940s Britten assimilated Shostakovich's musical language in the style of Mahler,[26] then Shostakovich's late style betrays elements of Britten's musical language, again through a Mahlerian prism. Without Mahler a comparative study of the music of Britten and Shostakovich loses in dimension, depth and inherent meaning, since for both of them Mahler was the embodiment of eternal values, of that 'blessed inheritance' (Osip Mandelstam), and of that soul-scorching sense of the modern world.

Thus, the 'dream' theme in *Grimes* was viewed at the beginning of this article as something internally pluralistic. Its familiar and semantically significant segments and elements spill over into adjacent areas of significance,

---

24 *Pis'ma k drugu: Dmitri Shostakovich – Isaaku Glikmanu* (Saint Petersburg: Kompozitor and DSCH Publishers, 1993).

25 Ibid.: 189.

26 See DMBA: 71–7; Donald Mitchell, 'What do we know about Britten now?', in BC: 27–38; Ludmila Kovnatskaya, '*Russian Funeral* through Russian ears: aural impressions and some questions', *International Journal of Musicology* 2 (1993): 321–32.

and thus become enriched by association. The unique nature of the theme as musical text is very much a result of Britten's individual, yet organic, fusion of these elements.

The predominant element of the theme, the motif of the rising ninth, in both its semantic significance and graphic form, dictates the 'monological' type of lyrical expression, inherent to the theme as a whole. None the less, this text communicates in 'various voices', relating both to individual styles (Mahler, Shostakovich) and to historical styles (late- and post-Romanticism). In other words, under the veil of 'monology' we can perceive a 'polylogic' complexity and ramification of meanings. This effect serves to activate our perception and awaken greater possibilities of interpretation.

Translated by Nick Winter and the author

19

The Making of Auden's
Hymn for St Cecilia's Day

EDWARD MENDELSON

Auden wrote his *Hymn for St Cecilia's Day* in the summer of 1940 as an out-of-season birthday gift for Benjamin Britten, who was born on St Cecilia's Day, 22 November, in 1913. The words that Britten eventually set were not the words that Auden originally wrote, and the unpublished earlier versions of the poem offer a glimpse of Auden's theories of music, theories that were explicitly part of Auden's emerging Christian theology and implicitly part of his continuing conversation with Britten about Britten's art.

Any ode on St Cecilia's Day written by an English poet inevitably recalls Dryden's *A Song for St Cecilia's Day*, set first by Antonio Draghi and then, famously, by Handel. And any ode on St Cecilia's Day set by an English composer inevitably invites comparison with both Purcell's and Handel's odes to the patroness of musicians. When Auden wrote texts for Britten in 1939 and 1940, he evidently thought of Dryden as his predecessor and rival. In writing the libretto for *Paul Bunyan* late in 1939, he incorporated echoes of Dryden's and Purcell's *King Arthur*, which was – until *Paul Bunyan* was finished – the first and only libretto written by a great English poet and set by a great English composer. In offering Britten a St Cecilia's Day ode, Auden invited Britten to join him in rivalling in the twentieth century the great ode that Dryden and Handel had separately created in the seventeenth and eighteenth.[1]

In his systematic way, Auden began planning the poem that he titled *Ode for St Cecilia's Day* some time before he began writing it. Around 15 June 1940, he wrote to his friend Mrs A. E. Dodds to report progress on the book that he published in 1941 under the title *The Double Man* in America and *New Year Letter* in Britain: 'I'm getting on with my book, doing the notes to the long poem (partly verse, partly prose), then a sonnet sequence and an ode for St Cecilia's day' (Bodleian Library). The long poem was *New Year*

---

1   Britten had already considered the possibility of a piece in praise of St Cecilia's virtues, although not to a text by Auden, in 1935. His diary for 19 January notes: 'I'm having great difficulty in finding Latin words for a proposed "Hymn to St. Cecilia". Spend morning hunting'; and later in the month, on the 25th: 'I have the scheme but no notes yet for my St. Cecilia Hymn'. See DMPR: 939.

Letter; the sonnet sequence was *The Quest*. He included both of these in *The Double Man*, and at one point he apparently also planned to include in the book both the St Cecilia's Day Ode and his radio play *The Dark Valley*, for which Britten had written incidental music. Sometime in the summer or autumn of 1940 he wrote out a list of titles that is clearly a sketch of the contents of the book: 'Letter/Notes/Play/Sonnets/Ode'.[2]

Probably three weeks later, in early July, he finished his first version of the poem and posted it to Britten, with a note at the end of the manuscript: 'Here is the Ode as promised.'[3] When Britten read it, he asked Auden to add to the text. Auden was then summering in Magnolia, Massachusetts, where Britten and Peter Pears planned to visit him, and he wrote to Britten on 15 July 1940: 'Of course I shall be delighted too to enlarge St Cecilia; I was only afraid of making her too fat. I will wait though till you come and I can discuss with you exactly what is best.'[4]

Britten did not visit at this time, but Auden wrote to him again around 31 July 1940: 'Have been expecting you now for many days. Here is another movement for the Cecilia Ode. I tried to do yet another but it didn't come off. If you really need it, though, I'll try again.'[5] Britten and Pears finally visited him in late August and early September, where the final version of the text took shape.

Much of Auden's first completed version of the poem, the version sent to Britten in early July 1940, disappeared in later revision. This first text exists in two forms. A fair copy is in a spiral-bound notebook now in the Kurt Weill Foundation for Music in New York; it differs only slightly from the fair copy that Auden sent Britten and that is now in the Berg Collection. The version sent to Britten in is three parts. In the Weill Foundation notebook, the text is in two parts; there, the first part consists of Parts I and III of the version sent to Britten, and the second part (in short unrhymed quatrains) is the same as Part II in the version sent to Britten. The text that follows is the one sent to Britten; the notes list the more important variants from the earlier version:

Song for St Cecilia's Day
Part I
(Chorus, solo and orchestra)

Chorus. Dear daughter of our double misery,
        Whole innocence begotten by our crime,
        Freedom released by our captivity,
        O timeless joy of all who weep in time,
        Our wish for heaven as we plunge to hell,

---

2   W. H. Auden and Chester Kallman, *Libretti and other Dramatic Writings by W. H. Auden 1939–1973*, ed. Edward Mendelson (London: Faber and Faber, 1993): 741.
3   Manuscript in the Berg Collection, New York Public Library.
4   Postcard in the Berg Collection; quoted in DMPR: 1039.
5   Letter in the Berg Collection; quoted in DMPR: 1039.

Our doubt when we believe in our disgrace,
O deep vow of return, O long embrace
Of those who bid eternally farewell,
O look into our lives, release, foretell.[6]

Solo. O dear white children, casual as birds,
Playing among the ruined languages,
So small beside their large confusing words,
So gay against the greater silences
Of dreadful things you did. O hang your head,
Impetuous child with the tremendous brain,
O weep, child, weep. O weep away the stain,
Lost innocent who wished your lover dead,
Weep for the lives your wishes never led.

Chorus. Pure song whose creatures cannot wish to fall
In your calm spaces unafraid of weight,
Where Sorrow is herself, forgetting all
The gaucheness of her adolescent state,
And Hope within the altogether strange
From every outworn image is released,
And Dread born whole and normal like a beast
Into a world of truths that never change,
Restore our fallen day, O re-arrange.

Solo. Descend into your night of tribulation
Take the cold hand of terror for a guide
O hear in the black pool of desolation
The nameless Horror roaring for a bride;
Approach the foetor of its wild unrest.
And as the huge deformed head rears to kill,
Echo its craving with a clear 'I Will';
And wake, a child in the rose-garden, pressed
Sobbing and happy, to your lover's breast.

Chorus. O cry created as the bow of sin
Is drawn across our trembling violin.

Solo. O weep child, weep. O weep away the stain.

Chorus. O sentence that our hearts drum out to still
The insolence of our anarchic will[7]

Solo. That what has been may never be again.

Chorus. O flute that throbs with the thanksgiving breath
Of convalescents on the shores of death.

---

6   In the Weill Foundation notebook, this line reads: 'Bring us clear water from your wishing well.'
7   In the Weill Foundation notebook: 'O law drummed out by hearts against the still/Long winter of our intellectual will.'

Solo.   O bless the freedom that you never chose.

Chorus. O trumpets that unguarded children blow
         About the fortress of their inner foe

Solo.   O wear your tribulation like a rose.

Part II
(solo)

I cannot grow
I have no shadow
To run away from
I only play.

I cannot err
There is no creature
Whom I belong to,
Whom I could wrong

I am defeat
Any defeat when it
Knows it can do nothing
By suffering.

All you have lived through
Dancing because you
No longer need it
For any deed.

I shall never be
Different. Love me.

Part III
(chorus)

Open your gates, discover us, Daughter of Song;
   O comprehend our defeat.
Attend the festivals where sorrow shows herself; visit
   the attics of the shivering self-isolated spirits.
Seek out the mute; who famish in the wilderness of
   an inarticulate silence.
Seek out the deaf; immured within the noises of rage
   and envy.[8]
Seek out the fearful who have learnt a safer life by heart;
   O give them back their doubt.
Seek out the humble; O whisper them salutation
   and comfort,
Those solitary devoted lives; upon whose unseen Glory
   depends all human greatness.
Go forth, O Daughter of Song; go towards life.

8   In the Weill Foundation notebook: 'within the noises of their anger'.

O gather the societies together; gather them to the dance.
For what the heart-beat of a mother promises her
    unborn child, your rhythm, shall repeat; that
    the otherness of the universe is not against us.
And your harmony is a re-assurance: that, though
    we are always solitary, we are never abandoned,
And your beauty, O daughter, a witness;
    to the reality of the Required.
O gather the finite creatures into that choir;
    through whom the Uninhibited rejoices for ever.
That its determined moment of gladness; may possess
    each tiny resonant structure,
Its life be echo; and its nature praise,
Acknowledging the attributes; of one immortal,
    one infinite substance.

The internal balance of this version is drastically different from that of the final poem, but its themes and arguments are essentially the same. Part I praises music in terms that identify it as an analogue of the condition of forgiveness and grace: it exists because of the Fall, and exists in order to make it possible for the Fall to be overcome. It points toward freedom, and is itself free, because we are not free and because we look away from freedom.

The nature of music's freedom is the subject of its own quiet credo in Part II. There it says, in a learned pun, that it can only *play*, because it can not be put to use either to hurt or connect, because it can achieve nothing through the suffering that human beings must endure in order to change, but can only be itself, in a world outside of time. Yet it is not sufficient unto itself. It asks a version of the pardon that it gives: when it asks for love in its simple demand, it asks to be loved for what it is now, and not, as in much human love, loved for some promise of what it might be someday.

In the opening stanzas of Part I, music is praised by a chorus that stands for everyone, while the responsive solo (identified in the Weill Foundation notebook as a soprano) is the voice, not quite the voice of music, but of Cecilia, commanding the repentance and courage that she herself makes possible by offering images and models. In the background of the dialogue that begins 'O cry created' are the illustrations of the emotional power of music in Dryden's *A Song for St Cecilia's Day*, but where Dryden praises music's power to raise and quell passions, Auden, in the midst of his return to the Anglican Church of his childhood, praises music's power to prompt self-knowledge, to quell doubt, to integrate the recalcitrant self with the world. Dryden's trumpets, on the Day of Judgement, will untune the sky. Auden's trumpets, on this day, topple the walls that exclude forgiveness and love.

Because music can topple those walls, it can bring about the unity that is praised in long unrhymed lines of Part III – the same kind of long lines, with biblical rhythms and strong caesuras, that Auden had earlier used for the choruses of his plays. Here music can command inner and outer peace because its harmony and order are a model of what that peace would be like if the world could achieve it, and its continuity and coherence are a sign of an ultimate completeness and unity that the poem describes in explicitly theological language.

In the Weill Foundation notebook, Auden wrote the first version of the poem on the right-hand pages of his notebook. On the left-hand pages, facing the pages with the first part of the first section, is a fair copy of the five untitled stanzas that constitute the additional 'movement' that Auden posted to Britten on 31 July 1940. He evidently intended these stanzas to precede the text he had written earlier; the final version of the poem, devised in August or September, opens with a revised version of these added stanzas. In writing the new stanzas, Auden belatedly remembered to allude to the season in which Cecilia's feast occurs. The text that follows is the fair copy sent to Britten, and now in the Berg Collection:

> The cold of Autumn comes on the water,
> And winds are bitter and the weather grey,
> But let our voices with loud rejoicing
> Remember saintly Cecilia's day.
>
> In a garden shady this holy lady
> With happy cadence poured forth her song.
> In celebration of her Creator
> To whom both the day and the night belong.[9]
> By ocean's margin this innocent virgin[10]
> Built also an organ to enlarge her prayer
> And with notes tremendous from her great engine
> Thundered out on the Roman air.[11]
>
> Blond Aphrodite rose up excited,
> Moved to delight by the melody,
> White as an orchid, she rode quite naked
> In an oyster-shell on top of the sea
> And athletic Apollo in his rocky hollow
> Who till then had been god of the musical art
> Swore he'd never felt a touch so gentle
> As now was melting his expert heart.
>
> Her hymns of thanksgiving astounded the evening
> And brought peace between all created things,[12]
> Bears and beggars and toads and tigers
> And owls and eagles and cats and kings.
> At sounds so entrancing the angels dancing
> Came out of their trance into time again,
> And around the wicked in Hell's abysses
> The huge flame flickered and eased their pain.

9 In the Weill Foundation notebook: 'To whom unnumbered worlds belong.'
10 In the Weill Foundation notebook: 'modest virgin'; and in the version sent to Britten, before being deleted and replaced with the text above, 'clever virgin'.
11 In the Weill Foundation notebook: 'Possessed with thunder the trembling air.'
12 In the Weill Foundation notebook: 'living things'.

> Blessed Cecilia, appear in visions
> To all musicians, appear and inspire.
> Translated Daughter, come down and startle
> Composing mortals with immortal fire.[13]

These stanzas, in which music alters the world of time, do not contradict the original stanzas in which music stands outside the world of time and change. But here music prompts change within the world of time, and the change is specifically the great historical change of the Incarnation of Christ. The flames of hell retreat as in the Harrowing of Hell. The efficient and expert Apollo is astounded by the mercy and gentleness of the new dispensation, and the Olympian gods, freed from the heartlessness of their power by the arrival of the first merciful God, feel a delight that was hitherto unavailable to a Greek pantheon that lacked hope. Auden's equation of Cecilia with Christ, in its daring baroque extravagance, deliberately recalls the English Baroque that began at the time of Dryden and ended with the death of Handel.

Probably no further revision took place until Auden and Britten worked together in August and September 1940 and gave the poem its final form. Much of the original Parts I and III and a substantial portion of the stanzas added afterward were dropped, and the interplay between solo and chorus from 'O cry created' to 'O wear your tribulation' was moved to the end. Auden and Britten worked from the original manuscript, on which Auden deleted the first and fourth stanzas of the original Part I, and placed a circled '1' next to the second stanza, a circled '2' next to the third stanza (after first marking them, respectively, '2' and '1'), and a circled '3' next to the dialogue in couplets and single lines at the end of this part. All these became the basis of Part III of the finished text, but not until Auden further revised the two stanzas that he had chosen to retain. A pencil draft of the revised versions is in a notebook now in the Berg Collection, and a typescript of the finished Part III is among Auden's letters to Britten in the same collection. The original Part III disappeared entirely.

Auden, always economical, reused some of the lines that he abandoned. The solo's command to descend into the night of tribulation reappeared, with minor changes, in *For the Time Being*, the Christmas oratorio that Auden wrote in the hope that it would be set by Britten. The line about the attributes of one immortal, one infinite substance found its way into the 'Epilogue' to *The Double Man*. As for the final text of the Cecilia Ode, it can be found in any edition of Auden's collected poems, but readers of this book will prefer to hear it – as Auden intended – sung to the music that Britten completed in March 1942, on his return journey from America to England. Except for two minor excerpts from *For the Time Being* and 'Out on the lawn' from *Look, Stranger!* (in the *Spring Symphony*), the *Hymn to St Cecilia's Day* was the last of Auden's poems that Britten set. When their friendship ended, so did the second, and still the last, collaboration between a great writer of English poetry and a great composer of English music.

---

13 In the Weill Foundation notebook: 'And touch these mortals with immortal fire.'

20

Edinburgh Diary 1968

KATHLEEN MITCHELL

Wednesday, 14 August 1968

Don & I have come to Edinburgh a day or two before Ben & Peter to open the house & have a look round. Tonight, we're ensconced in a lofty ceilinged bedroom (double bed – bad start!) & the empty rooms around us are all lofty & lovely. The house obviously belongs to a Fettes school master & reminds one of the Housemaster's House. There's a coat of arms & heraldic reaches into Goldilocks [i.e. the Goldie-Scotts] history hanging on the landing. But the best part of the house is the garden & the view of it from the kitchen. A soft green lawn & low grey wall with a magic door in it leading to a kitchen garden. I've seen two plump artichokes, picked armfuls of sweetpeas & collected a few pretty branches for the kitchen & downstairs sitting room. There's a workmanlike rather shabby sitting room downstairs which will be splendid for us to work in. Upstairs rather a charming grand salon with a Bechstein upright which Ben & Peter can use, & a choice of bedrooms. We've left a quiet room for B. & P. at the back. The main road passes the door but traffic has slowed down this evening.

Yesterday at this time we were in our little bunks on the train. The Motorail works splendidly (except for execrable food – an overworked dour little Scots waiter who was run off his feet serving tired salad & lukewarm coffee). There's rather a splendid view from the Caledonian Road station – it may of course be of the prison, but there's a church spire & industrial chimneys as well and a grey & pink enchantment in the view, even in the rain. English families going on holiday are always interesting to observe. One mother had her two children in the ubiquitous jeans & denim jackets & it was very difficult to make out whether they were boys or girls or one of each. However, it soon was apparent that the long-haired bold-faced one was the son – his feet were bigger & he had a definite proprietorial air with his mother – and the soft-faced gentle creature was the daughter. I suppose they were 12 & 10, or 13 & 11. The boy amused me as he showed off so, lolling back & making faces & exaggerated gestures – all to impress his mother. O Oedipus.

It rained all night & we slept, soundly or fitfully according to our several versions. The steward brought in tea & biscuits at 6.30 & the morning indeed looked grey & bleak. We were in a siding, facing one of those Scottish stone walls. I'd forgotten about the grey & its particular quality, but there was plenty of it in Perth. The station itself good old Scots baronial. We drove smartly to the station hotel & had an excellent breakfast of kippers. Don even went so far as having porridge – just to show we really were in Scotland.

It's a beautiful drive to Edinburgh from Perth, through green forested glens & past the charming Loch Leven. Don spied an unusual white house which looked Mackintoshian, so we drove off in quest of it & found ourselves driving through a farmyard with a wonderful beehive barn to a Scottish castle – tall, narrow, turreted, but all white & serenely overlooking the distant hills. A pretty house, but not Mackintosh though it's easy to see where he drew his inspiration from.

It was exciting to drive over the Forth Bridge – the first time we have. Beautiful views of the river & the shore. The head winds must be strong in the winter. And then on into Edinburgh to search for Inverleith Gardens, which turn out to be part of Ferry Road. Same old grey stone, but a green garden, thank goodness & it may be that the sun will shine tomorrow.

Thursday, 15 August

A grey blustery day. Where is the fine weather that Scotland has been enjoying while we have been washed away in the South? We found a note from Teresa who is going to come in to clean. She left a phone number, but when I rang it turned out be be a building site where no women work or have worked. 'The Goldie-Scotts have known me for 20 years and I have never let them down,' she said in her note. Not that she had known them. Not a democratic country apparently!

However, without Teresa but with the hope of her arriving some time we got on with our shopping & breathing life into the house. The Goldie-Scott children (4 of them) all hang in romantic *Women's Pictorial* style in our sitting room. The artist, one Lena Alexander, has one prettified style for all her sitters & the faces are without any character. Perhaps their rooms will give off more of their ambience.

At lunchtime a shaft of sunshine appeared & we drove to Granton along the coast towards Cramond & had a picnic looking over the Forth. The trees by the water & the green grass with the view of the hills beyond are very fine. Driven back to the house by rain. Put on the heating in the sitting room & enjoyed Scotch pancakes & tea. Don made lots of phone calls. Rather a dreary evening to go out into, but we ventured as far as Daniel Brown's in George Street. Not a thing in Rae Mackintosh's window except single copies of the librettos of *The Prodigal Son*, *Curlew River* and *The Burning Fiery Furnace*. Perhaps he doesn't know the Festival starts in 3 days' time!

We've made up a diary of rehearsals & performances. The first thing I looked for was for a day or two free of concerts! There is ONE only – Sunday, 25th August. I hope we can keep it for an excursion.

Friday, 16 August

Up early in glorious weather. There's a marvellous view from the back of the house. We feel we are preparing for a royal visit or command performance! Don has shoals of invitations for Ben & Peter. Flowers have arrived from the Festival Director & there's an air of flurry while the phone rings constantly. We wonder how it will be when they are here!

A charming encounter with Mr Johnstone, the fishmonger, who calls here twice a week with fish fresh from the quay (?Leith) in his van. He cut me 2lb from the best part of a salmon (poor fish had only been out of the water for 3 hours) & I got stocked up with kippers & herrings which I couldn't resist. Mr J. walked into the kitchen, found the appropriate dishes & told me about his fish, his family, Edinburgh & Scotland in a few broad minutes.

We were just eating the herrings lightly cooked in butter (absolutely delicious) when Rachel [MacFarlane] arrived. Great relief all round. Her fish was added to the pan & we all felt at home & happy with each other within moments. More flowers, telegrams, phone messages, shopping, menu planning, house arranging & then in a burst of glorious sunshine Ben & Peter & Graham [Nicholson] arrived. All in good shape after the 400-mile drive (how is it further from Aldeburgh to Scotland than from London? must look at the atlas). B. & P. delighted with the house & garden & Scotch pancakes for tea. These last are going to become a pernicious habit & death to weight-watchers. A consultation over bedrooms resulted in Ben finally deciding that he'd prefer the room with the large bed in front of the house on the traffic side! So Rachel & I did a big move round & made up the beds. Peter liked the idea of having the bed-sit (I'm sure a student stays here – the style is different from the rest of the house).

Ben & Don off to the King's Theatre for a *Peter Grimes* rehearsal at 6 pm, while Peter worked & rested. We all met for a late supper – Rachel's first delicious meal – (the salmon I'd bought in the morning). Ben tried to conceal his anxiety over the *P.G.* They were both low-spirited about the rehearsal, & particularly about the young man singing Peter Grimes – Richard Cassilly – who not only has a bad cold but is ill-suited to the part & says he'll never be able to sing it. Ben is inclined to agree & looks exceedingly rueful.

Saturday, 17 August

Saturday morning found us all having breakfast at 8.30 with the smiling Rachel complimented on excellent Scottish kippers (from Mr J.). A morning on work & schedules for rehearsals: roses from Tertia [Liebenthal] for Peter. It's fortunate that the Goldie Locks have so many vases in their armoury. Colin [Graham] to lunch, he having lost the way only had ½ hour to eat his. The first concert tomorrow – *Voices for Today*, Violin Concerto & the *Spring Symphony*. There were two rehearsals for this concert at the Usher Hall & another *Peter Grimes* rehearsal – first night Monday.

Such a beautiful evening that Rachel & I drove to the coast & to the Forth Bridge. Stupendous views. Edinburgh is a beautiful city.

No one in till late for supper. We had cauliflower cheese but decided not to eat cooked cheese so late another time. Meal times in the evenings are going to be very flexible. Most evening receptions after concerts have been refused, but tomorrow, Sunday, we all go to the Scottish Academy after the opening Britten Concert. We shall be able to look at the Boudins while we drink the champagne (if any).

Sunday, 18 August

Sunday rehearsal 10–1 left everyone famished for roast beef. It was a most beautiful day, brilliant sun, cloudless skies, dramatic shadow on the castle hill. Goldie Locks never seem to sit in the garden – there are no garden chairs in sight, except an extraordinary camping contraption of table & seat. We must buy a chair or two tomorrow.

A little rest & then a drive to the Forth Bridge because I wanted everyone to see N. Queensferry & gaze at the Firth through the old bridge & the new. A tiny settlement of people – now not all fisherfolk apparently as a betting shop counts itself as the only amenity beside the pub. The new bridge is delicate & slender. I like the old bridge with its Meccano No. 10 design.

Back to dress for the opening concert. Armed with emergency store of whisky for the interval. Peter came on later, so we four went ahead. Not all sitting together. There seems to have been a muddle over the seats. It was amusing that Ben was not sitting where Kertész expected him to be, so he solemnly bowed & waved his hand at the end of *Voices* [*for Today*] towards Peter Diamand and Miss Rosenberg who were sitting next to Graham & me. Arthur Oldham has done wonders with the chorus & the boys' choir. They looked cherubic in tartan kilts & white shirts & sang superbly. Very strong in the *Spring Symphony*. Ben had been very nervous about the Violin Concerto. In fact, listening to a performance is as much agony as performing or conducting – perhaps more. In the event Yehudi [Menuhin] managed quite well & looked as if he loved the music. My first sound of the Violin Concerto – it is an amazingly difficult piece full of virtuoso passages. At the interval Ben told us the sad story of the man for whom it was written. He seems to have fallen on to stony times. We all managed to find the whisky room at the interval & then the joy of hearing the *Spring Symphony*. Peter in marvellous voice; Helen [Watts] dark & vibrant & the Dutch girl, Elly Ameling, tremendously bright & vivacious. There was a mad cheer at the end & Ben took several calls to a great upsurge of applause & cheering.

It's a great thing here to have somewhere to park the car near to the Concert Hall & Don has been clever & got passes which require the police to give us every possible assistance. It seems to work wonderfully.

Later to the Scottish Academy where the pictures were more interesting to look at than the guests. It was fun to see the Scottish Academicians in their robes, with splendid flat hats & gold chains.

Peter knew a lot of the painters & has one or two McTaggart paintings at the Red House. So he had a special hug of welcome from Sir William & Lady M. Lady Rosebery in full fig and full of raillery. She told Ben 'what fun' it was to have the recording of the *War Requiem* . . . his smile didn't slip perceptibly! She called Don a 'cad' for speaking to Lord & Lady Harewood at Hamburg! However, cad or not, we've all been invited to tea later in the week.

Monday, 19 August

Monday: a rehearsal day with *Peter Grimes* tonight.

A quiet morning with Ben & Don off to a press conference at 12.20. Peter wandering along George St. to find a present for Colin tonight & calling in at Grants & the Wotruba Exhibition. The *Winterreise* rehearsal in the afternoon. We heard definitely that Cassilly won't sing tonight – a great relief for Ben. A dressing-up occasion with promise of an interval room with some whisky!

Rain fell in torrents in time to soak everyone in Edinburgh – 3 first nights: *Peter Grimes* at the King's Theatre, LSO with Kertész at the Usher Hall and *Hamlet* at the Assembly Hall.

But inside the theatre all was excitement & expectancy: an absolutely crowded house. The young man singing Grimes was really very good & he was totally involved in the part, looked absolutely right & even sounded right most of the time. Colin's production is fine, especially in the crowd scenes. I thought of Don's talk at the Battersea Library about *Peter Grimes* as the name came ringing out – the first words sung in the opera & the last hysterical sobbing from Peter Grimes as he repeats the name that has tracked him down in the manhunt. Ben wasn't especially displeased with it all, but there was no doubt that the Scottish Opera had a great success scored with the audience. So we all came home after Ben had taken six or seven curtain calls to vociferous applause & had a quiet cold supper here at Rosetta. No party attending because of the *Winterreise* tomorrow.

A lot of talk about the performance. Ben really very gay, & rather hoping this young man will do the other performances.

We saw Beth [Reiss] & [her son] Nicholas at the opera & Maria. Beth had driven up from Aldeburgh specially & is coming to lunch tomorrow after the *Winterreise*.

Tuesday, 20 August

A great air of expectancy in the morning. Ben on Complan but Peter in good spirits. Freemasons' Hall packed to overflowing with queues of people waiting for returned tickets. A marvellously sunny morning. It's not possible to say how extraordinarily moving this performance was. Although I have heard Ben & Peter perform this cycle on several occasions it seemed almost too painful in its spiritual despair. There could hardly have been a dry eye in the audience. Poor Maria sitting beside me, found it hard to restrain her tears, especially in 'Einsamkeit'. Ben played as if he were the frozen-fingered old man in 'Der Leiermann'. Everyone was carried away & the applause enormous.

A tremendously light-hearted lunch because nothing more to worry about today. Peter Diamand & Maria coming in at 5 when a call to Moscow is going to try to find out what has happened to Slava Richter from whom Ben has had a strange telegram warning him of a possible breakdown in his appearance Thursday week in the Piano Concerto. *Hamlet* tonight with Tom Courtenay playing Hamlet & this afternoon a drive along the coast.

Still sunny this afternoon after Ben & Peter had had a little rest so we drove off through Leith & Portobello & meant to reach North Berwick but actually only got as far as a nature reserve where all those sound in wind & limb strode off across the marshes to the sea. Lots of interesting birds but no one had remembered to bring the glasses so there was only wild guessing & counter-guessing. It was sad to have to rush back to drive to Edinburgh & in fact we were ten minutes late for Peter Diamand who was due at 5 pm. No signs of Peter fortunately but hardly had we dropped our coats than the bell rang & he appeared, rather reproachful. However the call booked to Moscow wasn't lost. There was an incredible muddle ringing through to find if it had already come through, re-ordering it, cancelling it because of 2 hours' delay on the line to Moscow & in between all this the original call came through, quite undeterred by orders made & countermanded. It makes me think a HOT LINE is a real necessity. One can imagine declarations of peace or war going through by default otherwise. However, the news from Moscow is not reassuring. The Richters are away on a 'holiday' presumably to try to recover from whatever Slava is suffering from. Peter Diamand very put out by this & by Maria being there for tea. He made his escape quickly telling Peter on the way out that he was not able to make social calls with Maria. A most difficult situation as they were together last night at *Peter Grimes*. This seems a fatal city for marriages, especially for the Directors'.

However, we all had a reviving drop of Crabbies (a whisky Don has discovered) & launched out to *Hamlet*, where the Manager received his distinguished guests & invited us all to his room at the interval where the other distinguished chaps were Prof. & Mrs Barenboim, papa & mama of Daniel (who is aptly named if ever anyone was) & Gervase de Peyer and a Scottish couple whose name I can't recall – v. vivacious wife who talked to Peter & a distinguished-looking husband, both introduced as patrons of the arts. Ben got caught by Daddy Barenboim & barely survived.

We all enjoyed *Hamlet* enormously. It was very plainly done & one had to strain one's ears to hear all the words as Tom Courtenay gave such a self-questioning performance. But he looked wonderfully right & was marvellous in the great scene with his mother. The King & Gertrude very well cast.

Talked a lot about the play at supper afterwards. Don took us all out to the Café Royal, Rachel too, so the whole family had an outing & our over-worked washing-up machine had a rest.

Wednesday, 21 August

Czechoslovakia invaded during the night.

The news came on the radio & has left us all stunned & bewildered. Ben thinking particularly of Slava [Rostropovich] & Galya [Vishnevskaya]. How on earth can one go on thinking about concerts & planning menus & arranging flowers when this terrifying thing is happening? Don very good, & a rock of confidence for Ben who worked at home all the morning. Rehearsals in the afternoon at Leith T.H. for the Thursday concert with Dieter Fischer-Dieskau & John Alldis's choir. Peter & Don went to see the Rennie Mackintosh exhibition. I stayed at home wanting to listen to hourly bulletins & did manage this during the afternoon, but all the news was bad.

On the practical side, Don had a fairly testing time at the rehearsal with worry about a standing platform for the choir & the sound being muffled by curtains. However by the evening it had all been resolved (by dint of telephone pressure on Don's part) & the evening rehearsal went very well. Six hours' rehearsal in one day is a heavy load. Ben very tired, but wonderful at the rehearsal – calm & tremendously patient & courteous & encouraging. What a magnificent voice Dieter has! The *Cantata Misericordium* is going to be marvellous. We ate late, trying not to talk too much about Prague but thinking about it all the time.

Some amusing things have happened. Ben spent two nights in the big bed & then decided it was after all too noisy a room, so we switched round bed-rooms again, flying to & fro with shirts & sheets & shoes. I think we shall all end up wearing each other's clothes. The bathroom door doesn't lock very well so caution has to be exercised in bursting in. 'Come in, but Not Now', the classic story Peter told of ? who was interrupted when sitting on the loo. I've started to call Don Ben, & Ben Peter & Graham Brian & so we are all likely to emerge from this period with some change of name if not personality.

Late supper is the best time for talk about music. Ben talks a lot & tells interesting stories which Don will remember better than I can.

Wednesday, 28 August

Mr Dubček: 'We need even more order & discipline'.

The weeping Mr Dubček, returning to Prague to appeal to his people for restraint to avoid further bloodshed the main item of news, & the main topic of conversation at breakfast. Ben & Peter inclined to equate Russian occupa-tion of Czechoslavakia with the American 'occupation' of Bentwaters [USAF

base near Aldeburgh]. So we had a lively discussion. The only hope is that
the more sophisticated Czechs in their greater political maturity will pull off
the incredible feat of maintaining a communist country that cares about
individual freedoms. How wonderful if such a development were possible!

The ruthless use of power, of terrorism & gangsterism was the theme of
Arturo Ui, the powerful Brecht play that Rachel & I saw this afternoon. A
brilliant idea to satirize the rise of Hitler in the setting of a Chicago gangster
who corners the market in cauliflowers! The play full of verbal play &
Shakespeare misquoted – & a Marlowe 'Is this the face that launched a
thousand tricks?' However, in the circumstances it was almost too brutal to
bear, especially the Dullfeet assassination (Dollfuss). The Glasgow Citizens'
Theatre an excellent company & Leonard Rossiter a brilliant Ui.

We rushed back to find everyone slightly on edge & the eggs boiling
timelessly. The rehearsal for tomorrow (Amadeus) hadn't gone too well.
But tea & eggs & Scotch pancakes restored morale. Ben & Don & I off to
St Cuthbert's Church for Slava's recital (two Bach suites & Britten): Peter to
rehearse at 6:15 for *The Prodigal Son*. A marvellous recital with a truly
exciting performance of Ben's Cello Suite. He looked terribly pleased. The
Serenata & the *March* most wonderfully played. Don was annoyed because
no reserved seats had been kept & we had to find side aisle seats, but
we heard very well! It's a strange church – really rather unpleasing with a
marble bas-relief of the Last Supper behind the altar. Marvellous views
through the side aisle doors of the castle hill with its dark green sides & grey
fortress. As I came out I heard a blues being played in the Festival Gardens.
A strange world of sound after the Bach & the Britten.

Rachel met me & we went to St Mary's to help Rod [Roderick Biss,
Production Manager at Faber Music] for ½ hour with the sale of the
librettos. A misty night. There's been no sun since Sunday. The cast of the
P.S. very lively outside the church. Peter saying 'boo' to Rachel from his
cowled head! We sold a lot of librettos & brought Rod back for a drink & a
sandwich.

The Goldie Scotts have arrived back. Everyone very nervous lest they
disturb our peaceful occupation of the house. I can't see 4 children & a dog
& 2 adults being entirely invisible!

Ben has felt better today & seems more cheerful. The Prague business
weighs heavily on us all. Slava had requested a prayer & blessing at the
church tonight, which was simply & movingly offered by the rector before
& after the recital.

The Cello Suite No. 1 an amazing piece. I especially was excited by the
Serenata & the *March*. The cello speaks in all tongues. Slava was apparently
transfixed by *The Prodigal Son* tonight to which everyone went after the
Cello Suite. Rachel kindly collected me & it was heaven to come home quietly
& sit down for ½ hour.

The Prodigal Son (1968): Peter Pears as The Tempter

Thursday, 29 August

Concert day.

A bad beginning for Ben who hadn't slept. However, Complan and Don kept him in one piece & they both went off early to rehearse – a balance test as this morning's concert is being broadcast. The Amadeus played with Ben a Purcell cantata 'When Night her purple veil' – & Don was turner-over-in-chief, a nerve-shattering task as he had to turn for Norbert as well as Ben on the piano. The Quartet went very well & we were all well prepared for the Blake songs after the interval. Dieter's English seems much better – even 'wrath' came through well. Christina Pugel (Dieter's fiancée) sat next to me and I introduced her to Galya & Slava in very bad Aldeburgh Deutsch. However, she speaks German so communication was instant, though not overwarm.

Peter had a *Prodigal Son* performance at 6.30 & Ben was rehearsing in the afternoon, so there was not much rest for anyone. Rod & Dorothy [Rod's wife] couldn't come over to sell librettos tonight so Rachel & I went to do it. But unfortunately everything worked badly. The first performance (*P.S.*) was splendidly arranged: another tremendous performance – Peter, the Tempter (his last performance), John Shirley-Quirk, the Father & Bernard Dickerson the Younger Son. Rachel & I were right up at the front. The best positions though are further back. Afterwards Rachel rushed home to put on the soup & I came on with Graham & Peter. All the silver in the cash tin showered over Peter as the tin skidded off the car shelf as Graham cornered sharply on the corner of Arboretum. P. was deluged with half-crowns & shillings but was very sweet about it. What a marvellous man Peter is. A noble person, full of charity, wisdom, kindness, but full of fun & perception. His care for Ben is extraordinary. He is never over fussy or obtrusive, but is ever there, as a guardian angel, alert & responsive.

The libretto business for the second performance broke down because of time. Rachel & Graham kindly went back but missed the opening of the doors. I stayed back with Peter to have the supper ready for Ben & Don who were at a rehearsal till after 9.30. It was idiotic of me to have left the church. I should have sat outside on my chair & sold for the *B.F.F.* & then gone to the performance. As it is, I've missed the *B.F.F.* which is sad, & annoyed Don by not organizing the libretto sales properly.

Friday, 30 August

The weather has let us down this week. Even in the rare intervals between rehearsals & concerts, there is no encouragement to go into the garden. The Prague situation dominates all our thinking. After breakfast is the time for most lively discussion. Galya & Slava are coming to supper tonight, after Slava's second recital at St Cuthbert's. There are rehearsals all day for Ben & Peter. The Kubelik telegram has caused great perturbation. Ben didn't sign it, as he wasn't in favour of severing the life lines between artists in Britain & in the invading countries. It's very clear that Slava Rostropovich is as anguished over the invasion as we all are. Giulini seems to have been one of the 36 musicians signing but what happens, then, to the *War Requiem* & Galya? The grey weather doesn't help us all. I think Ben may write to Kubelik to explain his attitude which is wholesale condemnation of the invasion & all Russian tactics but belief in keeping cultural & intellectual links strongly forged between individuals, who might between them be able to make some impression on a country's policy. The Chicago Democratic Convention out-rages filled the papers this morning – another terrible inhumanity & threat. Everyone feels very tired today: the skies are grey; the castle is blotted out. Hope for the Czechs is blotted out: hope in America is fading. On a less important level, Slava Richter is definitely not coming to fulfil his engage-ment for Th. 5th (Ben's Piano Concerto & Mozart K. 450). This also means that he won't be at Aldeburgh for the two w'end concerts (the '48'). Consternation all round & many messages to Stephen Reiss. All this with rehearsals going on for Sunday & Monday.

I don't know why I seem to have absolutely no time to write a postcard or go shopping. Did manage a brief dash to Highland Industries & the hair-dresser this pm. Bought a beautiful rug of soft heathery colours & sent one to the newly Starcross[1] weds (Tom Jones). Ben slept for a couple of hours so we had only half the cello programme. Slava played Ben's second Cello Suite after the interval. The two Bach suites took a tremendous long time & we hung about in the grey green churchyard, feeling rather disembodied our-selves in the cold wind, before seeking refuge in the back of the church. Mollie & Peter [du Sautoy] have arrived, looking very tired, but pleased with their hotel & happy to be away on holiday for a few days. The car, waiting for Slava (which was intended to take Galya to Arthur Oldham's house for a rehearsal), was ordered to arrive at 7 pm & waited till 7.45. Then came a desperate message that it was having to leave for another job at 8. Fortunately Don managed to get out in time to prevent the driver leaving, & I hopped out too to placate him. In the end, Galya was safely sent off with typewritten instructions where to go & a letter to Arthur to bring her back. Slava & Ben in our car off home very happy & pleased with the perfor-mance. The *Ciaccona* came off marvellously. Slava told me (before) that he thought this Second Suite more wonderful than the first. The first was wonderful, but it exacted the limit from the instrument but the second explored all the beautiful sounds.

We had an amusing few moments bringing Slava into the house & giving him a drop of Don's special Laphroaig whisky which he had bought as a particular (& rare) treat. Slava drank a glassful straight down, as if it was water, & poured out another glass & downed that, all the while roaring with

---

1   Starcross, the comprehensive school in Islington where KM was headmistress for ten
    years.

laughter, removing his jacket, stripping a banana & eating it, detaching a bunch of grapes & dropping them down his throat & finally biting juicily into a peach. Another glass of Laphroaig & he went gaily upstairs with Ben to rehearse the Cello Sonata! We had all watched awestruck, sipping our own little glasses of Crabbie & Laphroaig in our usual tentative Anglo-Saxon fashion! Rachel's ducks looked marvellous & she was just putting the finishing touches to the feast we were all going to enjoy later. Peter had bought glorious lobster but out of deference to Ben's quite violent dislike of shellfish (the night before we had supped off crayfish in their shells before his fascinated & horrified eyes) the lobster had all been taken from the shell & harmlessly served on reassuring plates with obscuring salad! Don & I tore ourselves away from these delights to dash to St Mary's to relieve Rod & Dorothy for ½ an hour & give them some sustaining Crabbie. They were doing very well again – a tremendous audience – & had been quite bowled over by the B.F.F. at 6.30. I sold librettos to people I had seen at other performances of the church operas. It seems as if the same people keep coming & they are all completely captured by the works. St Mary's is a very good church for the performances. The sound is excellent & the size allows a very large audience to congregate & share the experience. Our little 17/6d table did great work again. Rod very competent & cheerful, as is Dorothy. They were very grateful for the Crabbie & Don was v. grateful to them for coming over from Glasgow. We dashed back in high spirits to hear even higher spirits evident upstairs in the drawing room. Galya had arrived & all the transport plans had worked well. (Unlike the Festival arrangements which often don't – imagine – a car was sent to the N. British Hotel for Galya, who was waiting for it over an hour. It turned out that the hotel didn't realize that Vishnevskaya was staying there! They had booked in Mr & Mrs Rostropovich.) Loud voices & laughter upstairs, a wonderful spread downstairs. Everyone soon gathered round the table & to general murmurs of appreciation we feasted our way through lobster (avocado for Ben which, he asserted was NOT RIPE – it's no good trying to get one ahead of the maestro) & cold duck, orange salad, & rice salad & other delicious cold dishes. Slava drinking toasts to Ben & Peter, Peter drinking toasts to Galya & fondly loving her, Slava, very serious, choosing whisky to drink a toast to the friends of Ben & Peter, because the friends declare the man. Anyway, whichever Russian or English proverb it was there was a good deal of toasting to friendship & to the survival of art despite political and national differences. Slava adores Ben & adores his music & speaks always of his tremendous genius & of his overwhelming admiration for him. We all drank again to Ben & indeed to his genius. And there it is, residing in this slight delicate man through whose brain & fingers flow all these masterworks. Being the chief composer of the Festival is a somewhat daunting role, & it's sometimes hard to remember that the charming companion at the breakfast table, joking about his post, having a second sausage & mopping up the toast is the same gifted creature whose hands draw magic sounds from the piano & whose works are performed daily before audiences of hundreds, some of whom have travelled thousands of miles for the experience. There's no doubt that the rich field of friendship between the Rostropoviches & Ben & Peter is growing marvellous flowers. Ben's Aldeburgh Deutsch is tremendously fluent & marvellously grammatical. He amuses me as his spoken cadences remain exactly the same whether he is speaking English or German. We had all eaten, drunk & felt too much & staggered to bed after Don had driven S. & G. home with Ben. The rest of us enjoyed feeding the washing-up machine & talking about the evening, during which Slava had discovered a new gadget – the Tweeny – the waste-disposal unit – whose voracious maw fascinated him & Rachel had difficulty in preventing his putting his fingers in to feel the blades! Peter is sure he will be in Harrods on Wed morning buying one for the dacha.

Saturday, 31 August

A black day for me. No letter from Mark [Livingston, KM's son] & no phone call. An early start for the household as rehearsal for the *War Requiem* started at 9.30. Ben is not very pleased with the Melos – Gervase was reading a newspaper throughout yesterday's rehearsal – & Ben has mentioned this at least four times. So he's going to be slow to forgive this insult. His immersion in his music is total & he can't conceive how a musician could read a newspaper while waiting for his entries! Don came back with Ben fairly early & found me rather tearful. I'd had a singularly absurd conversation with Mark who had asked me where I was! So off Don whisked me into town. I'd hunted down copies of Boswell's *Life of Johnson*, which we thought we would give to Ben. He has been reading a house copy at night in bed, & in the morning regales us with one of the Doctor's choicest remarks from the previous night's instalment. Peter is reading the *Confessions of St Augustine* & he seems to have been rather a darling man. His prayer to be 'continent' but NOT YET amused us all, & proved the origin of the family joke with the upstairs bathroom where the door won't lock. It was rather a wet & tearful morning altogether – however John Grant's bookshop restored my spirits a bit & we not only got a mint set of Dr J. but a marvellous edition of Johnson's *Dictionary* for Peter. We had a little present giving at lunchtime. Ben & Peter were very pleased with their books as we are with our beautiful watercolour [by W. G. Gillies]. Don takes it upstairs to see it when he's in bed. During the day it is propped up on the mantelpiece. It's a beautiful painting, in the tender greens & blues & browns that we love most. There wasn't much time for admiring anything though except our excellent lunch (Rachel keeps up a fantastic standard – no failures – today a 'nursery' lunch of mince & vegetables & rice pud. so that no one will have indigestion with rehearsals piling up for the whole afternoon). I slept my depression away & had tea in bed alone & felt restored enough to go & sell librettos for the last performance of the *P.S.* at 8. Robert Tear is the Tempter tonight. Don took Peter & Ben to the Usher Hall for the Schubert

Mass, & came back in time to watch the church opera. It was a pretty cold
blustery night, but we sold a lot of books & recognized a lot of people who
had been at every performance during the week. The atmosphere was closer
to Aldeburgh than Edinburgh with the whole audience aware of one another
in a most curiously intimate way. Again our seats were up in the front. Just
before the lights were lowered, père Barenboim & Mrs Barenboim arrived,
& were most fussily escorted to a front seat from which he stood up, turned
round & surveyed the audience & made lightning signals all round. He was
pretty expressive during the performance, but whether with ecstasy or pain
was difficult to judge. The people in the church have been most extraordinarily helpful & kind. Not only with us & our librettos, but with finding
seats for Tertia out of the crowd, & in helping people to their places in the
pleasantest way. A great contrast to St Paul's, where it was impossible to get
in, & once in, impossible to get out.

We were all home round about the same time, & supped off asparagus
soup & coddled eggs with much satisfaction. Ben is tired & full of dread for
Sunday night.

Sunday, 1 September

There is great expectancy in the air today. The *War Requiem* is the performance many hundreds of people in Edinburgh have been waiting for. But we
woke to a sunny morning, Ben longing to sit in the green garden & not leap
up at 9.30 for a long rehearsal till 1 pm. They were off before I could extri-
cate myself from chores, but in any case I had to stay behind to get on with
some school work. At the same time the washing machine got busy on everyone's shirts – the last load, I suspect. Picked lots of flowers & arranged them
for the various rooms, made an analysis of exam results & had a chat with
Rachel, by which time Ben & Peter & Don & Graham were back. It had
been a wonderful rehearsal apparently. Galya in tremendous voice. Ben very
pleased. He even praised Peter & called him 'old thing', a term of great
affection. So drinks all round & much relaxation & happiness. This was
increased by a really fabulous lunch of roast lamb & onion sauce, superbly
cooked, and as Don said, the work of a genius. Rachel couldn't have had a
more appreciative family to feed. A rest upstairs for Ben & Peter, downstairs
for Don & Graham (I meanwhile slaving away on my wretched exam
papers) while outside the sun shone & made us all think longingly of Loch
Tay, and the Sunday before.

It's a dress-up night. Rachel's special roller in great demand for the
evening clothes. It's an excellent device, although when I used it on Don's
suit, the knob flew off & got lost under the bed. Trust me. Rachel's sharp
eyes found it fortunately. We are all going tonight & are going to smuggle
Rachel in. Reception afterwards at City Hall. Ben managed an egg & seemed
fairly steady, though as we drove off I held his hand in the car & could feel
him trembling all over. What a fantastic crowd at the Usher Hall. Every seat

was taken & every stair provided further perches. People stood all round the back. I wondered who among all these people was Mrs Blanka Heriton, the S. African lady who had written so plaintively to Ben to help her get a ticket. 8 o'clock came & the expectancy was intense – but minutes passed & no one came on to the platform except for the singers (already seated) & the orchestra who went on tuning their instruments. 8.10, 8.15 – still nothing. Don looked v. anxious & I wondered if he were going to leap out & downstairs – had someone been taken ill? At 8.20 a slight movement & shuffling among the brass & William Waterhouse slipped into place with his bassoon. Ironical cheering from the audience. We looked at each other aghast & thought of Ben's fury, waiting there in a state of tension, on such a night & with such a work. Speedily Peter, Galya, Dieter appeared – Galya in a glorious white satin gown with an embroidered coat – then, curiously, the leader of the New Phil. Tuning all over again! Then Ben & Giulini took their places & the tolling bells solemnly introduced the mourning march of *Requiem aeternam*. The boys' voices most thrillingly beautiful, Peter singing 'What passing bells for these who die as cattle' like an angel. I don't think I shall ever forget this performance. At such a time as this, the music had an impassioned & emotional impact that can't be described but which gripped us all. All three soloists in wonderful voice: Galya soaringly beautiful in *Libera me*. Peter sang 'Move him into the sun' wonderfully. Dieter most extraordinary in 'Strange Meeting'. He is a marvellous singer & sang tonight with such heart & love & compassion.

No easy thing to move out after such an experience. There was applause after all – vociferous applause – so apparently Ben's little note to announce that there should be no clapping was not regarded. Giulini had the chorus singing from their souls. He is a graceful conductor to watch – all flow & poetry. Ben's Melos in marvellous voice. He & Giulini together as if they had one heart beating instead of two.

The scenes behind after these big concerts give one a little time to come down to earth. A great crowd of admirers, autograph hunters, friends. Everyone absolutely overcome by this tremendous work. Ben & Peter finally hustled into the car by Don & Graham; Rachel & I followed in hers & off to the City Hall.

The amusing thing about this non-event was the Deputy pro-acting Provost whose name escapes me. He stumbled into a welcoming speech not really knowing which of his distinguished guests were which. The occasion was to honour the Scottish Festival Chorus, Maestro Giulini & Ben. The huge City Chamber was filled with a throng of black-garmented guests – rather a grisly sight – whose eyes were rather naturally turned to the long tables on the side laden with the supper they were longing to eat. But first there were formalities to get through. Ben knew he would have to speak, & had gone through tortures preparing his few words, & had been rather cross with us all for not taking this part of his public duties too seriously. He had just finished conducting an immaculate performance of the chamber orchestral section & the soloists of the *War Requiem* & was now pale with anticipation at the horrors of saying graceful words to the Scottish chorus & their redoubtable choral master, Arthur Oldham. The Deputy Provost apologized very clumsily for his presence & the Provost's absence (due to fatigue!) & looked at Arthur Oldham mistaking him for Ben in welcoming him & thanking him. It was one of those protracted graceless public speeches that are so painful to hear, & one gazed at the floor fearful of catching someone's glazed eye. I was seated just behind Ben, who suddenly sat on the arm of my chair & clasped my hand in desperate supplication. And that was not all. When the Vice had droned on for about 20 minutes, the lamp of oratory was handed to another chap – a member of the chorus – who in broad Scots made an awful fool of himself by cracking in-chorus jokes for 15 minutes before remembering what he was supposed to be doing. He was obviously the 'card' of the chorus & everyone roared while we gazed rather stonily ahead. However, he finally spoke most sincerely & simply about Ben's music, which they had all loved performing, & said very nice things. Ben, of course, replied superbly, & made a brief & witty speech, quite confounding his old doppelganger. An equally brief reply by Arthur & Maestro Giulini & off we went, leaving all the blackbirds to eat their pie.

What a relief to get back to Rosetta & have Rachel's super soup & mull over the evening, the performance, the chorus, the conductor, the soloists, Arthur, the vice provost & the Speech. Ben & Peter in excellent form & everyone relaxed & happy.

Monday, 2 September

The beginning of the last week. In a way, everyone rather enervated & anti-climactic, after Sunday night. Ben very testy about going to the *Sinfonietta* at Freemasons' Hall at 11. Actually his rehearsal for *Winter Words* (or at least, a balance test) early on gave him a good excuse for not going. In the end, I went to the Concert & wrote a note which I took round to Gervase to wish them all well & apologize for Mr B. possibly not being able to make it. Actually I enjoyed myself very much. It was a glorious morning & it was marvellous to be out. The Clarinet Quintet had been put in as an extra item, first, & was marvellous to hear again. I'm always very moved by it – not only because it's so beautiful but because of its associations when so long ago Don used to play it in the top room at Croxted Road when we thought there was little likelihood of any shared future. Saw Tony Gishford at the interval & had a long chat. He's staying at Dalmeny where we are supposed to be going for tea, but Heaven knows when. Ben's piece a tremendous *tour de force*; lovely music for an unusual combination of instruments. What an amazing genius he is! This piece was no 'early work'. It was the work of a master, though an 18-year-old one. The age was quite irrelevent, except to amaze us ordinary earthbound creatures. Mollie & Peter to lunch. They had been to the concert & were able to tell Ben about it (he knows better than to trust my judgement, which is always favourable).

Mollie has had a v. difficult time during the summer with her mother who has broken both hips, the first in a fall at home, the second in a fall at the nursing home that was mending the first. Extraordinary. Anyway, the poor lady is very confused, very difficult & cantankerous & Mollie has been charging up & down between Devon (where it rained all the time) & Brighton trying to mend the situation. So she was worn out, & glad to be here in Edinburgh for two or three days to enjoy the music & escape all the rigours of her responsibilities.

We all had a pleasant lunch & talk & enjoyed their visit. The house seems so much ours now that we all have a proprietorial attitude towards it & enjoy asking people in for a drink or to lunch. This six-sided life has gone on so long that I can't remember any other. We have become a family, with our jokes, our special words & phrases, our exaggerations & our drawbridges up protecting us.

* * *

In 1989 when Kathleen Mitchell presented the manuscript text of *Edinburgh Diary* to the Britten–Pears Library, DM realized the diary would be incomplete unless he provided an account of his and Britten's trip to Glasgow for a rehearsal, followed by a visit to Lady Rosebery back in Edinburgh, all of which took place on a day when KM was absent. Thus, over twenty years later, DM wrote a postscript to complete the story of those extraordinary weeks with Britten and Pears in Edinburgh during the troubled summer of 1968. [PR]

Thursday, 5 September

The last event of the Festival for Ben was a performance of his Piano Concerto, which he was going to conduct with the BBC Scottish Orchestra. The original intention was that Richter would be the soloist. But we had news of his cancellation during the Festival and it was decided to keep the performance in place but with Peter Frankl replacing Richter. Ben, naturally, was not particularly happy about the substitution but agreed none the less to conduct. It would have been particularly awkward for him to have cancelled because this was to be his last appearance at the Festival.

The performance entailed a trip to Glasgow, to visit the BBC Studios there and rehearse with the orchestra.

We had to leave the house fairly early in the morning. Kath was not with us because she had already left to spend the day at school in London to see her exam results; she was returning that night. Nor was Peter with us on this occasion. I think he'd pushed off somewhere to see friends or perhaps spend some time visiting the picture galleries in Edinburgh. Rachel had chosen to make this her day off. These absences perhaps have some bearing on the events of the afternoon.

I had taken the precaution of looking up the route to Glasgow and pin-pointing the location of the Studios and the journey passed off without incident. It was a rather showery day but there were some sunny moments. The weather in fact throughout the Festival period had not been half bad and on the day we made our trip out of Edinburgh for a picnic we had very fine weather indeed. None the less, whenever Ben recalled the time he spent at Edinburgh he always said, 'The only thing I remember was that it was always raining.' Demonstrably untrue, but somehow typical.

When we got to the Studios – we'd arrived a bit on the early side – the orchestra was still rehearsing with its conductor, James Loughran, who, if I remember rightly, was just coming to the end of a Beethoven symphony (the programme reminds me that it was in fact the Eighth). As soon as he was done, Loughran came over to us and greeted Ben and also told us that this was in fact the very first time he had conducted this particular symphony of Beethoven's. Ben made some polite response to this but I saw his eyebrows ascending when Loughran went on to add that the BBC were inviting him now to conduct a whole Beethoven cycle even though he had only conducted one or two (at most) of the symphonies before and now of course the Eighth. I don't think Ben could think of any particular reply to make to this pronouncement but when we were eating our sandwiches, which Rachel had prepared for us, in the nearby Glasgow Botanical Gardens, he remarked to me how very odd he found this bit of information: 'Rather strange, don't you think, Donald, to pick as conductor for a Beethoven cycle someone who has scarcely ever conducted Beethoven before.' We reflected on this, while enjoying our sandwiches.

The rehearsal had gone very well. Ben was very nice to Peter Frankl who, the next evening, was to give a thoroughly acceptable performance of the concerto. It was not unforgettable, as it might have been had we had Richter, but it was thoroughly musicianly and accurate. Ben was not at all displeased with it. The orchestra was not of the first rank, but it had been decently prepared, was an enthusiastic collaborator and, like most orchestras, took to Ben's highly economical and professional, unfussy rehearsal methods.

After the lunch break, we drove back to Edinburgh. By this time it was raining hard and Ben's spirits noticeably lowered on the return journey. This ensuing afternoon and evening were about the only free time we had in this final week, and I am sure Ben thought the weather was making certain our sabbatical afternoon and evening were going to be damp ones.

I am not quite sure now how it was that we met up with Peter. We probably went back to the house and found him there. There was a feeling that we ought to do something, though Edinburgh on a rainy afternoon did not seem to offer too many possibilities. Furthermore, Ben and Peter had entered into some kind of understanding with Lady Rosebery – the legendary Countess of Rosebery – éminence grise of the Festival, so it was said – that they would take tea with her at Dalmeny House. With this in mind, though, neither Ben nor Peter seemed ecstatic about the idea, we decided to go out for a while in the car, for a drive, and then call in at

Dalmeny on the way home. We drove out towards Cramond and the Forth Bridge but the weather was dispiriting, visibility poor and morale, by now, very low indeed. I am not quite sure why this was. There hadn't been a quarrel or a conflict of wills. It may have been bound up, possibly, with the sudden relaxation of tension after the preceding two weeks of more or less continuous high energy and unbroken activity. Suddenly no one seemed to know what to do with the longed-for break; and tea with Lady Rosebery seemed to excite less and less enthusiasm as we rather unpurposefully drove along.

Normally I saw to it that Ben and Peter got to wherever they ought to be on time; and by nature they were both extremely punctual and indeed punctilious people. But I fear that on this occasion we got towards teatime and indeed well beyond it without noticeably getting any nearer to Dalmeny. After a good deal of 'shall we' and 'shan't we', we finally decided that the call ought to be made; and by this time I was ready to welcome a change from the damp driving and above all a cup of tea. So we found our way to Dalmeny. As we drove up the long and dripping drive and the house came into view I remember thinking that it was all rather like a Charles Addams cartoon.

This impression was sustained somewhat when we reached the house. The front door was opened by a sombre butler who announced, somewhat forbiddingly, that 'Her Ladyship had been expecting us'. He led us to the drawing room and announced our arrival at the very same time that he opened the door. I have never forgotten the scene that was disclosed, for there, outlined against the window – with the falling rain outside – was Her Ladyship's back, a back that registered eloquently her displeasure at our late arrival. For an appreciable few seconds she did not turn round to greet us, which left us disconcerted and somewhat flustered, as no doubt she intended.

I cannot remember now whether there were signs that she, at least, had embarked on the tea that was laid out, that had doubtless been laid out for us. Now, however, there was no question of our participation. She was extremely put out and after the exchange of a few courtesies and mutual enquiries, conversation ran thin and finally expired altogether. We withdrew, back to the car and the rain, and drove back to the house.

In other circumstances, perhaps we should have found the whole affair comical rather than a disaster. But somehow the day seemed to be dogged by misfortune. I kept thinking that things might not have gone so badly if either Kath or Rachel had been around to help us out. But they were not, which meant there was no dinner at the house and we had to find somewhere to eat in Edinburgh. I think either Peter or Rachel had booked a table for us at a restaurant that I dare say on any other occasion might have proved to be perfectly agreeable. But Ben was beyond recovery, Peter had given up and I could think of no way myself of rescuing the dinner or the latter part of the day. It was now raining metaphorically as well as actually.

I ought to have gone to the airport with the car to meet Kath, but again indecision overtook the group – 'shall we', 'shan't we' made a further and last appearance, as a result of which I left it too late to get to the airport and the message I sent never reached Kath who was understandably annoyed to find no one at the airport to greet her. So when we all finally got home, there was an outraged Kath awaiting us, which provided the final touch to a depressing afternoon and evening. We all went off to bed, slightly at odds. But next morning Rachel was back and had a marvellous Scottish breakfast on the table, spirits were high again, Lady Rosebery's back was like some troubling dream, and we set about enjoying what was in fact the last day we were all to spend together in Edinburgh.

The concert in the evening at the Usher Hall went well. The Concerto made a lively, brilliant impression and the soloist, I thought, acquitted himself well. It can't have been easy occupying Richter's vacant shoes. Ben and Peter had spent the day, or part of it at least, packing. They took their bags to the hall in the evening and as soon as the Concerto was over, Ben changed out of his tails in the Green Room and within minutes of having conducted his work he was in the car with Peter and driving off to their next destination. I think they were going to stay overnight with a friend. I was rather amused at the speed of their exit. Suddenly all they wanted to do was to have the dust of Edinburgh off their feet and to be on their way. No time for reminiscences or going over the events of the past three weeks. It was just a terrific rush to get in the car and get away.

I had been much impressed by the Concerto and was also naturally moved by the thought that this was the last concert, the last Britten event in what had been an extraordinary two weeks, because it had been in truth a most extraordinary experience living at close hand with these two remarkable artists and experiencing in such a concentrated period the range and wealth of Ben's gifts in a whole series of works. In those last minutes of turmoil and escape, as Ben was struggling into his jacket, I embraced him and said, 'I think you're a very great composer and I love you very much.' To which Ben replied, without a moment's hesitation: 'I'm grateful for the second half of what you've just said, Donald, but about the first half – I'm not so sure.' A minute or two after that, and they were on their way.

21

Towards a Genealogy of *Death in Venice*

CHRISTOPHER PALMER[1]

One mellow autumn evening in 1892 a gondola drifted through the lagoons of Venice. Its owner, a middle-aged English writer, lay back absorbed in the melancholy reflections appropriate to his romantic surroundings. Suddenly his attention was riveted by the extraordinary beauty of the figure sturdily rowing a passing tourist boat, a bronzed *faccino* in the broad black hat and white costume then fashionable among gondoliers. Slowly the boat drew away, the youth disappeared from view, and the man was left with a sense of deprivation. His biographer notes that

> It was typical of John Addington Symonds to seize upon a fleeting encounter like this as a revelation of significant truth . . . the symbol of a lost ideal . . . The boy . . . became intricately fused with Symonds's feeling for Venice and his response to the landscape of the lagoons . . . His precise mood of melancholy had to be recaptured, 'one of those sad

---

1 As this volume was in preparation, one of its contributors, Christopher Palmer, died at the age of forty-eight after a long battle against Aids. One of his last pieces of published writing was the introductory essay 'Thinking Like a Composer', which he contributed to Donald Mitchell's *Cradles of the New: Writings on Music 1951–1991* (London: Faber and Faber, 1995), a project he had dreamed up and to which he had devoted much of the precious time that remained to him. Knowing of Christopher's state of health, I did not at first approach him to contribute to the present *Festschrift*; his work on *Cradles* constituted his own tribute to DM, a friend for over thirty years. But, as time passed, I began to regret my original exclusion of Christopher and accordingly made the appropriate invitation. Characteristically, he was delighted that a *Festschrift* was being assembled and without a moment's hesitation agreed to participate, despite his precarious and unpredictable medical condition.

Christopher set to work on a piece entitled 'Britten and the Anglican Tradition', an article that would offer further illumination on areas already touched on in his earlier 'The Ceremony of Innocence' (BC: 68–83). Only an unfinished torso of this piece remains, which, while full of Palmeresque enthusiasms, insights and unexpected connections, would do justice to neither its author nor its dedicatee were it to be published. To keep Christopher's place in the *Festschrift*, and to do honour to the originality of his contribution to our understanding of Britten and his music, I have chosen instead to reprint what seems to me one his most fascinating cross-cultural essays, 'Towards a Genealogy of *Death in Venice*', which first appeared in BC: 250–67. I am most grateful to Faber and Faber Ltd, publishers of BC, and to Christopher's executors for permission to include the essay in the present volume. Christopher's posthumous tribute to DM will also have to stand as an epitaph for himself. [PR]

moods, in which all life seems wasted, and the heart is full of hidden want, and one does not even know what one desires, but a sense of wistfulness is everywhere – one of these moods has been upon me several days'.[2]

In June 1926 A. E. Housman wrote to his sister Kate:

I was surprised to find what pleasure it gave me to be in Venice again . . . certainly there is no place like it in the world: everything there is better in reality than in memory. I first saw it on a romantic evening after sunset in 1900. and I left it on a sunshiny morning, and I shall not go there again.[3]

Meanwhile, in May 1911, another writer had been to Venice ('the incomparable, the fabulous, the like-nothing-else-in-the-world', as he called it), and immortalized his visit in his novella *Death in Venice*. Thomas Mann, his wife Katja and his brother Heinrich had planned a holiday on Brioni, off the Dalmatian coast. That turned out badly and, on an impulse, they went to Pola and took a steamer for Venice, where they spent a week at the Hôtel des Bains, on the Lido. Here Mann encountered the original of the beautiful boy whom the elderly writer Aschenbach fatally loves in *Death in Venice*.[4] In May 1932, when his children Erika and Klaus were staying in Venice at the same hotel, Mann felt he had to write to them,

. . . because the place is so important to me and I am glad to think of your being there. In spirit I am with you leading that unique life between the warm sea in the morning and the 'ambiguous' city in the afternoon. Ambiguous . . . is wonderfully relevant in all its meanings, and for all the city's modern silliness and corruptness . . . this musical magic of ambiguity still lives . . . You mention that it must have been lovely in the middle of the last century. But Platen was already saying: 'All that is left of Venice lies in the lands of dreams' . . . For certain people, there is a special melancholia associated with the name of Venice . . . my heart would be pounding were I there again.[5]

'Platen', August Graf von Platen-Hallermünde (1798–1835), a late-Romantic poet with strong classical affiliations (and, like Housman and Symonds, homosexual), was one of those for whom Venice had a 'special melancholia'. In *Death in Venice* Aschenbach, approaching Venice from the sea, thinks of the 'melancholy and susceptible poet who had once seen the towers and turrets of his dreams rise out of these waves': the poet is Platen. According to

2 Phyllis Grosskurth, *John Addington Symonds* (London: Longman, 1964): 1.
3 Henry Mass (ed.), *The Letters of A. E. Housman* (London: Rupert Hart-Davis, 1971): 238.
4 In the early 1960s a Polish count aged sixty-eight proved from photographs and recollections that he had been that boy. Mann himself stated, in *A Sketch of My Life*, that all the people and incidents of the story were drawn from life. [See 'I was Thomas Mann's Tadzio', in Donald Mitchell (ed.), *Benjamin Britten: Death in Venice* (Cambridge: Cambridge University Press, 1987): 184–5.]
5 *The Letters of Thomas Mann*, Vol. 1, selected and tr. Richard and Clara Winston (London: Secker & Warburg, 1970): 187.

W. D. Williams, 'his passionless objectivity, his extreme cultivation of formal values, is a cloak thrown over his natively romantic sensibility; indeed it is more, it is a necessary form of self-protection against the threat of disintegration'.[6] He chisels out statuesque, marmoreal verses, perfectly proportioned, but devoid of human feeling and sensuous appeal. Such are his fourteen sonnets on Venice: verbal reflections of the ornate and grandiose palaces, the still canals, the plethora of classical paintings and sculptures. Yet he is also everywhere conscious of the worm within the rose, the all-too-perfect ripeness poised on the brink of decay. This is the 'ambiguousness' of Venice to which Mann refers and which accounts for its appeal to all 'double-natures' (as Ernst Bertram describes them in his Nietzsche book) like Platen, Nietzsche and indeed Mann himself. Platen's Venetian sonnet which ends

> Dann stört mich kaum im schweigenden Reviere
> Herschallend aus entlegenen Kanälen,
> Von Zeit zu Zeit ein Ruf der Gondoliere[7]

reads like a classical pre-echo of Nietzsche's better known

> An der Brücke stand
> Jüngst ich in brauner Nacht.
> Fernher kam Gesang;
> goldner Tropfen quoll's
> über die zitternde Fläche weg.
> Gondeln, Lichter, Musik –
> trunken schwamm's in die Dämmerung hinaus . . .
>
> Meine Seele, ein Saitenspiel,
> sang sich, unsichtbar berührt,
> heimlich ein Gondellied dazu,
> zitternd vor bunter Seligkeit.
> – Hörte jemand ihr zu?[8]

Here we are aware of the intense *musicality* of Nietzsche's poetic gift. In the lines immediately before the introduction of this poem in *Ecce Homo*, he says: 'Were I in search of a synonym for music, I would say Venice. For me tears are music, music tears; and I know what bliss it is not to be able to think of the South without trembling in anticipation.' For Nietzsche and for Mann (one of his most ardent disciples) music meant above all Wagner, and

---

6   'August von Platen', in Alex Natan (ed.), *German Men of Letters*, Vol. 5 (New York: Oswald Wolff, 1969): 135 ff.
7   Then the gondoliers' cries, intermittently ringing from distant canals, scarcely disturb my silent reverie.
8   Just now I was standing on a bridge, the evening brown around me. Singing came from the distance; it flowed away in drops of gold over the trembling surface. Gondolas, lights, music – it swam, drunk with rapture, far out into the twilight.
    My soul seemed a lyre, invisibly moved, trembling with radiant bliss, it sang a gondola's song secretly to itself. Was anyone listening?

Wagner meant above all *Tristan und Isolde*. And here we return to Count Platen, for his most famous poem also bears the name of Tristan.

> Wer die Schönheit angeschaut mit Augen
> Ist dem Tode schon anheimgegeben.[9]

In effect: he who experiences essential beauty no longer belongs to life. In his essay on Platen, Mann discusses the poem in terms that bear directly on his own *Death in Venice*. The soul-world entered by Platen, he says,

> . . . is a world in which the imperative to live, the laws of life, reason and morality are nothing; a world of drunken, hopeless libertinage, which is at the same time a world of the most conscious form, the most deathlike rigidity; which teaches its adept that the principle of beauty and form does not spring from the sphere of life . . . [What conditions this world] is the idea of beauty and death, the idea that the arrow of beauty is the arrow of death and eternal pain of yearning: only there does it find full expression. Death, beauty, love, eternity: these are language symbols for this at once platonic and intoxicatingly musical soul-miracle so full of fascination and seduction . . . And those who on earth wear the order and are the knights of beauty are knights of death.[10]

This is the world of *Tristan*, Mann's *Death in Venice* and Britten's *Death in Venice* (and, in a sense, *Billy Budd*), all poems of unquenchable, endless love which issues in death, which *is* death, because it can find no release, fulfilment or expression on earth.[11]

Wagner and Britten may seem an unlikely juxtaposition, but perhaps their meeting on other than technical levels is brought about through Thomas Mann as intermediary. Wagner's personal links with Venice were as strong as Britten's. He orchestrated the *Tristan* love duet there and died there; a few weeks before his death, while staying with him at the Palazzo Vendramin, Liszt wrote his two extraordinary solo piano pieces entitled 'La lugubre gondola', early archetypes of Impressionistic water music. In *Death in Venice* Aschenbach feels himself impelled to write, in Tadzio's presence, a

---

9   He who once has looked on Beauty has lost himself irretrievably to Death.

10 *Essays of Three Decades* (London: Secker & Warburg, 1947): 261.

11 That Platen was one of Thomas Mann's models for Aschenbach is made abundantly clear by the passage from the same essay describing how the poet, with immense patience and devotion, 'had wrought out of the golden shield of language the most splendid and enduring things; he had . . . performed miracles of stylistic and intellectual perfection, single-handed, all in order to become worthy to fall asleep to the gods on the knee of the little Theoxenos'. Platen himself proclaimed, 'Der Kunst gelobt' ich ganz ein ganzes Leben,/Und wenn ich sterbe, sterb' ich für das Schöne.' ['I have spent my entire life in ceaseless devotion to Art; and when I die I shall die for Beauty.'] Platen was, like Aschenbach and, one suspects, perhaps a little like Britten himself, in a similar case to Melville's Captain Ahab in *Moby Dick*: 'gifted with the high perception, I lack the low enjoying power. Damned most subtly, and damned most malignantly! Damned in the midst of Paradise!'

piece on a certain 'cultural phenomenon' with which he is familiar and which means much to him. This fits an essay Mann wrote when he was in Venice in 1911, which was on Wagner: 'Auseinandersetzung mit Richard Wagner' ('About the Art of Richard Wagner'). Some of the manuscript paper bears the letterhead 'Grand Hôtel des Bains, Lido – Venice', and it is tempting to think that it was written in the real-life Tadzio's presence, on the beach.

It is certainly more than coincidence that water and the sea play so large a part in the work of both Wagner and Britten. Nietzsche was one of the first to associate the 'Dionysian' music of *Tristan* with diving, swimming and drowning, and later writers, notably Baudelaire ('la musique souvent me prend comme une mer'), Swinburne, D'Annunzio and Mann,[12] followed suit. Wagner himself constantly used water metaphors in relation to *Tristan*; for example when the latter was incubating he was much occupied in studying Liszt's symphonic poems, and told the composer that each time he read through one of the scores he felt as though he had dived down into some crystal water. Later he observed that in *Tristan* he had 'poured himself out in music'.[13] In *Death in Venice* the sea is omnipresent. To it Mann attributes the same 'dangerous fascination' (Nietzsche's phrase) as to music. Aschenbach's love of the ocean has its source, we are told, in a 'yearning . . . for the un-organized, the immeasurable, the eternal – in short, for nothingness'. This Nirvana-urge, which Wagner described as one of the sources of *Tristan*, is found in many *Tristan*-derived scores in which the sea of water is a ruling force: in d'Indy's *L'Etranger*, in Delius's *A Village Romeo and Juliet* in which the young lovers drown themselves, and in Debussy's *Pelléas et Mélisande*, where the sea is symbol of the womb and chaos of things whence we arose, and whither we return. So too in Mann's and Britten's *Death in Venice*: Aschenbach watches Tadzio bathe and then run out of the sea against the water,

> . . . churning the waves to a foam, his head flung high. The sight of this living figure, virginally pure and austere, with dripping locks, beautiful as a tender young god, emerging from the depths of sea and sky, outrunning the element – it conjured up mythologies, it was like a primeval legend, handed down from the beginning of time, of the birth of form, of the origin of the gods.

The end comes on the beach too: Aschenbach dies, slumped in his chair, watching Tadzio,

---

12 In her introduction to Blackwell's German Texts edition of *Tonio Kröger* (Oxford: Oxford University Press, 1943): xlv, Elizabeth M. Wilkinson points out that 'the sea, its rhythms, its musical transcendence, vibrates in the language of all [Mann's] books, even when there is no talk of it; and no German since Heine . . . has written of it so that we not only hear its rush and roar, but feel the spray and the salt tang on our lips and crush the shells beneath our feet.' The same is true in England of Britten's music.
13 See Elliott Zuckerman, *The First Hundred Years of Wagner's Tristan* (New York: Columbia University Press, 1964): 10.

> ... a remote and isolated figure, with floating locks, out there in the sea and wind, against the misty inane ... It seemed to him the pale and lovely Summoner out there smiled at him and beckoned ... pointed outward as he hovered on before into an immensity of richest expectation.

The sea, as symbol of the nothingness which is everythingness, is the ultimate appeaser of Eros, that simultaneous longing for the senses' fulfilment and their extinction; and in Britten it is the be-all and end-all not only of *Death in Venice* but also of *Peter Grimes*[14] and *Billy Budd*. Here is the crux of the affinity between Wagner and Britten. 'The only fulfilment is that of personal passion; this cannot be achieved except by separation from the conditions of the material world (society, civilization, domestic loyalties) ... finally ... it cannot be achieved within Time at all.' Wilfrid Mellers's account of the literary-dramatic aspect of Wagner's adaptation of the *Tristan* myth[15] applies equally, *mutatis mutandis*, to *Death in Venice*, *Grimes* and *Budd*. All three are set on or by the sea, their heroes all go down to a watery grave, and in all the sea acts ambivalently both as Alma Mater and as aggressor or agent of destruction. And when we recall that Wagner in *Tristan* was the first to explore through in-depth musical expression the related areas of night, sleep and dreams – related not only to each other but also to the *sea* as symbols of infinity, of the ultimate spiritual reality – and when we recall how frequently the idea of redemption recurs in both Britten's operas and Wagner's, then we can begin to make out a case for describing Britten as a Wagnerian composer. He is certainly an artist of the Wagnerian kind, in whom the creative impulse originates in a need to understand himself and reveal his self-understanding to the world, however he may thus paradoxically be *mis*understood by the world. It is important to note too that sex in one form or another is clearly a basic preoccupation of all the works mentioned in the preceding pages; apropos which Mann in his Platen essay quotes Nietzsche to the effect that the degree and kind of a man's sexuality permeate the very loftiest heights of his intellect.

Surveying the scene from the purely aesthetic point of view we find that sensibilities have always been ravished by the waters of Venice. Shelley noted the fairy-tale qualities of its sunsets; Symonds in his chapter on Venice in *The Renaissance in Italy* speaks of the 'vaporous atmosphere' which makes the city a unique theatre for sunsets, and describes the elemental conditions for Venetian art as light, colour, air, space; Henry James refers in his *Foreign Parts* to the 'inscrutable flattery of the atmosphere' which renders everything pictorial and harmonious; and all connect this quality of light with the presence of water.

For hundreds of years artists and writers have been attempting to capture the magic of Venice in colour and word. Music had to wait until the late

---

14 PETER: What is home? Calm as deep water. Where's my home? Deep in calm water. (*Peter Grimes*, Act III scene 2).
15 *Caliban Reborn* (London: Gollancz, 1968): 36.

twentieth century for those descriptive or rather evocative passages in *Death in Venice* which are among the finest in the work: the music of the open sea as Aschenbach approaches Venice on the boat, in which the feel as well as the sight of the 'low-lying clouds, unending grey' is conjured up in the heterophonic, diatonic string texture (whose heterogeneous homogeneity is partially achieved through free bowing); the sea motif, heard for the first time as the Hotel Manager shows Aschenbach the view of the sea from his room; Aschenbach's contemplation of the prospect when he is left alone: the *Grimes*-like thirds interweave and overlap in woodwind solos – an aural equivalent of the sound, shape and colour of the 'long low waves, rhythmic upon the sand' [see Fig. 65]; the gondola music, with its lolling, lapping rhythm and 'Serenissima' motif refracted in dipping figures; the gondoliers' cries, hauntingly re-created from authentic sources; the moment when Aschenbach pursues the Polish family in a gondola, with the tuned percussion that signals Tadzio's presence sounding the 'Serenissima' motif while, deep down below, in the lagoon (as in Billy's lullaby), the oozy liquidity of bass clarinet and harp keeps the music in water-motion [see Fig. 228].

If we return to the beach we find those *Grimes*-like thirds participating not only in the music of wind and water itself but in the siren-like chorus of offstage women's voices calling not so much to Tadzio as for and on behalf of him, and, indeed, in this case helping to lure an innocent man to his doom.[16] Tadzio is identified with the elements. In Britten's musical catechism 'elements' mean the 'elementary' triad, compounded of major and minor thirds, and for him chains of thirds seem to be associated with the elements: not only with water and the sea – as in *Grimes*, *Death in Venice*, the ballet of sea-horses, fish-creatures and waves in Act II of *The Prince of the Pagodas*, 'Afton Water' in *A Birthday Hansel*, and the sea-girt *Golden Vanity* – but also with sunlight (Act II, scene 2 of *The Rape of Lucretia*). Here, in *Death in Venice*, the third is insidiously 'sweet and wild', a perfect musical incarnation of Tadzio's name which 'with its softened consonants and long-drawn *u*-sound, seemed to possess the beach like a rallying-cry . . .' (Mann). The music seems to sweep like a great wave or surge of water over the beach – or rather over the star-struck Aschenbach, whose 'heart and soul and senses,/ World without end, are drowned'[17] [see Fig. 99].

But in Venice, it seems, darkness, dis-ease and death are never far away. James in *The Aspern Papers* (1888) evokes the city's façade of glamour and enchantment: 'See how it glows with the advancing summer; how the sky and the sea and the rosy air and the marble of the palaces all shimmer and melt together.' But the narrator is an unscrupulous scholar determined to

---

16 The effect of the offstage chorus, heard at varying proximity, is not unlike that of the last act of *Grimes*; and indeed there is a basic similarity, for each is a chorus of predators searching for their victim. The parallel is reinforced in the last scene of *Death in Venice* when the warning voice, the danger signal, of the tuba enters the scene. In *Grimes* the tuba represents a foghorn, both danger signal and siren song.
17 Housman, *A Shropshire Lad*, XIV.

charm the letters of a dead American poet out of two desiccated spinsters whose lives are crumbling away along with the old *palazzo* they inhabit. In Arthur Symons's *Extracts from the Journal of Henry Luxulyan* (1905) the eponymous hero begins, like Aschenbach, by yielding to the city's seductiveness: 'I must sink into this delicious Venice, where forgetfulness is easier than anywhere in the world . . . it is all a sort of immense rest, literally a dream, for there is sleep all over Venice.' Soon, however, signs of distemper begin to declare themselves:

> Does the too exciting exquisiteness of Venice drive people mad? Two madhouses in the water! It is like a menace . . . every day I find myself growing more uneasy. If I look out of the windows at dawn, when land and water seem to awaken like a flower, some poison comes to me out of this perhaps too perfect beauty . . . I have never felt anything like this insidious coiling of water about one. I came to Venice for peace, and I find a subtle terror growing up out of its waters . . .

Three years later Symons succumbed to a nervous breakdown in Venice. And Helen Waddell, after seeing the dungeons in the Doge's Palace, wrote to her sister that 'you open a door and come straight into the great court, blazing with light . . . and thank God you don't live in the fifteenth century. It is the combination of two things – the perfect sensuous imagination of beauty, and that dank cruel horror existing side by side . . .'[18]

So Venice is an embodiment in both its physiognomy and its inner being of the antithesis between beauty and ugliness, good and evil, darkness and light and all the extremes experienced throughout his history by ethical man. It was, therefore, a perfect setting for Mann's variation on the archetypal theme of the corruption of sense by the senses, the mind by the body, man by the animal. Others who had developed the theme before him included Goethe, in *Elective Affinities* and Mann's own brother Heinrich, in *Professor Unrat* (1905), about the downfall of a respectable schoolmaster at the hands of a night-club tart (later a famous film wth Marlene Dietrich, *The Blue Angel*). If in tracing the lineage of *Death in Venice* we look further afield, to Norway, we find a striking parallel, to which Donald Mitchell has drawn attention,[19] in Ibsen's *When We Dead Awaken* (1899–1900), his last play, consciously written as a final statement – like Britten's *Death in Venice*. In Professor Rubek, Ibsen draws a man who has sacrificed Irena, his true love and inspiration, for the sake of what he persuades himself is his art. Irena in real life was Rosa Fitinghoff, with whom Ibsen, at seventy, had fallen in love – a 'später Abenteuer des Gefühls', like Aschenbach's. Like Aschenbach's too are the sentiments voiced by Rubek when, at the height of his

18   Quoted in Monica Blackett, *The Mark of the Maker* (London: Constable, 1973): 42. Cf. also Byron (*Childe Harold*): 'I stood in Venice, on the Bridge of Sighs;/A palace and a prison on each hand.'
19   'A Billy Budd Notebook', *Opera News* (New York) 43 (31 March 1979): 12–13. [See also MCPR: 168.]

fame, talk about the artist's vocation and mission begins to strike him as hollow and meaningless. Instead he wants life. 'Isn't life in sunshine and beauty altogether more worthwhile than to go on till the end of one's days in some damp clammy hole, tiring oneself to death wrestling with lumps of clay and blocks of stone?' He confesses to Irena that, in his youth, he had been filled with the conviction that if he touched her, or desired her sensually, his vision would be so desecrated that he would never be able to achieve what he was striving for – the work of art came first, flesh and blood second. 'In those days my great task dominated me completely – filled me with exultant joy.' Aschenbach all over.[20]

Even more remarkable as a harbinger of *Death in Venice* is Walter Pater's short story *Apollo in Picardy*, first published in 1893. Here we find 'a cold and very reasonable spirit disturbed suddenly, thrown off its balance, as by a violent beam, a blaze of new light, revealing, as it glanced here and there, a hundred truths unguessed-at before, yet a curse, as it turned out, to its receiver, in dividing hopelessly against itself the well-ordered kingdom of his thought.' This 'receiver' is a monk, Prior Saint-Jean, the author of a dry, strict treatise on mathematics, astronomy and music, his vocation being the abstract sciences; poets he regards as miscreants and demons. But his health becomes affected by long and rigorous intellectual application (compare Aschenbach), and he is sent to an *obédience* in Picardy. A friend warns him that there 'the mere contact of one's feet with the soil might change one' (as in Venice). Disturbed by thought of the coming journey, the Prior dreams of hell-fire (compare Aschenbach's vision of the jungle). He takes with him a young novice, Hyacinth; and immediately they arrive 'the atmosphere, the light, the influence of things, seemed different from what they knew' (as in Aschenbach's first contact with Venice). Climbing up one night into the solar of the Grange, Prior Saint-Jean finds a youth asleep, and seems

> . . . to be looking for the first time on the human form, on the old Adam fresh from his Maker's hand . . . could one fancy a single curve bettered in the rich, warm limbs; in the haughty features of the face, with the golden hair, tied in a mystic knot, fallen down across the inspired brow? And yet what gentle sweetness also in the natural movement of the bosom, the throat, the lips, of the sleeper! Could that be diabolical, and really spotted with unseen evil, which was so spotless to the eye?

(Compare Tadzio.) Then the Prior, his moral constitution undermined by the 'luxury of the free, self-chosen hours, the irregular fare, the doing pretty much as one pleased' after the severe discipline of the monastery ('self-discipline my strength' Aschenbach mocks himself), becomes more and more infatuated with the boy, Apollyon, encountering in him, for the first time in

---

20 A similar late realization of the loss of human warmth for the sake of formal perfection is recorded of her father by Imogen Holst in *Gustav Holst* (Oxford: Oxford University Press, 1938): 141.

his life, 'the power of untutored natural impulse, of natural inspiration'. Vocation, scholarship, reputation – all go for nothing (Aschenbach: 'all folly, all pretence'). The narrator wonders if the Prior, on his way from the convent, 'passed unwittingly through some river or rivulet of Lethe, that had carried away from him all his so carefully accumulated intellectual baggage of fact and theory?' The metaphor would fit perfectly in *Death in Venice*: in fact Aschenbach passed through just such a river, rowed in the coffin-black gondola by a Charon-like gondolier who did as he pleased, left no name and took no money. The weather at the Grange (as in Venice) becomes 'fiery and plaguesome', the 'first heat of veritable summer come suddenly'.The implication is that a triangular situation develops between the two young men, Apollyon and Hyacinth, and the Prior. A catastrophe becomes inevitable, and when it arrives is both gory and erotic. Apollyon challenges Hyacinth to a naked, moonlight game of quoits. A sudden icy blast of wind takes control of Apollyon's quoit, it lodging in Hyacinth's skull and killing him instantly. Mann's Aschenbach sits in the park and watches Tadzio at play,

> . . . and at such times it was not Tadzio whom he saw but Hyacinthus, doomed to die because two gods were rivals for his love. Ah yes, he tasted the envious pangs that Zephyr knew when his rival, bow and cithara, oracle and all forgot, played with the beauteous youth; he watched the discus, guided by torturing jealousy, strike the beloved head; paled as he received the broken body in his arms and saw the flower spring up, watered by that sweet blood and signed for evermore with his lament.

And similarly in Picardy, the blood of Hyacinth, mingling with the rain, colours the grass around his body, and the following morning the Prior beholds a marvel of blue flowers. Apollyon makes off, and the Prior is arrested on suspicion of murder and dies mad. Apollyon and Tadzio are both Angels of Death.

While I am not trying to claim *Apollo in Picardy* as a hitherto unrecognized source of *Death in Venice*, the parallels are consistent and striking. Possibly the link is to be found in classical scholarship. In *Plato and Platonism* Pater touches on the Spartan festival of the *Hyacinthia* and describes Plato in terms that suggest not only Pater himself but also Aschenbach: 'Austere as he seems, and on well-considered principle really is, his temperance or austerity, aesthetically so winning, is attained only by the chastisement, the control, of a variously interested, a richly sensuous nature.' And as T. J. Reed has shown in the introduction to his Oxford University Press Clarendon German Series edition of *Death in Venice*, Mann used two Platonic dialogues (the *Symposium* and *Phaedrus*) and Plutarch's *Eròtikos*, in his novella.

Here we might suppose this particular branch of the genealogical tree to come to an end; yet not quite so. For both Pater's *Apollo in Picardy* and his thematically similar *Denys l'Auxerrois* were once considered as possible opera librettos by Szymanowski, who greatly admired him. Here the long arm of coincidence apparently grows to phenomenal proportions; for in the early summer of 1911 Szymanowski made a memorable journey to Sicily and Italy. On 30 April he was in Palermo announcing his intention to reach, during the ten days following, Naples, Rome, Florence and finally Venice. He was in Vienna by the time Mahler died (18 May), so at some time between the end of April and the middle of May 1911 he was in Venice. He may even have seen 'Tadzio', his fellow countryman. His path could not have crossed Mann's, since the latter did not arrive in Venice until the end of May (he had followed the newspaper accounts of Mahler's last hours on Brioni). Yet how extraordinary that these two artists, much akin in spirit, should have just missed each other in Venice in the month of Mahler's death: for if Mann's Italian trip engendered *Death in Venice*, Szymanowski's travels in the south, particularly in Sicily, produced his opera *King Roger* (1918–25) – which is virtually identical in theme with *Death in Venice*. The twelfth-century king is irresistibly attracted by a handsome young shepherd who preaches a cult of beauty and sensuous delight and who later reveals himself as Dionysus; whereas the king, of course, thinks to bear the 'Apollonian' insignia of law order and decency. The king yields to the shepherd, but – and here the story diverges radically from *Death in Venice* – comes to realize that the Dionysian religion of pleasure is ultimately just as constricting and *restricting* in its way as the dogmatic rigidity of the Church, and he rejects both. The tensions are resolved in the last act which is set in a Greek temple overlooking the sea. A picture of dawn on the face of the deep leads to Roger's apostrophe to the sun (in the 'basic', 'Brittenish' key of C major) and the opera ends with the spirit of regenerated man merging with sun and sea in a burst of 'elemental' ecstasy.

There is not scope in this discussion for a comparison of Britten's *Death in Venice* with Mann's; in such a comparison Mahler would be a key figure, as Mann's model for Aschenbach's facial features[21] and as a lifelong source of musical inspiration to Britten. Britten worked on *Death in Venice* – the story of an artist's dissolution and death – at the end of his life with Mahler's portrait looking down on him from the wall of his study; and both Britten and Mahler died of a chronic heart condition. In Britten's *Death in Venice*, as in late Mahler, the music longs for, yearns towards, death, yet regrets intensely the leaving of life; messages of farewell are everywhere. (Actual reminiscences of Mahler in *Death in Venice* are neither more nor less frequent than elsewhere in Britten, but circumstances naturally make us more conscious of them, e.g. the drone-struck music of slow dawn and dispersing shadows, of waking from heavy slumber to a sense of ultimate reality, which unveils Act II; and, of course, the final *Adagio*.)

---

21 In 1921 Wolfgang Born's nine coloured lithographs for *Death in Venice* were published in Munich. Born knew nothing of the part Mahler had played in the genesis of the novella, and so Mann was amazed to discover that Aschenbach's head in the last picture, 'Death', unmistakably revealed the Mahler type. See *The Letters of Thomas Mann*, op. cit.: 100–102 [and Philip Reed, 'Aschenbach becomes Mahler: Thomas Mann as film', in Donald Mitchell (ed.), *Benjamin Britten: Death in Venice*, op. cit.: 180–81].

But in considering the relation of Britten to Mann I propose to bypass Mann's *Death in Venice* and turn to its aftermath. In his letter of 4 July 1920 to Carl Maria Weber, a kind of apologia for *Death in Venice*,[22] Mann sets forth his attitudes to eroticism in general and homosexuality in particular. He quotes his own *Betrachtungen eines Unpolitischen* on the relationship between mind and life, and then asks

> but what else have we here if not the translation of one of the world's most beautiful love-poems into the language of criticism and prose, the poem whose final stanza begins: 'Wer das Tiefste *gedacht*, liebt das *Lebendigste*'. This wonderful poem contains the whole justification of the emotional tendency in question, and the whole explanation of it, which is mine also.

This 'wonderful poem' is none other than Hölderlin's 'Sokrates und Alcibiades' set by Britten as the third of his *Sechs Hölderlin-Fragmente* (1958) to music of the serenest, sweetest triadic simplicity; it is another rainbow-arch of chords (as Eric Walter White describes the music of Vere's interview with Billy in *Budd*),[23] except that the determining melodic line is not this time formed from the constituent notes of any one triad but is a repetition of the same melody which had accompanied (unharmonized) the first part of the poem, which calls Socrates to account for the court he pays to Alcibiades. Metaphorical harmony is the result of adding literal harmony, chords, to a melodic line which in its unaccompanied state is questioning, unfulfilled. It is perhaps significant, in the light of Britten's use of the triad in those two instances as a symbol of beauty, that very few bars in *Death in Venice* actually make use of the pure triad, two of which comprise Aschenbach's (initially) happy acceptance of his love for Tadzio: 'So be it!'

A similar and profounder coincidence in this chapter of coincidences involves Mann's last major work, *Doktor Faustus*. This epic story of a fictitious contemporary composer (Adrian Leverkühn), set against the backdrop of the rise and fall of the Third Reich, was begun in May 1943 and finished in January 1947. During the summer of 1944 Mann worked on chapter 20, which describes the first compositions Adrian completed after making his pact with the Devil. Among them were settings of Verlaine and Blake – 'Chanson d'Automne' (which had been one of the fourteen-year-old Britten's *Quatre Chansons Françaises*) and, uncannily, 'The Sick Rose', which Britten had composed as part of the *Serenade* for tenor, horn and strings in 1943, at the very time Mann was beginning his novel. The sexual metaphor of this latter poem is ironically appropriate in Leverkühn's case, whose pact with the Devil manifests itself as syphilitic infection; but the poem is also a verbal distillation of 'ambiguity' of the kind that Mann saw in Venice. That Mann was conscious of an underlying affinity of theme between *Faustus* and *Death in Venice* is shown by the warmth of his response to a seventieth

22 *The Letters of Thomas Mann*, op. cit.: 93–7.
23 *Benjamin Britten: His Life and Operas*, revised edn (London: Faber and Faber, 1983): 162.

birthday article by George Lukács which described *Death in Venice* as signalling the danger of a barbarous underworld existing within modern German civilization as its necessary complement'.[24] Nor is the connection between Blake and Venice missing from Britten's music, in which the major/minor antithesis – the variable third – is an archetypal symbol for good versus evil, and is as all-pervasive in 'The Sick Rose' as in *Death in Venice*; in both cases the idea is that of a cancer which has spread through every part of the organism.[25]

It is uncanny that these two creative artists, who never met or worked together, should turn to the same poetic text at virtually the same moment. Furthermore, another Blake poem which Mann has Leverkühn set – 'A Poison Tree' – was actually set by Britten, both earlier (1935) and much later (in the 1965 *Songs and Proverbs of William Blake*). Mann's comment on Leverkühn's treatment can be applied to Britten's: 'The evil simplicity of the verse was completely reproduced in the music.'

A final point to be made in connection with *Doktor Faustus* is the wholly Brittenish character of the 'Echo' episode. Echo is an enchanting small boy, half Hermes (like Tadzio), half Christ, a vision of 'adorable loveliness which was yet a prey to time, destined to mature and partake of the earthly lot', such as Britten would surely have warmed to as readily as Leverkühn. But part of Leverkühn's covenant with Satan is that he is not permitted to warm to anyone; and because he does, Echo dies, horribly, of cerebro-spinal meningitis, but not before he has inspired in Leverkühn some settings of Ariel's songs from *The Tempest*.[26]

Echo is in fact one of those young sacrificial victims, agents of salvation, that people Britten's scores – Lucretia, Billy, Isaac, Miles, the Madwoman's son in *Curlew River*, the Cabin-boy in *The Golden Vanity*, Owen Wingrave – all Angels from Heaven, but, as Vere says, 'the Angel must hang'. Tadzio is rather a destroyer, bringing Aschenbach to ruin and death in abject humiliation. But then so in their way are Billy and Miles – and Echo. Billy kills Claggart, dies and condemns Vere to a lifetime of self-laceration ('O what have I done?'); Miles dies, after (we imagine) driving the Governess insane and irremediably corrupting Flora. Echo dies – but his death causes Leverkühn to commit his ultimate act of creative negation, the 'taking-back' or 'un-writing' of the Ninth Symphony, in the form of his last work, the

---

24 Quoted in Thomas Mann, *The Genesis of a Novel* (London: Secker & Warburg, 1961): 115.

25 In an address given during the period of his writing *Doktor Faustus* (published in *Thomas Mann's Addresses* (Washington: Library of Congress, 1963)), Mann claimed for Romanticism a 'peculiar and psychologically highly fruitful relationship to sickness. Even in its loveliest, most ethereal aspects, where the popular mates with the sublime, Romanticism bears within its heart the germ of morbidity, *as the rose bears the worm*. Its innermost character is seduction, seduction to *death*.' (My italics.)

26 *The Tempest* was a project that Britten had often contemplated undertaking. At one time he had thought of writing the music for a film version of the play to be directed by Richard Attenborough and shot in Bali, with Sir John Gielgud as Prospero.

Lamentation of Dr Faustus. This in turn precipitates his final, complete mental and physical breakdown.

* * *

Over the years Venice seems to have offered a kind of common meeting-place of the mind to many artists whose temperaments involved them as closely with the life of the senses as with that of the intellect. Their age-old problem is stated with devastating simplicity in *Carmina Burana*:

> So short a day
> And life so quickly hasting,
> And in study wasting
> Youth that would be gay.[27]

In Britten the problem is that of the child shut out of the Kingdom of Heaven or the Garden of Paradise: he cannot re-enter unless he discards the 'disease of feeling' (Hardy) which is an inevitable consequence of growing up.[28] Neither Mann nor Britten offers a solution to these problems, which are by their nature insoluble; but by stating or crystallizing the matter in a unique and memorable fashion and creating works of art *about* men who create works of art they modify our perception of the world about us. They open our eyes to aspects of human experience, to immemorial truths; they teach us that life as we know it as 'civilized' human beings is absurd, that men are interested in things they were never meant to be interested in, pursuing aims they were never meant to pursue. And if artists affect ordinary people in this way, must they not also exert a profound influence on each other, and determine and modify each other's ways of feeling, thinking and expressing? How else can we account for the appeal of the thoroughly 'sentimentalic'[29] Mann to the 'naive' Britten? The result of this appeal was one of the master-pieces of twentieth-century music, one that, surely, Mann himself unwittingly adumbrated in his essay on Wagner written on the Lido within sight of the real-life Tadzio. He envisioned the masterpiece of the twentieth century as eminently un-Wagnerian; distinguished by its logic, form, and clari-ty; austere and yet serene; more detached, nobler and healthier than Wagner's operas; 'something that seeks greatness not in the colossal and the

---

27 Translated by Helen Waddell in *Medieval Latin Lyrics* (London: Constable, 1929), 203.
28 As Thomas Mann's son Klaus says in his autobiography *The Turning Point* (London: Gollancz, 1944): 16: 'No matter how hard we try to capture the bliss of paradise, it is only our own longing for the paradise lost we succeed in finding . . . there is no happiness where there is memory, To remember things means to yearn for the past. Our nostalgia begins with our consciousness.'
29 In his preface to HOBB, Hans Keller applies to composers the distinction drawn by Schiller between the 'naïve' artist – he who is 'in tune with nature, expressing it, its laws, its truths spontaneously' and the 'sentimentalic' (= Schiller's *sentimentalisch*, also a coinage) artist who is 'the perpetual striver, who thinks it better to travel than to arrive'. Into the first category Keller puts Mozart, Bruckner and Britten; into the second, Beethoven, Mahler and Wagner.

baroque, and beauty not in the ecstatic'. The musical substance of Britten's last opera corresponds to every one of these prescriptions, and it is supreme (and happy) irony that it is based on the very work that was taking shape in Mann's mind as he wrote his Wagner essay. In an unpublished letter to Britten dated 14 September 1970 (mainly concerned with the Mann family's positive response to Britten's desire to compose *Death in Venice*) Thomas Mann's son Golo wrote, 'My father . . . used to say, that if it ever came to some musical illustration of his novel *Doktor Faustus*, you would be the composer to do it.'

The Turn of the Screw, Venice, 1954:
Jennifer Vyvyan (The Governess) and Peter Pears (Quint)

22

Venice, 1954

MYFANWY PIPER

Fawley Bottom, October 1994

Dear Donald,

You were not associated with the English Opera Group in the far-off days when we opened at the Fenice Theatre with *The Turn of the Screw* and so you didn't experience, although I'm sure you must have heard about, the mixture of passion, mistakes and hilarious jokes that attended its realization.

Quite early in the months when Ben and I were discussing the text Basil Douglas had a letter from the Intendente of the Fenice which was as bizarre as it was unnerving. He sent it on to me in a great state of anxiety. The letter itself must, I think and hope, be somewhere in the Red House Archive since I can't find it in mine. The gist of it was that he hoped I could assure him that we were not going to present him with a specific tale of unnatural affections. I can't remember what I wrote to soothe his sensitive imagination but it seemed to do the trick and when we all met on our arrival in Venice the atmosphere was good: smiling, calm and full of friendly anticipation.

Our introduction to the stage and auditorium was a piece of pure theatre: everyone who had anything to do with the production was ushered on to the stage. The iron was down, the stage got fuller and fuller, at last the Intendente raised his hand for silence. At a slight gesture from him the iron went up; we gasped with delight then cheered and clapped. He bowed, we cheered and clapped again. It was a typical piece of Italian showmanship and pride.

What we saw was perhaps the most beautiful small theatre in the world. On the first night its architectural perfection was embellished with red roses on every box – it is almost all boxes.

Our stage staff and theirs were soon on the best of terms, one of them, Douglas, commonly known as Duggie, reduced them to rapturous laughter because Duggie in Venetian dialect means 'I stab myself' and they would rush about with pens or pencils or bits of wood making stabbing motions towards their hearts. As they rushed they called out *Duggi Duggi Duggi*.

When the first night was over and we had eaten at the delectable Fenice restaurant we walked back across St Mark's Square, starlit and silent except for the sound of the melancholy little café bands so wonderfully evoked by Ben in *Death in Venice* who were beginning to pack up and go.

Suddenly there was a wild and beautiful sound: Arda Mandikian (Miss Jessel) cast off her stage cloak of gloom and sang, at the top of her voice, the folk songs of her native Greece all the way back to the hotel. A perfect ending.

With love,

Myfanwy

23

On the Sketches for *Billy Budd*

PHILIP REED

Usually I have the music complete in my mind before putting pencil to paper. That doesn't mean that every note has been composed, perhaps not one has, but I have worked out questions of form, texture and character, and so forth, in a very precise way so that I know exactly what effects I want and how I am going to achieve them.

Benjamin Britten, 1963 [1]

The quotation above encapsulates something of Britten's own view of the complex creative processes involved in giving birth to a fresh composition. Evidently it was a procedure that progressed from generalities to specifics – from ideas formed in the mind to notes on the page. The present chapter explores some of the tangible by-products of Britten's compositional labours, i.e. the assorted musical sketches and drafts which can be thought of as the physical 'remains' of the mental procedure, to allow us some understanding of the creative process.

The pattern of Britten's working methods hardly ever varied and the disciplined routine adopted in early adulthood was maintained with unfailing regularity with only very few exceptions. Britten's business-like timetable for the working day is well attested: two main periods of composition at his desk, one in the morning, the other in the late afternoon/early evening, framed a long 'thinking' walk in the first part of the afternoon. He always mistrusted working at night, although scoring might be undertaken if a deadline were fast approaching. By adhering to this rigorous schedule, Britten was usually able to gauge the amount of time needed to complete a composition with unnerving accuracy.

A new work would take shape on the page as a through-composed short-score draft written in pencil, the orchestral texture reduced on to two, three or perhaps four staves with the vocal lines occupying their own staves. In the case of works involving voices and orchestra, it might resemble

---

1 Murray Schafer (ed.), *British Composers in Interview* (London: Faber and Faber, 1963): 123. Another first-hand account of Britten's creative process can also be found in 'Mapreading: Benjamin Britten in conversation with Donald Mitchell', in BC: 91.

something approaching a conventional vocal score at first glance. The instrumentation was indicated on the draft by abbreviations – 'str.', 'trbn', 'ww', etc. – at the time of composition, ready for instant retrieval when the moment came for the full score to be made. This simple technique was effective in allowing Britten to press on to the end of a piece before making the full score, safe in the knowledge that the work was virtually written. In the case of complex stage works this method made provision for an assistant to follow behind the composer, using the draft as a basis for the all-important vocal score from which the principal singers and chorus would learn their roles. Once a new piece was complete in draft form, the business of making the corresponding full score was largely a calligraphic labour; the majority of the problems had already presented themselves and been solved.

Throughout his career Britten preferred to work in pencil when composing because of the freedom it offered for change; the use of pencil was a significantly liberating factor to the composer's creativity since anything that was committed to paper might easily be rubbed out and rewritten. Almost every leaf of the composition draft of *Billy Budd* shows evidence of liberal use of the eraser, demonstrating unequivocally how closely Britten tested his original ideas. While generally speaking it is not very easy to read the rubbed-out notes, occasionally one can discern the impression made by Britten's pencil of what had at first been written.[2]

Two other, related, methods of making changes to a work can be found on any of Britten's composition drafts. Rather than erasing passages, particularly if they were more than a couple of bars, Britten would prefer to cross through a longer section he wished to delete. Occasionally, if the deleted passage amounted to a full page he might prefer to detach it and use the available blank verso elsewhere in the manuscript draft. If more than one page was rejected then Britten would almost always remove the offending passage from the main draft and place the particular folio(s) to one side. These discarded draft leaves form an important category of substantial earlier versions of the music.

The principal holograph draft of *Billy Budd* (GB–ALb 2–9300892) comprises 108 folios of 28-stave manuscript paper measuring 36.5 x 27.2 cms; the rastral span is 34.1 cms. The folios divide as follows: Act I – fol. 1–31;

---

2   A significant example of this type of deleted material is cited by Mervyn Cooke ('Britten's "Prophetic Song"', in MCPR: 98–9): 'At Billy's impressment . . . Billy's stammer trill . . . occurs on F. The alternation of F and G♭ (subsequently replaced by the C♯/D trill universally adopted elsewhere in the score) marked an even more obvious identification with the Phrygian F minor characterizing Claggart, a fitting reminder of Forster's description of Billy's impediment as "the devil's visiting card".'

   At the 'stammer' motif's first appearance (in the Prologue) the level of erasure evident on the composition draft suggests that Britten returned to this passage after having rewritten its subsequent appearance at Billy's impressment. The case for this theory is strengthened by the existence of a discarded draft for the passage from the Prologue appearing on fol. 14 (see p. 238 below), i.e. at the very point in the composition draft at which the 'stammer' motif makes its second appearance.

Act II – fol. 32–59; Act III – fol. 60–93; Act IV – fol. 94–108. It is written throughout in Britten's customary pencil with one insignificant revision made in red ballpoint (on fol. 12). This document was given by the composer to his amanuensis, Imogen Holst, on 23 December 1952; the cover (fol. 1) is inscribed: 'For dear Imo, / in place of a *proper* / copy of Budd which / will come later / with my great love & / admiration / Ben / *Xmas 1952*'. It remained in Miss Holst's possession until 1983 when she presented it to the Britten–Pears Library, Aldeburgh, as a gift, along with the holograph composition draft of *The Prince of the Pagodas*.

In addition to the holograph draft, two collections of discarded leaves from the main draft are of significance. Until 1967 both remained in the composer's possession; however, following the Decca recording sessions for *Billy Budd*, Britten presented 13 folios to his friend and trusted producer at Decca, John Culshaw. Once again he inscribed the first page of the manuscript: 'ODD SKETCHES FOR BILLY BUDD / For John Culshaw / – a memento of a long period of sessions together – & / in hopes of more in the future (either here or there) / with admiration, affection & gratitude / Benjamin Britten / Xmas 1967'. After Culshaw's death in 1980, these discarded drafts were bequeathed to the Imperial Cancer Research Fund on whose behalf they were sold at auction; they were purchased by the Austrian National Library, Vienna (Mus. Hs. 38.741). The other discarded folios (*GB–ALb* 2–9300892) remained with the composer and now form part of the substantial manuscript collection at Aldeburgh.

In the following discussion references to these three documents may be distinguished thus:

fol. 1: from the main composition draft
discd fol. 1: from the discarded drafts in Aldeburgh
Vienna fol. [1]: from the Austrian National Library's discarded drafts[3]

Although our account so far of Britten's working methods has suggested that he eschewed sketching material in the manner of Beethoven – i.e. the composition was thought out chiefly in advance in the head rather than on the page – there are a number of miscellaneous, more fragmentary sketches scattered among the principal sources which can be considered immediately.

Some of the most interesting examples are to be found in the Vienna manuscript, fol. [3] and [6*v*] (see Exx. 1(a)–(e) which have been transcribed precisely as they appear in Britten's manuscript). Exx. 1(a) and 1(b) belong to Claggart's aria, 'O beauty, o handsomeness, goodness, would that I never encountered you' (Fig. 105). Ex. 1(b) is clearly an early thought for the beginning of the contrasting middle section (Fig. 107), marked in the printed

---

3   The Vienna folio references are shown in square brackets because I have been unable to consult the original document and have relied on a microfilm of the manuscript held at the Britten–Pears Library (Mic. X3), filmed when the material was still in Culshaw's possession. The foliation is therefore editorial.

Ex. 1

(a)

(b)

I   am doomed to   an-hi -   el - ate   you

(c)

score 'Quick and determined – *Allegro con brio*'. The rising scales which
Britten first considered for the words 'I am doomed to annihilate you' (note
the composer's wayward spelling on his sketch!) were postponed for subsequent phrases where they appear in a modified form (see Ex. 2). Ex. 1(a)
is much less easy to pinpoint but its general shape suggests the same aria,
possibly at the opening.

Ex. 1(c) depicts an early version of the shanty used as part of the orchestral interlude between scenes 2 and 3 of Act I (Fig. 76). The melodic line is
very close to Britten's ultimate notation (see Ex. 3) – the triplet rhythm has
yet to be dotted and only one pitch at the end of the tune to be changed – but
the counterpoint is rather conventional and less imaginative. It makes no

Ex. 1 (contd)

(d)

(e)

play of the adjacent semitonal dissonances (except for the perfunctory, implied 7–6 resolution in bar 4) which set up such resonances with the remainder of the opera. In March 1951 Britten sent a version of this melody to Kenneth Harrison, who had supplied the words for the Act II shanty 'We're off to Samoa', as a suitable vehicle for another shanty, 'As gloomy, homesick and nostalgic as you like,' as the composer told Harrison.[4]

---

4   Britten to Kenneth Harrison, 2 March 1951. See Philip Reed, 'From First Thoughts to First Night: A *Billy Budd* Chronology', in MCPR: 65–6. Neither of the opera's librettists, E. M. Forster and Eric Crozier, had been successful in drafting shanties. Harrison was a friend and colleague of Forster's at King's College, Cambridge.

Ex. 2

CLAGGART
cantabile

I   will wipe you   off   the   face   of   the   earth! _____

Ex. 3

quietly, but a little more flowing – *tranquillo, ma un poco più andante*

Ex. 1(d) is probably the first notation of 'Billy in the darbies' (Act IV in the 1951 version; Act II scene 3 (1960)). Reading from the tenth bar of the scene, the sketched version given here matches Billy's words beginning at 'Through the port comes the moonshine astray' as far as 'I must up [too]'. The melodic profile is not identical to the final version – for example, the tension of Billy's A♭s is missing from bars 6–7 of the sketch version – although much of the harmonic detail of Britten's final thoughts is the same. Two further points: the evocative piccolo interpolations which break up the phrases throughout this scene were apparently a later consideration; and, unlike Exx. 1(a)–(c), Britten's earliest suggestions for instrumentation are indicated. The published score, however, does not precisely match the instrumentation given here: the low horn C is preserved (to be doubled by harp), while the bass clarinets and divided cellos combine with the other divided lower strings. But clearly, here is an example of how, even on a very early sketch, Britten's musical ideas were already matched to specific, if not always fully worked out, instrumental colours.

Ex. 1(e) encapsulates the principal choral idea that dominates the battle scene in Act II scene 1 (Fig. 15). Britten's working copy of the libretto (not fully complete for this scene) indicates that the choral element was interpolated amid the general milieu of the battle after much of the text had been fixed. Perhaps, then, this sketch was made to show the librettists the kind of melody for which they needed to find words. In any case, the fragmentary and transposed presentations it receives in the final version of the scene probably meant that Britten would make a complete notation of it beforehand. Interestingly, it is never heard in the opera in the key given in this sketch; the rhythm and pitches of the second half of the melody were subsequently refined. Vienna fol. [3] also includes a two-bar sketch for the complex superimposition of fanfares which greet Billy's first entrance in Act I scene 1 (Fig. 19).

A further example of such (principally) melodic sketching can be found on discd fol. 1 where the shanty tune for 'We're off to Samoa' is notated in 8/8 in E♭, rather than the G major of the published score (Fig. 82). Perhaps this sketch is an early version of the melody sent to Kenneth Harrison in order for him to write suitable words.[5] Although Britten abandoned E♭ for this catchy melody – labelled 'Shanty II' in the sketch – its tonality was transferred to the previous shanty in the score, 'Blow her away', and for much of the orchestral interlude.

The final example of this type of preliminary sketching concerns the opening bars of the opera in a sketch headed '*Prologue*' (discd fol. 1: see Ex. 4). The crucial oscillating muted string figuration is already established in spite of a notation in semiquavers in a *Lento* 4/4 metre. Absent from this early notation are the repeated A♭s from the brass over the simultaneously sounding B♭/B minor dyads on woodwind and harp. Evidently this idea grew out of the sketch's fermata in bar 3. Interestingly, even Britten's main composition draft for this passage (fol. 2) does not quite correspond in all details to the published score: for example, the tempo marking is *Poco Lento* (♩) rather

Ex. 4

---

5   See Reed, op. cit., in MCPR: 64–8.

Ex. 5

than 'Slowly moving – *Andante* ($\downarrow$ = 56), and the B♭/B minor motif is notated in quavers in 2/2 rather than in 4/4. Evidence of erasure and two deleted bars on the main draft indicates the care Britten took over this important passage.

The remainder of the discarded manuscript sketches relate directly to the principal composition draft and comprise far more substantial passages of music. They are noted in the order of their appearance in the opera rather than necessarily in their position within the three sources. Our discussion is limited to the most significant drafts.

Fol. 14 from Britten's main draft comprises a ten-bar discarded version of a passage for Vere from the Prologue, 'There is always some flaw in it, some defect' (see Ex. 5). The rhythm of Vere's vocal line is virtually identical to the final version but the melodic profile is far less wide-ranging, centred firmly on C♯ and therefore matching the trill. This draft also demonstrates Britten's earlier and far cruder thoughts for the woodwind figurations that comprise Billy's 'stammer' motif.

The exchange between the First Mate, the Four Midshipmen and Donald (after Fig. 9) resulted in some insignificant alterations visible in the main draft (fol. 6*v*); Vienna fol. [4] contains a related four-bar draft for Donald in which his *pianissimo* falsetto phrase, 'Teach 'em to play upon a man of war!', appears in a different version using the voice's normal register.

Claggart's interrogation of Red Whiskers was the next section of the opera to be subjected to more substantial redrafting (Fig. 20). Britten's first version of the ten bars from Fig. 20 was, in many respects, very similar to what appears in the published score – the agitated string accompaniment was a feature of the first draft although its impact was softened by the B major key signature; Red Whiskers's objections followed a descending scalic contour accompanied by two-part string counterpoint (violins 1 and 2?), rather than agitated recitative over a held chord. Later in the same scene Britten rethought the opening bars of Claggart's F minor 'Was I born yesterday?' (Fig. 36), refining the instrumentation of the oscillating crotchets (horns replaced bassoons) and altering the vocal line in order that it should emerge from the same pitch as the dark-sounding horns. Even for the final version of these bars – a total of eight in all – there is evidence of substantial rubbing out: Britten clearly strove hard to perfect this crucial opening of Claggart's first solo.

Ex. 6

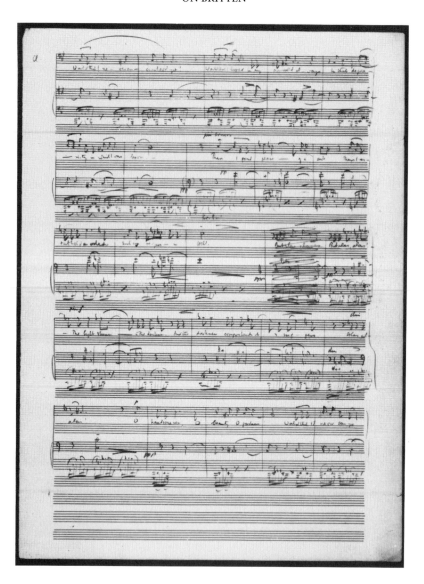

Above and facing: two discarded pages from Britten's composition draft of
Claggart's aria 'O beauty, o handsomeness . . .' (A–Wn Mus. HS. 38.741).
Reproduced by permission.

In scene 2 of Act I Vere's original toast to the French (Fig. 66) turned the tonality towards C major – Vere's key and one of the principal tonalities of this scene – rather than B major, the tonal centre associated with mutiny, as in the published score. Britten also used as accompaniment a transposed version of the opening chords from the beginning of the scene. The linking orchestral interlude between the scene in Vere's cabin and that below decks is founded on quasi sea-shanties deployed by Britten to tremendous effect. This episode proved at first something of a stumbling block to the composer, revealed by discarded material in both the main draft and the Vienna leaves. The difficulties with this instrumental transition may well have been caused by the delay on the librettists' part in finding an appropriate text for the second shanty, 'We're off to Samoa'; while Britten had finished the original Act II (i.e. scenes 2 and 3 of Act I in the 1960 version) in December 1950, the problem of the missing shanty text remained unresolved until February/March 1951. Ex. 1(c) has already indicated Britten's first ideas for material used in the interlude; Ex. 6 gives what is probably the second, fuller expression of this memorable material. A comparison with Britten's conceptual sketch (Ex. 1(c)) immediately throws up relationships, notably in the bass counterpoint. Comparison of Ex. 6 with the final version of this passage – the sketch exactly matches the number of bars between Figs. 76 and 77 – reveals other, related connections: the counterpoint is at first developed in a way approaching the rhythmic profile of the final version but, unlike the published score, Britten at first abandoned the basic two-part texture in favour of fuller triadic harmonies in a rising progression.

Fol. 39*v* includes six discarded bars (at Fig. 77) which originally led not to fol. 40 *et al.*, but to Vienna fol. [5–6], i.e. the first version of the conclusion of the orchestral interlude, the climax of the E♭ shanty, and the transition 'We're off to Samoa' where the draft peters out. While the fundamental shape of Britten's earlier attempt is very similar to the published version, it has none of the latter's care in respect of the placing of the E♭ tonality nor the overwhelming E♭ chord four bars after Fig. 78. This draft may have progressed no further than the opening phrases of the jaunty G major shanty because at the time of writing (the end of October 1950) a finished text had yet to be provided.

We have observed elsewhere how the music of Claggart's aria offended Forster and how the composer, seriously disturbed by this upset, put it to one side, grudgingly revising it in July 1951 when most of the draft had been completed.[6] The revisions to which 'O beauty, o handsomeness . . .' was subjected are reflected in the manuscript sources which are divided between the principal draft (fol. 47–51) and the Vienna sketches (Vienna fol. [6*v*–7*v*]). The complexities of the interrelating leaves from the draft may be represented as follows:

6   Ibid.: 61.

First version	*Revised version*
fol. 46*v* [last 3 bars]	
Vienna fol. [7]	fol. 47
Vienna fol. [7*v*]	fol. 47*v*
fol. 48	fol. 48
fol. 48*v*	fol. 49*v*
	fol. 49 revised as fol. 50 ⟶
	fol. 50*v*
fol. 51	fol. 51

It is evident from the diagram alone that the aria was expanded in its latter part, roughly in accordance with Forster's criticisms – 'I looked for an aria perhaps, for a more recognizable form. I liked the last section best, and if it is extended so that it dominates my vague objections may vanish.'[7] In fact what Britten gave him in the aria's original form was not Peter Evans's plausible 'sonata movement' reading of this music,[8] but something closer to a straightforward ternary structure capped by the identical F minor 'credo' coda ('I, John Claggart'). Whereas in his first draft Britten allowed the B section to return to the A reprise by the same brass chordal progression that effects the recapitulation in the published score (cf. the twelve bars leading up to Fig. 110), he indulges in only a rather half-hearted, quasi development of material rather than the heightened dramatic development (in E♭, at Fig. 109) of the final version. The reprise of the A major first section was originally as long in its number of bars as the revised version, but part of its text was transferred to the new development section (Fig. 109). The text for this revised passage – 'For what hope remains if love can escape? If love still lives and grows strong in a land they cannot enter. What hope is in my own world for me' – is placed (in a revised version) in the new reprise of the A section (see Fig. 110).

Britten's second attempt at this troublesome passage – i.e. his *first* revision – comprises fol. 49*v* and fol. 49 (in that order) and follows the musical text of the final version fairly closely, but displaces the libretto text rather in the manner of his earliest attempt. It was only in the final draft of this passage that Britten redrew the musical–textual relationship to produce the finely wrought, almost Verdian, set-piece aria that Forster was evidently seeking.

Britten's rethinking of the principal A section of the aria also demonstrates the care which he lavished on this crucial, revelatory passage. In comparison with Vienna fol. [7–7*v*] (see pp. 240–41), the revised draft makes more dramatic use of the identical text. The earlier version is not so obsessive in its

---

7 Forster to Britten, early December 1951. See Mary Lago and P. N. Furbank (eds.), *Selected Letters of E. M. Forster: Volume Two, 1921–1970* (London: Collins, 1985): 242–3.

8 See Peter Evans, *The Music of Benjamin Britten* (London: Dent, 1979): 178, where a diagrammatic representation of Claggart's aria may be found. In his diagram Professor Evans refers to figure numbers which appear only in the now unavailable four-act vocal score. The references may, however, be simply converted by reading Fig. 45 as Fig. 105, etc.

Above and facing: Discarded drafts from Vere's aria, 'I accept their verdict'
(*GB–ALb* 2–9300892 (p. 244); *A–Wn* Mus. HS. 38.741 (p. 245).
Reproduced by permission

use of the interval of the fourth and its interlocking references to other motivic cells from the opera. Clearly the trombone obbligato and accompaniment figuration, while loosely similar, have in fact been drafted afresh to accommodate the newly spun vocal line.

Before the end of the act Britten evidently found problems with two further passages. In December 1950 he told Forster he was finding difficulties with the encounter between the Novice (under Claggart's malign influence) and Billy, when the Novice attempts to lure Billy to mutiny by offering him foreign gold.[9] Vienna fol. [8–8v] comprises a first draft of this passage (from Fig. 117) setting an earlier version of the libretto (Britten's working copy of the libretto is heavily annotated at this point, with at least two layers of pencil revisions before a rewriting of the dialogue was undertaken). Presumably it was a textual difficulty that needed to be solved. Both versions of the passage make use of the same rhythmic motif (Ex. 7) and the sparse orchestration, allowing through the important words, is also common to both. The second problematic passage belongs to the final bars of the act. Fol. 58v is an incomplete sketch belonging to the Billy–Dansker duet; the lack of a text, however, prevents its precise location. It probably derives from an earlier version of the libretto because, like the Novice–Billy scene, the text has been much revised by the composer in his working copy of the libretto.

Ex. 7

Act II (in 1951, Acts III and IV) proved to be less problematical. An abandoned draft of 16 bars exists for the opening of scene 1 (disced fol. 2) which is very similar to the published score. When writing to Pears in January 1951, Britten admitted he was having problems, largely textual, with the battle scene:[10] evidence of his difficulties can be found among the discarded Vienna draft pages (Vienna fol. [9–9v]) which match the finished draft fol. 63–63v (Fig. 6), when the first exchange between Claggart and Vere is interrupted by the sighting of a French ship. (This passage was subsequently reconsidered by Britten as part of the 1960 revisions.)[11] Essentially the first draft is very similar to that appearing in the 1951 score, but two points of detail are absent in the original draft: the clarinet figure six bars after Fig. 6, and the orchestral accompaniment given to the Maintop's cries of 'Deck ahoy!'

9   Reed, op. cit., in MCPR: 62.
10   Ibid.: 62.
11   See Philip Reed, 'The 1960 Revisions: A Two-act *Billy Budd*', in MCPR: 76–8.

Ex. 8

At the end of the battle scene Vere's cry of despair, 'Ay the mist is back to foil us' (seven bars after Fig. 34), was subjected to careful redrafting. Ex. 8 transcribes Britten's first attempt at this passage: the chorus's cries of 'The mist' continue underneath a more elaborate vocal line for Vere; the conflict between B♭ and B minor is present, though not perhaps as finely honed as in the ultimate version of these bars. We should note too the prominent C major chords – Vere's key – in the third bar of his solo.

Ex. 9

Some insignificant reworking of the Vere–Claggart exchange around Fig. 41 ('Mutiny? Mutiny? I'm not to be scared by words') can be seen on the main composition draft, and the orchestral interlude between scenes 1 and 2 required some reworking before Britten was altogether satisfied. The sequence of twelve pitches on Vienna fol. [9v] (see Ex. 9) probably relates to arpeggiated chords announced at the start of the interlude (cf. Fig. 50).

Vere's 'Justice must be done' (Fig. 79) was revised: in the first draft (Vienna fol. [10–10v]) Britten allowed the repeated Cs to continue and persist more readily, and at Fig. 80 with the move to F minor, his first sketch clearly indicates the peculiarly spaced F minor chords that are associated throughout with Claggart. That sound persisted in the *Grave* instrumental link where Britten, in the published score, preferred only the dark, low sonorities of F minor.

A crucial passage in Vere's F minor aria, 'I accept their verdict', proved tricky to resolve. Two discarded drafts exist for the link into the *Allegro* section at Fig. 100, following Vere's climactic 'I, Edward Fairfax Vere, Captain of the *Indomitable* lost with all hands on the infinite sea'. Pages 234 and 235 show the first and second attempts respectively (fol. 91v and Vienna fol. [11]). The second version is very close to the published score, but after a few bars of the *Allegro* the ideas became far less assured and exiguous. The first draft is even more sketch-like in outline and while we can detect the similarity between Britten's ideas here and in the subsequent versions, even the first part of the draft is substantially different.

Act II scene 3 (Act IV scene 1 in the 1951 score) held few anxieties for the composer: the nine bars before Fig. 117 from Billy's B♭ aria ('And farewell to ye, old *Rights o' Man!*') were redrafted to achieve a better placing of the phrase's climax, and the trumpet fanfares from the interlude linking scene 3 to scene 4 were also slightly reworked. The passage following Billy's cry 'Starry Vere, God bless you!' was rethought to achieve a more satisfactory transition into the crew's wordless chorus of rebellion.

The principal difficulty with the final scene concerned the rebellious

Ex. 10

(a)

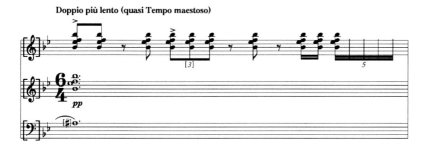

Doppio più lento (quasi Tempo maestoso)

pp

(b)

Slow and solemn – *Grave* ♩ = 66
perc and str pizz.

pp

chorus and the transformation of the final scene into Vere's Epilogue. Vienna fol. [12–12*v*] comprises a rejected version of the 36 bars leading up to Fig. 140 (the beginning of the Epilogue). Of crucial interest are the bars around the start of the Epilogue (Ex. 10(a)) which show that Britten originally modelled the Epilogue's opening on the percussion figure from the beginning of scene 4 (Ex. 10(b)). The rewriting of this passage must be associated with the exchange of correspondence between Britten and Forster in August 1951 when Forster assured the composer of the wise dramatic sense in recalling the opera's Prologue at this juncture.[12]

Vere's music from Fig. 143 until the end of the opera ('I was lost on the infinite sea') was entirely redrafted sometime shortly after the completion of the composition draft on 10 August 1951. The intention of the musical and dramatic climax is virtually identical in both versions but in his reconsideration of this music Britten achieves what many of the changes previously discussed reflect: a consistent awareness of the subtle dramatic inflexions of Forster's and Crozier's text coupled to a strengthening of the overall musico-dramatic shape. While his first version of 'I was lost' (Ex. 11) sets out the identical harmonic progressions that can be found in the second attempt, it is the missing element, the detail of the rippling quaver motion (itself an organic

12 See Reed, 'From First Thoughts to First Night', in MCPR: 67.

Ex. 11

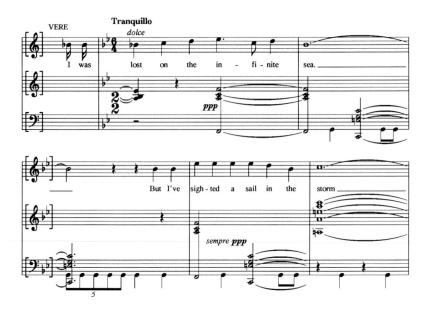

development of the Prologue's quavers), that adds immeasurably to the impact of this passage. Furthermore, Britten's ultimate refinement of this music finds him providing an even more tumultuous B♭ climax (cf. Ex. 12(a) and (b)) towards which, in a sense, the whole opera has been moving.

Ex. 12

(a)

Ex. 12 (contd)

(b)

24

'Abraham and Isaac' Revisited:
Reflections on a Theme and Its Inversion

ERIC ROSEBERRY

The ideas come easily enough but it is more difficult to find the right
notes to fit them . . . Its conception and formal plan came almost at once;
discovering the notes was the real problem.

Britten on War Requiem *in 1963*

The inter-relationship of the settings of the Owen poems (solo tenor and
baritone with chamber orchestra) with the liturgy of the Requiem Mass (solo
soprano, chorus and orchestra, boys' voices with organ) has always struck
me as a crucial and indeed undervalued aspect of Britten's *War Requiem*.
Britten's inspired choice of poems, the way in which they provide the
associative image-'cue' for their location (in one memorable instance, that of
the *Agnus Dei*, for a simultaneous *overlaying* of the Latin text) remain a
subject of extraordinary fascination. 'What passing bells', 'Bugles sang', 'Be
slowly lifted up, thou long black arm' – in each case the context, the passing
from Latin text to English poem and vice versa is born of a mastery of the
art of *transition* that goes back – via *A Midsummer Night's Dream*, the
Nocturne and *The Turn of the Screw* – to the three-in-one cycle of the
Sinfonia da Requiem. If 'finding the right notes' was by no means a painless
process (and a perusal of the sketches would seem to confirm this) yet, as the
sequence unfolds, the notes are discovered in a process of organic thinking,
reflection, motivic economy. Subtle, minute connections and cross-references
abound. By means of overlap, transformation and allusion to previous material
the music achieves a density of thematic/motivic weave and consistency of
style (rhythmic, harmonic, polyphonic) that give the entire work a cumula-
tive resonance. The Owen settings are sometimes referred to as 'a cycle within
a cycle', but their engagement with the liturgy, their manifest derivation
from its music require closer definition. The tension between the Latin
('a language turned to stone' in Stravinsky's formulation) and the tone of
personal protest in Owen hinges on the poems acting as a kind of
questioning commentary on the traditional rhetoric of worship and prayer
embodied in the liturgy – sometimes almost a dissident parody of its images
of consolation. Can there be a rapprochement between man, the helpless
victim of war and persecution, and the official, dogmatic forms of religion?

Britten's music, like Owen's poetry, would seem to leave the question open.

By way of introduction, let us attempt to describe briefly the formal–expressive relationship of the nine Owen settings to those of the liturgy in Britten's scheme of things:

I *Requiem Aeternam.* 'What passing bells for these who die as cattle?' transforms the foregoing symbols of religious consolation into a harsher reality before dissolving into the anxious tritone on 'Kyrie Eleison'.

II *Dies Irae.* In this vast movement the four Owen poems play contrasted (if relatively secondary) roles in accordance with their expression. Parenthetical their role may be, but the sheer weight of their accumulation tends to provide a strong, reflective pull against the current of the liturgy. Thus 'Bugles sang' is a nostalgic intermezzo, transforming the bugle calls of the *Dies Irae.* 'Out there, we walked quite friendly up to death' forms a rough-hewn march-cum-dance episode for the two male soloists, the false heartiness of its A major standing out against the A minor formalities of the preceding. 'Be slowly lifted up' is saturated in motifs recalled from the music of the liturgy: for example – the timpani figure transforming the preceding 'Confutatis maledictis' into a quintuplet figure, the tritone in the voice part at the end of phrases 1, 2 and 4 and the punctuating fanfares. This functions as retransition into the return of the G minor *Dies Irae* at full throttle, so to speak. Finally, each stanza of 'Move him into the sun' stands in expressive parenthesis to the cadence points of a soprano aria with chorus, the *Lacrimosa.*

III *Offertorium.* This is a fugal scherzo on a G major/E minor axis whose central trio section (in E major) is a paraphrase, abridged and transformed, of Britten's *Canticle II: Abraham and Isaac. The Parable of the Old Man and the Young* is a monstrous subversion of the Bible story. Owen's paraphrase takes precedence over the words of the liturgy, which, musically speaking, serve as introduction and frame for Britten's central 'scena' depicting Abraham's turning away from God.

IV *Sanctus.* The Owen poem 'After the blast of lightning from the east' forms a despondent postscript to a brilliant A–B–A choral fanfare of praise and thanksgiving. Its music negates the preceding positive shapes, and the movement ends in fragmentation.

V *Agnus Dei,* the shortest movement of all, superimposes the aria of the Owen poem *At a Calvary near the Ancre* above the choral ground *Agnus Dei.* This forms the quiet climax of *War Requiem* and is the clearest possible expression of the supremacy of Owen's pacifist message for Britten.

VI *Libera Me.* The final and longest of the Owen poems is here placed strategically as a reflective transition from the G minor climax of the *Dies*

Irae to the peaceful Lydian D major 'resolution'(?) of 'Let us sleep now' as it intermingles with 'In Paradisum'.

In no place is the tension between the 'official' liturgy and the private, dissenting Owen more apparent than in Britten's juxtaposition in the *Offertorium*. Here is a prayer for deliverance and eternal life that is poisoned by Owen's poem – itself a bitterly ironic comment on the Old Testament parable of Abraham and Isaac. The composer seizes his chance with both hands, so to speak, in taking one of his most beautiful Canticles and recycling, inverting, *emotionally deconstructing* its material to destroy the serenity and joy, the tender humanity and affirmation of the original. (At the end of the Owen poem the music literally breaks itself to pieces.) Britten's works, like Owen's verse, are rich in the poetry of disillusion. The irony of the *Offertorium*, with its dashing of high hopes, its sense of 'what was not to be' is by no means without precedent: one recalls the march-parody finale of the Piano Concerto or the tragic transformation of 'Happy were he' at the end of *Gloriana*. (Even the fairy music of 'All shall be well' at the end of the second act of *A Midsummer Night's Dream* would seem to touch on the fragility of human happiness.) But in *War Requiem* the musico-dramatic irony of the *Offertorium* breaks a hitherto self-contained mould of inter-reference. Just what is the nature of the relationship of the war piece to its extra-referential antecedent? In concentrating on a closer reading I found myself led back to *Canticle II* in order to discover precisely what use Britten makes of his original material. Reading the later piece in the light of its predecessor, how does this influence our understanding of its motifs, themes, pitches and tonality, the way in which these elements operate musico-dramatically? How successfully does Britten work on the earlier material so that it does not become mere self-pastiche, but a true member of its new context? How relevant is the concept of self-parody to our response? Can one detect a consistency of aims and method between the earlier and the later Britten? Finally, in what sense does the later piece reveal an organically developing style?

* * *

Let us begin with some account of the basic material of the Canticle – the setting of the voice of God, a kind of 'exposition' that proves to be the motivic kernel of the entire piece. In the Canticle it immediately and unequivocally establishes the tonality – E♭ major, God's 'key' – and focuses on the primal 'image' of a (fifthless!) major third. (Bruckner called it 'a gift from God'.) The two-part vocal (alto and tenor) characterization yields important further configurations, for although the words are always sung in rhythmic unison and tend to pivot on the notes of the major third E♭–G in the two parts, there is a constant ebb and flow of gentle diatonic dissonance between them – the product of stepwise motion against its converse.

The rising arpeggio (dominant) seventh ('And in Sacrifice offer him to me' [motif *x*]) and falling third cum rising step sequence set against a descending scale ('For aught that may befall' [motif *y*]) form crucial shapes in the drama to follow. One other musico-dramatic symbol must not escape our attention, and that is the *Ursatz* of the tonic–dominant–tonic 'statement' in this prologue, confirming at a higher level what is implicit in the dominant orientated (E♭–D, G–A♭) two-part opening. Already embodied in the prologue's gentle flow is Britten's symbol of God's authority: a fundamental law of harmonic progression whose full impact will be felt only when the 'sonata form' of its drama reaches the reprise. That long-postponed V⁷–I harmonic resolution in E♭ carries with it all the moral force of a Beethovenian gesture! The strength of this supremely explicit harmonic move, clinching the optimistic message of the Canticle (we shall see how, ironically, it also clinches the pessimistic message of the *Offertorium*), is all the more strongly felt at the end of a piece that is encrusted with V–I gestures as a melodic/harmonic symbol in more or less localized contexts. (The V–I (A♭–D♭) ostinato that underpins the duet beginning 'Father do with me as you will' is a case in point.)

After the E♭ prologue, the tonal shift is a step down to D♭, which is the key of Abraham's obedient submission to God's will and, associatively, both the key of Isaac's farewell to his father and the pitch which (as a pedal C♯) is destined to underpin the preparations for sacrifice. (This same D♭ stands in mediant relation to its satellite A major,[1] the key of 'Father I am all ready'.) Abraham's 'neighbour note' key appears first ('Lord to Thee is my intent') as a pivotal shift from E♭, not a functionally established new region. And, with a fitting symmetry, God's key of E♭ (which makes several brief but telling appearances in the context of other tonal regions throughout the Canticle, notably A major and D minor) returns as a shift back from D♭ when (on a bass tremolo poised between E♭ and D♭!) Abraham is on the point of killing his son. As an example of one of Britten's minute subtleties let it be noted that in this return to the pure E♭ major music of the prologue, Abraham's D♭ is now freshly incorporated in the tenor at 'That of thy son has no mercy well wot I'. In Abraham's joy at God's command his 'obedient' D♭ sounds again, first as a flat seventh in E♭, then as a localized shift of key, as at the beginning ('Thy bidding shall be done'). Joy transports him to an affirmative C major where in the declamatory piano octaves (motifs *x* and *y* conflated) D♭ (as C♯) still has a place. The *y* motif is tellingly redirected towards B♭ and thence to the dominant seventh on B♭ (all the more powerfully commanding in its provisional C major context) as a pointer to the conclusive E♭ of the *envoi*. In which key Abraham and Isaac become as it were at one with God, and in which the tonic–dominant relationship is celebrated in a swinging harmonic ostinato. D♭ has no place in this divine order of things – unless as some unheard remote overtone.

---

1   But see Peter Evans, *The Music of Benjamin Britten* (London: Dent, 1979): 406, who notes the key's symbolic polarity with E♭.

The D♭ neighbour-note relationship to E♭ is a foreground phenomenon; but there is another, higher level context in which to understand theoretically the pitch D (whether natural or flat) in Britten's Canticle. For D♭ is the seventh in the arpeggiation motif x on E♭, and at one crucial juncture ('Ah! Isaac, Isaac, I must thee kill!') we are led (via a chain of dominants – God's will again!) to expect a resolution on to D♭ but instead move into an agitated 'off key' D minor. A♭ here forms a 'false dominant' to D minor and sounds the tritone 'alarm' that will manifest itself again at the climax of the sacrifice. Here indeed are pre-echoes of *War Requiem*'s tonal symbolism!

Although (perhaps not altogether co-incidentally?) the notes E♭–D♭ form the starting point of Britten's *Offertorium* (and, as will be seen below, return in the prayerful intervention of the 'Hostias' at the end of the 'Abraham and Isaac' episode), it is – on the deceptive face of things – in G major and its surprise mediant E major/minor that Britten pitches his parodistic paraphrase of the Canticle in *War Requiem*. (G minor has already identified itself with the *Dies Irae*, so inter-referentially speaking we are in familiar territory.) The E♭–D♭ sonority, symbol of obedience to God's will in the Canticle, now becomes a 'false dominant' to G that derives from the tritone leitmotif of the *War Requiem* as a whole. And – as we shall soon know – G is to prove a deceptive tonic resolution that will be replaced by E major/minor.

Perhaps we should pursue the symbol of the perfect cadence in both pieces a little further. To my ears, parody is apparent at 'Sed signifer sanctus Michael', not least in the 'false dominant' wrench of its destined 'resolution' into the G major of 'quam olim Abraham promisisti'. The jaunty rhythm of the rising bugle fanfare, the strangeness and menace of its bony heterophony, the mechanical repetition – these features are not consonant with a 'straight' reading. One wonders if Britten ever came across *Soldier's Dream*, an extremely uncomplimentary poem about Michael the standard-bearer which Owen had written in 1917. Too casual – even farcical – in tone to fit into the context of the *Offertorium*, Britten would none the less have surely relished its sardonic humour.

> I dreamed kind Jesus fouled the big-gun gears;
> And caused a permanent stoppage in all bolts;
> And buckled with a smile Mausers and Colts;
> And rusted every bayonet with His tears.
>
> And there were no more bombs, of ours or Theirs,
> Not even an old flint-lock, nor even a pikel.
> But God was vexed, and gave all power to Michael;
> And when I woke he'd seen to our repairs.[2]

I would suggest that, as in Owen, Britten's conception of Michael the standard-bearer is something of a caricature, the choral-orchestral militarism of the

2   Jon Stallworthy (ed.), *Wilfred Owen: The Complete Poems and Fragments* (London: Chatto & Windus/Hogarth Press/Oxford University Press, 1983): 182.

Old Testament God of 'righteous' battles breaking in rudely on the celestial sound of boys' voices and organ. The dissonant configuration of two divergent 'series' founded on the C♯–D♯ sonority of the preceding and constructed out of gapped, quasi-pentatonic patterns of seconds and thirds is a far cry from the harmonious pentatonicism of the Canticle. Indeed we have here a near twelve-note situation (nine notes, to be precise) not untypical of the later Britten whose 'resolution' will be on to one of the three missing notes, G.[3] The as yet far-off return of the lower series of this complex hexatonic series 2 (i) (see Ex. 1) on boys' voices and organ in the *Hostias* is destined to strike a further (and qualitatively different) dissonance in the brutal context of the E major 'Half the seed of Europe'.

So the lead-in to the fugue on 'Quam olim Abrahae' may be construed as parodistic, a perversion of the 'natural' V–I, the 'fiat' of God's will in the Canticle, as abrupt in its effect of arriving on G as the $\hat{5}\ \hat{6}\ \hat{5}\ \hat{4}\ \hat{3}\ \hat{2}\ \hat{1}$ melodic descent into it is a barren cliché. The fugue subject is a close but rhythmically destabilized adaptation of Isaac's 'Father I am all ready' and in its formal pairing of entries at the fifth and strict inversions suggests an automaton-like response to the text. As if this were not enough, Britten's perpetual accompaniment of rhythmically broken scale patterns (both rising and falling) in the orchestra as a 'countersubject' serves only to enhance the impression of the (baroque) academic model of fugue being guyed. And when the final, climactic section launches into contrary-motion fifths between the two pairs of voices the sense of a cod fugue is hard to resist. If the Canticle is full of 'straight' canonic duets abounding in pairs of entries at the fifth then this fugue would seem to mock such agreeable symmetries.

With the conclusion first time round of the fugue we reach the transition to E major: the true, and in this case tragic home key for Owen's retelling of the Genesis story that finds its musical analogue in Britten's 'deconstruction' of his Canticle. We have reached the 'trio' section of our fugal 'scherzo'. Much of the Canticle's material finds a new place in the scheme of things. Alto and tenor in the Canticle are transposed (for the essentially narrative mode of Owen's poem) to tenor and baritone. The innocent journey to the place of sacrifice in the Canticle, with its sostenuto two-part right-hand piano part (now in the middle register of the string section) and gentle arpeggio ostinato (motif *x*) in the bass (now heavy timpani and *pizzicato* bass) is treated with a sense of urgency and menace in the chamber ensemble. Abraham's outbreak of anguish 'Oh my heart will break in three' in the Canticle is the phrase and – in the minor mode – key that Britten takes up and refashions for Isaac's words 'My father, behold the preparations'. The voice of God, reassigned to the description of the angel's intervention in Owen, is now a central, not an initiating event, presented as a dramatic interrupted cadence on C (V–VI♭) in

---

3   For a perceptive commentary on Britten's tonally orientated traditionalism in his use of twelve-note dissonance, see Erwin Stein 'Britten against his English Background' in his *Orpheus in New Guises* (London: Rockliff, 1953): 154–5.

Ex. 1

Heterophony in *Offertorium*: 'Sed signifer sanctus Michael'

Linear reduction of above

Derivation from above in 'Hostias et Preces'.
Series 2 (i), inverted and shaped into quasi-medieval
tune by means of passing and neighbour notes

'Hos-ti- as et pre-ces ... fac -   e-as, Do-mi-ne, ... pro-mi-sis- ti

259

E major. The preceding build-up over the dominant pedal B (its murderous tension recalling the significance of the same pitch in Berg's *Wozzeck*) is overlaid with new associations such as the fanfares from the *Dies Irae* and the 'shrapnel' motif from 'What passing bells'. The Canticle's arpeggio 'sacrifice' motif x begins (solo bassoon) on the same pitch – D – as in the Canticle, its pitch acquiring a new cogency in the present context through its identity with the last note of the tenor's phrase. The final phrase of this build-up, 'And stretched forth the knife to kill his son' is an inversion of a key phrase (motif y) in the Canticle that will reappear at the end of the Angel's words 'Offer the Ram of Pride instead of him'. The latter notes, incidentally, appear in Britten's sketches without these words attached. The long ascending scale of the bass part emphasizes the idea of stepwise motion as a leading feature of Canticle and *Offertorium*, linking up with the rising scale as an inversion of that prominent motif in the *Dies Irae*. For me, it sums up – motivically and expressively – the inverse ratio of the two pieces to each other:

Ex. 2

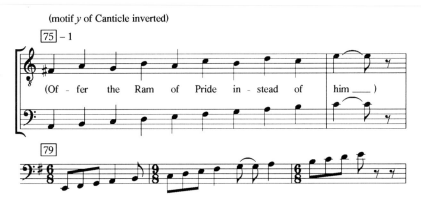

(motif y of Canticle inverted)

But the dramatic interruption merely postpones the inevitable perfect cadence in E. What was the God-given symbol in the Canticle now becomes a musico-dramatic image of man's hell-bent folly. The *Dies Irae* fanfare returns on muted horn, the flattened seventh B♭ emphasizes the unstable tritone (how different from the E♭–D♭ relationship at the same point in the Canticle!), what were Abraham's joyful transports of his motif are now invested with a sinister impulse and the pedal B returns – this time to carry forward, uninterrupted into a baleful return of the E major sacrifice. The brutalization of the repeated E major chords, hammering home the tonality, is like some parody of classical convention. Meanwhile another celestial intervention 'Hostias et preces' on choir and organ (deriving from the 'Et signifer Michael' – see Ex. 1) is not to be dismissed. And the formal perfection of this spiritually remote, overlapping retransition to the scherzo's repeat (now about to serve not as a 'false dominant' to G but as a retransition to E minor) is a fine example of the non-impressionistic economy and cogency of Britten's harmonic thinking.

The inverted recapitulation of the fugue, sotto voce in E minor, is the closing symmetry of this 'evil' scherzo,[4] unable to escape from the tragic implications of its 'trio'. A ghost of its former self, it is led into by the symbolic rising scale that links the Abraham and Isaac motif *y* to the cold fury of the *Dies Irae*. 'Inversion' in this piece – the inversion of all that was good in the Canticle – surely represents perversion of God's will, just as in the Canticle inversion (of the arpeggio motif *x* on God's 'For thou dreadest me, well wot I' etc.) symbolizes all that is good and merciful.

Nevertheless the perfect cadence, the *Ursatz* of God's will in the Canticle, remains the musico-dramatic symbol *par excellence* that Britten stands on its head in the *Offertorium*. In the former, the stability of God's E♭ major is assured; in the latter, E major/minor takes centre stage as the key of Man's folly – all else proves to be deception. In each case the music is 'about' a key

Ex. 3

Canticle II ('God's law')

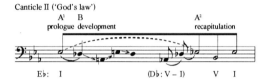

Offertorium ('Man's folly')

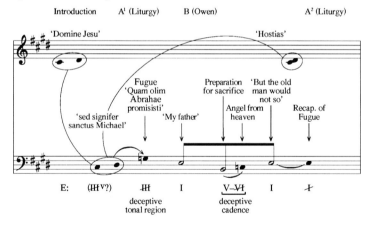

---

4 If Shostakovich remains unique in the music of this century for his portrayal of 'evil' through parody in the scherzo genre (see, for example, the Eighth, Tenth and Fourteenth Symphonies), then Britten's dances and marches of death (in, for example, *Our Hunting Fathers* and the *Sinfonia da Requiem*) disclose one of the many parallels between these two composers.

and its dominant. But stability is fatally undermined in the *Offertorium* through assigning the *Ursatz* to man, not God. The analytical sketch (see Ex. 3 above) attempts a graphic explanation.

*   *   *

In Britten classical symmetry is axiomatic; not for nothing was Mozart's Symphony No. 40 in G minor one of his sacred texts. An almost Bartókian symmetry is a *sine qua non* of the *Offertorium*, and the symmetrical principle governs its first section, the antiphonal setting for two-part boys' chorus of 'Domine Jesu Christe'. Here the organ C♯–D♯ sonority provides the pivot notes for the mirror inversions of the boys' antiphon, which in their turn launch the hexatonic series of 'Sed signifer sanctus Michael'. The formal symmetries of the *Offertorium* are pointed up through the use of a variety of scale patterns, now ascending now descending. Whether the scale patterns are diatonic, twelve-note chromatic, whole-tone, pentatonic or near-octatonic in nature, the 'image' of the stepwise rising fourth and its consequent descent (taken from the formally symmetrical 'Father, I am all ready' in the Canticle) is ubiquitous. The musical connection between Canticle and *Offertorium* is, from this point of view, a strong one, for scales, stepwise motion that fills in the 'arpeggiated' space of third, fourth or fifth tend to define the melodic character of each and every significant motif in both pieces. Moreover the scalic tendency of the melodic/harmonic configurations of *War Requiem* are well established by the time we have reached the *Offertorium*, and continue to be so, as Ex. 4 serves to demonstrate.

Ex. 4

(i)

Minor and octatonic (*Requiem Aeternam*)

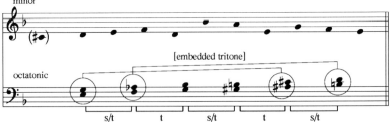

(ii)

Octatonic ('When I do ask white age')

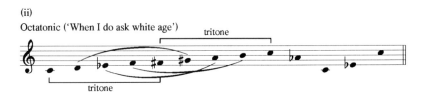

(iii)
Mixed-mode segments (*Dies Irae*)

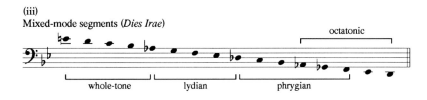

(iv)
Overlapping pentatonic (*Offertorium*)

Overlapping hexatonic

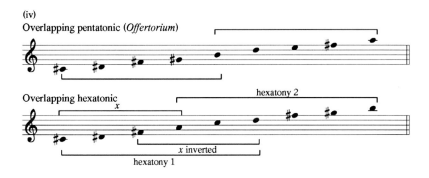

(v)
12-note pentatonic segments ('Pleni sunt coeli')

(vi)
Whole-tone ('Te decet hymnus')

(vii)
Mixed-mode (*Agnus Dei*)

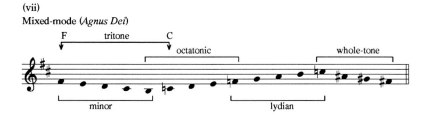

263

Such a 'regressive' feature of a musical style at a time when English musical life was buzzing with the discovery of Schoenberg allies Britten to Berg (whose twelve-note thinking favoured scalic and tonally arpeggiated configurations) rather than the more anguished expressionistic angularity of the twelve-note master and his radical pupil, Webern. And the pronounced tendency of *War Requiem* towards a loosely twelve-note mode of operating with scalic patterns is a mark of the 'developing' Britten not to be encountered in the earlier, limpidly diatonic Canticle. And yet even in the earlier piece we may note a tendency towards an octatonic type of chromaticism that transforms the classical diatonic scale. The following passage from *Abraham and Isaac* is an interesting quasi-octatonic descent towards a phrase that unites

Ex. 5

Scalar reduction of above
(i) Descending octatonicism

(ii) Eb major embedded in D minor octatonic segment

tritone

Isaac's D minor fear with God's E♭. (N.B. The tritone D–A♭: again a pre-glimpse of *War Requiem*.) A and C are the 'missing' two pitches needed to complete a twelve-note 'row' freely deployed; they turn up in the luminous context of a pentatonic F major that will follow (Ex. 5).

In *War Requiem* such situations are more explicit, first in the 'mixed modal' run-up to the interrupted cadence on C (the note needed to complete a twelve-note ascent), and then in the terrible confirmation of the perfect cadence 'But the old man would not so' (another twelve-note ascent to the 'missing' note G♯) (see Ex. 6).

Ex. 6

This close and unrepentantly subjective reading of a model in the context of what I take to be its parody may not recommend itself to those who prefer to concentrate on the music of a given piece as a hermetically sealed process. Criticism here takes issue with Analysis – a subject upon which Joseph Kerman has been eloquent both in critical practice and as commentator on the musicological scene.[5] As we listen to *War Requiem* there is certainly not time to indulge in the kind of activity that has taken place in this essay without losing track of immediate events. But any consideration of a composer's style must engage in the reflective mode of thought that looks beyond the boundaries of the individual work, seeking to view the *oeuvre* as a stylistic whole. For example (and I am sure that the dedicatee of this essay would be the first to agree with me), the analyst denies himself essential insights if he/she refuses to consider Mahler's First Symphony as some kind of symphonic trans-formation of the experience of *Lieder eines fahrenden Gesellen*. Similarly – less positivistically – to interpret the first movement of Tchaikovsky's Sixth Symphony as a kind of long-range – if unconscious and deeply subjective – 'parody' of his *Fantasy Overture: Romeo and Juliet* is not, perhaps, without its bearing on the tormented expression of the former late piece, with its

5   See, for example, Kerman's chapter on Musicology and Criticism in his *Musicology* (London: Fontana/Collins, 1985): 113 *et seq*. Kerman's masterly study of *The Beethoven Quartets* (London: Oxford University Press, 1967) remains a virtuoso display of multi-contextual critical/analytical readings in style.

undisclosed programme. Where, ultimately, is the boundary line of 'context' in the evaluation of a composer's style to be drawn? (In the preceding discussion I have only touched on the notion of *War Requiem* as a Mahlerian choral symphony, for instance.) As I hope to have shown, Britten's treatment of the parable of authority in Requiem and Canticle offers a rewarding study in the making of a mirror image, in a concept of self-parody that can enrich our separate perceptions of the music of a great English composer at two different stages of his development.

25

Not All the Way to the Tigers:
Britten's *Death in Venice*

EDWARD W. SAID

Donald Mitchell has quite justifiably, I think, raised the question of whether Britten's *Death in Venice* can be regarded as being in more than a chronological sense a *last* work. Moreover he presents convincing evidence that Britten had not intended the opera to be his final, and therefore summary statement about the genre. But, Mitchell concedes, it is a *late* testamentary work nevertheless by virtue of its subject matter.[1] Britten's frail and even precarious health, the opera's compressed and often difficult style, which Mitchell describes as belonging to the genre of 'parable art', the catastrophe that befalls Gustav von Aschenbach: these converge in Britten's choice of the solitary figure of the German (but symbolically European) artist, a brooding and celebrated author beset by a 'late' impulse to flee Munich for a new locale largely because (in Thomas Mann's words) 'his work had ceased to be marked by that fiery play of fancy which is the product of joy'.[2] Within Mann's novella then, Aschenbach's half-aware and yet inevitable voyage to Venice induces in the reader the sense that because of various premonitions and past associations (e.g. Wagner's own death there in 1883) and its own peculiar character, Venice is a place where one finds a quite special finality. Everything that Aschenbach encounters in the tale – especially that whole range of demonic characters, from his strange fellow passenger on the boat to the overly amiable barber – accentuates the feeling we have as spectators that he cannot ever leave Venice alive.

Mann himself wrote nothing for ten years after *Death in Venice* was published in 1911. But within his *oeuvre* the work is a relatively early one, all the more paradoxical for its autumnal and even at times elegiac qualities. Britten came to it at a late point in his life and career: we know, as Rosamund Strode points out, that he had it 'well in mind by 1965' although

1 Donald Mitchell, 'An Introduction in the Shape of a Memoir', in Donald Mitchell (ed.), *Benjamin Britten: Death in Venice* (Cambridge: Cambridge University Press, 1987): 21.
2 Thomas Mann, *Death in Venice and Seven Other Stories*, tr. H. T. Lowe-Porter (1911, reprinted New York: Vintage Books, 1954): 67.

its completion and first performance took place about nine years later.[3] The striking thing about both opera and novella though is how extraordinarily much they beseech, and yet, by means I want to explore in this essay, they also reject a principally or exclusively autobiographical interpretation. Both deal with crises, challenges, and complexities unique to the artistic life, and these certainly were experienced by Mann and Britten. We know of course that homosexuality for both men energized their explorations of their own creativity as artists: opera and novella do not shy away from this at all. More important, however, is that both works in effect represent the triumph of artistic achievement over the final degeneration and terminal submission to disease and to illicit (or at least unconsummated) and irrational passion to which Aschenbach arrives. The old man dead on the beach in both works represents a carefully distanced object – pathetic and sad it is true – from whom author and composer have already departed; this, they seem to be saying, is *not* me, despite the numerous parallels and suggestions.

According to Dorrit Cohn, Mann accomplished this by means of a 'bifurcating narrative schema' through which 'the narrator [who is not Aschenbach] maintains his intimacy with Aschenbach's sensations, thoughts and feelings, even as he distances himself from him more and more on the ideological level'.[4] Cohn takes the further step, however, of also separating Mann's narrator from Mann himself: 'The author *behind* the work is communicating a message that escapes the narrator he placed *within* the work.'[5] Unlike Mann whose ironic mode undercuts any simple moral resolution of Aschenbach's experience, the narrator constantly employs a morally judgemental rhetoric, which some commentators (she cites T. J. Reed) want to associate with Mann's failure of nerve: having conceived the tale 'hymnically', he now wants to resolve it 'morally', with the result, says Reed, that the tale is ambiguous in a bad sense, uncertain of its own meaning, disunited.

Like Cohn, however, it is preferable for us to view the novella's apparent moral resolution as answering to the narrator's own needs and not to Mann himself, for whom an ironic distance between himself and the narrator is maintained scrupulously. Very plausibly Cohn asks us to think ahead to *Doktor Faustus*, the only other of Mann's full-length explorations of the artistic predicament.[6] Neither Serenus Zeitblom nor the narrator of *Death in Venice* is capable of having 'created' Adrian Leverkühn and Aschenbach respectively.

Mann's 'irony in both directions' – between himself and the narrator, between the narrator and protagonist – is achieved by literary, narratological means not readily available to the musical composer. And I think this rather simple, indeed elementary realization must be thought of as constitutive to

---

3 Rosamund Strode, 'A *Death in Venice* Chronicle', in Mitchell, op. cit.: 26.
4 Dorrit Cohn, 'The Second Author of *Der Tod in Venedig*', in Inta M. Ezergailis (ed.), *Critical Essays on Thomas Mann* (Boston: G. K. Hall & Co., 1988): 126.
5 Ibid.: 137.
6 Ibid.: 140.

Britten's whole undertaking in *Death in Venice*, an *askesis* imposed necessarily on him in the transfer of the novella from one medium to another. His librettist Myfanwy Piper admits as much throughout her valuable chronicle of how she constructed the opera's 'book' out of Mann's, the latter 'a dense and disturbing', endlessly evocative, ambiguous and referential text, the former a translation of 'very elaborate poetic prose' into the forms of the stage.[7] Accordingly, she comments on how a great deal of what she did involved cutting, para-phrasing, condensing. What resulted was a libretto specifically designed to be mounted in the theatre as the staging of story *and* music together.

What the very skilfully shaped opera story jettisons is Mann's narrator, the mocking, moralizing, explicitly ironizing voice that both describes what Aschenbach does or thinks, and tries to direct our thoughts about it. For example, as the protagonist wanders through the city (he has just uttered his 'I love you'), the narrator refers to him as 'our adventurer', and goes on to describe Aschenbach's unhinged behaviour, all the while of course standing further (and more disapprovingly) away from him. This particular device is not to be found in the opera. Indeed, according to Britten's early sketches, it was deliberately forgone: the original plan had been to provide a sort of external narrative for the opera by having Aschenbach appear at times to be *reading* from his diary (seeming like a narrator to stand back from the action) but this was changed into a sung recitative accompanied by the piano. The outer narrative dimension was thus absorbed into the music, sub-merged so to speak in the musical element, and especially into the orchestra.

Another particularly interesting change concerns a very early moment in the novella. Aschenbach has already seen the exotic man in the mortuary chapel portico, and this inspires him (the man himself actually says nothing) to formulate his desire to travel south. The narrator then describes Aschen-bach's thoughts, noting the cautionary limits Aschenbach imposed on him-self: 'He would go on a journey. Not far – not all the way to the tigers.'[8] The reference is to 'the eyes of a tiger' gleaming in the hallucinatory vision stimulated in him by the exotic man. In the opera both the cautionary idea of not going as far as the tigers and the outer narrative frame are dropped. The exotic man speaks directly of 'a sudden predatory gleam, the crouching tiger's eyes' as part of his injunction (again, a direct one) to Aschenbach to 'travel south' where his 'ordered soul shall be refreshed at last'. This is pre-ceded by a few questioning lines of doubt about whether or not he should break with his orderly life, which soon after he does in fact break with.

Here the opera seems immediate and explicit, where Mann's text is circumspect and even ironically devious, since it will be precisely the tiger's world – that of the exotic Orient – that finally overtakes him in Venice in the form of an Eastern plague. 'Not going all the way to the tigers' is one of those odd bits in the narrative that might be a part of Aschenbach's interior

7   Myfanwy Piper, 'The Libretto', in Mitchell, op. cit.: 50.
8   Mann, op. cit: 8.

monologue, or it could be something introduced by the ironically observant narrator. In reading it 'normally' we rush past it, a tiny detail that is quickly left behind. The act of solitary and consciously interpretative re-reading, however, allows for moments of pause and return; we come back over the text, we make distinctions, we move forward and back, and, occasionally, we discover these instances of ambiguity and even instability, where words may belong in one or another level of discourse. The sequential temporality of written (and hence of read) prose permits, indeed encourages, this sort of inward non-sequential activity. *Death in Venice* is in fact a text whose density, range of references, and highly wrought texture requires a slow, extremely deliberate decipherment very different from a reading produced under the pressures of theatrical musical performance, with its urgent succession of recitative, scenes, arias, ensembles.

On the other hand, more than all other musical genres opera delivers the largest amount of direct information to be processed by the audience. Words, notes, costumes, characters, physical movements, orchestra, dance, setting: these hurtle across the proscenium directly at the spectators who must make sense of what is happening even though the sheer quantity of material nearly defies absorption and understanding. Britten's *Death in Venice* also carries with it the considerable weight of Mann's novella, the knowledge of which is perforce present as the opera unfolds. So what we see and hear therefore is a complex simultaneity of memory and actuality, all of it dominated by the presence of Aschenbach whose first words – 'My mind beats on' – make explicit the ineluctable forward movement of his story. Mann's work interiorizes the action, whereas by necessity of course Britten exteriorizes it: Aschenbach's thoughts are always audible in the opera, to be heard and seen, whereas in the novella Aschenbach is above all *legible*, scripted in that odd too-and-froing between his own thoughts and those of the narrator that I mentioned earlier.

Despite their differences, however, both works in the end convey a feeling of overpowering solitude and, also because in both works Aschenbach nowhere consummates his love for Tadzio, of great sadness. Aschenbach's failure to possess Tadzio physically is contrasted with the enactment of actual physical coupling and intimacy that goes on between Tadzio and his friend–antagonist, Jaschiu. And as in the last scene Tadzio seems to wander out to sea, the now terminally infected Aschenbach – grotesquely perfumed, coiffed, primped – sits in his lonely chair passively watching him, and then expires. This literal gap between lover and beloved is maintained throughout *Death in Venice*, as if author and composer want to keep reminding us that although Aschenbach travels south he does not quite make it to the tigers, that is, he never arrives at that wild, presumably unrestrained region where desires are realized, fantasies fulfilled. For both Mann and Aschenbach Venice of course is where he ends up, a southern city but not quite a truly Oriental one, a European but most definitely not a really exotic locale. The question remains, however, for both Mann and for Britten, who sticks quite closely to his great predecessor: why not in fact allow

Aschenbach to go the whole way, and why the choice of Venice in particular?

Aside from its immediate anecdotal association with Wagner's death Venice carries with it an astonishing, formidably dense cultural history, which is the subject of a remarkable book by Tony Tanner, *Venice Desired.* More convincingly than anyone before him, Tanner shows that Mann's city is the inheritor of a rich history of the nineteenth-century imagination: Byron, Ruskin, Henry James, Melville, Proust before Mann located in Venice a special quality that drew to it 'appreciations, recuperations and dazzled hallucinations', most of them capitalizing on the city's peculiar appearance and its decline, as well as its power for attracting *desire.* 'In decay and decline', Tanner says,

> (*particularly* in decay and decline), falling or sinking to ruins and fragments, yet saturated with secretive sexuality – thus emanating or suggesting a heady compound of death and desire – Venice becomes for many writers what it was, in anticipation for Byron: 'the greenest island of my imagination'. When Byron left Venice two years later, it had become a 'sea Sodom'. Venice had a way of turning on her writerly admirers as no other city does.[9]

Venice's reality as a city combines two extremes almost without transition: a glorious, unexampled and shining creativity on the one hand with, on the other, a history of sordid, labyrinthine corruption and profound degradation. Venice as quasi-Platonic sovereign republic; Venice as city of prisons, sinister police forces, internal dissension, and tyranny.

The special force of Tanner's book, which treats Venice synoptically in such a way for the first time, is how he demonstrates that despite the enormous diversity of his writers, a certain troubling consistency in Venice's image keeps recurring. One is (Tanner speaks here of Ruskin) how in Venice 'the transition from gorgeousness to garbage [the city's two extremes] is swift indeed'.[10] He quotes the following passage from *The Stones of Venice*:

> Venice had in her childhood sown, in tears, the harvest she was to reap in rejoicing. She now sowed in laughter the seeds of death. Thenceforward, year after year, the nation drank with deeper thirst from the fountains of forbidden pleasure, and dug springs, hitherto unknown, in the dark places of the earth. In the ingenuity of indulgence, in the varieties of vanity, Venice surpassed the cities of Christendom as of old she has surpassed them in fortitude and devotion; and as once the powers of Europe stood before her judgment-seat, to receive the decision of her justice, so now the youth of Europe assembled in the halls of her luxury, to learn from her the arts of delight.
>
> It is needless as it is painful to trace the steps of her final ruin. The ancient curse was upon her, the curse of the Cities of the Plain, 'Pride, fulness of bread, and abundance of idleness'. By the inner burning of her own

9   Tony Tanner, *Venice Desired* (Cambridge, Mass.: Harvard University Press, 1992): 5.
10 Ibid.: 121.

passions, as fatal as the fiery rain of Gomorrah, she was consumed from her place among the nations; and her ashes are choking the channels of the dead, salt sea.[11]

This rapid oscillation between paradise and Inferno, Tanner shows, is central to Ruskin's vision. How suggestive it is for *Death in Venice*! Clearly Mann and Britten both seized on and each in his own way reappropriated this topos for each of their works.

The second feature of Venice's image is the way in which the city is always written about from the outside (by a visitor from the outside), and is therefore *already* 'grounded in an image which in turn was nourished by a textually based text. Venice is always the already written as well as the already seen, the already read.'[12] Thus Proust in a sense inherits Venice from Ruskin by reading about it, and in turn writing it, so to speak, in his own idiosyncratic way. Tanner remarks:

> Fairness is all. In terms of Proust's novel, Venice (the word-name) both represents and *is* the indefinable and unconfinable pleasure of absence, a pleasure which is indistinguishable from pleasure deferred, or that deferral which is pleasure. Venice present is Venice lost . . . But again perhaps losing is a prelude to another finding – a finding *again* – in another mode . . . The pleasure of Venice is no unambiguous matter.[13]

Mann belongs in this formation too, using, or rather causing Aschenbach to use, Venice as a distant place to return to, and to locate or find in it that immense reservoir of cultural memory contributed to by his predecessors; in addition Mann's own work is a regaining, 'a finding again in another mode', of the Venice lost through time and distance. Britten's opera is yet another prolongation, or regaining of Venice, much more explicit than Mann's in that it is unabashedly based on an already-there literary text which Britten reuses to explore the peculiar splendours of the city in terms of an artist's coming to terms with his own inner (and dark) sensual impulses.

In a rather intriguing way then for Britten Venice is not only approached from outside via another text very much in keeping with the artistic image of Venice so persuasively analysed by Tanner, but also by virtue of its history of glory and degradation it is a pre-eminently *late* setting for a mature opera, for which a crystallized, much worked over style conveys in itself an allegory (Mitchell's word is *parable*) of the artistic/personal predicament of coming to a place, theme, or style at a late period in one's life, coming there not as to Prospero's island, but rather to an old, much excavated, extremely worldly place, visited *again*, as if for the last time. We must remember that the problematic of allegories, and even of parables, is that *what* they allegorize is

11 Ibid.: 124.
12 Ibid.: 17.
13 Ibid.: 24.

always viewed retrospectively, the fable or allegorical narrative coming *after* an experience or theme that is conveyed by the subsequent performance, so to speak, in a different, more attenuated and coded form.

I noted earlier that Mann's *Death in Venice* employs an ironizing narrative device to distance Aschenbach from the *persona* who recounts the story of his infatuation with Tadzio, and that this *persona* is used by Mann to place even more distance between himself as author and Aschenbach, his character. Britten's composition, however, uses the Mann novella without these narratological devices. So on the one hand *Death in Venice* the opera allegorizes its German 'original', but does so on the other hand in what is in effect an actualized present, or operatic time, unfolding before us in Venice (except for the two scenes at the beginning of Act I that precede the orchestral 'Overture', entitled *Venice*).

Now, unlike a literary text such as Mann's *Death in Venice*, the opera is a collaborative work, although Britten's role was quite clearly the dominant one: the music he wrote takes up the libretto, devises a total aural vocabulary, and finally shapes the work's aesthetic existence down to its smallest orchestral and vocal detail. Venice, however, remains central to the opera, although it too is absorbed into the work's musical fabric, its unfolding and actual present. But its role is quite a different one than in its literary antecedents. The orchestral prologue identifies the music directly with coming to the city, which is not only talked about before but presented, or rather enacted, as a sensuous part of what the audience sees and hears *immediately*: thereafter Venice is where we are along with Aschenbach. So Britten's music accomplishes not only the approach to Venice (in the first two scenes) but also overcomes geographical distance and gives us Venice as a musical–theatrical environment, minus ironizing narrator and self-conscious scepticism.

Britten's technique of using opera to provide direct and immediate non-ironic identifications of the sort that Mann's narrative art struggles quite consciously to avoid is clearly seen, I think, in his instructions that one baritone was to play seven distinct roles, all of them kept quite distinct (albeit obviously related to each other internally) by Mann. Intermittently, but unmistakably, we are reminded by Britten that Venice is the setting of the action. It too is seen to embody numerous, simultaneously present identities: the polyglot hotel clientele, its staff, the various Venetian characters encountered by Aschenbach, etc. But Britten's Venice is also revealed to be the site of a divine contest or *agon* (prepared for in the games of Apollo that end Act I) between Apollo and Dionysus. But when Dionysus actually sings in his own voice, it is as an outsider ('the stranger god'), although his dream appearance occurs just after Aschenbach has allied himself with Venice's underground self: 'The city's secret, desperate, disastrous, destroying, is my hope.'

By this time – to be more exact, a scene earlier – the city itself has been invaded by an Asiatic plague, described in great detail by the English travel clerk to whom Aschenbach comes for information. What Aschenbach experiences in the opera is therefore an accumulation of identities (much as the single baritone accumulates several identities throughout the work) all of them anchored in Venice, Venice as glorious city of Christendom *and* City of the Plain, Venice as European *and* Asiatic, as art *and* chaos. So too does Britten's 'ambiguous' tonal idiom deliver a European and an Oriental orchestra – polytonal, polyrhythmic, polymorphous. It is as if Britten's purpose in the work was to set himself a series of obstacles, and even ordeals to go through in Venice, which its ambiguous nature, part Inferno and part Paradise, necessarily entails and from which Britten does not flinch.

I would then speculate that Britten's *Death in Venice* is a late work to the extent that it uses Venice as an allegory to convey not only a sense of recapitulation and return for a long artistic trajectory, but also in its representation as a site for this opera, as a place where for the main character at least irreconcilable opposites are deliberately collapsed into each other threatening complete senselessness. Tanner very aptly suggests that for Mann's Aschenbach the music he hears in Venice is an anti-language, an idiom completely given over to a disturbing, distasteful and bestial assault on the clarity of consciousness and conscious artistic communication.[14]

In his opera Britten cannot really separate word and music, or the textual and the extra-textual, and therefore devises a music for the opera that draws on his past work as well as non-European sources. This music incorporates normally discordant elements (much as Venice does) into an eccentric, that is, unexpected and rare, amalgam whose purpose for Britten is that it allows him intimately, and at very close quarters, to explore the limits of the artistic enterprise, maintaining and even prolonging those opposites whose basic difference goes back to the struggle between Dionysus, the stranger, and Apollo, the luminous sense-giver. Thus even though the opera does not go as far as 'the tigers' – to the eradication of all sense – it does not *resolve* the conflict, and therefore, in my opinion, Britten provides no redemptive message or reconciliation at all. When Aschenbach is forced to the limit of both his mortality and his aesthetic capacities, Britten presents his protagonist's fate as that of a man neither able to draw back from nor fully to consummate his desire for the beloved, yet elusive, object. And this, I would finally argue, is the essence of Britten's *late work* which is perhaps most poignantly and terminally embodied in the space we see between the seated Aschenbach and the increasingly distant Polish boy. Adorno, analysing late Beethoven, calls such a composite figure of nearness and distance both 'subjective and objective. Objective is the fractured landscape, subjective the light in which – alone – it glows into life. He [the artist] does not bring about their harmonious synthesis. As the power of dissociation, he tears them apart in time, in order, perhaps, to preserve them for the eternal. In the history of art late works are the catastrophes.'[15]

14 Ibid.: 355.
15 Theodor Adorno, 'Late Style in Beethoven' (1937) tr. Susan Gillespie, *Raritan Review* XIII 1 (Summer 1993): 107.

26

A (Far Eastern) Note on *Paul Bunyan*

SOMSAK KETUKAENCHAN

Balinese music was first introduced to Benjamin Britten during his years in America (1939–42) by Colin McPhee, the Canadian composer, then living in the USA, and an authority on Balinese music.[1] In 1934 McPhee first transcribed *Balinese Ceremonial Music* for two pianos in Western notation which both Britten and McPhee later performed and recorded in 1941. It therefore can be assumed that Britten's involvement with Far Eastern music originated during this period. It was an involvement that was eventually to have a deep influence on his composing techniques.

The first appearance of a Far Eastern influence on Britten can be heard in *Paul Bunyan* (libretto by W. H. Auden), Britten's first opera, composed while he was in America. It was written a year after he had met McPhee, and McPhee's influence on Britten is revealed in a rather surprising way: from Fig. 11 in the Prologue to Act I we encounter a kind of gamelan ensemble playing a heterophonic texture in order to create a special effect when the chorus sings: 'Look at the moon! It's turning blue.' This is the moment when Paul Bunyan, the mythical hero, is born.

Chou Wen Chung, the Chinese ethnomusicologist, defines a gamelan composition as: 'A nuclear theme played simultaneously with several layers of elaboration on the theme in different registers and different paces.'[2] In what respects does Britten's gamelan composition in *Paul Bunyan* correspond to this definition? We find a slow nuclear motif in the lower register and faster variations in the higher registers. At the start, the nuclear motif, E, F♯, G, F♯, is played by the second trombone and the harp in minims, each statement of the motif occupying two bars. The motif, in different rhythms and different

---

1 Colin McPhee (1900–1964) was born in Montreal, Canada. He studied music at the Peabody Conservatory in Baltimore and also in Paris with Paul Le Flem. He spent most of his time in America and Bali. One of his well-known orchestral works is the toccata for orchestra, *Tabuh-Tabuhan*, based on Balinese music. He also wrote three books, *A House in Bali* (1946), *Dance in Bali* (1948) and finally *Music in Bali* (1966). See also Carol J. Oja, 'Colin McPhee: A composer turned explorer', *Tempo* 148 (March 1984): 2–7.

2 See Chou Wen Chung 'Asian Music and Western Composition', *Dictionary of Twentieth-Century Music* (London, 1971): 22.

Ex. 1

Ex. 2

(a)

(b)

speeds, is repeated again and again by the other instruments. The nuclear motif is never transposed except to different octaves. Ex. 1 shows all these features. Such music, in which all the parts are derived from and elaborate on a nuclear motif, is a perfect example of the heterophonic principle. (The nuclear motif is marked x on Ex. 1.) The unusual scoring of this passage for woodwind, brass, percussion, harp and piano only (no strings) represents Britten's way of trying to achieve the sound of a gamelan with the conventional instruments of the Western orchestra. The relationship between the nuclear motif and its elaborations is very simple. At the beginning of the passage, the simpler and slower elaborations enter first, and then, after all the parts have entered, they drop out one by one until only the basic motif remains. (See Exx. 2(a) and (b).) The simplest elaboration is in the horns, which play the motif at double speed (i.e. crotchets instead of minims) but displaced so that the motif begins on the last beat of the 4/4 bar instead of on the first beat (see Ex. 2(a)). While the horn is playing the nuclear motif like an ostinato, the top woodwind (piccolo and flute) are playing a speeded-up semiquaver version of the basic motif which includes one statement and three repetitions of the basic motif. In the oboe, bass clarinet, bassoon and piano (left hand) we have a quaver triplet version of the motif which includes one statement and two repetitions of the nuclear motif. In the clarinets and harp there is yet another version of the basic motif, this time in quavers, each bar of which includes one statement and one repetition of the basic motif. The second trumpet meanwhile plays a syncopated version of the motif (one statement in each bar) and the trombone continues the motif in ornamentation. The piano (right hand) sustains a tremolo in each bar made up of all the notes of the basic motif. This gives us a mathematical sequence as follows:

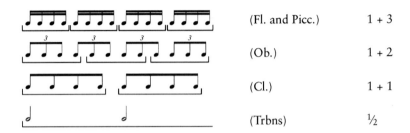

(Fl. and Picc.)	1 + 3
(Ob.)	1 + 2
(Cl.)	1 + 1
(Trbns)	½

The nuclear motif itself is derived from the opening chorus of the Prologue, which begins in C major (see Ex. 3a). But this soon becomes the nuclear motif itself, motivically, and also through using the Lydian fourth (F♯) in C (see Ex. 3b).

Ex. 3

(a)

Ex. 3 (contd)

(b)

Although this example of the gamelan influence on Britten is comparatively simple, it also shows very many subtleties. It clearly derived from what he learned from McPhee and the two-piano transcriptions of *Balinese Ceremonial Music*.[3] The influence was to become much richer and more flowing in his ballet *The Prince of the Pagodas*, composed about sixteen years later.

3   The heterophonic principle is found throughout the *Balinese Ceremonial Music* (New York: Schirmer, n.d.). For example, see *Taboeh-Teloe*, the last system on p. 4, where all the parts, different though they are in rhythm, are derived from this same scale or nuclear motif:

27

Writing and Copying: A Superficial Survey of Benjamin Britten's Music

ROSAMUND STRODE

'Another copy, please.' Easy to say, and easy to put into effect in 1995, when office copying machines, so obliging with their ever-increasing range of facilities, will yield up instant clones of the submitted original. But life hasn't always been governed by electronic devices, and one of the aspects of Benjamin Britten's work that becomes increasingly fascinating as one handles the manuscripts and other materials is the way in which, in common with other composers of his age, his active *writing* career encompassed so many changes (or, if you like, advances) of technology.

Putting aside for now the musicians whose work is transmitted solely by an aural tradition (or by its modern counterpart, the ubiquitous eaves-dropping recording apparatus), all composers must set down their music on paper so that it may be performed and distributed and thus, with luck, survive for future generations. For Benjamin Britten, once he had reached that point of putting something down, this involved several distinct stages: (i) the original manuscript composition sketch or draft; (ii) developments from that in order to obtain a performance, e.g. the full score (entirely or mainly autograph), vocal/instrumental score, parts, etc. (fair copies often entirely or partially made by a copyist); (iii) revisions (often based on experience gained at the first performance), edited copies, printers' proofs etc. (i.e. interim materials) leading to (iv) the publication of the first edition, available on sale to the public. The text of this would be corrected when reprinted, or it might even be succeeded by (v) a reset second edition. All of these stages – except perhaps the first – involved the use of different technical means at various times throughout Britten's creative life, which began in 1919 and was to continue until shortly before his death in 1976.

Fortunately he lived in the age of pencil and rubber[1] (an advantage denied to many earlier generations of composers, obliged to use pen-and-ink and a

---

1   This friendly word is, of course, the short form of 'India rubber', which described the substance when, at the end of the eighteenth century, this indispensable use for it was first realized. Now not necessarily made of rubber at all, the more accurate description should perhaps be the prim 'pencil eraser' – but that smacks of stationers' catalogues.

knife blade) and all his life habitually used pencil, particularly for his composition sketches. And the little boy who wrote a play called *The Royal Falily* [*sic*][2] had a very clear idea of what publication meant; the author's name and address appear at the foot of the title-page though he had not then (aged six) set up the 'publishing house' – HOME SERIES – used three or four years later for 'Beware!' in its earliest 'published' version, and again (as HOME SONGS) for the 'collected edition' of his own songs which Britten wrote out for his mother in 1924.[3]

Britten was not unique in dressing up presentation copies of his earliest works, written out with laborious childish care, as if they were 'real' music: it seems to be a stage through which many very young composers pass, though not always with the addition of a 'publisher'. The British Library has examples by the six-year-old Mr R. Williams (a four-bar piano piece composed in 1878/9 entitled *The Robin's Nest*) and by the visiting Austrian prodigy, then aged nine, Mr Wolfgang Mozart, whose only setting of an English text 'God is our refuge' marked his visit to the British Museum in 1765. (Though *he* was helped to write it out by his indefatigable father Leopold, always anxious to show off his son in the best possible light.)

In his first years as an apprentice composer Britten had several notions about the way that music should look; for instance he firmly believed that a piece had to finish at the bottom of a page, so he would (he said) carry on composing until it did. (Publishers please note: it must have been the excellent page layout of the piano editions used by the young Britten that led to this conviction.) Then there was a period when, at around the age of eleven (perhaps having seen an adult signing or initialling changes on cheques) any small alteration to the current composition was carefully endorsed by E. B. Britten with a stylish autograph, a prudent practice reminiscent of the composer's or publisher's stamps of authenticity to be found on printed music of the late eighteenth and early nineteenth centuries.

---

2 Reproduced in full in PFL, Plate 19.
3 See PFL, Plates 28–9. The full title of the collection is: *Twelve/SONGS FOR THE MEZZO-SOPRANO/AND CONTRALTO VOICE/MUSIC BY E. B. Britten/ WORDS/BY FAMOUS POETS ETC./. . . N.B. All these songs are dedicated to My Mother Mrs. E. B. Britten/Published by "Home Songs"/21 Kirkley Cliff Rd/ Lowestoft.* (Mrs Britten's middle name was in fact Rhoda: the second initial here is, one supposes, a subliminal slip on the part of the composer, whose signature is placed immediately below.)
    Ten piano pieces from the collection of *WALZTES* [*sic*]/. . . *Opus 3/1925/dedicated to My Father:/R. V. Britten Esq.* were slightly revised by the composer when published by Faber Music in 1970, with a cover design based on the front of the original 1925 manuscript book (*GB–Lbl* Add. MS. 60624). This time there is no domestic 'publisher' on the front – the details there for A. Weekes & Co. Ltd, sellers of the manuscript book itself, are copied from its back cover – but a nice touch is the addition of this significant line: 'copyright for U.S.A.' On the 1970 edition the publishers' names are given as 'Home Publications in association with/FABER MUSIC LTD, LONDON' – and the characteristic mis-spelling of 'Walztes' is there retained. Alas, both of these jokes were removed from the second edition (1992): too subtle and irritating for music dealers and cataloguers to handle.

While still at a preparatory school in Lowestoft and before he began to study with Frank Bridge, Britten relied on the local music shop for supplies of manuscript paper, where he obtained the 12-stave quarto books widely distributed by various London music publishers. There would, one supposes, have been occasional gifts of other sizes (including some of closely ruled orchestral paper) to satisfy his insatiable demands and his sisters begged from their friends the unwanted small manuscript books issued by their school. When not using pencil to write with, a penholder with nib dipped into a bottle of ink or an inkwell would, in common with most children of his time, have been used by E.B.B.; fountain pens were exotic possessions not to be expected before a 'responsible' age was reached and besides, most teachers thought that they were not good for the handwriting of younger children and banned them from school work. But once at Gresham's School, Holt, in 1928, a fountain pen became Britten's norm and with it he generally used one of the pale-blue so-called 'washable' inks which many boarding schools (including Gresham's?) actually required. The private possession of bottles of ordinary ink would have brought imaginable hazards.

Several interesting compositions date from July 1930 – interesting both for their musical content and (in this context) for their superficial appearance; these include the original version of *A Hymn to the Virgin*.[4] After working exceptionally hard that school year Britten took (and won) an open scholarship examination to the Royal College of Music in June and his School Certificate exams in the second half of July;[5] those who knew him in later life are not surprised to learn that, having overdone things somewhat, he had to be taken out of school at the beginning of July to spend some days in the sanatorium. While there he was, characteristically, writing away (the *Hymn* is just one of several pieces) but, having run out of manuscript paper, had to make do with a block of plain writing paper and rule up the staves for himself. From the way in which these dip at the right-hand margin it rather looks as though he didn't even have a good flat surface to write on – or did he use a book-edge as a ruler?

It was during those two years at Gresham's that Britten began to involve others in trying over his compositions, and so moved seriously into the business of supplying performing material. Usually this meant copying out single parts for instrumentalists or singers, though in the case of another of the compositions dating from July 1930 he did make an attempt to save time and, aided by his mother's sister, to mass-produce the voice parts for two works intended for a little group of his mother's friends to sing at a Musical Evening at home on 3 January 1931.[6] The duplication involved his trying to

---

4   Part of this manuscript is reproduced in Imogen Holst, *Britten* (London: Faber and Faber, 1966): 24. When published by Boosey & Hawkes in 1935, the *Hymn* was transposed down a semitone into A minor.

5   See DMPR: 131–3 and 135–6.

6   'O, fly not, pleasure' to a poem by W. S. Blunt, with Walter de la Mare's 'I saw three witches' composed on 5 November 1930. See DMPR: 149.

align some pages of 12-stave manuscript paper with blue carbon paper sandwiched in between and then write firmly on the top page in pencil: not an experiment he repeated. The inexperienced singers could neither sight-read nor understand the music; a disaster both for them and for the composer, but from it he learned something about the importance of good, readable copies if you want your work to go well. (He couldn't do much about the total unsuitability of the singers on that occasion.)[7] Rather more professionally produced music was used (apparently made by an office typing agency) when *Two Choral Songs* were performed by the Lowestoft Musical Society a few days later.[8]

Once at the Royal College of Music in September 1930, the real business of being a composer began for Britten and apart from refinements to his musical handwriting (which assumed its familiar adult form around 1933) he settled into grown-up habits most of which were to last for many years.[9] The pencil drafts had small corrections made with the help of a rubber; larger unwanted passages were crossed out but usually remained visible. He would use separate bifolia of paper one at a time (i.e. four pages) and if a whole leaf (two pages) were to be scrapped it was torn away from its twin. A single loose leaf in the middle of a Britten manuscript otherwise consisting of bifolia should send one looking for the 'missing' half.

Occasionally traces of ink appear on a pencil composition sketch – alterations or the addition of small details; the composer's ink fair copy always matches these, both as to ink colour and in the musical text.[10] The thrifty-minded Britten used any paper that came to hand – no composer wastes expensive manuscript paper, especially when there's usable space on it – and he had early become ingenious, in those pre-Sellotape days, in using up stamp-paper and tiny strips of gummed tape to hold his work

---

7   This sorry tale was recalled by one of the participants, the late Mrs E. M. Walker, when interviewed (by RS) in Lowestoft in November 1985 (transcript at the Britten–Pears Library).

8   *A Hymn to the Virgin* and *I saw three ships*, the latter published in 1968 as *The Sycamore Tree*. The foolscap-sized copies, printed on to Gestetner paper by (presumably) a rotary duplicator, were, however, not without fault. Britten, using Indian ink, had provided a specially written fair copy which must then have been carefully traced over with a sharp stylus on to a wax-coated stencil before the words were typed in below the music. In his diary for 23 November 1930 Britten (rather unfairly) complains: 'I spend most of the rest of the day altering the 54 copies of the songs (about 26 alterations in each copy) that I think are very badly done.' (This careful labour paid off and he was pleased with the performance; see DMPR: 150.)

9   When attempting to date a piece by its look, a great deal has to be taken into consideration in addition to the conjectured age of the writer. Tools and materials (a change of pen nib, especially) and haste or other circumstances can all conspire to mislead; a child's handwriting is especially prone to sudden change, and can just as suddenly revert back to an earlier style.

10   *Peter Grimes* provides an interesting example, as the ink used for the full score is of a distinctive blue. Although the complete full score is in the Library of Congress, Washington, DC (ML30.3c2.B75case), a few discarded pages are in the Britten–Pears Library (2–9300936) where they may be compared with the composition draft (2–9401098).

together[11] and, quite often, to join the edges of leaves embracing substantial cuts instead of using paperclips or tearing out the unwanted pages. Boyhood work from the age of eleven shows that he had already learned the trick of drawing long, straight barlines across all the staves from top to bottom of a page without using a ruler, a facility he was to retain all his life.

When it came to the provision of copies, the student, however busy, had just to settle down and make them, as had every generation of composers before him; hard work, and duplicates of several of Britten's earlier official compositions were copied out again by himself. There are, for instance, two autograph fair copies of the full score of the *Sinfonietta*, Op. 1[12] – a substantial work running to well over a hundred pages – and in June and July 1933 the composer wrote out a set of nine voice parts for a try-through by the BBC's Wireless Singers (using single voices) of *A Boy Was Born*; each part, as he pointed out in a letter to his parents on 2 July, consisted of 'at least 14 closely written pages'.[13] These fair copies and performing parts were always in ink (Britten had, by now, abandoned the 'washable' pale blue ink of his school days and thereafter used blue-black for preference): thirty years later, in the 1960s, the tremendous advances of copying processes were to allow the successful reproduction of pencil originals.

In 1932 the Oxford University Press published the first of Britten's works to appear in print, the Three Two-part Songs for boys' or women's voices, to texts by Walter de la Mare. These 'studies in canon' were engraved, just as music had been reproduced for two hundred years, though the actual processes of printing had moved on a good deal. (One must remember that until the development of photo-lithography early in the twentieth century, this was virtually the *only* way of obtaining multiple copies for larger works.) In 1995 the laborious skills of the engraver have quite vanished from London, and even the master craftsman, Jack Thompson, who worked alone in producing the beautiful vocal score of *Death in Venice* published in 1975, has taken to more modern methods and no longer engraves.[14] In the

11 Fortunately: modern self-adhesive tapes are a nightmare to all bookbinders and - conservators.
12 *GB–ALb* 2–9800019 and *GB–LBl* Add. MS. 60593. The latter was copied in November 1932 for submission (via Oxford University Press) to the ISCM Festival Committee.
13 See DMPR: 307. These voice parts are now in the British Library (*GB–Lbl* Add. MS 59798). Britten wrote in his diary (10 July 1933):
    ... to B.B.C. where I hear end of rehearsal of wireless singers (8 + 2 for boys pt.) doing my Boy. That from 12–12.45; & again aft. lunch back here 2.30–3.30, then a run through for the B.B.C. music staff to hear. I am relieved to say that it all comes off splendidly. They sang it excellently considering they were sight-reading it from M.S. parts (copied at 5.30 in morning!). I am very pleased & bucked.
14 In 1963 or 1964 I was lucky enough to see the engravers' shop at Boosey & Hawkes with half-a-dozen men, under Mr Price, working in good light at a long bench below a window. It was fascinating to see how this exacting task was carried out (with everything in reverse, and often done by people who knew nothing at all about music) and understanding a little about its difficult techniques certainly helped when it came to proof correcting.

1960s and 1970s Britten was usually favoured by his publishers when it came to proofs of an engraved work; of course the final set of corrected pages of an engraved publication was painstakingly produced in the traditional manner before being printed by the offset lithographic method, but by the 1960s quick proof pages were often made with white notes on a coloured background (generally green) – far more difficult to read.[15] Plaintive grumbles from Britten would sometimes bring along the traditional sort he preferred.

Composers are always on the look-out for reliable copyists, and the need must have been far greater in the 1930s (as in earlier centuries) when, for instance, every individual orchestral part for a new work still had to be written out by hand. Not much fun with a large string section to provide for, though at least good copyists saw to it that the page-turns were staggered so that only one player turned at a time. Britten was often fortunate in enlisting a friend to help him out when the need arose, especially when pressed for time. In 1936, at a particularly busy moment, the composer Grace Williams copied out parts for some of the movements of *Temporal Variations*, Britten himself dealing with the rest.[16] And in the spring of 1939 Lennox Berkeley helped with the vocal score of two songs destined ultimately for *Les Illuminations* – 'Marine' and 'Being Beauteous' – for Sophie Wyss, who broadcast them on 21 April;[17] Britten and Peter Pears sailed for North America a week later. *Les Illuminations* was not resumed until July and not finished until October that year, but it bears an example of a typical Britten compositional battle-scar: the insertion into a work at a relatively late stage of an extra number or movement (in this case No. 5a 'Phrase'), assigning to it the number of a neighbouring movement, and then distinguishing between the two with 'a' and 'b'.[18] The same device, which derived from last-minute changes to the incidental music for screen, stage and radio, also appears (for instance) in *Paul Bunyan* and *A Ceremony of Carols*.[19]

Not surprisingly, technology in the USA in 1939 was in many ways much further advanced than in England and Britten tried out several (to him)

---

15 For the final pulls, black ink is rubbed into the engraved plate and the surface then cleaned off, leaving ink only in the punched and engraved areas. Damped paper is then rubbed well down on to the plate by hand (or the plate put into a press) taking up an impression off the ink. With 'quick' proofs, ink is applied lightly over the surface of the plate with a roller so that the (uninked) engraved areas print out white, as with a lino-cut.

16 The choice of movements copied by Grace Williams looks odd until one realizes that Britten must have been working simultaneously from the composition draft (*GB–ALb* 2-9500568), so couldn't release it for her to use. In fact the fair copy (*GB–ALb* 2-9500569) never did get finished and Adolph Hallis, the pianist at the first performance on 15 December 1936, played the last three movements from the composition draft.

17 See DMPR: 617–18.

18 See Britten's letters to Ralph Hawkes (3 June 1939) and Sophie Wyss (19 October 1939) for different examples of the composer's attempts to finalize the order of songs within the cycle (DMPR: 650–52 and 713–16).

19 See DMPB: 121–8, and DMPR: 1040–42.

innovative and labour-saving ways of reproducing work in manuscript. Although in 1939 and 1940 he did use semi-transparent paper (written on with black ink) for a few smaller pieces, he never really took happily to this method and did not continue with it; perhaps it needed 'modern' finishing not available for some time in England. Peter Pears, who had become Britten's in-house copyist for *Paul Bunyan* in 1940, wrote some of the vocal score on transparent paper so that multiple copies could easily be printed off; these were slightly reduced in size photographically.[20]

Most advances in reproduction were due to photographic processes of one kind or another – not merely the one-off small 'bromide' photographs, or cameras used as adjuncts to offset-litho printing for longer runs of any size, but also the early varieties of wet chemical photocopiers which were suitable for making just a few copies, especially of manuscripts. (The needs of technical drawings and architectural plans demanding, like full-sized music scores, large-sized reproductions, must certainly have brought about much of this progress, as also was the case with dyelines.) One photocopying method gave large, thin, paper prints each of which, when doubled over back-to-back, formed a single page. The free back edges were held together and bound between boards with a spiral wire spine, while the head and foot of each finished page remained open. A few copies of the *Seven Sonnets of Michelangelo* were made like this, one of them suitably inscribed and presented to Alma Mahler by the composer.[21]

Returning to England in 1942, Britten resumed pre-war methods of setting down his work. But of course he found that there were scarcities of everything, frustrations made worse by the fact that he had discovered excellent manuscript paper in the USA the like of which he was not able to obtain at home until some was made to order for him twenty years later. Although pre-war British papers had been adequate, some frankly substandard paper was produced both during and after the war. Unreliable and variable in quality with impurities in the paper, it tended to be a bad colour and slightly shiny on the surface; additionally the actual widths of the available rulings did not suit Britten's compact, neat hand. He found that the staves were usually too wide and that the unruled spaces between, as well as the upper and lower margins, were all far too cramped for his needs. Furthermore a rubber removed stave lines and paper surface in addition to the unwanted

---

20 A reduced-size facsimile of Britten's autograph full score of *Diversions*, photographically reproduced, was published (in the USA only) by the New York office of Boosey & Hawkes in 1941. Until the appearance of the limited edition of a replica of the composition sketch of *Children's Crusade* (actual size), with added illustrations by Sidney Nolan (London: Faber Music, 1973), this remained the only facsimile of a Britten work to reach the market. Since access to the original manuscript of *Diversions* has been severely restricted for many years, in its case the fortuitous existence of the 1941 facsimile has been particularly valuable.

21 This score is in the British Library (*GB–Lbl* part of Deposit 9353); see also DMPR: 1088 and 1095–6. There are also some early vocal scores of *Peter Grimes* made up in a similar manner.

pencil, so that the stave lines had to be replaced before work resumed.[22]

This brings the ballpoint pen on to the scene, for Britten was to find that a black one gave him the best results when repairing staves or, when necessary, extending them into the margins. Ballpoints, not at first reliable, were available in the USA from 1945 and came on to the market in England in 1950;[23] they were gradually to supplant the fountain pen and become Britten's most usual writing tool for correspondence and everyday life except for music, apart for the function mentioned above.[24] He continued to draft in pencil and to write full scores in ink (with Imogen Holst as his music assistant from 1952 to 1964), except in moments of real crisis when the far quicker pencil came to the rescue.[25]

In the mid-1960s, with the change of publishers (for new works) from Boosey & Hawkes to Faber Music,[26] came changes in production processes and consequently some small adjustments to Britten's writing habits. The use of dyelines for small runs of performing material,[27] such as vocal scores for

22 In 1963 Boosey & Hawkes produced manuscript paper with three special rulings for *Curlew River*, using a good quality white paper giving folio pages. The templates were ruled out by John Arthur, head of copying: two for instrumental parts (one ruling with systems of two bracketed staves and a cue-stave above (for harp and organ parts), the other a single part-line with cue stave for the remaining instruments) and one 'open' 16-stave ruling, used for the score and thereafter for practically all of Britten's work, except for large scores. This 16-stave paper was reprinted twice; in 1969, together with a 24-stave score ruling (by which time the original paper was, inevitably, unobtainable and I remember testing other possibilities by seeing how the surfaces withstood maltreatment), and again in 1972.
23 See Henry Petroski, *The Pencil: A History of Design and Circumstance* (London: Faber and Faber, 1990): 323.
24 After his illness in 1973 when his right hand would no longer function properly, Britten took to using a black fibre-tipped pen for correspondence; easier to manage than a ballpoint.
25 For instance the last pages of the full score of *The Prince of the Pagodas* (GB–ALb 2–9300932/4/5) are entirely in pencil, although this huge score is otherwise in ink. In the full score of *War Requiem* (GB–Lbl Add. MS. 60610), except for the last movement (again, entirely in pencil) the amanuenses (Imogen Holst and RS) used ink; all of Britten's scoring is in pencil. Both of these large works were written against time. A particular oddity is the full score of *The Turn of the Screw* (GB–Lbl Add. MSS 60603/4). Prepared in the usual way by Imogen Holst using ink (clefs, voice parts, some instrumental lines etc.) as instructed by the composer, he then completed the scoring – in pencil, for speed. She next made the set of instrumental parts, but when Britten came to conduct at rehearsals he found that he could not read the pencil of the full score under the prevailing low light conditions. Imogen Holst had, therefore, to ink over all the pencil work, presumably between rehearsals. History repeating itself, for Britten had had to ink over the full score of his Violin Concerto (GB–ALb 2–9500570). It was written early in 1940 in a particularly small, neat hand and the conductor (Barbirolli) found it impossible to read until most of the music had been clarified; it makes an interesting study. And the much used autograph manuscript full score of the Piano Concerto of 1938 (GB–ALb 2–9500571) serves to remind one what used to happen to composers' original scores; the days of quick replication rescued them from frequent use by different conductors.
26 See Peter du Sautoy, 'Donald Mitchell as Publisher': 167–9 above.
27 A method of actual-size reproduction based on transparencies. Either hand-written work on translucent paper may be used, or photographically produced 'autopositives' taken

an opera, had already become quite usual, though Boosey & Hawkes had their own printing shop and Britten's work was generally produced there in the more traditional way. Faber Music perforce relied on external printers, and, with Britten's agreement, did not attempt to put the final printed copies of his music on sale to the public until he was thoroughly satisfied with the text.[28] This led not only to delays (often deliberately planned, as for works with a period of performing 'exclusivity' guaranteed to a particular soloist) but also to a proliferation of on-hire interim copies, which met demand until sale copies were available. These interim copies, usually dyelines of a manuscript (though not necessarily one in Britten's hand), could circulate for several years; that applied, for instance, to the full scores of *Paul Bunyan* and *Death in Venice*. (Incidentally although the latter was written entirely in pencil, legible conductors' scores were made from it.) Original or early performing materials and proof sets preparing the way for final printed copies constitute other interim copies, all highly important to the proper understanding of how Britten actually worked.[29] With the development of electrostatic photocopiers from the 1960s the nature of proof sets issued to the composer changed to match. Specially prepared papers, not always producing a satisfactory or permanent copy, mercifully gave way to plain-paper copiers using ordinary office paper; a similar battle is currently (1995) being fought out with fax machines. Even so, no photocopied page yet supplies the hoped-for archival degree of permanence. And it is instructive to look down the list of twentieth-century manuscripts given to Peter Pears by the composers whose works he performed. Up to 1960 these were almost all handwritten, but (apart from special gifts) the later scores tended to be reproductions of one kind or another.

Over the years since Britten's death the pace of this kind of technology has galloped on; composers may now (if they wish) use their own computers for composition and a single software program can produce an elegant score, extract accurate parts from it (coping faultlessly with transpositions as required) and so on. But it is surely essential for the musicological research

from black-and-white originals. Copies may easily be printed off in any quantity, and corrections incorporated, if need be, on to the transparencies to update successive copies. (Autopositives are more difficult to correct and are rather fragile.) The final copies, printed on chemically coated bulky paper, unfortunately discolour with exposure to light and with age, and a reek of the ammonia sometimes used in the dyelining process can often be detected whatever the age of the prints. Dyelines also present acute conservation problems, as yet unsolved.

28 Several different motives lay behind this decision – uncertainties on Britten's part about the direction his work seemed to be taking and how best to set it down clearly (e.g. *Curlew River* and the later more freely structured pieces), business reasons, etc. – all outside the scope of this essay. Faber Music has, over the years, published works prepared in several different ways – engraved; hand-copied; the various processes developed and patented by firms such as Halstan & Co. Ltd, Caligraving Ltd and others; Notaset (rubbed-on dry transfer music symbols related to Letraset) – and so on. Computer-set music must now (1995) be added to the list.

29 Much of this interim material may be seen at the Britten–Pears Library.

of the future that these earlier, sometimes transitory, methods of the twentieth century should be accurately and helpfully charted. Will someone not write a comprehensive *Student's Guide to Twentieth-Century Reproductive Processes*? Though it may, of course, find its way on to the wrong shelf in public libraries . . .

*   *   *

Except for Alma Mahler's copy of the *Seven Sonnets of Michelangelo* and the set of vocal parts of *A Boy Was Born*, Britten manuscripts belonging to the British Library mentioned above are on loan to the Britten–Pears Library, Aldeburgh. Experts at Boosey & Hawkes and Faber Music have been most helpful with detailed information about past technology, and I am grateful to the Librarian and staff of the Britten–Pears Library for allowing me to renew my acquaintance with the Britten materials for the benefit of this essay.

28

Along the Knife-Edge: The Topic of
Transcendence in Britten's Musical Aesthetic

ARNOLD WHITTALL

Reviewing *Letters from a Life*,[1] Paul Griffiths felt an 'overwhelming sadness' coming from his observation of 'a sharp, eager mind withdrawing itself'. Around 1940, Griffiths suggests, there 'came a change not only in manner but in the whole musical outlook . . . Britten goes, with no transition, from boyhood into middle age.'[2] A similar point is made by Robin Holloway when he describes *The Prince of the Pagodas* as 'the only work of Britten's maturity (apart from the *Spring Symphony*) that realizes fully the gaiety and brio with which the Young Apollo's voice had disconcerted the melancholy water-meadows and coronation rhetoric of this country's musical norms in the interwar years'.[3]

In such comments we see the elements of what another writer, discussing another, younger composer, Oliver Knussen, has termed (unconvincingly, in my view) an 'aesthetic of avoidance',[4] and it is common to link that apparently decisive and permanent change to Britten's need to acknowledge, yet conceal, his sexuality. In Griffiths's diagnosis, 'the secrecy, the constant cautiousness about what was being revealed, left the music lamed', and Griffiths concludes that 'it is hard not to regret the lost possibility of a father-figure who could have revolutionized British music in the 1940s and 1950s'.[5]

In contrast to Griffiths, Philip Brett has argued that Britten turned the tension between acknowledgement and concealment to positive artistic ends:

> Prevented from any open discourse by the self-imposed silence on the matter of sexuality which he shared with most prominent homosexual men of his generation . . . covert treatment of the issues of sexuality may have offered itself as a personally effective remedy. The result was an

1   DMPR.
2   Paul Griffiths, 'A Mind Withdrawing', *The Times Literary Supplement* (28 June 1991): 15.
3   Robin Holloway, [Record review], *Tempo* 176 (March 1991): 32.
4   Ivan Hewitt, 'The Aesthetics of Avoidance', *Musical Times* 134 (December 1993): 712–13.
5   Griffiths, op. cit.

engagement in his work, first with the social issues of his experience of homosexuality, later with the metaphysical ones, that trod various fine lines between disclosure and secrecy, allegory and realism, public and private.[6]

It is not difficult to regard the 'fine lines' to which Brett refers as the principal location of those conflicts and ambiguities which, for many, are more than adequate replacements for that early 'daring and brilliance'. To put it another way, Britten engaged consistently in his work with established musical genres, some of which have an essentially social, or functional, resonance, others of which are primarily aesthetic, and it is the interaction between those genres, sometimes reinforcing tension, sometimes achieving integration, that actualizes and enhances the engagement with both social and metaphysical issues of which Brett speaks.

Brett claims that 'part of the attraction of Britten's art is the knife-edge it walks between the genuine and the sentimental, between honesty about life's difficulties and a longing for resolution and comfort'.[7] But Britten's art could walk this knife-edge only by means of compositional techniques capable of embodying the co-existent alternatives to which Brett refers.

Britten's music is usually defended against accusations of thinness and narrowness by reference to the composer's ability to integrate (and not merely juxtapose) a wide range of musical elements in an entirely personal way. In a striking obituary tribute, Robin Holloway wrote that

> the combination of lucidity, emptiness and tightness in the latter works, can reveal common ground between the most unexpected and unrelated sources. This music has the power to connect the avant-garde with the lost paradise of tonality; it conserves and renovates in the boldest and simplest manner; it shows how old usages can be refreshed and remade, and how the new can be saved from mere rootlessness, etiolation, lack of connection and communication.

All this is in the context of the judgement that, while Britten's style might not, by the standards of the mid-1970s, be 'central', 'it can show the way better than any other to a possible pulling-together'.[8]

Britten's powers of synthesis and integration should certainly not be under-estimated: as Holloway correctly observed in another context, 'it is Britten's extraordinary achievement in the church parables to have integrated the discoveries of serial and post-serial pitch organization into the fundamental unchangeables of the harmonic series'.[9] It is that impulse to integrate

---

6 Philip Brett, 'Britten's Dream', in Ruth A. Solie (ed.), *Musicology and Difference: Gender and Sexuality in Music Scholarship* (Berkeley: University of California Press, 1993): 263.

7 Ibid.: 276.

8 Robin Holloway, in 'Benjamin Britten: Tributes and Memories', *Tempo* 120 (March 1977): 5–6.

9 Robin Holloway, 'The Church Parables (II)', in BC: 218–19.

which does much to determine the ultimately 'classical' quality of Britten's aesthetic and technique. Yet it is no less characteristic, no less essential a part of Britten's creativity, for the tendency to synthesize to be countered, offset and even, on occasion, frustrated, by strong and irreducible ambiguities. Even when the 'language' appears unified, the form, the genre, may contribute to the creation of an ambiguous aesthetic result, and in no context is this process more striking or more characteristic than when what I've termed social genres confront aesthetic ones in ways that focus a confrontation between extra-musical and more purely musical concerns.

That confrontation is particularly unambiguous when Britten's concern is arrangement rather than 'free' composition. His treatment of the folksong 'The Ash Grove' is a famous example of what can happen when a twentieth-century composer, his ear sensitive to every psychological nuance of a text, decides to confront the unvaried strophic structure of the original tune. The result might be deemed a clear case of a composer subverting the simple (folklike) qualities of the original in order to do proper justice – 'proper' in the sense of what psychologically aware art music can achieve – to the expressive range of the text. Any attempt to claim that, on the contrary, there is no 'subversion' in Britten's treatment of the original, rather an enrichment and enhancement, by means of a logical yet sensitive transformation of its elements into something new, might well be countered with the argument that it is the very persistence of the original melody, superimposed in the voice against dissonant derivations in the piano, that is subversive and resistant to overall synthesis despite the final return to consonance between voice and piano. The social genre is disorientated by the over-mastering assertiveness of the aesthetic genre, and a narrative that, in the unaccompanied folksong, might appear, on musical grounds at least, to be recollected in tranquillity, is shown in the art song to be the source of persistent pain. Most of the time, however, Britten was a composer, not arranger, and the situations that arise when he alludes to a social genre within an essentially aesthetic one are likely to be more subtle and more complex than is the case with 'The Ash Grove', powerfully immediate though that work is.

Another strategy for defending Britten against accusations of thinness and narrowness stresses the emotional resonance of his references to musical archetypes deeply rooted in the psychology of his formative years. Christopher Palmer is one writer who has sought to emphasize the effect of what he has termed Britten's enchanted childhood on the composer's entire development, and it is also Palmer who introduces a discussion of hymnody, the particular genre with which the rest of this essay will be mainly concerned. Palmer brings his two topics together, asserting that 'Britten's lifelong attachment to hymnody' may well have 'remained throughout his life associated with the context in which he first encountered [hymns] as a boy'. Listing some of Britten's uses of, or allusions to, hymns and other sacred material, Palmer then declares that 'the hymns touch something deep down in our sub-conscious, something older than the present organization of our nature, something innocent of the fall from grace', in support of his thesis that 'Britten's child-like-ness was the mainspring of his creativity'.[10]

One could easily take issue with Palmer's recourse to unambiguous causality in his essay, yet my concern here is not to consider the cause so much as the nature of Britten's creativity, and the significance of the role of hymnody, as actuality and allusion, within it. Real hymns may be written by real composers, but they are not art music: they fulfil a function within church services that cannot, by definition, be in the least ambiguous, even though hymn texts may be poetically allusive in their use of metaphor and symbol. Like folksongs, hymns are normally strophic and non-developmental in structure, assuming that, even when a full four-part choir is present, the collective singing by choir and congregation of a repeated tune is the genre's most fundamental attribute. In this sense, therefore, for Britten, hymns are not simply representative of childlike innocence and certainty, but 'found objects' whose transference from church service to artwork inevitably under-lines the contrast between the generic role of the original and its possible function after that transference has taken place. The process of transference gives the composer the opportunity to exercise his imagination. Sometimes he may seek to integrate the 'found' material so closely into his own cultivated idiom that the gap is closed, the tension between the social and the aesthetic defused; in other contexts he may appear to stress the tension, so much so that the celebratory or meditative quality of the original generic association is, in part at least, subverted.

There is clearly a broader topic here, for it is a characteristic of relatively conservative twentieth-century styles, such as Britten's, that they can call on a rich variety of generic associations and allusions, both social and aesthetic. In Britten's case, a social generic allusion may on occasion stand for some-thing both innocent and desirable which arouses nostalgic, regressive emotions, but it may also represent a kind of 'otherness' which lies at the heart of the music's intensely personal dialogue between collective and individual impulses. The potential significance of such 'otherness' is all the greater if one acknowledges the tendencies, in the art-music context, for the boundaries of various contributory genres to blur. In an earlier study of Britten I have explored this blurring where associations with pastoral and lullaby are concerned.[11] It would be an enormous task to consider all the ramifications in Britten's work of genres relating to sacred and liturgical music – chant, anthem, canticle, chorale, as well as hymn – yet even with observations restricted to certain aspects of hymnody and chant, the potential richness of the topic can be clearly indicated.

As far as I am aware, no one has ever accused J. S. Bach of failing to

---

10 Christopher Palmer, 'The Ceremony of Innocence', in BC: 81–2.
11 'The Signs of Genre: Britten's Version of Pastoral', in Chris Banks, Arthur Searle and Malcolm Turner (eds), *Sundry Sorts of Music Books* (London: The British Library, 1993): 363–74.

integrate his chorale harmonizations into the unified musical fabric of his Passions and cantatas. The effect of their introduction is not the creation of degrees of ambiguity between Bach's 'real' music and these found melodies. Their function is to add to the range of contrasts within the formal and textural elements of the structure – to enrich the 'variety within unity' of the whole – rather than to disrupt unity, still less to prevent it from being established at all. The chorales place collective reflection alongside the individual reflection of the arias, as well as the narrative of recitatives and choruses, and the 'super-genre' of the whole remains, of course, a sacred one, finely poised as it is – or was in Bach's own time – between its social function and its aesthetic attributes.

The opposite extreme from such integrated variety is the kind of modernist superimposition we find at the end of Peter Maxwell Davies's opera *Taverner*, where John Taverner's real, sixteenth-century 'In nomine' – played by recorders – overlaps with, and ultimately outlives, Davies's own music, derived from the Taverner but radically remote from its stylistic and textural characteristics. Such an ending is powerfully symbolic – of an unresolved tension between doubt and faith, of the contradictory impulses to betray and affirm, and of the intense difficulty of celebrating integration in the real world of modern life and art. It might be claimed that Britten achieves a not dissimilar effect in Act II scene 1 of *Peter Grimes*, where the personal conflict between Grimes and Ellen stands in stark opposition to the collective conventions of the offstage church service. Yet simply because Britten is not a modernist, the degree of conflict within the musical fabric as a whole is less extreme than in the Maxwell Davies. Britten's response to the aesthetic issue of the 'space' between generic allusion and cultivated style is not so much to preserve and enhance the differences as to explore their interrelationship, if only, in the end, to cast a shadow over their integration even as he (ironically) affirms it.

Since hymns and chorales are, in essence, collective songs of praise and adoration, it is understandable that much rhythmically regular homophonic music which is not explicitly dancelike or otherwise determinedly secular should have the potential to carry a special expressive charge, and especially so when set to statements of belief in which the tone is elevated and the text acknowledges the transcendent. Obviously enough, composers may choose to set familiar hymn or carol texts in a wholly non-hymn-like style in order to underline their aesthetic freedom from the utilitarian constraints of the social genre, as Britten does with the first stanza of Christina Rossetti's 'In the bleak mid-winter' in *A Boy Was Born*. Something closer to hymn, or chorale, in that work appears in the setting of the fifteenth-century carol 'Jesu, as Thou art our Saviour', whose initial, four-fold repetition of 'Jesu' suggests the rapt simplicity of what is at first more like rhythmicized chant, with a single reciting tone. It is the evolving harmony of the three lower parts that brings chorale into the generic picture – that and the character of the text, with its description of Jesus as 'paramour', inevitably if anachronistically creating a frisson in the twentieth-century audience which the sensuous treble solo descant underlines. This is a prayer of longing rather than lament and, while not totally remote in atmosphere from the authentic, social hymn-tune style of Vaughan Williams's *Down Ampney* ('Come down, O love divine') it is clearly too intense, too contrived in terms of its consistently dissonant lines, for congregational singing. The initial, homophonic theme of *A Boy Was Born* is closer to orthodox chorale texture in its use of a melody/bass polarity, but again its extended tonality lifts it into the realm of art music. That status is confirmed in the glorious recomposition of the theme with which the work ends: it is not simply that the tune returns, but the whole texture is developed and enriched.

Britten's early ability to absorb allusion to the hymn or chorale genre into purely instrumental contexts, even when the mood is solemn, reflective, akin to lament, may be noted in the *Chant* of the *Frank Bridge Variations* and the concluding section of the Violin Concerto. But it is the adjacent opuses 26 and 27, the *Scottish Ballad* for two pianos and orchestra and the *Hymn to St Cecilia* for five-part unaccompanied chorus, that bring the generic topic highlighted in this essay into full focus. The *Ballad* employs the Scottish psalm tune *Dundee* as one important thematic factor in what is a thoroughly diverting, wholly secularized concert work: here the found object sheds all its generic content save its inherent nobility, which stands for one extreme of the *Scottish Ballad*'s aesthetic spectrum. The effect of the *Hymn to St Cecilia* is no less thoroughly secular, in keeping with Auden's highly refined poetic content, and even its more homophonic refrain passages cannot be claimed to allude to hymn as a social genre. If there is a social element, it is dance rather than prayer. On the evidence of these relatively early works, then, it might appear that it was the need to find convincing musical material for the social situations so crucial to his opera *Peter Grimes* that led Britten to consider the more 'realistic' use of hymns and hymn-like material in his works, and, given his particular enthusiasm for editing and arranging in the 1940s, he may well have been newly sensitive to the attraction and signi-ficance of enriching his own language with such alien elements at the time when he was composing *Grimes*.

Christopher Palmer has observed that in *Albert Herring* the children's 'Glory to our new May King' is clearly an intentionally comic hymn-tune parody (perhaps partly derived from Wesley's 'Hark how all the welkin rings' and W. H. Monk's tune *Würtemburg*).[12] But in 1948, in *Saint Nicolas*, parody gives way to full quotation. When *Saint Nicolas* was still relatively new, Donald Mitchell commented: 'It has always struck me as little short of miraculous that Britten could integrate two great English hymns into *Saint Nicolas* without any stylistic or formal discrepancy and, more importantly and astonishingly, without causing any sort of psychological discomfort to the audience.'[13] On one level, this 'miracle' is a tribute to the adaptability of

12 Palmer, op. cit.: 81.
13 Donald Mitchell, 'The Musical Atmosphere', in Donald Mitchell and Hans Keller (eds),

the hymn: what we learn from *Saint Nicolas* is not that Britten's musical language, all along, has been devised to fit perfectly with that of the original hymn tunes, but rather that the hymn settings can be absorbed by Britten's style without losing any of their essential attributes, and without those attributes being turned into objects of parody or distortion. Here, and even more powerfully in *Noye's Fludde* a decade later, Britten demonstrated that hymnody could adapt itself to quite radical if not downright modernist musical techniques without seeming to be totally subverted in the process. It will not do, after all, to regard *Saint Nicolas* and *Noye's Fludde* as attacks on established religion, even if one might conclude from them that Britten is preaching a gentle sermon on the need for congregational church music to move with the times: one need not abandon Victorian tunes, but one might at least question Victorian attitudes to dissonance. Such a strategy can even be construed as Britten warning of the dangers, in religion as in other aspects of the social life, of mindless conformity and unthinking support for convention. If so, the most striking example of this strategy in his work must be his treatment of *Mount Ephraim* in *Winter Words*.

In 'The Choirmaster's Burial', Britten treads a particularly fine line between the harmonic defamiliarization of a hymn and the positive use of its generic essence within his music. Given Hardy's unambiguous critique of the bluff Dorset vicar and the local worthies who simply do as they are told, Britten might have been tempted to hold up the blinkered and insensitive attitudes of the Established Church to ridicule by using, but distorting, the original harmonization of the hymn tune. Such a procedure could have intensified the gulf between the original object and the contemporary (to Britten) commentary upon it. In the event, however, Britten preferred the integrating path, offering an otherworldly version of the tune from the beginning – a harmonization, provided by the angels of Hardy's verse, in Britten's own style. The result is that the emotional and psychological significance of the hymn is enhanced: it is not to be dismissed as obsolete, but transferred into a newly expressive musical world. Britten deploys his critique of convention and pomposity by transfiguring rather than subverting the genre of hymnody, and this has less to do with paradigms of lost innocence than with that vision of a wider social tolerance and justice which can be glimpsed in so many of his later works.

Britten's use of the *St Denio* tune ('Immortal, invisible') for the final movement of the Suite for Harp, Op. 83, underlines the flexibility of the hymn genre, since here the tune serves a purely formal, aesthetic purpose, as *Dundee* did in the *Scottish Ballad*, and extra-musical associations presumably do not extend beyond the shared Welshness of *St Denio* and the Suite's dedicatee, Osian Ellis.

Such generic flexibility enables Britten to work with that particularly

Benjamin Britten: A Commentary on His Works from a Group of Specialists (London: Rockliff, 1952): 52.

penetrating ambiguity which arises when aspects of a genre are simultaneously evoked and resisted. Peter Porter has described the *Sechs Hölderlin-Fragmente* as 'Britten's masterpiece about art',[14] and has discussed (as other writers have) the generic contexts within which Britten places his settings of Hölderlin's poetry. The aphoristic sermon on the nature of limitations of human life that ends the work – 'Die Linien des Lebens' – summons up explicit connections with Bachian chorale, and chorale fantasy, in a way that reinforces the text's expression of faith in an eternal life, even one presided over by 'a god' rather than 'God'. Yet it is the third song in the collection, 'Sokrates und Alcibiades', that has been generally, and surely correctly, recognized as expressing perceptions about life and feeling closer to Britten's own. For Porter, the line that begins the second stanza – 'Wer das Tiefste gedacht, liebt das Lebendigste' – 'sums up Britten's artistic creed',[15] in the way it brings truth and beauty into association as things available to the living.[16] The thought is transcendentally aesthetic rather than religious, and so it is appropriate that the hints of hymn here are more ambiguous than they are in the final song. Indeed, I can imagine some scepticism about the claim that this supremely beautiful harmonized melody can be linked to the hymn genre at all. Clearly, the degree of technical stylization relative to that genre is considerable: in other words, the character of the music would change significantly if the piano chords were transformed into alto, tenor and bass choir parts with enough repeated notes for the four voices to sing all the words. Yet it is the transcendent, mystic–mysterious tone that matters, and that for me creates a valid generic link. This is a rare moment – for Britten – of unambiguous serenity. More usually, Britten the uncertain Christian,[17] walking the knife-edge separating aesthetic self-confidence from social self-doubt, directed his generic allusions towards those moments of purely human self-understanding and illumination that have their own transcendent expressive force. It is, after all, the great tragic irony at the heart of the triumphantly integrated music drama that is *Death in Venice* that Aschenbach's profession of faith in his 'Hymn to Apollo' leads him not to the fulfilment of love, but to a lonely death, with no hint of Christian consolation.

Paul Griffiths is right: Britten did not turn into a 'father-figure who . . . revolutionized British music in the 1940s and 1950s'. As we can now appreciate, his own steadily evolving ability to explore fruitful interactions

14 Peter Porter, 'Composer and Poet', in BC: 278.
15 Ibid.
16 All the German editions of Hölderlin that I have been able to consult have 'Hohe Jugend' – not 'Hohe Tugend' – in the second line of the second stanza of *Sokrates und Alcibiades*. The 1943 dual-language edition used by Britten is the only one I've seen to have 'Tugend' (*Poems of Hölderlin*, tr. Michael Hamburger (London: Nicholson & Watson, 1943): 104).
17 See the various comments collated by Humphrey Carpenter in *Benjamin Britten: A Biography* (London: Faber and Faber, 1992): 583.

between relatively traditional and relatively radical technical features (as described by Holloway) has, since his death, become part of a wider dialectic in which the Britten synthesis stands alongside the more expressionistic practices of, in particular, Birtwistle and Maxwell Davies as a field of force within which younger composers can find stimulus and models. That Maxwell Davies can speak of his own harmony, since the mid-1980s, as 'clearer and more directional, and feeling its way towards the possibility of serious modal expression in the twenty-first century'[18] is just one indication of how British music tends to proceed by evolution rather than revolution. Within that evolution, Britten has not just an honoured but an essential place, and while to excavate such a narrow generic path through his work as I have done in this essay is to risk obscuring rather than illuminating the wider landscape, I believe that the path in question, which may look narrow on the map but whose possibilities are multifarious when you actually stand on it, is at the heart of what it is that makes Britten's socially sensitive music a special source of aesthetic satisfaction.

18 Quoted in Stephen Pruslin, 'Peter Maxwell Davies's Symphony No. 4', *Musical Times* 130 (September 1989): 521.

A Bibliography of Donald Mitchell's Writings, 1945–1995

MAUREEN BUJA

This bibliography is presented in four categories:

I   Books and music editions (p. 300)
II   Articles (including his major work for the *Daily Telegraph* but excluding the numerous concert reviews) (p. 303)
III   Programme, publication and sleeve notes (p. 318)
IV   Broadcasting (p. 323)

I am grateful to Gaston Fournier-Facio for his earlier bibliography, prepared in 1975 at the University of Sussex. In addition, I would like to thank Paul Banks and Philip Reed of the Britten–Pears Library, Jenny Doctor for her advice on the BBC Archives, Belinda Matthews of Faber and Faber, and the music reference staff at the Library of Congress, the New York Public Library, the National Sound Archive and the British Library.

Abbreviations

AFPB Aldeburgh Festival Programme Book
MMR Monthly Musical Record
MO   Musical Opinion
MQ   Musical Quarterly
MR   Music Review
TLS   The Times Literary Supplement
MT   Musical Times

I Books and Music Editions

Books

Benjamin Britten, 1913–1976: Pictures From a Life: a Pictorial Biography, compiled by Donald Mitchell with the assistance of John Evans. London: Faber and Faber; New York: Charles Scribner's Sons, 1978, R1980.

Benjamin Britten (1913–1976): Three Lectures . . . for the British Council in China: Benjamin Britten: The Relationship of Life and Work; Benjamin Britten: The Musical Character; Benjamin Britten: From Bali to Shakespeare. Unpublished typescript: March 1983.

Benjamin Britten: a Commentary on his Works from a Group of Specialists, edited by Donald Mitchell and Hans Keller. London: Rockliff; New York: Philosphical Library, 1952; Corrected reprint, Westport, CT: Greenwood Press, 1972.

Benjamin Britten: Death in Venice, compiled and edited by Donald Mitchell, Cambridge: Cambridge University Press, 1987.

Benjamin Britten: the Early Years. Guilford, CT: Jeffrey Norton Publishers, 1984. Series: Sound seminars. BBC study tapes.

Britten and Auden in the Thirties, the Year 1936: The T.S. Eliot Memorial Lectures Delivered at the University of Kent at Canterbury in November 1979. London: Faber and Faber; Seattle, WA: University of Washington Press, 1981.

Cradles of the New: Writings on Music, 1951–1991, selected by Christopher Palmer, edited by Mervyn Cooke. London: Faber and Faber, 1995.

The Faber Book of Children's Songs, edited by Donald Mitchell and Roderick Biss, illustrated by Errol Le Cain. London: Faber and Faber, 1970; Boston: Gambit, 1970 as *The Gambit Book of Children's Song*; London: Faber Music in association with Faber and Faber, 1984, R1987, R1993.

The Faber Book of Nursery Songs, selected by Donald Mitchell, arranged by Carey Blyton, illustrated by Alan Howard. London: Faber and Faber, 1968, R1985, R1993; New York: Bonanza Books, 1968 as *Every Child's Book of Nursery Songs*; New York: Crown, 1968, R1985 as *Every Child's Book of Nursery Songs*.

Mahler, Alma. *Gustav Mahler: Erinnerungen und Briefe von Alma Mahler-Werfel. Gustav Mahler: Briefe an Alma Mahler*, edited by Donald Mitchell. Second edition: Frankfurt am Main: Ullstein/Propyläen, 1971; Third edition: Berlin: Propyläen Verlag, 1972; Ungekürtzte Ausgabe, Frankfurt am Main: Ullstein, 1978, R1980 as *Erinnerungen an Gustav Mahler*.
First published as: *Gustav Mahler: Erinnerungen und Briefe* (Amsterdam: Allert de Lange, 1940); Italian Translation of 1971 German edition: *Gustav Mahler: ricordi e lettere*, a cura di Luigi Rognoni, traduzione di Laura Dalla Piccola (Milan: Saggiatore, 2/1976).

Mahler, Alma. *Gustav Mahler: Memories and Letters*, edited by Donald Mitchell, translated by Basil Creighton. Second Enlarged edition: New York: Viking, 1967; London: John Murray, 1968, 1969; New York: Viking Press, 1969. Revised and Enlarged edition [= Second edition]: Seattle: University of Washington Press, 1971. Third Edition, further enlarged with a new appendix and chronology by Knud Martner and Donald Mitchell: London: John Murray, 1973; New appendix by Donald Mitchell: Seattle: University of Washington Press, 1975. Fourth edition, with additional notes and commentaries: Boston: Abacus (Little, Brown), 1990. London: Cardinal, 1990.

Translation of *Gustav Mahler: Erinnerungen und Briefe* (Amsterdam: Allert de Lange, 1940). Basil Creighton's translation was first published London: John

Murray, 1946. Foreign language translations based on the 1968 English and German editions: *Gustav Mahler: Minnen från ett Aktensap* (Stockholm: Natur och Kultur, 1977); *Gustav Mahler: Recuerdos y cartas* (Madrid: Edicione Taurus, 1978); *Mahler: Mémoires et Correspondance* (Paris: Editions Jean-Claude Lattès, 1980).

Gustav Mahler: the Early Years. London: Rockliff, 1958; revised edition, edited by Paul Banks and David Matthews. London: Faber and Faber; Berkeley: University of California Press, 1980; *R*1995 London: Faber and Faber; Berkeley, CA: University of California Press.

Gustav Mahler: Songs and Symphonies of Life and Death – Interpretations and Annotations. London: Faber and Faber; Berkeley, CA: University of California Press, 1985.

Gustav Mahler: the World Listens. Haarlem: TEMA Uitgevers, 1995.

Gustav Mahler: the Wunderhorn Years: Chronicles and Commentaries. London: Faber and Faber, 1975; Boulder, CO: Westview Press, 1976; *R*1980 Berkeley, CA: University of California Press; with one-page update *R*1995 London: Faber and Faber; Berkeley, CA: University of California Press.

The Language of Modern Music. London: Faber and Faber; New York: St Martin's Press, 1963; Second revised edition: London: Faber and Faber; New York: St Martin's Press, 1966; Third revised edition: New York: St. Martin's Press, 1970; New edition [= Fourth edition]: London: Faber and Faber, 1976; New edition [= Fifth edition]: introduction by Edward Said, London: Faber and Faber, 1993; Revised edition [= Fifth edition]: introduction by Edward Said: Philadelphia: University of Pennsylvania Press, 1994.

Spanish translation as *El languaje de la música moderna* (Barcelona: Lumen, 1972); Japanese translation as *Gendai ongaku no kotoba* (Tokyo: Ongaku-no-tomo, 1976); Greek translation (Athens: Epicouros, 1976); Serbo-Croatian translation as *Jezik moderne muzike* (Beograd: Nolit, 1983).

Letters from a Life: The Selected Letters and Diaries of Benjamin Britten, Volume I: 1923–1939; Vol. II: 1939–1945, edited by Donald Mitchell, assistant editor: Philip Reed, associate editors: Rosamund Strode, Kathleen Mitchell, Judy Young. London: Faber and Faber; Berkeley, CA: University of California Press, 1991.

The Mozart Companion, edited by H. C. Robbins Landon and Donald Mitchell. London: Rockliff; New York: Oxford University Press, 1956; Reduced photographic reprint of 1956 without the plates: London: Faber and Faber 1965, *R*1968; *R*1974–1993; Corrected edition: New York: Norton, 1969, *R* Greenport, CT: Greenwood Press, 1981.

Music Survey, new series, 1949–1952, edited by Donald Mitchell and Hans Keller. London: Faber Music in association with Faber and Faber, 1981. Reprint of the periodical, *Music Survey*, with the addition of a 'Preface in the Form of a Dialogue' by the editors as interviewed by Patrick Carnegy. Does not include the first six issues of the journal (1947–9), all of which were edited by DM alone, the first of which was entitled *Music Journal*; from the second issue *Music Survey* was adopted as a title because of the existence of another *Music Journal*, published by the Incorporated Society of Musicians.

Cosman, Milein. *Musical Sketchbook: Texts by Paul Hamburger, the Earl of Harewood, Hans Keller, Donald Mitchell, Charles Reid and others*, edited by Hans Keller and Donald Mitchell. Oxford: Bruno Cassirer, 1957. Articles by Donald Mitchell: 'Igor Stravinsky', p. 10; 'Aaron Copland', p. 28; 'Arthur Honegger', p. 32; 'Georges Enesco', p. 42; 'Sir Adrian Boult', p. 52; '[Enrico] Mainardi and [Pierre] Fournier', p. 58; 'Paul Hindemith', p. 92; 'Sir William

Walton', p. 104; '[Dennis] Brain and [James P.] Bradshaw', p. 112; 'Vaughan Williams', p. 114, 116.

Réti, Jean. *Notes on Playing the Piano, illustrated with "Scenes from Childhood" of Schumann*, Edited by Donald Mitchell. Athens: Special Collections, Main Library, University of Georgia, 1974.

Supplement to 'Gustav Mahler: The Wunderhorn Years'. University of Southampton, PhD thesis: 1977.

Wolfgang Amadeus Mozart, 1756–1956: a Short Biography. London: Decca Record Co. Ltd, 1956

Music Editions

Mahler, Gustav, *Seventh Symphony*. Facsimile edition, with essays by DM. Amsterdam, Rosbeek: 1995.

Schubert, Franz, *Streichquartett in D-moll (D. 810): Der Tod und das Mädchen, Bearbeitung für Streichorchester von Gustav Mahler*, edited by David Matthews and DM. London: Josef Weinberger, 1984.

II Articles

'About Mahler's Early Symphonies', *The Listener* 61 (26 February 1959): 393.
'An After-note on Strauss' *Ariadne auf Naxos*', *Music Survey* 3/2 (1950): 123–4.
'An Afterword on Britten's "Pagoda": the Balinese Sources', *Tempo* 152 (March 1985): 7–11.
'Aim and Achievement', *Daily Telegraph* (3 February 1962).
'An *Albert Herring* Anthology' compiled by Eric Crozier, Donald Mitchell, Philip Reed and Rosamund Strode; edited by Donald Mitchell, *Glyndebourne Festival Programme Book 1985*: 113–23.
'Albert Roussel: French Symphonist', *The Listener* 52 (14 October 1954): 645.
'The Aldeburgh Festival', *MO* 75 (1951–52): 652.
'Aldeburgh Festival, 1950', *Music Survey* 3/1 (1950): 43–4.
'Aldeburgh, England', *Opera News* 15/1 (16 October 1950): 18–20. [*Let's Make an Opera, The Beggar's Opera, Albert Herring*].
'Benjamin Britten: *An American Overture*', *AFPB* (1984): 71–2.
'Another Side of Haydn', *Daily Telegraph* (4 July 1959).
'Around and About the Heterophonic Thais', *AFPB* (1991): 93–5.
'Artistic Parallels', *Daily Telegraph* (4 August 1962).
'Bach's Triumphant Tragedy', *Daily Telegraph* (8 February 1964).
'The Background to Busoni's Harlequinade', *The Listener* 52 (15 July 1954): 114.
'The Background to Recent German Music', *The Listener* 46 (4 October 1951): 572.
'Balancing the Amateur Diet', *Daily Telegraph* (28 October 1961).
'Bangkok Diary II: January 1978', in *Cradles of the New* (London: Faber and Faber, 1995): 235–40.
'Bangkok Diary, June 1976', *Newslink: Faber and Faber Staff Magazine*, 12–13 (1976): 9–10. Reprinted as 'Bangkok Diary I: June 1976' in *Cradles of the New* as (London: Faber and Faber, 1995): 231–4.
'Bartók, Stravinsky and Schoenberg: Periods: Early, Middle and Late', *The Chesterian* 28 (1953–54): 9–16.
'BBC Radio: Benjamin Britten: St. Nicolas', *Music Survey* 2/4 (1950): 278.
'BBC Symphony', *Music Survey* 3/3 (1951): 203–4.
'BBC Symphony Orchestra', *Music Survey* 1/6 (1949): 210.
'BBC Symphony Orchestra', *Music Survey* 2/3 (1950): 198.
'BBC Symphony Orchestra and Chorus', *Music Survey* 2/4 (1950): 274–5.
'The BBC's Victory over Schönberg' by Hans Keller with a footnote by DM, *MR* 13 (1952): 130–32.
'Behind the Rumpus over *Figaro*', *Daily Telegraph* (6 July 1963).
'Benjamin Britten b.1913', in *The Decca Book of Opera* (London: Werner Laurie, 1956): 121–9. [On *Peter Grimes, Let's Make an Opera, The Turn of the Screw*].
'Benjamin Britten: *Billy Budd*', *Tribune* [London] (14 December 1951): 15.
'Benjamin Britten: *Cantata academica*, "Carmen basiliense" op. 62 (1959)', in *Komponisten des 20. Jahrhunderts in der Paul Sacher Stiftung* (Basel: Paul Sacher Stiftung, 1986): 268–72.
'Benjamin Britten: l'innovatore silenzioso', *Programme book for 51o Maggio Musicale Fiorentino (1988)*. Reprinted as 'Benjamin Britten: the Quiet Innovator' in *Cradles of the New* (London: Faber and Faber, 1995): 305–37 (original English text).
'Benjamin Britten's New Opera *Owen Wingrave*', *The Listener* 85 (13 May 1971): 626–7.

'Benjamin Britten [obituary]', *Australian Journal of Music Education* 20 (April 1977): 30.

'Benjamin Britten: Three Letters to Anthony Gishford', *Tempo* 120 (March 1977): 7–9.

'A *Billy Budd* Notebook', *Opera News* 43/19 (31 March 1979): 8–14; revised as 'A *Billy Budd* Notebook (1979–1991), in Mervyn Cooke and Philip Reed, *Benjamin Britten: Billy Budd* (Cambridge: Cambridge University Press, 1993): 111–34.

'A Birthday Card in Music', *Daily Telegraph* (13 September 1963). [Benjamin Britten: *Cantata Misericordium*]

'A Bite in the Ballad', *Daily Telegraph* (9 February 1963).

'Bohuslav Martinu (b. 1890)'; 'Hans Pfitzner (1869–1949)'; 'Max Reger (1873–1916)', in *The Music Masters*, edited by A. L. Bacharach (London: Maurice Fridberg, 1954, R1957): 205–10; 227–31; 281–90.

'Boyd Neel Orchestra', *Music Survey* 2/3 (1950): 203.

'Breakdown of Communications', *Daily Telegraph* (9 March 1963).

'The Brilliance of Mr. Britten', *Disc* [Bristol] 4 (1951): 149–53. [on BB's operas in general].

'Britische Musikfest', *Musik der Zeit* 4 (1953): 25–8. Issue is entitled "England–Heft".

'British Festivals: Some Comments on their Customs', *Tempo* 16 (1950): 6–11.

'Britten a jeho Rekviem o Válce', *Hudební Rozhledy* 16 (1963): 846.

'Britten and Auden in the Thirties' *TLS* (15 February 1980): 179–82. [part of DM's T. S. Eliot Memorial Lecture.]

'Britten and his Performers', *Aldeburgh Gala Concert: Securing the Future* (7 March 1990): 30–31.

'Britten and the Ballet: Music and Movement', *London: Covent Garden: Royal Opera House* (December 1989). Reprinted as 'Britten and the Ballet: *The Prince of the Pagodas*' in *Cradles of the New* (London: Faber and Faber, 1995): 407–18.

'Britten at Aldeburgh', *Daily Telegraph* (30 June 1963).

'Britten, (Edward) Benjamin, Lord Britten (1913–1976)', in *The Dictionary of National Biography 1971–1980* (Oxford: Oxford University Press, 1986), 83–6.

'Britten on Records I', *Disc* [Bristol] 5 (1951): 54–62.

'Britten on *Oedipus Rex* [Stravinsky] and *Lady Macbeth* [Shostakovich]', *Tempo* 120 (March 1977): 10–12.

'Britten to Japan', by DM and Philip Reed, *AFPB* (1991): 18–19.

'Britten's Chamber Music', *Snape Maltings: Benson & Hedges Music Festival Programme* (26 September–2 October 1977): 8–10

'Britten's "Dramatic" Legacy', *Opera* 28 (1977): 127–30.

'Britten's Latest Opera Opens at Covent Garden [*Billy Budd*]', *Eastern Daily Press* (3 December 1951).

'Britten's *Let's Make an Opera*, op. 45', *Music Survey* 2/2 (1949): 86–8.

'Britten's Revisionary Practice: Practical and Creative', *Tempo* 66/67 (Autumn–Winter 1963): 15–22. Reprinted in *Cradles of the New* (London: Faber and Faber, 1995): 393–406.

'Britten's Theatre Music' by Donald Mitchell and Jill Burrows, *AFPB* (1980): 9–12.

'Britten's *The Turn of the Screw* II', *MO* 78 (1954–55): 279, 281.

'Britten, Thou Art Translated', *Daily Telegraph* (4 March 1961).

'Broadcast Opera: *La Donna del Lago*', *Opera* 9 (1958): 744–5.

'Bruckner, Mahler and Reger', *The Listener* 49 (23 April 1953): 698.

'Busoni and the World of Ideas', *The Listener* 50 (3 September 1953): 402.

'Can a Passion Chorus be Too Big?', *Daily Telegraph* (1 April 1961).

'Carl Orff: a Modern Primitive', *MMR* 87 (1957): 10–12.

'The Case of Max Reger I', *MO* 76 (1953): 539–41. Reprinted in *Cradles of the New* (London: Faber and Faber, 1995): 52–60.

'The Case of Max Reger II', *MO* 76 (1953): 659–61. Reprinted in *Cradles of the New* (London: Faber and Faber, 1995): 61–9.

'Catching on to the technique in Pagoda-Land', *Tempo* 146 (1983): 13–24. Reprinted in Christopher Palmer (ed.), *The Britten Companion* (London: Faber and Faber, 1984): 192–210.

'Catching Up in Warsaw Too', *Daily Telegraph* (1 October 1960).

'The Chamber Music: an Introduction', in Christopher Palmer (ed.), *The Britten Companion* (London: Faber and Faber, 1984): 369–74.

'The Character of Lulu: Wedekind's and Berg's Conceptions Compared', *MR* 15/4 (1954): 268–74. Reprinted in *Cradles of the New* (London: Faber and Faber, 1995): 187–99.

'Chelsea Symphony Orchestra', *Music Survey* 2/1 (1949): 58.

'Cheltenham and After: Some First Performances', *Music Survey* 3/2 (1950): 117–18.

'Cheltenham Festival', *MT* 105 (1964): 672–3.

'The Cheltenham Festival – Britten Operas', *Manchester Guardian* (15 July 1950): 5. [*The Beggar's Opera* and *Albert Herring*].

'The Cheltenham Festival, 1949', *Music Survey* 2/2 (1949): 96–7.

'Cheltenham Festival, 1950', *MR* 11 (1950): 213–14.

'Chor– und Solo–Kantaten I: "Wedding Album"', *Musik der Zeit* 7 (1954): 31–3. [Issue is entitled 'Benjamin Britten'.]

'Christopher Palmer' [obituary], *Independent* (27 January 1995).

'The Church Parables (I): Ritual and Restraint', in Christopher Palmer (ed.), *The Britten Companion* (London: Faber and Faber, 1984): 211–14. Edited from the sleeve note for Decca SET 438 (1970).

'Comedy: the Mirror of Life', *Daily Telegraph* (7 July 1962).

'Coming Out of the Doldrums', *Daily Telegraph* (14 September 1963).

'Coming to Grips with M. Boulez', *Daily Telegraph* (29 February 1964).

'The Composer Among the Monuments: Review of Jerrold Northrop Moore: *Edward Elgar: a Creative Life*; Jerrold Northrop Moore: *Spirit of England: Edward Elgar in his World*; E. Wulstan Atkins: *The Elgar–Atkins Friendship*; Pauline Collett: *An Elgar Travelogue*', *TLS* (14 September 1984): 1011–12. Reprinted in *Cradles of the New* (London: Faber and Faber, 1995): 269–79.

'The Composer as Critic', *Daily Telegraph* (21 July 1962).

'Composing in Series [concerning Faber and Faber's translation of Pierre Boulez: *Pensier la musique aujourd'hui*]', *TLS* (28 July 1966): 671–2.

'Composition in Depth', *Daily Telegraph* (5 May 1962).

'Concerts and Opera: Beethoven and Mozart', *MR* 13 (1952): 220–21.

'Concerts and Opera: London Contemporary Music Centre; Gieseking; Strauss–Hindemith–Roussel–Britten', *MR* 12 (1951): 157–9.

'Concerts and Opera: Mahler Mis–performed: Van Beinum's *Das Lied von der Erde*; Gina Bachauer', *MR* 11 (1950): 153–4, 157.

'Concerts, Recitals and Opera: Mahler's *Das Lied von der Erde*', *MR* 11 (1950): 222.

'Concerts: BBC Symphony Orchestra', *MR* 10 (1949): 45.

'Concerts: Cantelli and the Philharmonia', *MR* 14 (1953): 60.

'Concerts: Hindemith's *Mathis der Maler*', *MR* 13 (1952): 140–41.

'Conductors II: Bruno Walter', *AFPB* (1988): 53.

'Contemporary Chronicle: (1) *Peter Grimes* Revived; (2) My New Year's Honours List' *MO* 77 (1953–54): 281, 283.

'Contemporary Chronicle: 1. The Aldeburgh Festival; 2. The Genesis of *Il Prigioniero* [Dallapiccola]', *MO* 77 (1953–54): 645, 647.

'Contemporary Chronicle: the Art of Compression I; II', *MO* 76 (1953): 409, 411; 274–5. [on *Saint Nicolas*].

'Contemporary Chronicle: the Art of Compression II', *MO* 76 (May 1953): 274–5.

'Contemporary Chronicle: Background, Middleground, Foreground', *MO* 78 (1954–55): 729, 731.

'Contemporary Chronicle: Bartók, Berg, Britten, Respighi, Shostakovitch and Strawinsky', *MO* 78 (1954–55): 153, 155.

'Contemporary Chronicle: The BBC's Light Programme Music Festival of 1954; *My Brother Died*; An Interim Note from Salzburg: Furtwängler's *Don Giovanni*', *MO* 77 (1953–54): 707, 709.

'Contemporary Chronicle: Britten and Marschner', *MO* 77 (1953–54): 217, 219.

'Contemporary Chronicle: Britten's *The Turn of the Screw* I; II', *MO* 78 (1954–55): 219, 221; 279, 281.

'Contemporary Chronicle: Clearing the Decks', *MO* 79 (1955–56): 25.

'Contemporary Chronicle: Contemporary Music on Discs' *MO* 78 (1954–55): 665, 667.

'Contemporary Chronicle: Functional Vulgarity', *MO* 79 (1955–56): 225.

'Contemporary Chronicle: Hindemith and the History of a Term', *MO* 79 (1955–56): 163.

'Contemporary Chronicle: The Holland Festival: I', *MO* 76 (1953–54): 721, 723.

'Contemporary Chronicle: The Holland Festival: II – Berg's *Lulu*', *MO* 77 (1953–54): 23, 25.

'Contemporary Chronicle: Mahler and his English Critics I; Mahler and his English Critics [II], Mahler at Manchester, Reger in London; Mahler and his English Critics [III], Musical Terms: a Call for a Conference', *MO* 77 (1953–54): 345, 347; 409, 411, 413; 475, 477.

'Contemporary Chronicle: Miscellany', *MO* 77 (1953–54): 155, 157.

'Contemporary Chronicle: Music and Youth', *MO* 79 (1955–56): 89, 91.

'Contemporary Chronicle: A Pocket Guide to *Gloriana*', *MO* 76 (1952–53): 603, 605. See also 'Letter to the Editor: *Gloriana*', *MO* 76 (1952–53): 711, and 77 (1953–54): 79.

'Contemporary Chronicle: Revaluations I; II: Vaughan Williams; III: Vaughan Williams; IV: William Walton; V: William Walton', *MO* 78 (1954–55): 345, 347; 409, 411; 471; 539, 541; 601, 603.

'Contemporary Chronicle: Schoenberg's *Moses und Aron*', *MO* 77 (1953–54): 533, 535.

'Contemporary Chronicle: Serial Topics', *MO* 77 (1953–54): 587, 589.

'Contemporary Chronicle: Side-shows at the Proms: Leoš Janáček (I); Politics and Panufnik, Side-shows at the Proms: Leoš Janáček (II)', *MO* 78 (1954–55): 23, 25; 89, 91.

'Contemporary Chronicle: The St Matthew Passion on Film', *MO* 79 (1955–56): 289.

'Contemporary Chronicle: Symphonies New and Old', *MO* 77 (1953–54): 91, 93.

'Counterpoint from Manchester' [Obituary of Henry Raynor], *Guardian* (7 August 1989): 37.

'Country Gardens Revisited', *Daily Telegraph* (18 April 1964).

'Cradles of the New: Paris and Vienna at the Turn of the Century', *Lecture at*

Fourth Tokyo Summer Festival (11 July 1988). Reprinted in *Cradles of the New* (London: Faber and Faber, 1995): 134–61.

'Criticism: a State of Emergency', *Tempo* 37 (Autumn 1955): 6–11. Reprinted as 'A State of Emergency' in *Cradles of the New* (London: Faber and Faber, 1995): 3–13.

'Death in Venice: the Dark Side of Perfection', in Christopher Palmer (ed.), *The Britten Companion* (London: Faber and Faber, 1984): 238–49. Edited from introduction to BBC Radio 3 performance of *Death in Venice*, 22 June 1973.

'Delius – the Last Impressionist', *Daily Telegraph* (27 January 1962).

'Delius – Twenty Years After', *The Listener* 59 (12 June 1958): 993.

'Delius and Opera', *The Listener* 59 (23 January 1958): 177.

'Delius: the Choral Music', *Tempo* 26 (1952–53): 8–17.

'Donald Mitchell Remembers Hans Keller', *London Review of Books* (3 September 1987): 8–11. Reprinted as 'Remembering Hans Keller' in *Cradles of the New* (London: Faber and Faber, 1995): 461–80.

'Dowland's Melancholy Muse', *Daily Telegraph* (19 October 1963).

'Down there on a Visit: Isherwood in California', *London Magazine* 32/1–2 (April/May 1992): 80–87. Reprinted as 'Down there on a Visit: A Meeting with Christopher Isherwood' in *Cradles of the New* (London: Faber and Faber, 1995): 441–9.

'Early and Mature Mahler' *The Listener* 68 (25 October 1962): 695.

'East Meets West at Palermo', *Daily Telegraph* (13 October 1962).

'The Edinburgh Festival', *MO* 73 (1949–50): 15, 17.

'The Edinburgh Festival', *MO* 74 (1950–51): 31, 33.

'Edinburgh: *The Turn of the Screw*. English Opera Group, September 5,' *Opera* 13 (Summer Festival Issue 1962): 95–6.

'Editorial', by Donald Mitchell and Hans Keller. *Music Survey* 3/3 (1951): 152–3.

'Editorial', by Donald Mitchell and Hans Keller. *Music Survey* 4/1 (1951): 317.

'Editorial: Professor J. A. Westrup – An Apology', *Music Survey* 3/4 (1951): 232.

'Editorial: The Edinburgh Festival', *Music-Journal* [= *Music Survey*] 1/1 (1947): 1–3.

'Elegy for Young Lovers [Henze]', *The Listener* 66 (13 July 1961): 73.

'Elegy in Memory of my Mother', in *Justa Catarinae Mitchell a quatuor moerentibus, amoris & recordationis causa*, London: s.n., 1945: 3–5.

'Elgar and the English Oratorio', *The Listener* 57 (28 February 1957): 361. Reprinted in *Cradles of the New* (London: Faber and Faber, 1995): 251–4.

'Elijah: the Problem of Belief', *The Listener* 55 (5 April 1956): 377.

'"The Emancipation of the Dissonance": a Selected Bibliography of the Writings of Composers, Theorists and Critics', *Music Book* 7 (1952): 141–52.

'An Enigmatic Piano Concerto [Busoni]', *The Listener* 63 (2 June 1960): 993.

'Eric Crozier' [obituary], *Guardian* (8 September 1994)

'Ernst Krenek: *Sonata for Organ, op. 92* in concert', *Music Survey* 2/4 (1950): 275.

'Experiments with Bad Mixers', *Daily Telegraph* (4 May 1963).

'Exploratory Concert Society', *Music Survey* 1/5 (1949): 171.

'Exploratory Concert Society', *Music Survey* 1/6 (1949): 213.

'Exploring the Limits of the Abstract', *Daily Telegraph* (24 October 1959).

'Ferrier, Pears, Britten [concert]', *Music Survey* 3/2 (1950): 138.

'Festival Springtime in Prague', *Daily Telegraph* (5 June 1963).

'Film Music: Roman Vlad: *Sunday in August*; Darius Milhaud: *La Vie Commence Demain*', *Music Survey* 3/3 (1951): 181–2.

'First Performances', *MR* 14 (1953): 297–8.

'First Performances', *MR* 15 (1954): 138.

'First Performances', *MR* 16 (1955): 145, 147–8.

'For Hedli: Britten's and Auden's Cabaret Songs', by DM and Philip Reed, in Katherine Bucknell and Nicholas Jenkins (eds), *W. H. Auden: The language of love and learning* (Auden Studies 2) (Oxford: Oxford University Press, 1994): 61–8.

'For Those who Sing Together', *Daily Telegraph* (3 March 1962).

'France's Other New Wave', *Daily Telegraph* (20 February 1960).

'*Die Frau ohne Schatten*: Size and Quality', *The Listener* 59 (17 April 1958): 673.

The French Connection: Britten–Poulenc–Milhaud', compiled and edited by DM and Philip Reed, *Aldeburgh October Britten Festival Programme Book* (1994): 8–17.

'Giulini: the Man Behind the Baton', *Daily Telegraph* (7 Nov 1962).

'A Gulf to Bridge at the Proms', *Daily Telegraph* (8 August 1959).

'Gustav Mahler' by Donald Mitchell and Paul Banks, in *The New Grove Dictionary of Music*, edited by Stanley Sadie, vol. 11 (London: Macmillan, 1980): 505–11.

'Gustav Mahler 1860–1911', *AFPB* (1975): 22–3.

'Gustav Mahler and Hugo Wolf', *Chord and Discord* 2/5 (1948): 40–46.

'Gustav Mahler: Prospect and Retrospect', *PRMA* 87 (1960–61): 83–97. Reprinted in *Chord and Discord*, 2/10 (1963), 138–48.

'Hans Keller 1919–1985', *Tempo* 156 (March 1986): 2–3. Reprinted in *Cradles of the New* (London: Faber and Faber, 1995): 457–60.

'Hans Pfitzner and his Opera *Palestrina*', *Listener* 42 (18 August 1949): 288.

'Hedli Anderson' [obituary], by DM and Philip Reed. *Independent* (10 February 1990)

'Hedli Anderson (1907–1990)', by DM and Philip Reed. *AFPB* (1990): 18–19.

'History Speaking', *Daily Telegraph* (15 August 1959).

'The Holland Festival', *MT* 94 (1953): 422–3.

'Holland Festival', *MR* 14 (1953): 303–4.

'The Holland Festival 1953: Berg's *Lulu*', *Tempo* 29 (1953): 5–7.

'The Holland Festival, 1954', *Tempo* 33 (1954): 6–7. See also 'Letter to the Editor', *Tempo* 34 (1954): 39.

'Holland Festival. 15th June–15th July', by Hans Keller and DM, *MR* 17 (1956): 249–51.

'Holland II; Mahler's Eighth Symphony', *MR* 15 (1954): 315–16.

'Honoured in Another Country', *Daily Telegraph* (15 October 1960).

'How Fast – or Slow – Makes Sense?', *Daily Telegraph* (19 November 1960).

'How Many Notes in a Serial', *Daily Telegraph* (6 May 1961).

'How Shall we Sing the Lord's Song?', *Daily Telegraph* (23 December 1961).

'In and Out of Britten's *Dream*', *Opera* 9 (1960): 797–801.

'In My Opinion: the Promenade Concerts', *MO* 76 (1952–53): 703–4.

'Incomparable Genius', *Daily Telegraph* (13 April 1963).

'Intellect and Intuition in Busoni's Operas', *The Listener* 58 (3 October 1957): 545.

'An Introduction', *Programme book for Mahler, Vienna and The Twentieth Century, London Symphony Orchestra* (Spring 1985): 4–6.

'An introduction in the shape of a memoir', in Donald Mitchell (ed.), *Benjamin Britten: Death in Venice* (Cambridge: Cambridge University Press, 1987): 1–24.

'An Introduction to Our Time', *Daily Telegraph* (17 September 1960).

'Isador Caplan', *AFPB* (1988): 86.

'Isador Caplan' [obituary], *Independent* (23 January 1995), reprinted in *Soundings* 28 (Spring 1995): 18–19.

'Jacques Orchestra', *Music Survey* 3/2 (1950): 138.

'Keeping the Cultural Frontiers Open', *Daily Telegraph* (18 May 1963).

'*Die Kluge* [Orff]', *The Listener* 57 (2 May 1957): 730.

'Kurt Weill's *Dreigroschenoper* and German Cabaret–Opera in the 1920's', *Chesterian* 163 (1960): 1–6.

'Kurt Weill's *Mahagonny* and "Eternal Art"', *Daily Telegraph* (9 February 1963).

'The Language of Contemporary Art', *The Listener* 63 (18 February 1960): 301–2.

'Larkin's Music', in Anthony Thwaite (ed.), *Larkin at Sixty* (London: Faber and Faber, 1982): 75–80. Reprinted in *Cradles of the New* (London: Faber and Faber, 1995): 450–56.

'The Later Development of Benjamin Britten I: Texture, Instrumentation and Structure; II ', *The Chesterian* 171 (1952): 1–7; 172 (1952): 36–40.

'LCMC [London Contemporary Music Centre]', *Music Survey* 2/1 (1949): 54–5.

'The Leeds Festival', *Music Survey* 3/2 (1950): 124–5.

'The Leeds Triennial Festival', *MT* 91 (1950): 440–41.

'*Let's Make an Opera*: Britten's Entertainment for Young People', *Making Music* 12 (1950): 9–10.

'Letter to Editor: Leppard's Realizations', *Opera* 21 (1970): 371–2.

'Letter to the Editor', *MR* 12 (1951): 268.

'Letter to the Editor: an Analogy of Music and Experience', *MR* 13 (1952): 168.

'Letter to the Editor: On review of H. F. Redlich: *Bruckner and Mahler*', *The Listener* 54 (10 November 1955): 805.

'Letter to the Editor: Quis Custodiet?' by Donald Mitchell, Hans Keller and Robert Donington, *MR* 11 (1950): 168.

'Letter to the Editor: Request for information on Gustav Mahler', *The Listener* 52 (8 July 1954): 65.

'Letter to the Editor: the PRS Controversy', *MO* 115 (1992): 340.

'Letter to the Editor: *The Language of Modern Music*', *TLS* (2 August 1963): 597.

'Letter to the Editor: *Wozzeck*', *MR* 10 (1949): 247.

'Listening in All Innocence', *Daily Telegraph* (28 January 1961).

'London Concerts', *MT* 95 (1954): 145–6.

'London Concerts', *MT* 96 (1955): 37–9; 91–3.

'London Concerts', *MT* 97 (1956): 316–18.

'London Concerts and Opera', *MT* 97 (1956): 90–92; 596–7.

'London Contemporary Music Centre', *Music Survey* 2/4 (1950): 273.

'London Music', *MT* 95 (1954): 380–82; 434–6; 612–15.

'London Music', *MT* 96 (1955): 209–11; 378–80; 433–4; 484–5.

'London Music', *MT* 97 (1956): 34–8; 147–51; 205–8; 371–5; 483–5; 539–40; 653–5.

'London Music', *MT* 98 (1957): 35–6; 90–93.

'London Music, Concerts and Opera', *MT* 97 (1956): 264–6.

'London Philharmonic Orchestra', *Music Survey* 1/3 (1948): 78–9.

'London Philharmonic Orchestra', *Music Survey* 1/3 (1948): 80.

'London Philharmonic Orchestra', *Music Survey* 2/1 (1949): 55.

'London Philharmonic Orchestra', *Music Survey* 2/2 (1949): 123.

'London Philharmonic Orchestra', *Music Survey* 1/6 (1949): 212.

'London Philharmonic Orchestra', *Music Survey* 3/1 (1950): 66.

'London Philharmonic Orchestra', *Music Survey* 3/3 (1951): 204.

'The Lyric, Hammersmith: Britten Season', *Music Survey* 3/4 (June 1951): 303–4. [*Albert Herring*]

'Maggie Hemingway [obituary]', *Guardian* (25 May 1993).

'Mahler', with Paul Banks, in *The New Grove Turn of the Century Masters:*

Janáček, Mahler, Strauss, Sibelius, by John Tyrrell, Paul Banks, Donald Mitchell, Michael Kennedy, Robert Bailey, Robert Layton (London: Macmillan, 1985): 81–181.

'Mahler Amid the Stars', *Daily Telegraph* (20 July 1963).

'Mahler and Freud', *Chord and Discord* 2/8 (1958): 63–8. Reprint of a script from BBC Third Programme, 28 March 1955.

'Mahler and Nature: Landscape into Music', *Lecture given at Musikwoche in memoriam Gustav Mahler, Toblach* (22 July 1986). Reprinted in *Cradles of the New* (London: Faber and Faber, 1995): 162–74.

'Mahler and The Concept of the Chamber Orchestra', *London Philharmonic Orchestra Programme Book* (7 December 1993).

'Mahler and the English', *The Listener* 63 (10 March 1960): 473.

'Mahler in Japan: das Tsuyama Festival, 1987', *Nachrichten zur Mahler–Forschung* 19 (March 1988): 5–7.

'Mahler on the Gramophone', *ML* 41 (1960): 156–63.

'The Mahler Renaissance in England: its Origins and Chronology', in Andrew Nicholson (ed.), *The Mahler Companion* (Oxford: Oxford University Press, forthcoming).

'Mahler under the Microscope: Review of Henry Louis de la Grange: *Mahler. volume I*; Michael Kennedy: *Mahler*', *TLS* (29 November 1974): 1349–51.

'Mahler's *Abschied*: A Wrong Note Righted', *MQ* 71 (1985): 200–204; reprinted in *Cradles of the New* (London: Faber and Faber, 1995): 181–6.

'Mahler's Enigmatic Seventh Symphony', *The Listener* 69 (11 April 1963): 649.

'Mahler's Hungarian *Glissando*', in *Cradles of the New* (London: Faber and Faber, 1995): 175–80.

'Mahler's Waldmärchen: the Unpublished First Part of *Das klagende Lied*', *MT* 111 (April 1970): 375–9.

'Mahler, Schubert, and the String Orchestra', *Sony Music Entertainment* (7 December 1993).

'Mahler: a Modern in Two Centuries', *Daily Telegraph* (23 January 1960).

'Mahlerian Afterthoughts', *Daily Telegraph* (3 November 1962).

'Malcolm Arnold', *MT* 96 (1955): 410–13. Reprinted as 'Malcolm Arnold I' in *Cradles of the New* (London: Faber and Faber, 1995): 98–106.

'Malcolm Arnold II', BBC Radio 3 (23 March 1977). Reprinted in *Cradles of the New* (London: Faber and Faber, 1995): 107–21.

'The Man and the Mind Within', *Daily Telegraph* (8 December 1962).

'Mapreading: Benjamin Britten in conversation with Donald Mitchell', in Christopher Palmer (ed.), *The Britten Companion* (London: Faber and Faber, 1984): 87–96. [On the writing of *Owen Wingrave*.]

'Max Reger', *Mandrake* [Oxford] 2 (1946): 25–33.

'Max Reger (1873–1916): an Introductory Musical Portrait', *MR* 12/4 (1951): 279–88. Reprinted in *Cradles of the New* (London: Faber and Faber, 1995): 41–51

'A Memorable Cantata by Britten', *Daily Telegraph* (2 September 1963). [*Cantata Misericordium*.]

'[Memories of Britten: Interview with Alan Blyth]', in Alan Blyth (ed.), *Remembering Britten*, (London: Hutchinson, 1981): 130–35.

'Mendelssohn Bartholdy: Review of Eric Werner: *Mendelssohn: a New Image of the Composer and his Age*', *MT* 106 (1965): 34–5.

'Michael Tippett: Divertimento on *Sellinger's Round* (1953–4)', in *Komponisten des*

20. Jahrhunderts in der Paul Sacher Stiftung (Basel: Paul Sacher Stiftung, 1986): 246–9.

'*A Midsummer Night's Dream* anthology', by DM and Philip Reed, *Glyndebourne Festival Opera 1989*: 133–41.

'Milein Cosman-Keller', *AFPB* (1988): 109.

'The "Modernity" of William Walton', *The Listener* 57 (7 February 1957): 245. See also 'Letter to the Editor', *The Listener* 57 (21 February 1957): 313.

'Montagu Slater (1902–1956): Who was He?', in Philip Brett (compiler), *Benjamin Britten: Peter Grimes* (Cambridge: Cambridge University Press, 1983): 22–46.

'More Off than On *Billy Budd*', *Music Survey* 4/2 (February 1952): 386–408. Reprinted in *Cradles of the New* (London: Faber and Faber, 1995): 365–92.

'Morley College Concert Society', *Music Survey* 2/1 (1949): 57.

'Mozart and Mahler', *AFPB* (1975): 19–20.

'Music and "Music": Review of Ernst Krenek: *Exploring Music*; William W. Austin: *Music in the 20th Century, from Debussy through Stravinsky*; *Contemporary Music in Europe*, edited by Paul Henry Lang and Nathan Broder; Fernand Ouellette: *Edgard Varèse*; Pierre Schaeffer: *Traité des objets musicaux*; Wolfgang Stockmeier: *Musikalische Formprinzipien*; Konrad Boehme: *Zur Theorie der Offenen Form in der Neuen Musik*; Friedrich Wildgans: *Anton Webern*', *TLS* (4 January 1968): 1–3.

'Music and the Literature of Childhood', *Music Survey* 1/4 (1948): 108–11.

'Music Critics and Criticism Today: the "Ideal" Music Critic', *MT* 101 (1960): 224.

'Music for Children and Amateurs', *AFPB* (1964): 28–9.

'Music in London', *MT* 96 (1955): 321–4.

'Music in Television I', *The Listener* 71 (4 June 1964): 927.

'Music of the Historian: Asa Briggs', *AFPB* (1993): 62.

'The Music of Karol Szymanowski', *The Listener* 48 (6 November 1952): 785.

'The Music of Richard Arnell', *The Listener* 41 (23 June 1949): 1084.

'The Musical Atmosphere', in Donald Mitchell and Hans Keller (eds), *Benjamin Britten: a Commentary on his Works from a Group of Specialists* (London: Rockliff, 1952; New York: Philosphical Library, 1953, R Westport, CT: Greenwood Press, 1972): 3–58

'Musical Terms: a Call for a Conference', *MO* 77 (1953–54): 475, 477.

'*My Brother Died*; An Interim Note from Salzburg [Furtwängler's *Don Giovanni*]', *MO* 77 (1953–54): 707, 709.

'Mythic Pears: *Idomeneo* and *Oedipus*', in Marion Thorpe (ed.), *Peter Pears: a Tribute on His 75th Birthday* (London: Faber Music in association with the Britten Estate, 1985): 67–8.

'The Need for a Crisis', *The Chesterian* 161 (1950): 58–62.

'A Neglected Masterpiece: Britten's *Gloriana*', *The Listener* 73 (14 November 1963): 809. Reprinted in Felix Aprahamian (ed.), *Essays on Music: an Anthology from 'The Listener'* (London: Cassell, 1967): 64–8.

'New Era Concert Society', *Music Survey* 1/3 (1948): 79.

'New Era Concert Society', *Music Survey* 3/3 (1951): 204.

'The New Language of Music: Review of Wilfrid Mellers: *Caliban Reborn*; Paul Doe: *Tallis*; Anthony Payne: *Schoenberg*; Peter Yates: *Twentieth Century Music*; H. H. Stuckenschmidt: *Twentieth-Century Music*; John Cage: *A Year from Monday*', *TLS* (9 October 1969): 1141–3.

'New Light on *Das Lied von der Erde*', *AFPB* (1985): 46.

'New Light on *Das Lied von der Erde*', in *Colloque international Gustav Mahler, 25. 26. 27. Janvier 1985* (Paris: Association Gustav Mahler, 1986): 20–29.

'Nietzsche, Wagner, and Mr. Newman', *Music Survey* [1]/2 (1948): 21–2.

'No Tricks in Opera in the Round', *Daily Telegraph* (6 June 1964).

'Nolan on Britten: in conversation with Donald Mitchell', *AFPB* (1993): 87–90.

'. . . Not a Hint of Zak', *Daily Telegraph* (2 September 1961).

'Not Too Old to be New', *Daily Telegraph* (7 October 1961).

'A Note on Tchaikovsky's *Queen of Spades*', *The Chesterian* 166 (1951): 86–9.

'A Note on the Catalan Songs (1928) [Roberto Gerhard]', *The Score and I.M.A. Magazine* [London]17 (1956): 11–12.

'A Note on the "Flower Aria" and "Passacaglia" in *Lucretia*' *Music Survey* 3/4 (1951): 276–7.

'A Note on *St Nicolas*: Some Points of Britten's Style', *Music Survey* 2/4 (1950): 220–26.

'Notes from Abroad: Holland', *MT* 95 (1954): 493–4.

'Notes from Abroad: Holland', *MT* 97 (1956): 435–6.

'"Now Sleeps the Crimson Petal": Britten's Other *Serenade*', *Tempo* 169 (June 1989): 22–7. Reprinted in *Horn Call* 22/1 (October 1991): 9–14; reprinted in *Cradles of the New* (London: Faber and Faber, 1995): 345–51.

'Obituary: Arnold Schoenberg, 1874–1951', *Music Survey* 4/1 (1951): 316–17.

'Odd Goings-on in an Attic', *Daily Telegraph* (25 June 1960).

'Of Peacocks and Waterfalls: The Traditional Music of Thailand', in *Cradles of the New* (London: Faber and Faber, 1995): 241–7. Part I: reprinted from Prom Concerts Programme Book, 1981, pp. 27–9; Part II: reprinted from programme for performance of Thai Classical Music Group of Srinakharinwirot University, Bangkok, London: Royal Albert Hall: Henry J. Wood Promenade Concert (22 August 1981).

'On Bicycle and Podium: Review of *Gustav Mahler: Mahler's Unknown Letters*, edited by Herta Blaukopf', *TLS* (19 June 1987): 657–8.

'The One Quality Callas Lacks – a Great Voice', *Daily Telegraph* (12 August 1961).

'One-Time Radical', *Daily Telegraph* (23 March 1963).

'Opera and Concerts in London', *MT* 96 (1955): 658–60.

'Opera and Society Performances: *The Jacobin*', *Opera* 10 (1959): 476–7.

'Opera Audiences Catch Up', *Daily Telegraph* (14 January 1961).

'Opera Diary: *Figaro; La Clemenza di Tito; L'Histoire du Soldat* and *Boris Godunov; Il Segreto di Susanna* and *Zaide; Nelson; I Quattro Rusteghi* and *Pimpinone; A Tale of Two Cities; Armide; Der Freischütz; Albert Herring; Figaro* and *Lulu*', *Opera* 4 (1953): 49–51; 111–13; 115–19; 243–4; 245–6; 373–4; 376–7; 432–3; 484–6; 488–9; 547–51.

'Opera Diary: *Rigoletto*; BBC3 *Die Lustigen Weiber von Windsor* and *Abu Hassan*', *Opera* 8 (1957): 120–21; 323–4.

'Opera Diary: *The Cenci; Doktor Faust*; Television *The Turn of the Screw*', *Opera* 11 (1960): 61–2; 63–4; 162, 164.

'Opera Diary: *Wozzeck, Turandot, Salome, The Magic Flute, Billy Budd* and on BBC3 *Moses and Aron*; BBC3 *Fidelio; Madam Butterfly*', *Opera* 3 (1952): 309–12; 373–7; 502–3.

'Opera in London', *MT* 96 (1955): 36–7; 91; 150–51.

'Opera, Covent Garden: *The Magic Flute; Turandot* and the Truth; *Tristan und Isolde*; Tchaikovsky's *Queen of Spades*', *MR* 14 (1953): 64–5; 66–8; 160–61.

'Opera: Covent Garden: *Boris Godunov*', *MR* 9 (1948): 196.

'Opera: Covent Garden: *Rigoletto*', *MR* 10 (1949): 220.

'Opera: Mozart up the Garden Path', *MR* 11 (1950): 48–51.

'Opera: *Wozzeck, The Immortal Hour, Avon, Titus*', *Music Survey* 2/1 (1949): 49.

'The Operas of Karol Szymanowski', *The Listener* 53 (3 March 1955): 401.

'Operatic No-man's Land', *Daily Telegraph* (21 December 1963).

'The Origins, Evolution and Metamorphosis of *Paul Bunyan*, Auden's and Britten's "American" Opera', in W. H. Auden, *Paul Bunyan: the libretto of the operetta by Benjamin Britten* (London: Faber and Faber, 1988): 83–148.

'The Other Performances', *Opera* 3 (1952): 595–6, 633–4.

'Outline Model for a Biography of Benjamin Britten (1913–1976)', in Rudolf Elvers (ed.), *Festchrift Albi Rosenthal* (Tutzing: Hans Schneider, 1984): 239–51.

'An *Owen Wingrave* Anthology', compiled by DM and Philip Reed, *AFPB* (1993): 11–20.

'The Paradox of *Gloriana*: Simple and Difficult', in Paul Banks (ed.), *Britten's Gloriana* (Woodbridge, Suffolk: The Boydell Press and The Britten–Pears Library, 1993): 67–75.

'Patriotism is Not Enough: Review of László Eösze: *Zoltán Kodály: his Life and Work*', *MT* 104 (1963): 34–5.

'Pears, Peter (1910–1986)', in *The Dictionary of National Biography 1986–1990*, Oxford: Oxford University Press, forthcoming.

'A Permanent Seat in the Stalls', *Daily Telegraph* (30 December 1961).

'Peter: A Performer Remembered', *A Tribute to Peter Pears, 1910–1986: London: Covent Garden: Royal Opera House* (30 November 1986).

'A *Peter Grimes* Chronology', by DM and Philip Reed, London: English National Opera (1991)

'Peter Pears', *European Gay Review* 1 (1986): 33–5.

'The Philharmonia Lesson', *Daily Telegraph* (21 March 1964).

'Pioneer of Do-it-Yourself', *Daily Telegraph* (11 January 1964).

'Platform for Modern Experiment', *Daily Telegraph* (9 June 1962).

'The Poetic Image: a Note on Britten's *Wedding Anthem*', *Tempo* 25 (1952): 21–3.

'Prefatory Note', in *Benjamin Britten: a complete catalogue of his published works*, London: Boosey & Hawkes, 1963; Boosey & Hawkes/Faber Music, 2nd edition, 1973.

'Prevailing East Wind in Prague', *Daily Telegraph* (1 June 1963).

'The Private World of Frederick Delius', *MO* 76 (1952–53): 405–7. Reprinted in *Cradles of the New* (London: Faber and Faber, 1995): 297–301.

'Prokofieff's *Three Oranges*: a Note on its Musical–Dramatic Organisation', *Tempo* 41 (Autumn 1956): 20–24.

'Promenade Concerts', *MT* 94 (1953): 472.

'A Propos Picasso', *Daily Telegraph* (23 July 1960).

'Psychology and Character in *Così fan tutte*', *The Listener* 64 (22 December 1960): 1160. Revised and reprinted as 'The Truth about *Così*' in Anthony Gishford (ed.), *Tribute to Benjamin Britten on his Fifieth Birthday* (London: Faber and Faber, 1963): 95–9. Reprinted as 'Mozart: the Truth about *Così*' in *Cradles of the New* (London: Faber and Faber, 1995): 127–33.

'Public and Private Life in Britten's *Gloriana*', *Opera* 17/10 (October 1966): 767–74. Reprinted as 'Public and Private in *Gloriana*', in Christopher Palmer (ed.), *The Britten Companion* (London: Faber and Faber, 1984): 170–76.

'Radio Criticism: Early One Morning; Floreat Tippett; Olde English?; Morning Exercises; Finest Hour; Lambert Ho!; A la mode; On Disc; Aimez–vous Brahms?; Penny Dreadful; Extra-Metropolitan; Happy Birth Day; Mangled Eloquence; Adieu', *The Listener* 73 (7 January–15 April 1965): 32, 34; 83–4; 119–20; 163–4; 204–5; 240–41; 275–7; 312–13; 348–9; 382, 384; 428–9; 464–5; 534–5; 576–7.

'Ralph Vaughan Williams: *The House of Life* in concert', *Music Survey* 2/4 (1950): 275.

'The Real Background to *Palestrina*', *The Listener* 54 (28 July 1955): 161.

'Recital, Opera and Ballet: Pfitzner's *Palestrina*', *MR* 13 (1952): 315–16.

'Reply to a letter by H. F. Redlich', *Music Survey* 4/1 (1951): 380–81.

'[Request for information on] Gustav Mahler', *TLS* (25 June 1954): 409.

'Review of A. Horējs: *Antonín Dvořák: the Composer's Life and Work in Pictures*', *Tempo* 47 (1958): 34.

'Review of Adolfo Salazar: *Music in Our Time*', *Music Survey* 1/6 (1949): 202–4.

'Review of Alan Rawsthorne: *Street Corner Overture*', *Music Survey* 2/3 (1950): 192.

'Review of Alfred Einstein: *A Short History of Music*', *Music Survey* 2/1 (1949): 38.

'Review of Ann Phillips Basart: *Serial music: a Classified Bibliography of Writings on Twelve-tone and Electronic Music*', *Tempo* 63 (1962–63): 46, 48.

'Review of Arthur Oldham: *Violin Sonata* in concert', *Music Survey* 2/4 (1950): 273.

'Review of Artur Schnabel: *My Life and Music*; Neville Cardus: *Sir Thomas Beecham*; Charles Reid: *Thomas Beecham*', *MR* 23 (1962): 331–2.

'Review of Béla Bartók: *Concerto for Orchestra*, Concertgebouw Orchestra of Amsterdam/Eduard van Beinum (Decca).' *Music Survey* 1/6 (1949): 215.

'Review of Benjamin Britten: *Spring Symphony, op. 44*; *Let's Make an Opera, op. 45*; *A Wedding Anthem (Amo Ergo Sum), op. 46*', *Music Survey* 3/1 (1950): 49–50. See also Erwin Stein's rebuttal to review in *Music Survey* 3/2 (1950): 144–5 and DM's reply ibid., 145–6.

'Review of Carlo Gatti: *Verdi: the Man and his Music*', *Tempo* 41 (1956): 30–31.

'Review of Charles Stuart: *Peter Grimes*', *Music Survey* 1/3 (1948): 71.

'Review of Donald N. Ferguson: *A History of Musical Thought*', *Music Survey* 1/5 (1949): 152.

'Review of Douglas Turnell: *Harmony for Listeners*', *Music Survey* 3/1 (1950): 58–9.

'Review of E. Priestley and J. H. Grayson: *A Music Guide for Schools*', *Music Survey* 1/2 (1948): 47.

'Review of Ernest Newman: *Handel*', *Music Survey* 1/2 (1948): 47.

'Review of Ernest Newman: *Wagner Nights*', *Music Survey* 2/4 (1950): 266.

'Review of Franz Grasberger: *Johannes Brahms*', *MR* 15 (1954): 83–4.

'Review of Franz Schubert: *Octet in F Major*, The Vienna Octet (Decca)', *Music Survey* 1/6 (1949): 215.

'Review of Gramophone Records', *MR* 10 (1949): 160–62; 322–4.

'Review of Gramophone Records', *Music Survey* 3/1 (1950): 76–7.

'Review of Gramophone Records', *MR* 11 (1950): 75–8; 160–62; 338–9.

'Review of Gramophone Records', *MR* 12 (1951): 175–7; 259–62; 342–3.

'Review of Gramophone Records', *MR* 14 (1953): 86–8; 167–8.

'Review of Gramophone Records', *MR* 15 (1954): 165–6; 327–9.

'Review of Gramophone Records', *MR* 16 (1955): 354–7.

'Review of Gramophone Records', *MR* 17 (1956): 347; 350–55.

'Review of Gramophone Records', *MR* 18 (1957): 258–60; 263.

'Review of Gramophone Records: Operatic Miscellany; Mahler: *Das Lied von der Erde*', *MR* 13 (1952): 76–7; 328–9.

'Review of H. C. Robbins Landon: *The Symphonies of Joseph Haydn*', *Tempo* 39 (1956): 32–3.

'Review of Hector Berlioz: *Evenings with the Orchestra*, translated and edited by Jacques Barzun', *Tempo* 47 (1958): 34.

'Review of Homer Urlich: *Symphonic Music: its Evolution since the Renaissance*', *Tempo* 30 (1953–54): 31.
'Review of Humphrey Searle: *Twentieth Century Counterpoint: a Guide for Students*', *Tempo* 34 (1954–55): 35–6.
'Review of Igor Stravinsky: *Concerto in D for String Orchestra*', *Music Survey* 1/3 (1948): 77.
'Review of Irene Downes: *Olin Downes on Music*', *Tempo* 46 (1958): 34.
'Review of L. v. Beethoven: *String Quartet in F minor, op. 95*', Griller String Quartet (Decca)', *Music Survey* 2/4 (1950): 280.
'Review of Lillian Littlehales: *Pablo Casals*', *Tempo* 15 (1950): 36.
'Review of Norman Del Mar: *Richard Strauss: a Critical Commentary on his Life and Works, vol. 1*', *The Listener* 69 (17 January 1963): 130.
'Review of Norman Demuth: *An Anthology of Musical Criticism*', *Music Survey* 1/5 (1949): 160.
'Review of Norman Demuth: *Musical Forms and Textures: a Reference Guide*', *Tempo* 32 (1954): 37.
'Review of Otto Klemperer: *Minor Recollections*', *Tempo* 73 (Summer 1965): 33.
'Review of Paul Nettl: *The Book of Musical Documents*', *Music Survey* 2/2 (1949): 114.
'Review of Percy Colson: *Manon*; Hans Keller: *The Rape of Lucretia/Albert Herring*; Martin Cooper: *Carmen*; Alan Pryce-Jones: *Rosenkavalier*; Rupert Lee: *Magic Flute*; Eric Crozier: *Albert Herring* libretto', *Music Survey* 1/2 (1948): 47.
'Review of Prokofiev: *Cinderella*, Royal Opera House Orchestra/Warwick Braithwaite (Columbia)', *Music Survey* 2/2 (1949): 131.
'Review of Ralph Vaughan Williams: *Some Thoughts on Beethoven's Choral Symphony*', *Tempo* 32 (1954): 36.
'Review of Roland-Manual: *Maurice Ravel*', *Music Survey* 1/2 (1948): 46.
'Review of Sergei Prokofiev: *Third Piano Concerto in C, op. 26*', *Music Survey* 2/4 (1950): 260.
'Review of Victor I. Seroff: *Rachmaninoff: a Biography*', *Tempo* 24 (1952): 35–6.
'Review of William Ashbrook: *Donizetti*', *Tempo* 76 (1966): 29.
'Review of William C. Smith: *Concerning Handel: Essays*', *Tempo* 13 (1949): 44–5.
'Review of *Grove's Dictionary*: "Gustav Mahler"', *MR* 16 (1955): 80–82.
'Review of *Hinrichsen's Musical Year Book 1947/48*', *Music Survey* 1/2 (1948): 49.
'Review of *Hinrichsen's Musical Yearbook, Vol. IV*', *Music Survey* 2/2 (1949): 119.
'Review of *Music and the Amateur: a Report Prepared by the Standing Conference of County Music Committees*', *Tempo* 30 (1953–54): 30–31.
'Review of *Practical Music for All (A Symposium)*', *Music Survey* 1/3 (1948): 71.
'Review of *The New Oxford History of Music. I: Ancient and Oriental Music*, edited by Egon Wellesz', *Tempo* 47 (1958): 33.
'Richard Strauss: *Tod und Verklärung, op. 24*', *Music Survey* 3/3 (1951): 189.
'Royal Opera House: *Die Meistersinger*', *Music Survey* 1/3 (1948): 82.
'A Russian Composer Speaks [Aram Khachaturyan]', *MT* 96 (1955): 33.
'La Scala, Milan', *Music Survey* 3/2 (1950): 126.
'Schoenberg', *Music Survey* 2/4 (1950): 251–2.
'Schoenberg in Lowestoft: a chronology compiled from Britten's pocket diaries (1928–1939)', in Chris Banks, Arthur Searle and Malcolm Turner (eds), *Sundry Sorts of Music Books: Essays on the British Library Collections: presented to O. W. Neighbour on his 70th birthday* (London: British Library, 1993): 354–62.
'Schoenberg the Traditionalist', *The Chesterian* 159 (1949): 1–6.
'Schoenberg, Chamber Symphony, op. 9 – II. Style', *Music Survey* 3/3 (1951): 177–8.

'Searching for the Typically American', *Daily Telegraph* (29 August 1959).

'The Season's Balance Sheet', *Opera* 3 (1952): 474–9.

'A Second Renaissance for English Music'; 'Shostakovich and his Symphonies'; 'Britten's Church Parables'; 'Double Portrait: Some Personal Recollections', in Ronald Blythe (ed.) *Aldeburgh Anthology* (Aldeburgh: Snape Maltings Foundation in association with Faber Music, 1972), 88–92; 215–18; 251–6; 431–7.

'A Second Renaissance for English Music?', *AFPB* (1965): 58–60.

'The Serenades for Wind Band', in H. C. Robbins Landon and Donald Mitchell (eds), *The Mozart Companion* (London: Rockliff, New York: Oxford University Press, 1956, R Greenport, CT: Greenwood Press, 1991; Reduced photographic reprint of 1956 without the plates: London: Faber and Faber 1965; Corrected edition: New York: Norton, 1969): 66–89.

'The Serious Comedy of *Albert Herring*', *Glyndebourne Festival Programme Book 1986*, 105–11; reprinted in *Opera Quarterly* 4/3 (Autumn 1986): 45–59; reprinted in programme book for *London: Covent Garden: Royal Opera House* (1 March 1989); reprinted in *About the House* 8/2 (1989): 32–6; reprinted in *Performing Arts: Music Center of Los Angeles County* 26/4 (April 1992); reprinted in *Cradles of the New* (London: Faber and Faber, 1995): 352–64.

'The Shadow of the Librettist', *Daily Telegraph* (11 November 1961).

'Shostakovich and his Symphonies', *AFPB* (1970): 9–12.

'Side-Shows at the Proms: Leoš Janáček I; II', *MO* 78 (1954–55): 23, 25; 89–91.

'Sidney Nolan' [obituary], by DM and Philip Reed. *Independent* (19 December 1992).

'Sir Lennox Berkeley (1903–1989)', *AFPB* (1990): 92.

'Small Victims: *The Golden Vanity* and *Children's Crusade*', in Christopher Palmer (ed.), *The Britten Companion* (London: Faber and Faber; New York: Cambridge University Press, 1984): 165–9. Edited from notes to Decca SET 445 (1970).

'So They Said', *Music Survey* 2/4 (Spring 1950): 272–3. [review of reviews of first English performances of the *Spring Symphony*].

'Some First Performances', *MT* 94 (1953): 576–7.

'Some First Performances', *MT* 95 (1954): 31–2; 92–3; 201–2; 266–8; 324–5; 490–91.

'Some First Performances', *MT* 96 (1955): 151–3; 266–9; 601–3.

'Some First Performances: Vaughan Williams – Stevens – Lambert – Arnell', *Music Survey* 3/3 (1951): 207.

'Some Notes on Gustav Mahler (1860–1911)', *Chord and Discord* 2/6 (1950): 86–91.

'Some Notes on Mahler's Tenth Symphony', *MT* 96 (1955): 656–7.

'Some Observations of William Walton, i: Point of Departure – *Façade*; ii: Walton and Conservatism: Attractions and Revulsions (a Partly Psychological Analysis)', *The Chesterian* 169 (1951): 35–8; 170 (1952): 67–72.

'Some Observations on *Gloriana*', *MMR* 83 (1953): 255–60.

'Some Thoughts on Elgar (1857–1934)', *ML* 38 (April 1957): 113–23. Reprinted in *Cradles of the New* (London: Faber and Faber, 1995): 255–68.

'Something for Everybody's Taste', *Daily Telegraph* (19 January 1963).

'Still in Search of the American Composer', *Daily Telegraph* (17 December 1960).

'The Strauss Festival: ii: Strauss the Conversationalist', *Opera* 4 (1953): 658–62.

'Strauss' *Ariadne auf Naxos*', *Listener* 44 (17 August 1950): 249.

'Stravinsky and Neo-Classicism', *Tempo* 61/2 (Spring–Summer 1962): 9–13. Excerpt from the forthcoming *Language of Modern Music*.

'Stravinsky at the Proms', *Daily Telegraph* (28 July 1962).

'A Suggested Anatomy of Twentieth-Century Art', *MR* 23/2 (1962): 89–102. From the forthcoming *Language of Modern Music*.

'Summer Festivals: *A Dinner Engagement* and *Love in a Village*', *Opera* 5 (1954): 478–81.

'Summer Festivals: *Von Heute auf Morgen* and *Erwartung*', *Opera* 9 (1958): 567–71.

'Summer School's Lure – and its Dangers', *Daily Telegraph* (13 August 1960).

'Teaching to Enjoy', *Daily Telegraph* (17 November 1962).

'The Third Programme and Hans Pfitzner', *Tempo* 27 (1953): 19–20.

'Three First Performances', *MT* 95 (1954): 555.

'Time for a Gesture to Bartók', *Daily Telegraph* (25 August 1962).

'*Tito* at Oxford', *MO* 76 (1952–53): 205.

'Too Early for Life-Saving', *Daily Telegraph* (8 July 1961).

'A Touch of Zagreb at Covent Garden', *Daily Telegraph* (19 June 1963).

'Tragic Conflict Unresolved', *Daily Telegraph* (15 September 1962).

'*Troilus and Cressida*: Two Further Opinions', *Opera* 6 (1955): 88–91.

'The Truth about *Così*', in Anthony Gishford (ed.), *Tribute to Benjamin Britten on his Fiftieth Birthday* (London: Faber and Faber, 1963): 95–9. Reprinted as 'Mozart: the Truth about *Così*' in *Cradles of the New* (London: Faber and Faber, 1995): 127–33.

'*The Turn of the Screw*: a Note on its Thematic Organization', *MMR* 85 (1955): 95–100.

'*The Turn of the Screw*', *Opera* 13 (Autumn 1962): 95–6.

'Two Symphonic Novelists: Mahler and Shostakovich', *Polyphone [Tokyo]* (21 September 1992)

'Two Violinists: Szigeti and January Damen', *MR* 14 (1953): 61–2.

'Under the Influence', *Daily Telegraph* (18 November 1961).

'Under Thirty Theatre Group', *Music Survey* 3/4 (1951): 297.

'Unwritten Music of the Heart: Review of *Edward Elgar: The Windflower Letters* and *Elgar and his Publishers: Letters of a Creative Life*, edited by Jerrold Northrop Moore', *TLS* (26 May 1989): 587–9. Reprinted in *Cradles of the New* (London: Faber and Faber, 1995): 280–94.

'The Valen Society', *MR* 14 (1953): 152.

'Vaughan Williams and the English Tradition', BBC Third Programme (25 April 1965). Reprinted as 'Vaughan Williams' in *Cradles of the New* (London: Faber and Faber, 1995): 87–97.

'Venetian Chaos', *Daily Telegraph* (21 April 1962).

'"VW" Against Three Yardsticks', *Daily Telegraph* (10 June 1961).

'Wedding Anthem', *Musik der Zeit* 7 (1954): 31–2.

'Werner Egk: Man of the Centre', *The Listener* 60 (24 July 1958): 141.

'What do we Know about Britten Now?', in Christopher Palmer (ed.), *The Britten Companion* (London: Faber and Faber, 1984): 21–45.

'What Does the Public Want?', *Daily Telegraph* (12 January 1963).

'What is Expressionism', *Professorial Inaugural Lecture, University of Sussex* (13 March 1972). Reprinted in *Cradles of the New* (London: Faber and Faber, 1995): 203–27.

'What is Wrong with Cheltenham', *Daily Telegraph* (22 July 1961).

'The World of Hans Pfitzner', *The Listener* 49 (15 January 1953): 118. See also 'Letter to the Editor', *The Listener* 49 (29 January 1953): 184.

'The World of Paul Hindemith', *The Chesterian* 28 (1953–54): 35–41. Reprinted in *Cradles of the New* (London: Faber and Faber, 1995): 70–81.

'The Young Person's Composer', *Making Music* 17 (1951): 11–13.

'Youth Versus Convention', *Daily Telegraph* (16 November 1963).

III Programme, Publication and Sleeve Notes

ARNOLD

Malcolm Arnold's Sixty–fifth Birthday Concert (21 October 1986). Reprinted as 'Malcolm Arnold III' in *Cradles of the New* (London: Faber and Faber, 1995): 122–3.

BRITTEN

Alla marcia for string quartet: Note by DM and John Evans (Unicorn-Kanchana DLP 9020, 1983; UKCD 2060, 1993).

American Overture: Introductory note (London: Faber Music, 1985); City of Birmingham Symphony Orchestra/Rattle (EMI CDC 7 47343 2; EMI EL 7494801; EMI EL 7494804, 1986).

Ballad of Heroes: AFPB (1989): 111–12. Revision of section from *Britten and Auden in the Thirties* (London: Faber and Faber, 1981).

The Beggar's Opera: 'The Beggar's Opera – an Introduction'; 'Documents', compiled by DM and Philip Reed; 'A Commentary on the Music', by DM and Philip Reed. Aldeburgh Festival Ensemble/Bedford. (Argo 436 850–2, 1993).

A Birthday Hansel: Pears/Osian Ellis (Decca SXL 6788, 1976).

Blues (arr. Runswick): 'Britten's Blues and Cabaret Songs' (Unicorn-Kanchana DKP(CD) 9138, 1993).

The Burning Fiery Furnace: AFPB (1989): 78–9; 'Britten's Church Parables'. English Opera Group/Britten and Tunnard (London OSA 1163 and OS 26049, 1967; Decca MET 356 and SET 356).

Cabaret Songs: Introductory note (London: Faber Music, 1980); a revised note appears in the second edition [1992]; AFPB (1990): 21 (with Philip Reed); 'Britten's Blues and Cabaret Songs' (Unicorn-Kanchana DKP(CD) 9138, 1993).

Canadian Carnival: City of Birmingham Symphony Orchestra/Rattle. (EMI ASD 4177, 1982).

Canticle IV: The Journey of the Magi: Bowman/Pears/Shirley-Quirk/Britten (Decca SXL 6608, 1973).

Canticle V: The Death of Saint Narcissus: Pears/Ellis (Decca SXL 6788, 1976).

A Charm of Lullabies: Watts/Britten (BBC Records REGL 417, 1981).

Children's Crusade: Wandsworth School/Britten/Burgess (Decca SET 445, 1970), revised as 'Small Victims: *The Golden Vanity* and *Children's Crusade*', in Christopher Palmer (ed.), *The Britten Companion* (London: Faber and Faber; New York: Cambridge University Press, 1984): 165–9.

Christ's Nativity: Preface by DM and Philip Reed (London: Faber Music, 1994).

Church Parables: Decca SET 438 (1970), revised as 'The Church Parables (I): Ritual and Restraint', in Christopher Palmer (ed.), *The Britten Companion* (London: Faber and Faber, 1984): 211–14.

The Company of Heaven: Foreword to vocal score (London: Faber Music, 1990); a revised note appears the second edition, [1992]; R in full score (London: Faber Music, 1993).

Curlew River: 'Curlew River: the Background', English Opera Group/Britten and Tunnard. (London A 4156, OSA 1156, OS 25959, 1965; and Decca MET 301 and SET 301, 1966).

Death in Venice: 'Britten's Concerto for Tenor Voice and Orchestra', *Royal Opera House, Covent Garden* (March/April 1992); 'An Introduction to *Death in Venice*', English Chamber Orchestra/Bedford (Decca SET 581–3; London OSA 13109 and OS 26403–26405, 1974).

Diversions, for piano (left hand) and orchestra: Julius Katchen/London Symphony Orchestra/Britten (London LL 1123, 1955).

Gloriana: 'Fit for A Queen? The Reception of *Gloriana*' and (with Philip Reed) 'The Creation of *Gloriana*: Excerpts from Britten's Correspondence, 1952–3', Welsh National Opera/Mackerras. (Argo 440 213–2, 1993).

The Golden Vanity: Wandsworth School/Britten/Burgess (Decca SET 445, 1970; London 425 161–2, 1989), revised as 'Small Victims: *The Golden Vanity* and *Children's Crusade*', in Christopher Palmer (ed.), *The Britten Companion* (London: Faber and Faber; New York: Cambridge University Press, 1984): 165–9.

Les Illuminations: New Symphony Orchestra/Goossens (London LL 994; Decca LXT 2941, 1954; Decca SXL 6110, 1964; London OS 26161, 1971). ECO/ Bedford, 'Introduction', 'Musical Commentary' by DM and Philip Reed (Collins Classics 70372, 1994).

The Little Sweep: English Opera Group Orchestra/Britten (London A4107; Decca LXT 5163; Decca Eclipse ECM 2166, 1956).

Moderato & Nocturne from Sonatina Romantica: Introductory note (London: Faber Music, 1986).

Nocturne: AFPB (1993): 85–7; 'Introduction', 'Musical Commentary' by DM and Philip Reed (Collins Classics 70372, 1994).

'Now sleeps the crimson petal': Notes by DM and Philip Reed. Scottish Chamber Orchestra/Bedford. (EMI CDC 7494802; EL 7494801; EL 7494804, 1988).

Occasional Overture: Introductory note (London: Faber Music, 1984); City of Birmingham Symphony Orchestra/Rattle (EMI CDC 7 47343 2; EMI EL 7494801; EMI EL 7494804, 1986).

On This Island: Pears/Britten (BBC Records REGL 417, 1981).

Our Hunting Fathers: London Symphony Orchestra/Britten (BBC Records REGL 417, 1981); reprinted in *Cradles of the New* (London: Faber and Faber, 1995): 338–44; revised for *AFPB* (1990): 108–9.

Owen Wingrave: 'Owen Wingrave and the Sense of the Past: Some Reflections on Britten's Opera'. English Chamber Orchestra/Britten (Decca SET 501–502, 1971); reprinted as '*Owen Wingrave* and the Sense of the Past', in *Cradles of the New* (London: Faber and Faber, 1995): 419–38.

Paul Bunyan: Publisher's note, vocal score (London: Faber Music, 1978); revised version appears in the full score (London: Faber Music, 1993); 'Synopsis', 'Paul Bunyan: Britten's and Auden's "American" Opera'; 'Paul Bunyan: the Music' by DM and Philip Reed. Plymouth Music Series/Brunelle. (Virgin VCD 7 90710–2, Virgin Classics 353 243–232, 1988).

Phaedra: 'Introduction', 'Musical Commentary' by DM and Philip Reed (Collins Classics 70372, 1994).

Phantasy Quartet: Note by DM and John Evans (Unicorn-Kanchana DLP 9020, 1983; UKCD 2060, 1993).

Phantasy Quintet in F minor: Note by DM and John Evans (Unicorn-Kanchana DLP 9020, 1983; UKCD 2060, 1993).

The Prince of the Pagodas: Orchestra of the Royal Opera House/Britten (London LL 1690–1691, 1957; Decca LXT 5336–7, n.d.; Ace of Diamonds GOS 558–559, 1968; London STS 15081–15082, 1969).

The Prodigal Son: English Opera Group/Britten and Tunnard (Decca SET 438, 1969; London OSA 1164 and OS 26145, 1971; Decca 425 7132, 1990).

Quatre Chansons Françaises: City of Birmingham Symphony Orchestra/Rattle (EMI ASD 4177,1982); 'Introduction', 'Musical Commentary' by DM and Philip Reed (Collins Classics 70372, 1994).

Rossini Suite: Notes by DM and Philip Reed. Scottish Chamber Orchestra/Bedford. (EMI CDC 7494802; EL 7494801; EL 7494804, 1988).

Russian Funeral: Introductory note by John Evans and DM (London: Faber Music, 1981).

Scottish Ballad: City of Birmingham Symphony Orchestra/Rattle (EMI ASD 4177, 1982).

Second Lute Song from *Gloriana*: Pears/Ellis (Decca SXL 6788, 1976).

Serenade, for tenor, horn and strings: New Symphony Orchestra/Goossens (London LL 994; Decca LXT 2941, 1954; Decca SXL 6110, 1964; London OS 26161, 1971). Scottish Chamber Orchestra/Bedford, notes by DM and Philip Reed (EMI CDC 7494802; EL 7494801; EL 7494804, 1988). ECO/Bedford, 'Introduction', 'Musical Commentary' by DM and Philip Reed (Collins Classics 70372, 1994).

Seven Sonnets of Michelangelo: Pears/Britten (London LL 1204, 1955; Decca LXT 5095, 1956).

Sinfonia da Requiem: Danish State Symphony Orchestra/Britten (London LL 1123, 1955); *AFPB* (1988): 102–3; City of Birmingham Symphony Orchestra/Rattle (EMI CDC 7 47343 2; EMI EL 7494801; EMI EL 7494804, 1986).

Suite for Harp, Op. 83: Pears/Ellis (Decca SXL 6788, 1976).

Suite on English Folk Tunes 'A time there was . . .': City of Birmingham Symphony Orchestra/Rattle (EMI CDC 7 47343 2; EMI EL 7494801; EMI EL 7494804, 1986).

Symphony for Cello and Orchestra, Op. 68: *AFPB* (1970): 67–8.

Temporal Variations: Note by DM and John Evans (Unicorn-Kanchana DLP 9020, 1983; UKCD 2060, 1993).

Three Divertimenti, for string quartet: Note by DM and John Evans (Unicorn-Kanchana DLP 9020, 1983; UKCD 2060, 1993).

The Turn of the Screw: English Opera Group Orchestra/Britten (London XLL 1207–8; Decca LXT 5038–9, 1955). *AFPB* (1972): 63; reprinted in *AFPB* (1983): 29. 'The Screw Keeps on Turning', 'Synopsis and Musical Commentary' by DM and Philip Reed (Collins Classics 70302, 1993).

Two Insect Pieces: Note by DM and John Evans (Unicorn-Kanchana DLP 9020, 1983; UKCD 2060, 1993).

Two Scottish Folk Songs: Pears/Ellis (Decca SXL 6788, 1976).

Winter Words: Pears/Britten (London LL 1204, 1955; Decca LXT 5095, 1956).

Young Apollo: Prefatory note by DM and John Evans (London: Faber Music, 1979); City of Birmingham Symphony Orchestra/Rattle. (EMI ASD 4177, 1982).

BRUCKNER

Symphony No. 5 in B♭ major: Vienna Philharmonic Orchestra/Knappertsbusch (London CMA 7208 C; CSA 2205; SA 6114–15; LL 1527–8, 1956; and London STS 15121–2, 1971).

GRIEG

Holberg Suite: Stuttgart Chamber Orchestra/Karl Münchinger (London CS 6088, 1959; London STS 15044 and CM 9195, 1968).

MAHLER

Des Knaben Wunderhorn: Symphony Orchestra of the Vienna Festival/Prohaska (Vanguard VRS 1113 and VSD 2154, 1963; Vanguard SRV 285 SD, 1968; Vanguard CSRV 285, 1983).

Das Lied von der Erde: *AFPB* (1985): 50.

Lieder eines fahrenden Gesellen: Introduction (London: Josef Weinberger, 1977); *Mahler, Vienna and the Twentieth Century Programme Book* (Autumn 1985): 28–9.

Symphony No. 1: *AFPB* (1994): 165–8.

Symphony No. 2: 'Mahler's Longest Journey: Symphony 2', Chicago Symphony Orchestra/Abbado. (Deutsche Grammophon 427 262–2, 1993).

Symphony No. 4: *Henry J. Wood Promenade Concerts* (26 August 1991).

Symphony No. 5: *Henry J. Wood Promenade Concerts* (20 August 1991); reprinted for same series 9 May 1993; Berlin Philharmonic Orchestra/Abbado (Deutsche Grammophon 427 254–2, 1993).

Symphony No. 6: 'The Only Sixth', *Mahler, Vienna and the Twentieth Century Programme Book* (Autumn 1985): 61–3; Chicago Symphony Orchestra/Abbado (Deutsche Grammophon 2707 117 1MS, 1987); *Henry J. Wood Promenade Concerts* (28 August 1990); *BBC Symphony Orchestra Programme Book* (1990/1 season).

Symphony No. 7: Chicago Symphony Orchestra/Abbado (Deutsche Grammophon 413 773–2, 1984); *Henry J. Wood Promenade Concerts* (3 September 1989); reprinted for same series 6 August 1990; *AFPB* (1991): 142–3.

Symphony No. 9: *Henry J. Wood Promenade Concerts* (12 October 1989); 'Dualities, Contrasts, Conflicts: New Formal Thinking in Mahler's Last Symphonies', Vienna Philharmonic/Abbado (Deutsche Grammophon 423 564–1/2/4, 1988).

Symphony No. 10: 'Dualities, Contrasts, Conflicts: New Formal Thinking in Mahler's Last Symphonies', Vienna Philharmonic/Abbado (Deutsche Grammophon 423 564–1/2/4, 1988).

Todtenfeier: *AFPB* (1994): 20–22.

Wunderhorn Songs: Fourteen Songs to Texts from Youth's Magic Horn: Introductory note (New York: G. Schirmer, 1968).

MOZART

Divertimento No. 11 in D major, K. 251: Stuttgart Chamber Orchestra/Karl Münchinger (London LL 1393, 1956; London CS 6169, 1968).

Divertimento No. 15 in B♭ major (K. Anh. 287): Members of the Vienna Octet (London LL 1239, 1963; London 9352 and 6352, 1963).

Eine kleine Nachtmusik, K. 525: Israel Philharmonic Orchestra Strings/Solti (London CS 6066, 1959; London STS 15141, 1971); Academy of St Martin-in-the-Field/Marriner (London Jubilee JL 41010, 1981).

Quintet in E♭ major, K. 452: Members of the Vienna Octet/Panhoffer. (London CM 9181, 1960; London CS 6109, 1961; London STS 15059, 1969).

Les Petits Riens (K. Anh. 10): Stuttgart Chamber Orchestra/Münchinger (London CS 6088, 1959; London STS 15044 and CM 9195, 1968).

Piano Concerto No. 27 in B♭ major, K. 595: Vienna Philharmonic Orchestra/Karl Böhm (London LL 1282, 1956; London CS 6141, CM 9140 and STS 15062, 1968).

Piano Sonata No. 11 in A major, K. 331: Backhaus (London LL 1282, 1956; London CS 6141,CM 9140 and STS 15062, 1968).

Piano Sonatas Nos. 16, K. 545; No. 11, K. 331; No. 13, K. 333: Katchen (London LL 1164, 1956).

Serenade for Orchestra in D major, K. 203: New Symphony Orchestra of London/Maag (London LL 1206, 1955).

Trio in E♭ major, K. 498: Members of the Vienna Octet/Panhoffer. (London CM 9181, 1960; London CS 6109, 1961; London STS 15059, 1969).

Die Zauberflöte: 'Synopsis', Vienna Philharmonic Orchestra/Böhm (London OS 25046 and A–4319 [X.5180–2], 1958; London OSA 1397, OS 26189–91, 1970).

PURCELL

Suite of Songs, for high voice and orchestra (arr. Britten): notes by DM and Philip Reed. Scottish Chamber Orchestra/Bedford. (EMI CDC 7494802; EL 7494801; EL 7494804, 1988).

SCHUBERT

'Die Forelle' (orch. Britten): notes by DM and Philip Reed. Scottish Chamber Orchestra/Bedford. (EMI CDC 7494802; EL 7494801; EL 7494804, 1988).

SCHUMANN

'Frühlingsnacht' (orch. Britten): notes by DM and Philip Reed. Scottish Chamber Orchestra/Bedford. (EMI CDC 7494802; EL 7494801; EL 7494804, 1988).

TCHAIKOVSKY

Serenade in C major for string orchestra, Op. 48: Israel Philharmonic Orchestra Strings/Solti (London CS 6066, 1959; London STS 15141, 1971).

WAGNER

Siegfried Idyll: Vienna Philharmonic Orchestra/Knappertsbusch (London CMA 7208 C; CSA 2205; SA 6114–15; LL 1527–8, 1956; and London STS 15121–2, 1971).

IV Broadcasting

Radio

'The Background to Mahler's Wunderhorn Settings', *BBC Radio 3* (16 March 1988; rebroadcast 24 Aug 1988).
'Background to Music: Mahler's Fourth Symphony', *BBC Third Programme* (20 June 1961).
'Background to Music: Mahler's Fourth Symphony', *BBC Third Programme* (27 June 1961).
'Background to Music: *Peter Grimes* by Benjamin Britten', *BBC Third Programme* (10 November 1959).
'Background to Music: Schönberg: *Moses and Aron*', *BBC Third Programme* (28 September 1960).
'Benjamin Britten (radio adaptation of documentary film *Britten at 50*), *BBC General Overseas Service* (5 October 1964).
'Benjamin Britten and the English Tradition', *BBC Third Programme* (17 July 1952).
'Benjamin Britten interviewed on his work with references to opera on television', *BBC Third Programme* (1970).
'Benjamin Britten: review of recently published book on Benjamin Britten', *BBC Third Programme* (29 January 1953).
'Benjamin Britten: the Early Years', *BBC Radio 3* (2 January 1980, 14 January 1980, 4 April 1980).
'Brahms' Fourth Symphony (Interval Talk)', *BBC Home Service* (1 January 1947).
'Britten and Parody', *BBC Radio 3* (25 March 1972; rebroadcast 29 June 1979 and 31 Oct 1979).
'Britten in Retrospect', *BBC Radio 3* (13 March 1979).
'Britten's Balinese Ballet', *BBC Radio 3* (20 June 1988).
'Charles Ives and the Vernacular', *BBC Third Programme* (19 May 1960).
'Comment: Donaueschingen Music Festival', *BBC Third Programme* (22 October 1959).
'Concert Calendar: Forthcoming Musical Events', *BBC Third Programme* (17, 18, 19, 20, 21 November 1969).
'Concert Interval: Britten's Cello Suite No. 2 in relation to Suite No. 1 and to Bach', *BBC Third Programme* (17 June 1968).
'Current Series of Third Programme Thursday Invitation Concerts', *BBC Third Programme* (4 February 1960).
'*Das Lied von der Erde* (Prom talk with Nicholas Kenyon)', *BBC Radio 3* (1 September 1985).
'Discussion on Britten's *The Burning Fiery Furnace*', *BBC Transcription Service* (recorded 1 July 1966; transmission date unknown).
'Discussion on Britten's working methods and years in the USA (with Hans Keller)', *BBC Radio 3* (December 1978).
'Edinburgh Festival (interview)', *BBC European Service* (26 August 1968).
'Elgar and His Music (interview)', *BBC European Service* (recorded 6 April 1965; transmission date unknown).
'Elgar's Second Symphony', *BBC Third Programme* (15 January 1967).
'The Faculty of Music: Introduction', *BBC Radio 3* (5 May 1972).
'The Fairy Queen (discussion)', *BBC Third Programme* (25 June 1967).
'Focus: Schoenberg's *Moses and Aron*', *BBC European Service* (recorded 20 July

1966; transmission date unknown).

'Focus: Sibelius (interview)', *BBC European Service* (8 December 1965).

'Great Recordings', *BBC General Overseas Service* (17 January 1964).

'Great Recordings: Beethoven Symphony No. 7 in A', *BBC General Overseas Service* (2 June 1962).

'Great Recordings: César Franck Symphony in D minor', *BBC General Overseas Service* (9 April 1963).

'Great Recordings: Mahler Symphony No. 1 in D', *BBC General Overseas Service* (29 June 1963).

'Great Recordings: Mahler Symphony No. 4 in G', *BBC General Overseas Service* (22 December 1962).

'Great Recordings: Mendelssohn's Symphony No. 4 in A (Italian)', *BBC General Overseas Service* (15 August 1960).

'Great Recordings: Mozart Clarinet Concerto in A, K. 622', *BBC General Overseas Service* (17 October 1960).

'Great Recordings: Mozart The Marriage of Figaro', *BBC General Overseas Service* (1 May 1961).

'Great Recordings: Mozart's Piano Concerto in A, K. 488', *BBC General Overseas Service* (11 April 1960).

'Great Recordings: Rimsky-Korsakov *Sheherazade*', *BBC General Overseas Service* (27 February 1961).

'Great Recordings: Schumann Symphony No. 4 in D minor', *BBC General Overseas Service* (13 September 1962).

'Gustav Holst', *BBC German Service* (30 March 1966).

'The Idea was Good: a Study of Britten's *War Requiem* (with others)', *BBC Radio 3* (17 February 1986).

'In discussion before a performance of Benjamin Britten's *Burning Fiery Furnace*', *BBC Third Programme* (11 June 1966, 1 July 1966).

'*In Short*: Britten the Innovator', *BBC Radio 3* (5 May 1978; rebroadcast 9 September 1978).

'Interview on the 44th Aldeburgh Festival', *BBC Radio 3* (22 June 1991). Recording held at the Britten–Pears Library.

'Interviewed by Peter Paul Nash, at The Red House, Aldeburgh, June 1990', *BBC Radio 3* (8 June 1990).

'Introduction to Busoni: *La Sposa Sorteggiata*', *BBC Third Programme* (27 October 1957).

'Introduction to a Concert of Thai Classical Music', *BBC Radio 3* (24 March 1981).

'Introduction to a Programme of Benjamin Britten's Cabaret Songs', *BBC Radio 3* (17 June 1981).

'Introduction to a Programme of Early Works by Benjamin Britten', *BBC Radio 3* (15 June 1981).

'Introduction to Britten's *War Requiem*', *BBC General Overseas Service* (6 December 1962).

'Introduction to *Die Entführung aus dem Serail* (Mozart)', *BBC General Overseas Service* (28 July 1957).

'An Introductory Talk: Max Reger – The Man and his Music', *BBC Third Programme* (22 January 1951; a series of 10 programmes organized by DM, broadcast on 25, 28 January; 9, 12, 21 February; 2, 4, 13, 21, 31 March 1951).

'James Bowman: A Twentieth-century Voice (interview with Brian Kay)', *BBC Radio 3* (16 May 1992; rebroadcast 12 January 1993).

'The Language of Contemporary Art', *BBC Third Programme* (25 January 1960).

'*Letters from a Life*: discussion of the Britten Letters with Michael Berkeley', *BBC Radio 4* (17 June 1991).
'The Lively Arts: Aldeburgh Festival', *BBC European Service* (7 June 1969).
'The Lively Arts: Aldeburgh Festival', *BBC English Service* (7 June 1969).
'The Lively Arts: Revival of *Peter Grimes*', *BBC English Service* (24 May 1969).
'The Lively Arts: Revival of *Peter Grimes*', *BBC European Service* (24 May 1969).
'*Lulu*', *BBC Third Programme* (6 February 1960).
'Mahler and Freud', *BBC Third Programme* (28 March 1955).
'Mahler and the Fourth Symphony', *BBC Home Service* (19 May 1965).
'Mahler's Chinese Sources', *BBC Radio 3* (29 July 1988).
'Mahler's First Symphony: Unknown Last Movement', *BBC Third Programme* (18 June 1967).
'Mahler: Song Cycle and Symphony', *BBC Third Programme* (13 March 1960).
'Malcolm Arnold and the Curse of Popularity', *BBC Radio 3* (28 February 1977; rebroadcast 4 March 1978).
'Man, Myth and Music: Interview with John Amis', *BBC General Overseas Service* (27 April 1965).
'Mozart: *The Marriage of Figaro*: Introductory Talk', *BBC General Overseas Service* (11 June 1958).
'Music All Day: Discussion about the BBC Music Programme', *BBC Home Service* (21 March 1965).
'Music Club: The Waltz', *BBC Light Programme* (23 November 1953).
'Music in Television (discussion)', *BBC Third Programme* (1 May 1964).
'Music Lover's Diary: The Music of Max Reger, 1873–1916', *BBC Home Service* (7 July 1946).
'Music Lovers' Bookshop: Review of Books on Music', *BBC General Overseas Service* (13 May 1962).
'Music Magazine', *BBC Radio 3* (30 May 1971).
'Music Magazine', *BBC Radio 3* (12 December 1972).
'Music Magazine: Beethoven: a Portrait of himself and his contemporaries', *BBC Home Service* (25 November 1951).
'Music Magazine: Book Review *Western Man and His Music*', *BBC Home Service* (23 September 1962).
'Music Magazine: Book Review: Two Books about Mozart', *BBC Home Service* (30 October 1960).
'Music Magazine: Book Review: *The Death of Music since Debussy*', *BBC Home Service* (5 November 1961).
'Music Magazine: Book Review: *Bach's Brandenburg Concertos*', *BBC Home Service* (23 May 1964).
'Music Magazine: Britten and Rostropovich', *BBC Third Programme* (5 May 1967).
'Music Magazine: Britten's Chamber Music', *BBC Home Service* (10 November 1957).
'Music Magazine: Britten's *The Turn of the Screw*', *BBC Home Service* (19 February 1961).
'Music Magazine: Bruckner and Prokofiev: Book Review', *BBC Home Service* (7 May 1961).
'Music Magazine: Centenary Edition for Gustav Mahler', *BBC Home Service* (3 July 1960).
'Music Magazine: Cheltenham Festival', *BBC Home Service* (12 July 1964).
'Music Magazine: Cheltenham Festival: Interview with Thomas Hillbish', *BBC*

Home Service (12 July 1964).
'Music Magazine: From Music Magazine', *BBC Radio 3* (8 February 1972).
'Music Magazine: Holst Today', *BBC Home Service* (24 May 1964).
'Music Magazine: Ives and Hindemith', *BBC Third Programme* (14 March 1965).
'Music Magazine: Mahler's Second Symphony', *BBC Home Service* (8 March 1959).
'Music Magazine: Mahler's Seventh Symphony', *BBC Radio 3* (6 February 1972).
'Music Magazine: Mahler's Third Symphony', *BBC Third Programme* (24 April 1966).
'Music Magazine: Mahler's Unfinished Symphony', *BBC Home Service* (24 March 1963).
'Music Magazine: Mahler's *Das Lied von der Erde*', *BBC Home Service* (28 December 1958).
'Music Magazine: Max Reger (1873–1916)', *BBC Third Programme* (8 May 1966).
'Music Magazine: Miscellaneous Records for April', *BBC Home Service* (16 April 1950).
'Music Magazine: Mozart and the Italian Opera Seria', *BBC Home Service* (31 May 1959).
'Music Magazine: Mozart's Chamber Music', *BBC Home Service* (8 April 1956).
'Music Magazine: Musical Profile· Francesco Malipiero', *BBC General Overseas Service* (14 March 1957).
'Music Magazine: Record Review', *BBC Home Service* (8 December 1963).
'Music Magazine: Record Reviews', *BBC Home Service* (12 December 1954).
'Music Magazine: Record Reviews', *BBC Home Service* (18 June 1961).
'Music Magazine: Record Reviews', *BBC Home Service* (15 December 1963).
'Music Magazine: Reger and Hindemith Records', *BBC Home Service* (11 February 1951).
'Music Magazine: Review of Miscellaneous Records', *BBC Home Service* (18 May 1952).
'Music Magazine: Review of New Records', *BBC Home Service* (16 May 1953).
'Music Magazine: Review of New Records', *BBC Home Service* (18 October 1953).
'Music Magazine: Review of New Records', *BBC Home Service* (13 June 1954).
'Music Magazine: Review of New Records', *BBC Home Service* (13 March 1955).
'Music Magazine: Review of New Records', *BBC Home Service* (12 June 1955).
'Music Magazine: Review of New Records', *BBC Home Service* (10 July 1955).
'Music Magazine: Review of New Records', *BBC Home Service* (16 October 1955).
'Music Magazine: Review of New Records', *BBC Home Service* (19 February 1956).
'Music Magazine: Review of New Records', *BBC Home Service* (13 May 1956).
'Music Magazine: Review of New Records', *BBC Home Service* (8 July 1956).
'Music Magazine: Review of New Records', *BBC Home Service* (21 October 1956).
'Music Magazine: Review of New Records', *BBC Home Service* (17 February 1957).
'Music Magazine: Review of New Records', *BBC Home Service* (7 April 1957).
'Music Magazine: Review of New Records', *BBC Home Service* (19 May 1957).
'Music Magazine: Review of New Records', *BBC Home Service* (15 December 1957).
'Music Magazine: Review of New Records', *BBC Home Service* (16 March 1958).
'Music Magazine: Review of New Records', *BBC Home Service* (22 June 1958).
'Music Magazine: Review of New Records', *BBC Home Service* (20 July 1958).
'Music Magazine: Review of New Records', *BBC Home Service* (15 February 1959).
'Music Magazine: Review of New Records', *BBC Home Service* (10 May 1959).
'Music Magazine: Review of New Records', *BBC Home Service* (19 July 1959).
'Music Magazine: Review of New Records', *BBC Home Service* (11 October 1959).

'Music Magazine: Review of New Records', *BBC Home Service* (16 October 1960).

'Music Magazine: Review of Orchestral and Instrumental Records for March', *BBC Home Service* (16 March 1952).

'Music Magazine: Review of Orchestral Music', *BBC Home Service* (13 July 1952).

'Music Magazine: Review of Recent Records of Concertos by Mozart', *BBC Home Service* (15 February 1953).

'Music Magazine: Schoenberg's *Pierrot Lunaire*', *BBC Home Service* (10 April 1960).

'Music Magazine: Scriabin's Piano Concerto', *BBC Home Service* (9 November 1958).

'Music Magazine: Some Books on Music for Christmas', *BBC Home Service* (15 December 1963).

'Music Magazine: Some New Records of Contemporary Music', *BBC Home Service* (9 April 1961).

'Music Magazine: Strauss's *Elektra*', *BBC Third Programme, BBC Home Service* (25 May 1958).

'Music Magazine: Stravinsky and Tchaikovsky', *BBC Third Programme* (11 June 1967).

'Music Magazine: Stravinsky and the Old Testament', *BBC Third Programme* (22 February 1968; rebroadcast 7 April 1968).

'Music Magazine: Stravinsky *The Flood*', *BBC Home Service* (29 September 1963).

'Music Magazine: Stravinsky's Middle Period', *BBC Radio 3* (13 June 1971).

'Music Magazine: Stravinsky's Piano Music', *BBC Third Programme* (18 May 1969).

'Music Magazine: Stravinsky's *Oedipus Rex*', *BBC Third Programme* (1 February 1970).

'Music Magazine: The Music of Szymanowsky', *BBC Home Service* (30 December 1962).

'Music Magazine: Tribute to Igor Stravinsky', *BBC Radio 3* (17 April 1970).

'Music Magazine: Tribute to Stravinsky', *BBC Radio 3* (4 April 1971).

'Music Magazine: Two Books about Music', *BBC Home Service* (16 June 1957).

'Music Magazine: Two Romantic Composers', *BBC Third Programme* (6 November 1966).

'Music Magazine: Vaughan Williams and the Symphonies', *BBC General Overseas Service* (7 October 1957).

'Music Magazine: Virgil Thomson', *BBC Home Service* (25 November 1956).

'Music Now: Britten–Pears School for Advanced Musical Study (interview)', *BBC Radio 3* (1 June 1979).

'Music Now: Time for Benjamin Britten (interview)', *BBC Radio 3* (4 June 1980).

'Music Questions', *BBC Home Service* (13 August 1961).

'Music Questions', *BBC Home Service* (5 August 1962).

'Music to Remember', *BBC Home Service* (2 April 1963).

'Music Weekly: Britten, *Curlew River*, and the Church Parable', *BBC Radio 3* (1 June 1986).

'Music Weekly: Mahler the Arranger', *BBC Radio 3* (14 September 1986).

'Music Weekly: Mahler's Chinese Sources for *Das Lied von der Erde*', *BBC Radio 3* (4 December 1983).

'Music Weekly: Mahler's Fifth Symphony', *BBC Radio 3* (18 March 1984).

'Music Weekly: Mahler, Vienna and the Twentieth Century', *BBC Radio 3* (10 March 1985).

'Music Weekly: The Britten Archive in Aldeburgh', *BBC Radio 3* (21 April 1985).

'Music Weekly: The Music of Thailand', *BBC Radio 3* (18 January 1987).
'The New Britten Opera (Mitchell and Britten in Conversation)', *BBC Radio 3* (10 May 1971).
'New Light on Mahler', *BBC Third Programme* (24 September 1957).
'New Records: Concert Edition', *BBC General Overseas Service* (23, 30 August 1959).
'New Records: Concert Music', *BBC General Overseas Service* (22, 29 December 1958; 5, 12, 19, 26 January; 2, 9, 16 February; 2, 9, 16 March 1959).
'New Records: Concert Music', *BBC General Overseas Service* (31 December 1961; 7, 14, 21, 28 January; 4, 11 February 1962).
'New Records: Concert type', *BBC General Overseas Service* (22, 29 September; 6, 13, 20, 27 October; 3, 10, 17, 24 November; 1, 8, 15 December 1958).
'Opera: *Wozzeck* at Covent Garden', *BBC Third Programme* (8 December 1960).
'Orchestral Concerts (introduction)', *BBC Home Service* (22 September 1952).
'Orchestral Concerts: Introduction to German Music (Schools scripts)', *BBC Home Service* (22 September 1952).
'The Originality of Percy Grainger', *BBC Third Programme* (12 June 1966).
'Outlook (interview)', *BBC European Service* (23 June 1965).
'Poulenc's Opera: *La voix humaine*', *BBC Third Programme* (2 September 1960).
'Quotation in *Cosi fan Tutte* (interval talk)', *BBC Radio 3* (14 March 1978)
'The Radical Years: Schoenberg and Mahler', *BBC Third Programme* (2 March 1970).
'Record Review', *BBC Home Service* (30 July 1961).
'Record Review: Building a Library: Mahler's Symphony No. 1', *BBC Third Programme* (19 March 1963).
'Record Review: Building a Library: Mozart 'Haffner' Symphony', *BBC Third Programme* (2 January 1962).
'Record Review: Building a Library: Mozart Piano Concerto in C minor', *BBC Third Programme* (22 May 1962).
'Record Review: Building a Library: Mozart Piano Concerto No. 27', *BBC Third Programme* (17 July 1963).
'Record Review: Building a Library: Bruckner', *BBC Third Programme* (14 February 1959).
'Record Review: Building a Library: *Cosi*', *BBC Third Programme* (23 February 1961).
'Record Review: Building a Library: On Choosing a Mozart Piano Concerto', *BBC Third Programme* (15 February 1958).
'Record Review: Building a Modern Library: Review of Recordings of Works by Mendelssohn', *BBC Third Programme* (26 July 1958).
'Record Review: Comparative Review of All the Available Recordings of Bartók's Piano Concerto No. 3', *BBC Third Programme* (21 July 1960).
'Record Review: Critic's Choice', *BBC Third Programme* (18 December 1962).
'Record Review: Discussion-review of all the available recordings of Mendelssohn's Italian Symphony', *BBC Third Programme* (4 December 1958; recorded but not broadcast).
'Record Review: Introduction to Mahler: Review of Records of Works by Mahler', *BBC Third Programme* (29 November 1958).
'Record Review: Introduction to Our Time', *BBC Third Programme* (24 November; 1 December 1960).
'Record Review: Mahler's Symphonies', *BBC Third Programme* (22 January 1963).
'Record Review: Mozart Symphony No. 36 in C', *BBC Third Programme* (16

October 1962).

'Record Review: Recent Chamber Music Records', *BBC Third Programme* (4 May 1961).

'Record Review: Recent Operatic Records', *BBC Third Programme* (9 November 1957).

'Record Review: Review of Current Recordings of Mozart's Symphony No. 39 in E♭', *BBC Third Programme* (9 September 1957).

'Record Review: Review of Kurt Weill *Mahagonny*', *BBC Third Programme* (6 October 1960).

'Record Review: Review of Recent Records of Chamber Music', *BBC Third Programme* (14 July 1959).

'Record Review: Review of Recent Records of Instrumental Music and Songs', *BBC Third Programme* (27 September 1958).

'Record Review: Review of Recently Issued Recording of Bartók's *Bluebeard's Castle*', *BBC Third Programme* (9 June 1960).

'Record Review: Review of Recently Issued Records of Instrumental Music', *BBC Third Programme* (3 December 1959).

'Record Review: Review of Recently Issued Records of Instrumental Music', *BBC Third Programme* (17 March 1960).

'Record Review: Review of Recordings of Recent Chamber Music', *BBC Third Programme* (24 May 1958).

'Record Review: Review of Records of Works by Mahler for the Mahler Centenary Edition', *BBC Third Programme* (25 August 1960).

'Record Review: Traditional Songs of Spain, Early English Keyboard Music', *BBC Third Programme* (4 October 1951).

'Report from London: Interview with a Flamenco Guitarist', *BBC Transcription Service for Pacific Service* (recorded 2 October 1961; transmission date unknown).

'Roger Smalley *Pulses* (discussion)', *BBC Third Programme* (7 November 1969).

'Second "Music Today" Concert at the Royal Festival Hall', *BBC Third Programme* (17 March 1960).

'The Strange Case of Piotr Zak', *BBC Third Programme* (11 September 1961).

'The Strange Case of Piotr Zak (with Hans Keller and Jeremy Noble)', *BBC Third Programme* (13 August 1961).

'Stravinsky and *The Rite of Spring*', *BBC Home Service* (20 May 1965).

'Studies in Interpretation: The Conductor's Art (Furtwängler)', *BBC Third Programme* (24 January 1952).

'A Time for Benjamin Britten (with others)', *BBC Radio 3* (4 June 1980).

'Vaughan Williams and the English Tradition: Personal Reactions to Two Recently Published Studies of Vaughan Williams', *BBC Third Programme* (25 April 1965).

'The Works of Gustav Holst (interview)', *BBC European Service* (25 July 1965).

'World Theatre: Britten's Music for *Johnson over Jordan*', *BBC Radio 3* (1987).

'The World Tonight: Britten's *Venite* (1961)', *BBC Radio 4* (30 September 1983).

'Young Musicians (interview)', *BBC Home Service* (28 April 1964).

'Younger Generation: Four Overtures: *Die Fledermaus* Overture', *BBC Light Programme* (26 March 1952).

'Younger Generation: Your Music Club: Music and the Gramophone – Collecting Records', *BBC Light Programme* (11 December 1951).

'Your Concert Choice', *BBC Home Service* (2, 9, 23, 30 September 1956).

'Your Concert Choice', *BBC Home Service* (31 December 1957; 7, 14, 21 January 1958).

Television

Death in Venice: the Opera by Benjamin Britten (London Trust Cultural
Productions/Tony Palmer, 1981)
From East to West: The Jade Flute (BBC Television/Barrie Gavin, 1986)
A Tenor Man's Story (Central Television/Barrie Gavin, 27 August 1985).
A time there was . . . : A Profile of Benjamin Britten (London Weekend
Television/Tony Palmer, 6 April 1980).
Young Apollo (BBC Television/Barrie Gavin, 2 November 1985).

Contributors

Paul Banks specializes in music of the nineteenth and twentieth centuries. He is Librarian of the Britten–Pears Library, Aldeburgh, and special professor in nineteenth-century studies in the department of music at the University of Nottingham. His publications include the revised edition of DM's *Gustav Mahler: The Early Years* (with David Matthews), the *New Grove* article on Mahler (with DM), and *Britten's Gloriana: Essays and Sources* (Aldeburgh Studies in Music 1).

Herta Blaukopf was born in Vienna. Her publications about literary and musical life in Vienna include *Gustav Mahler–Richard Strauss Correspondence 1888–1891* and *Mahler's Unknown Letters*, as well as several books and essays in German. Since 1959 she has been married to the socio-musicologist Kurt Blaukopf with whom she collaborated on *Mahler: His Life, Work and World* and a monograph of the Vienna Philharmonic Orchestra.

Asa Briggs (Lord Briggs of Lewes) is a distinguished historian. He was involved with the University of Sussex from its inception, serving as Vice-Chancellor from 1967 until 1976, when he became Provost of Worcester College, Oxford, a post he held until 1991. His numerous publications have been dominated by two areas of special interest – the nineteenth century and the BBC.

Maureen Buja was an editor and bibliographer for the *New Grove Dictionary of Opera*. She lives in New York and is currently completing a critical study of sixteenth-century music printing.

Jill Burrows is a playwright, publisher, editor and typographer. She has been associated with Aldeburgh and DM since the mid-1970s and has edited the Aldeburgh Foundation programme books since 1982. She is currently researching a history of the English Opera Group.

Mervyn Cooke teaches in the Music Department at the University of Nottingham. Among his publications are a Cambridge Opera Handbook on *Billy Budd* (with Philip Reed) and an edition of DM's selected writings, *Cradles of the New*. Forthcoming books include an important study of the influence of the musics of the Far East on Britten.

David Drew's unrivalled knowledge of the life and works of Kurt Weill has led to numerous collaborations with opera houses, festivals and concert organizations throughout Europe. His *Kurt Weill Handbook* (1987) attracted critical acclaim and he is currently completing two volumes on the German works of Weill. From 1975 until his resignation in 1992, he was in charge of contemporary music at Boosey & Hawkes.

Peter du Sautoy worked at Faber and Faber from the mid-1940s until his retirement (as Chairman). In 1965, with DM, he founded Faber Music, of which he was the first Chairman. He has lived in Aldeburgh for a number of years where he and his wife have worked tirelessly in the cause of the Aldeburgh Foundation and the Britten–Pears School for Advanced Musical Studies.

Peter Franklin has taught music at the University of Leeds since 1980. His publications include a case study of Mahler's Third Symphony, *The Idea of Music: Schoenberg and Others* and an edition of Natalie Bauer-Lechner's *Recollections of Gustav Mahler*.

Henry-Louis de La Grange has written about Mahler's life and works for the last fifty years. His monumental three-volume study, *Gustav Mahler: Chronique d'une vie*, was completed in 1984 and is soon to appear in English.

Gilbert Kaplan is a businessman whose lifelong interest in Mahler has led him to conduct and record (among other works) the Second Symphony and through the Kaplan Foundation to publish facsimile editions of the autograph full scores of the Second Symphony and the *Adagietto* from the Fifth.

Oliver Knussen is widely regarded as the leading composer of his generation. As a conductor, he appears regularly with leading orchestras and ensembles around the world. He has been an Artistic Director of the Aldeburgh Festival since 1983 and an Executive Director (with Steuart Bedford) since 1987.

Ludmila Kovnatskaya has lived and worked in St Petersburg most of her adult life. She is the foremost Britten scholar in Russia and has done much to promote interest not only in Britten, but in all aspects of twentieth-century English musical culture. She was Artistic Director of the 1993 St Petersburg Britten Festival, a major survey of Britten's *oeuvre* and the first event of its kind in Russia since Britten's and Pears's own visits there in the 1960s and 1970s.

Colin Matthews is a composer. He and his brother, David, assisted Deryck Cooke in the completion of Mahler's Tenth Symphony.

David Matthews is a composer. Apart from his work on the completion of the Tenth Symphony, David Matthews (with Paul Banks) was responsible for the revised edition of DM's *Gustav Mahler: The Early Years*.

Edward Mendelson teaches at Columbia University, New York. He is the literary executor of the Auden Estate, in which capacity he has generated an enormous amount of scholarly activity since the poet's death. Among Prof. Mendelson's publications are *Early Auden*, and the complete edition of Auden's writings, two volumes of which have thus far appeared.

Kathleen Mitchell read history at Birkbeck College, and later became a leading figure in London education. From 1974 to 1979, she was Headmistress of Pimlico School, with its Special Music Course, in which Britten took a close interest.

Eveline Nikkels studied musicology at Utrecht. She researched the music of Friedrich Nietzsche and wrote a thesis on the influence of Nietzsche on Mahler's music. She is currently a member of the board of the Gustav Mahler Society in the Netherlands.

Christopher Palmer (1946–1995), writer, orchestrator, arranger and producer, died while this book was in preparation. His many publications include *Impressionism in Music* and *The Britten Companion*. One of his last pieces of published writing was 'Thinking Like a Composer', his introduction to DM's *Cradles of the New*.

Myfanwy Piper is the librettist of three of Britten's operas: *The Turn of the Screw*, *Owen Wingrave*, and *Death in Venice*. She and her husband, the artist John Piper, were friends and colleagues of both Britten and Pears for fifty years.

Philip Reed is Staff Musicologist at the Britten–Pears Library, Aldeburgh. He and DM jointly edited the first two volumes of *Letters from a Life: The Selected Letters and Diaries of Benjamin Britten*, which were awarded a Royal Philharmonic Society Music Award in 1992. Other publications include *Benjamin Britten: Billy Budd* (with Mervyn Cooke) and an edition of *The Travel Diaries of Peter Pears, 1936–1978* (Aldeburgh Studies in Music 2).

Edward R. Reilly is professor of Music at Vassar College, Poughkeepsie, NY. He has written extensively on Mahler's works, particularly on manuscript studies.

Eric Roseberry is a freelance musician and writer. After a spell at the BBC as a music producer, he helped DM establish the music degree course at the University of Sussex. He has written extensively on the music of Britten and Shostakovich.

Edward W. Said is University Professor at Columbia University and chairs the doctoral program in Comparative Literature. He is the author of several book including *Beginnings: Intention and Method, Orientalism, The World, the Text and the Critic, Musical Elaborations,* and *Culture and Imperialism.* In 1993 he gave the Reith Lectures, published in 1994 as *Representations of the Intellectual.*

Peter Sculthorpe is one of Australia's leading composers. His major music-theatre piece, *Rites of Passage,* was premièred by the Australian Opera.

Somsak Ketukaenchan studied music in his native Thailand before coming to England to undertake postgraduate work at the University of York (on Britten, and the classical music of Thailand). He is currently head of the music department at Srinakharinwirot University, Bangkok. He is also one of Thailand's finest players of the *pi nai* (the Thai oboe).

Erwin Stein (1885–1958) was a pupil of Schoenberg, and a contemporary of Berg and Webern. After leaving Vienna in 1938, Stein came to London where he worked at Boosey & Hawkes as an editor and adviser, in which capacity he came into contact with Benjamin Britten. His many publications include a collection of essays, *Orpheus in New Guises,* and *Form and Performance* (published posthumously).

Rosamund Strode worked as Benjamin Britten's music assistant for many years, and was subsequently Keeper of Manuscripts and Archivist at the Britten–Pears Library. She is currently preparing a biography of Imogen Holst.

Marion Thorpe was born in Vienna where, through her father, the distinguished musician Erwin Stein, she was already as a child exposed to music of a great variety. Her family settled in London in 1938 where Erwin Stein established new musical friendships, notably with Benjamin Britten. Her publications include a highly successful series of piano-teaching books (with Fanny Waterman) and the *Tribute to Peter Pears on His 75th Birthday.*

Arnold Whittall is Emeritus Professor of Musical Theory and Analysis at King's College, University of London. His many publications include *Britten and Tippett: Studies in Themes and Techniques.*

John Williamson teaches at the University of Liverpool. His most recent publication is *The Music of Hans Pfitzner.*

Index

WORKS: *Albert Herring*, Op. 39, 154, 295, 303, 305, 309, 312, 315, 316; libretto, 315; performances, 153; sense of location, 154; *Alla marcia* (1933), 318; *An American Overture* (1941), 303, 318; 'The Ash Grove' (folksong arrangement), 292; *Ballad of Heroes*, Op. 14, 155, 318; *The Beggar's Opera* (Gay realization), Op. 43, 155, 303, 305, 318; 'Beware!' (1922/23), 281; *Billy Budd*, Op. 50, 216, 218, 225, 303, 304, 311, 312; composition, 231–52; interview chords, 224; libretto, 235, 235 n. 4, 236, 246, 249; publication, 236–7; recording, 233; *A Birthday Hansel*, Op. 92, 318; 'Afton Water', 219; *Blues* (arr. Runswick), 318; *A Boy Was Born*, Op. 3, 294–5; manuscripts, 284, 284 n. 13, 289; performances, 284, 284 n. 13; *The Burning Fiery Furnace*, Op. 77, 305, 316, 318, 323, 324; composition, 135–45; critical reception, 144–5; dedication, 137, 137 n. 4; libretto, 135–40; performances, 137, 137 n. 4, 141; publication, 194, 204; recording, 137 n. 4; *Cabaret Songs* (1937–9), 308, 318, 324; *Canadian Carnival*, Op. 19, 318; *Cantata Academica*, Op. 62, 303; commission, 156; *Cantata misericordium*, Op. 69, 304, 310; commission, 155; performances, 199; *Canticle II: Abraham and Isaac*, Op. 51, 225; analysis, 254–66; *Canticle IV: Journey of the Magi*, Op. 86, 318; *Canticle V: The Death of Saint Narcissus*, Op. 89, 318; *A Ceremony of Carols*, Op. 28; composition, 285; *A Charm of Lullabies*, Op. 41, 318; *Children's Crusade*, Op. 82, 316, 318, 319; publication, 286 n. 20; *Christ's Nativity* (1931), 318; *The Company of Heaven* (1937), 318; *Curlew River*, Op. 71, 153, 225, 305, 316, 318, 327; composition, 136, 287 n. 22; church parable conventions, 137, 138, 140, 141, 142, 143, 144, 145; critical reception, 145;

performances, 135; publication, 153, 194, 288 n. 28; sense of location, 154; *The Dark Valley* (incidental music), 187; *Death in Venice*, Op. 88, xvii, 175 n. 4, 184, 230, 307, 308, 318; commentary, 267–74, 297; libretto, 269, 333; publication, 284, 288; sources and related works, 216–27; television film, 330; *Diversions*, Op. 21, 319; publication, 286 n. 20; *Five Walztes* (1923–5/1969), 281 n. 3; folksong arrangements, 320, *see also individual songs*; *Gloriana*, Op. 53, 255, 306, 311, 313, 316, 319, 320; *The Golden Vanity*, Op. 78, 219, 225, 316, 318, 319; *Hymn to St Cecilia*, Op. 27, 295; composition, 186–7, 192; text, 186–92; *A Hymn to the Virgin* (1930), 282, 283 n. 8; *Les Illuminations*, Op. 18, 154 n. 6, 319; analysis, 170–71; composition, 153; manuscripts, 285; performances, 153–4, 285; 'I saw three witches' (1930), 282 n. 6; *Johnson over Jordan* (incidental music), 329; *The Little Sweep*, Op. 45, 303, 304, 309, 314, 319; *Let's Make an Opera, see The Little Sweep*; *A Midsummer Night's Dream*, Op. 64, 253, 255, 308, 311; *Mont Juic* (with Berkeley), Op. 12; composition, 162; *Nocturne*, Op. 60, 253, 319; 'Now Sleeps the Crimson Petal' (1943), 312, 319; *Noye's Fludde*, Op. 59, 296, 319; 'O, fly not, pleasure' (1930), 282 n. 6; *Occasional Overture* (1946), 319; *On This Island*, Op. 11, 319; *Our Hunting Fathers*, Op. 8, 182, 261 n. 4, 319; *Owen Wingrave*, Op. 85, 225, 303, 310, 313, 319; libretto, 333; *Paul Bunyan*, Op. 17, 313, 319; Auden's essay on, 149–50; composition, 148, 149, 285; gamelan elements, 275–9; libretto, 186; manuscripts, 286; première, 150; publication, 288; *Peter Grimes*, Op. 33, 152, 154, 154 n. 6, 162, 218, 219, 219 n. 16, 294, 295, 303, 306, 311, 313, 323,

Metropolitan Opera, New York, 5, 58, 59, 60, 63, 74
Mewton-Wood, Noel, 163
Mildenburg, Anna von, 29
Milhaud, Darius, 146, 152, 153–5, 156, 157, 308; *A propos des Bottes*, 155; *Ani maamin*, 155; *The Beggar's Opera* (Gay realization), 155; *Cantate de la croix de charité*, 154; *Cantate de la Guerre*, 155; *Le château de feu*, 155; *Christophe Colomb*, 153; *Cortege funèbre*, 155; *La création du monde*, 153; *Esther de Carpentras*, 154; 'Etude de hasard dirigé', 154; *Les Malheurs d'Orphée*, 154; *La Mort du Tyran*, 155; *Ode pour les morts*, 155; *Pacem in terris*, 154; *Pan et Syrinx*, 153, 154, 154 n. 6; *Un petit peu de musique*, 155; *Poèmes Juifs*, 153; *Saudades do Brasil*, 153; *La Vie Commence*, 307; Violin Concerto No. 1, 153
Minneapolis Symphony Orchestra, 63
Miró, Joán, 161
Mitchell, Catherine, 307
Mitchell, Donald, 41, 49–51, 101, 104, 107, 109, 114, 115 n. 1, 125; and Aldeburgh Festival, 40 n. 46; and Britten, 40, 115 n. 1, 137, 137 n. 4, 141, 167–9; and *Mahler-Feest*, 78; as critic, 40 n. 46, 42 n. 55, 50, 146, 147, 167, 220, 267, 272; as editor, 45, 45 n. 3, 50; as publisher, 45 n. 3, 167–9; at Edinburgh Festival 1968, 193–212; at University of Sussex, 41; bibliography, 300–330; *Gustav Mahler: Songs and Symphonies of Life and Death: Interpretations and Annotations*, 43; *Gustav Mahler: The Early Years*, 92, 115 n. 1; *The Language of Modern Music*, 167; *Letters from a Life* (ed., with Philip Reed), 290
Mitchell, Kathleen, 114, 137, 137 n. 4, 141, 209, 301, 333
Mitropoulos, Dimitri, 76
Mitterand, François, 90
Modern Music, 148, 151
Moll, Carl, 4, 5, 15 n. 47, 59, 119

Monk, W. H., 295; *Württemberg*, 295
Monteverdi, Claudio: *L'Incoronazione di Poppea*, 168
Moore, Herbert, 78
Moore, Jerrold Northrop, 305; *Edward Elgar: The Windflower Letters*, 317; *Elgar and his Publishers . . .*, 317
Moorhouse, Frederick, 111
Morgan, J. P., 60, 62, 66
Morley College Concert Society, 311
Moser, Koloman (Kolo), 4, 6, 10
Mount Ephraim (hymn tune), 296
Mozart, Leopold, 281
Mozart, Wolfgang Amadeus, xvii, 6, 8, 9–10, 53 n. 50, 129, 147, 226 n. 29, 262, 281, 301, 302, 305, 311, 312, 316, 321–2, 325, 326, 327; Clarinet Concerto in A (K. 622), 324; Clarinet Quintet (K. 581), 208; Clarinet Trio (K. 498), 321; *La Clemenza di Tito*, 312, 317; *Così fan tutte*, 6, 9, 10, 313, 317, 328; Divertimento in B♭ (K. Anh. 287); Divertimento in D (K. 251), 321; *Don Giovanni*, 6, 59, 306, 311; *Die Entführung aus dem Serail*, 6, 324; 'God is our refuge', 281; *Idomeneo*, xvii; *Eine kleine Nachtmusik*, 321; *Le nozze di Figaro* [*Die Hochzeit des Figaro*], xvii, 6, 9, 10, 59, 303, 312, 324, 325; *Les Petits Riens* (K. Anh. 10), 321; Piano Concerto in A (K. 488), 324; Piano Concerto in B♭ (K. 450), 203; Piano Concerto in B♭ (K. 595), 321, 328; Piano Concerto in C minor (K. 491), 328; piano sonatas, 321; Quintet in E♭ for Piano and Wind (K. 452), 321; Requiem, xvii; Serenade in D (K. 203); Symphony No. 35 in D (K. 385) ('Haffner'), 328; Symphony No. 36 in C (K. 425) ('Linz'), 329; Symphony No. 39 in E♭ (K. 543), 329; Symphony No. 40 in G minor (K. 550), 262; *Zaide*, 8, 312; *Die Zauberflöte*, 6, 312, 315, 321
Müller, Wilhelm, 25
Münchinger, Karl, 320, 321
Music Review, 146